MORTAL GODS 1

A Sword of Shadow and Deceit

USAT BESTSELLING AUTHOR LUCY SMOKE WRITING AS

LUCINDA DARK

"To beguile the time, look like the time;
Bear welcome in your eye, your hand, your tongue:
Look like the innocent flower,
But be the serpent under it."

— William Shakespeare, *Macbeth*

For the fighters and the survivors.

Developmental Edits by Lunar Rose Services

Line Edits by Your Editing Lounge

Proofreads by Rumi Khan

Cover Design by Simply Defined Art

CONTENTS

GLOSSARY/LIST
OF GODS

Axlan: (Lower God) God of Victory

Azai: (Upper God) God of Strength

Caedmon: (Upper God) God of Prophecy

Dea: (ancient language) endearment meaning either "goddess" or "fortune/treasure"

Demia: (Lower God) Goddess of Birds

Denza: money, currency

Divinity: magic or otherworldly abilities possessed only by those who are Gods or descended from Gods.

Dolos: (Lower God) God of Imprisonment

God City: a city chosen as tribute to the Gods, usually more opulent and wealthy than smaller cities that are ruled by God Lords.

God Lord: a God/Goddess that has been granted rights to rule over a specific town, city, or territory as its governing head.

Hinterlands: unsettled lands outside of mortal and immortal civilization inhabited by monsters and Nezeracians. The only piece of land upon the Anatol continent that is not ruled or inhabited by Divine Beings.

Maladesia: (Lower God) Goddess of Praise

Mortal God: a mortal with God/Divine ancestry

Narelle: (Lower God) Goddess of Scribes

Nezeracians: nomadic mortal tribes or individuals that usually live in the Hinterlands.

Talmatia: (Lower God) Goddess of Vanity

Terra: term used for the human/mortal servants that dwell and serve the Gods and God children within the Mortal Gods Academies.

Tryphone: (Upper God) King of the Gods

TRIGGER WARNINGS:

Child Death
Child Abuse
Suicidal Thoughts/Ideation
Servitude
Class System Prejudice
Attempted Rape (non-con and dub-con)
Self-harm
Torture
Humiliation
Death
Blood
Gore

CHAPTER 1

KIERA

It is a simple enough practice to distinguish a God from a human. Though they descended from the realm of the Divine to rule over the forsaken land of mortals, they've never lost their godly appearance. The Divine is a light that dwells within them, illuminating their features and making them appear *somehow* otherworldly. Beautiful. Dangerous.

It's easy to disguise if they choose to—a bit of brimstone on their person will do the trick if they're brave enough to keep something so dangerous to them so close, but otherwise, it's like staring at an ever-so-slightly distorted reflection of a human. The mirrored mirage looks human and moves like a human, but in essence, it isn't. There is always something foreign about the Gods' appearance that warns the human psyche that they are not what we are. They are predators masquerading as their prey. It's sickening. A predator should simply be a predator. I'd respect them more if they didn't pretend to be compassionate or even ... simply what they're not. *Mortal.*

Despite their hopes and imitations, their Divinity still makes it all too easy to differentiate them from the humans that surround them.

The only times I've ever truly had an issue with differentiating a Divine Being from the non-Divine is when they're a Mortal God.

Mortal Gods are not common in the countryside, though. If they choose to leave the God Cities at all then they have connections, but usually they only do so at the behest of their Masters. The precious dogs of the Divine Beings, happily ignoring the singular half of themselves that makes them not Gods at all, but *Mortal* Gods, if it means they live in the lap of luxury and freedom. I've thankfully only ever come across one in my life, and it's an experience I am all too happy to avoid repeating.

My ability to differentiate the Divine from the ordinary is a silly little game I've played for years to hone my skills. Ophelia used it as a teaching method to instruct her apprentices how to pick out targets from a crowd and follow them. Now, however, I find myself playing it from the shadowed corner of the Black Hat Tavern as a method to keep myself from disintegrating out of sheer boredom into the uncomfortable wooden chair I've been stationed in for the last two hours.

Patience is a virtue I do *not* possess. Ironic, considering my profession.

The game does little for me now but pass the time. Out here in the countryside, there are few Gods to pick out in the crowd of people who have gathered to get out of the downpour or to drink and forget their woes. Most Divine Beings prefer their God Cities to the mortal villages outside of their gilded castles. A few, on occasion, make their way out here—probably out of boredom or curiosity. Most are Lower Gods, Gods of less powerful origins, but still Divine nonetheless.

I scan the room once more and find two in the vicinity. *Like telling a donkey from a horse,* Ophelia had once said. Though both may be farm animals, one is clearly superior to the other. Taller. Broader. More aesthetically pleasing to the eye. It doesn't take a genius to figure out that Gods are the horses and humans are the donkeys in her analogy.

Uncanny, that's what I think of the Divine Beings who disguise themselves. *Disturbing.* Though they come in all heights and sizes and colors—like humans—the primary difference that distinguishes them from their mortal counterparts is their beauty. The effect of their Divinity. They shine internally. Their skin never ages. Their eyes are never dulled by disease or flaw. Their hair never loses its luster. They are as they have always been since the dawn of time— perfection personified.

At least on the outside.

It's wrong. Against nature.

I pinpoint the two Lower Gods in the room and, indeed, they're attempting to hide their Divinity. Though they've managed to shield it from the commoners here, their unblemished skin and clear eyes are a dead giveaway for me. It's no surprise to find that when entering these types of places—unless they're preceded by a posse of their godly acquaintances—most Divine Beings choose invisibility over audaciousness. It's easier for Gods to pass through these parts when they mask themselves, easier for everyone.

Still, I always spot them, and if they were my targets, they'd be dead in an instant for revealing themselves so recklessly. Lucky for them, I've got no current orders to attack and even if I detest their existence, I don't plan to give myself more work than I have to.

Another pass through the room with my gaze finds no more Divine Beings and I settle back against the spine of my seat with crossed arms and an irritated *hmph*. An easy game that is quickly over is no fun at all. I don't know why I even bothered.

From my darkened corner in the Black Hat Tavern, I watch the room beneath the hood of my cloak. Outside, rain pours down over the side of the awning and every once in a while, a new arrival will come in, stomping their muddied boots at the front as they shake off the thunderstorm from their heads.

My breathing stabilizes until I'm sure anyone passing by would merely assume I have fallen asleep here, resting between the table and wall. That is, if they can even see me. The long silvery strands of my hair have been carefully braided back and tucked beneath my hood. The cloak that covers the rest of me is large enough to envelop my slender frame, hiding the majority of my curves and stature. Thankfully, it must also hide my gender. Otherwise, I'd have already had to deal with a few of the drunken tavern customers by now.

I count the seconds until my mind begins to drift once more, and just when I'm about to give up for the night and go up to the rented room I've got waiting for me—and the bed calling my name—the chair across from mine skids across the floor as it's pulled from beneath the table.

My eyes shoot up and I curse. "*Fuck*—I didn't even hear you walk up," I mutter. It's irritating how he manages it every time, especially after all of my training.

Regis grins at my scowl, the corners of his mouth

tipping up with amusement. His sand-colored hair is pulled back away from his face and tied off at the base of his skull with a thin leather band, but a few strands have snuck free and sway on the sides of his slightly squared face. Regis reaches up, tucking one of the straight locks behind his ear absently, only for it to slip free once more as he tilts his head at me. "I know," he says with his usual smugness. "You should look into that—bad habit for one in your line of work."

My scowl deepens as he plops down into his seat. "No one else can manage it but you and Ophelia," I point out. "I don't think that's half bad for a decade of service."

"She'd be the first to tell you to do better," he replies, arching a brow at me. He's right. Ophelia's a firm taskmaster. Regis lifts a hand for one of the barmaids to stop by. It doesn't take long—he's a handsome man and he knows just how to use it to be noticed when he wants to be. Once he's assured that a maid will be along, he drops his hand and turns to me. "Have I kept you waiting long?"

"I'm practically wasting away with age," I deadpan, earning another grin from him. "Obviously this new job isn't all that important if you weren't in any rush to bring me the details of it."

"On the contrary," he replies coolly, "I think you'll find this new job is everything you've been hoping for."

I scowl. "Unless it pays my debt, then I doubt it."

He scoffs. "You act like you hate the Guild."

I pick at the edge of the table where splinters of wood have come off the grain. "Hard not to hate something you feel imprisoned by." I say it without much heat. The fact is —the Underworld is both a haven and a noose around my neck. If love and hate are each a side of the same coin, the Guild and Ophelia *are* the coin itself.

Regis shakes his head. "Even if you have a blood contract brand, you're the most well-treated servant I've ever met," he says.

As if lured by his words, my hand immediately reaches back to the place on my neck that often burns when I use my Divinity. It's smooth to the touch, save for the sliver of a scar where the brimstone remains that Ophelia embedded within me when she took me on as an apprentice and created the contract brand.

"You're practically a Guild servant in name only," Regis continues. "If anything, I think Ophelia is looking to you as a potential heir to the Guild."

I snort at that. "The only reason I'm treated so well is because I've proved myself and I'm more valuable this way. Ophelia is an investor and I'm her product." Just like him— except with far fewer options. "Besides, she has a son," I remind him.

"Carcel?" Regis rolls his eyes. "He's not nearly as good as you or I. He's definitely not Guild Master material."

A ruddy-faced barmaid approaches, interrupting any comment from me. "What can I get for you fine gentlemen?" she asks.

I move further back into my cloak, pulling it across my chest. When I was younger, I'd found it insulting to be mistaken for a man. Now, though, I recognize that it's more helpful than anything else, and besides, I *am* dressed like one. Quirk of the job. It's easier to go around killing people in trousers than dress skirts.

As if he can sense my thoughts, Regis shoots me a bemused glance before he turns his pearly whites on her and orders for us. He sticks up two fingers. "Two ales, if you please, my lady."

The barmaid blushes a little at the appeasing lady

comment. I don't even bother to resist the eye roll that overtakes me. "Is that all you'd like?" she asks, reaching back and tucking a stray strand of mousy brown hair behind her ear. The innuendo is not lost on Regis.

"For now," he hedges, his grin never ceasing.

She nods and scampers away, and once more, I'm alone with the womanizer. "Was that really necessary?" I ask.

He turns big, round eyes on me and blinks in pseudo-innocence. "Whatever could you mean, dear Kiera?"

I cough into my fist, adding a clear insult to the fake noise. "*Lecher.*"

Regis laughs and shakes his head. "Jealous?" he taunts. "Because I could satisfy her, but you ... well, you're not exactly equipped, good *sir.*"

With a bored look, I lift one hand out from my cloak and stick my middle finger straight to the sky, earning yet another laugh from him. "You can take your *equipment* and fuck right off, Regis," I comment dryly.

"Oh, but if I do that, then how will you ever get any information on the next job Ophelia has lined up for you?" he replies. "I promise you, it pays handsomely."

I arch a brow. "Ophelia knows good and well who's the more professional of us. If I miss out on a job, she'll know that it was never a result of *my* incompetence."

He releases a mock gasp and leans back. "Are you insinuating that *I* am incompetent?" he asks.

I blink back at him. "If you think I'm insinuating versus saying it outright, then I suppose the description fits better than I anticipated."

Regis shakes his head as the barmaid returns with two pints of ale. She slaps mine down haphazardly and the foam at the top spills over the rim, dripping down the semi-rusted metal exterior. Regis' drink, however, is gently placed before him as she bends over in front of him. She sucks in a quick breath, drawing it in so sharply that her breasts push tight against the neckline of her already low-cut dress. "If there's *anything* else I can get you, do let me know." She puts emphasis on 'anything.'

Regis smiles kindly. "Of course, darling," he replies. "I'd never leave a lady such as yourself wondering. Perhaps if you're not working later—" He doesn't even need to finish.

"I get off around midnight," she says quickly.

With a groan, I lift the mug of ale to my lips and drink. I gulp back mouthful after mouthful, half convinced that I'll be done with it by the time the barmaid twitters away from my companion. Regis turns and watches her go—or rather, he watches her ass sway back and forth as she walks away.

Had I called him a lecher? I'd been wrong; he's a down-right pig. Unfortunately, though, he's a pig with connections and a damn good throwing arm. That and the fact that he's been the only other assassin even remotely close in age to me when we'd grown up together, is really the only reason I call him my friend.

"Disgusting," I mutter, setting my ale back down.

Regis shrugs and turns back to his own mug. "You have to take your pleasures where you can get them in this life, Kiera," he replies. "We could all die tomorrow."

"My pleasures are found in work and making money," I snap. "Now, stop messing around and give me the information I came here for."

With a pathetic little huff, Regis sets his mug down and finally reaches into his worn leather satchel. He withdraws a small slip of yellowed paper barely the length of my longest finger and places it before me on the edge of the dirty table. Eyeing him with suspicion, I pick it up and unravel it to read the contents.

The paper is short and the lines even shorter to fit into the space. In Ophelia's messy scrawl are the basics of my next job.

God City of Riviere. MGA. Extended contract. Target: Unknown.

The lack of a target name or identification should be an immediate warning, but just as I read it and scan below to check the compensation for the job, my mouth drops open. When I read the number written under the payment, my eyes bulge.

"Is this a fucking joke?" I demand, my gaze shooting up to Regis who watches me with a grin on his face as he drinks from his mug. "If it is, it's not amusing." That kind of money is damn near impossible to come by even with years of back-alley debts and blood contracts. The bastard takes his time, finishing his unnecessarily long gulp before setting the metal cup back onto the surface of the table with a clank.

He leans forward. "No joke," he says, excitement permeating his tone. "Four *million* denza. It's the largest contract Ophelia's ever seen in her lifetime." Considering she's been the head of the Guild for the last twenty-plus years, I'm shocked, but it *is* a considerable amount of money. The things I could do with that kind of money. The freedom it could buy. Old desire fights its way back to the surface. It's by far more money than I've ever seen offered, even for a contract with multiple targets.

"Is it one target?" I demand as that thought slams into me. I look back to the scrap of parchment even as I ask the question. I scan the rest of the information, but unlike the previous jobs, there is no name or image attached to the paper. No target name or count. Though I've primarily taken on singular jobs, there have been occasions when I've been tasked with the eradication of a collection of people rather than individuals. Those are usually the higher compensation jobs. This one must have multiple targets. I can't imagine that it wouldn't. Not for that fucking much. "There has to be more information on something like this. Where's the rest?"

Regis' grin slips from his face as I fold the paper in half and lean over to the singular candle set on our table. I let the edge of the yellowed square catch fire, dropping it into a metal plate next to the candle where the ashes of men's cigars and smokes remain. The fire spreads, ripping through the ink and parchment until it's disintegrated into nothing but ash and dust. Only a memory in the minds of the recipient, the messenger, and the sender.

"Yeah," Regis replies, reaching back as he cups the back of his neck. "That's the only issue. What you saw written there"—he gestures to the remaining embers—"is all the information we have."

I narrow my gaze on him and wait.

He sighs. "The client won't say the target name until we agree to take on the job."

"That's not how it works," I remind him.

He nods. "I know—Ophelia knows—but ... the compensation, Kiera—Shit, even with the Underworld's cut, you'll be able to pay back your debt." Regis leans towards me. "You can't deny that it's tempting."

It's incredibly tempting. That's the problem. Ten years I've waited for this type of job, this opportunity. Most assassination jobs take anywhere from weeks to months to see through appropriately. It's risky business and being too quick to take one up isn't always safe. Not having all of the information initially almost certainly means there's a catch.

I'm not so naive to think that the compensation means anything else.

"It's dangerous, is what it is," I reply. "I need to know at least how many targets I've got to hit. I can't prepare adequately without that."

Regis grits his teeth but doesn't disagree. "Ophelia is working on finding that out. She didn't like it, but she didn't want to say no until you had the chance to make your own decision."

Shit. I turn away from him and stare out across the tavern. Ophelia is well within her rights as my owner to just order me to take the job. It isn't like I have the luxury of denying her. As brimstone is one of the few—if not the only thing of this world—that can counteract Divinity, the brimstone-infused contract mark within my body ensures that I have no other recourse than to do as she commands if I ever want it removed. Not only does it keep the majority of my power contained and my Divinity hidden, it acts as a tracking spell that allows her to always know my location.

Unchained though I am, I'm still indebted at the end of the day, bound by a blood contract that ensures my complete obedience. Though I might be a skillful and wildly successful blood servant that's made her a pretty fucking denza in the last decade, that doesn't erase the fact that if she wanted me to take this contract, there'd be no question. The indebted have no choice.

I might not be treated like one, and as Regis said, I certainly damn well don't act like one, but still, I wake every day with the knowledge that I could be called to her side and bound to her will with nothing more than an order. I glance down at my wrists, covered by my sleeves. Though invisible, the mark of the blood contract remains in my bones and blood and makes me feel as though I'm carrying around invisible shackles wherever I go.

This hit could be the thing that erases it. This job could set me free.

Her consideration and the illusion of choices she's given me have kept me by Ophelia's side. The very fact that I'm given the choice makes me want to take it. I doubt many other owners would have been so willing to offer me the chance at true freedom or to even keep my own earnings.

Another thought comes to mind, part of the earlier information she'd written. *MGA*. That acronym only stands for one thing. Mortal Gods Academy. "Wait—it's at one of the Academies?" I look back to Regis.

He nods. On one hand, that knowledge narrows down the type of target I'll be expected to kill—and it explains why I'm the only one who can take on the job. "Then it's either a God or a Mortal God," I say absently, considering.

"In all likeliness," Regis agrees.

I suck in a breath. "I'm sure she's already tried to get the information from the client, right?"

He nods. "She's still trying, but they're being obstinate. The extended contract means that you'll have to set up a false identity, infiltrate the actual Academy grounds, and lie low for a while to get close to your target before you get the rest of the job information."

Damn it. The fact that Ophelia had nothing else written means that regardless of her attempts, whoever it is, they still haven't caved. I grit my teeth.

"You can take some time to think about it," Regis offers, "but the client wants the job started by the harvest season."

Of course, I think, because that's when the Academy will be back in session. It's the only time of year that they open their doors to invite new servants into its inner walls. It only makes sense—if I'm to infiltrate that damnable Mortal God haven then I'll need to do so at the start of the next semester.

I don't like it. Not at fucking all.

Yet, the thought of four fucking million denza can't leave my mind. It'll pay off my debt. All of it, and there will still be enough to live on. I wouldn't have to take on another job for as long as I live. Shit, if I wanted, I'd be able to afford something small in one of the God Cities, not that I would—it'd be dangerous for me to settle down in an area teeming with Divine Beings—but the idea that I *could* remains an ever-present beacon of hope.

I drain the last of my mug and set down a few denza as payment, the coins clinking together as they land on the scarred table's surface, before standing up. Despite Regis' late arrival, I rode throughout the day to get here on time and my bones are weary from the travel. A good night's sleep might help me make my final decision.

"I'll meet you in the morning," I say, "and give my decision then."

Regis stares back at me as I tug the top of my hood down further, covering my face as I make my way out of the corner. He doesn't press and merely gives his consent with a nod.

Four million denza. It's a lot of fucking money. More than I've ever seen or heard of at once. The largest contract I've ever taken was a million. It'd been for ten targets. I can't possibly think that the client wants me to kill an entire battalion. No, it must be a high-ranking individual. The risk is high but so is the reward.

My head spins with the possibilities as I make my way through the tavern to the staircase leading up to the inn.

Under the creaking old wood of the steps, I let my mind wander to those possibilities.

Freedom has never been so close.

Will I regret it if I don't say yes? Or will I be choosing my own death?

CHAPTER 2

KIERA

The next morning comes pouring through the thin, worn brown curtains of my paltry, tiny-ass room, draping the space in a murky gray. Despite the early turn-in and the singular pint of ale I'd consumed the night before, a deep pounding starts up at the back of my head, dragging a frustrated groan from my throat—a sign that I should've eaten before retiring.

I toss a forearm over my eyes, muting the light, but the sounds of the world waking up outside soon become too much to ignore. Perhaps we should've chosen an inn a little more on the outskirts of Mineval. Though it's nothing more than a town between the God City of Riviere and the absolute Hinterlands of the wild, it still has a considerable amount of traffic. Traffic that likes to start its day early, apparently.

Finally, I remove my forearm and crack my eyes open. A small eight-legged creature makes its way down the side wall closest to the single bed I'm lying in. Without waiting, I lift a hand and press the tips of my fingers to the wall. The spider hurries towards me, speeding along the wood grain, and slips onto the edge of my finger, crawling up to my knuckle before stopping. I pull it closer to my face and close my eyes, focusing on the point of contact.

Blurry images invade my mind, making my head reel. It's probably not the best idea to do this so soon upon waking. It makes the world tip and tilt as the image I try to focus on is fractured into multiple different angles before zeroing in on my target.

Regis. I grimace as I catch sight of him rolling over, the sheet draped around his naked waist slipping down. I almost cut off the image the second I see his fucking dick pop out, but thankfully, the feminine body on the other side of the bed drapes over him, hiding the damn thing, and he turns once more. An arm circles his waist and nails drag down his back. It doesn't take a genius to know what's happening as his body arches up and moves over the woman in his bed.

Guess he really did get lucky with the barmaid the night before. No shock there. Objectively, I can say that Regis is a good-looking man. If he weren't such a fucking idiot and manwhore, I might even find him appealing personality-wise. I reopen my eyes and turn my hand towards the nightstand. The spider crawls onto the solid surface before skittering away, disappearing back to wherever it came from after having done its duty of checking in.

Now that I know Regis won't be looking for me anytime soon, I sit up and stretch my sore muscles. Knowing him, with a woman in his bed and no other job hovering on the horizon, he'll spend the next several hours lounging and catching up on the sleep he likely missed out on the night before. I, however, don't have the luxury of relaxing. I still need to consider my options on the latest proposition I've received. I also need to soothe the pounding in my head.

I crawl out of bed and dress in the same clothes from yesterday. Buckling a leather band about my middle, I tighten all of my straps and slip the smaller stilettos I carry into the pockets that line the inside. There's little to pack, but more time than I need before checking out later so I leave the remainder of my belongings in the room, locking the door at my back with a slender metal key that I hang around my neck as I make my way down the stairs and into the already bustling tavern dining room.

My stomach rumbles, but as I pass a few of the bleary-eyed men from the night before, hanging their heads over the slop of what looks like the tavern's breakfast offering, I decide to nix the thought and instead head for the market square.

Humans and Gods alike pass me by as I make my way out of the tavern and inn and into the streets of Mineval. Stalls are beginning to open and people are milling about, some running late for work as they rush along the sides of the cobblestoned streets. This early, few carriages and horses are clogging the roads, so it's easy enough for me to pass through.

Although Mineval is smaller than the God Cities like Riviere, I like it. It's not hard for me to differentiate the Gods hiding their Divinity out here in the country towns, but the fact that they live harmoniously with their mortal counterparts is what gives Mineval its appeal. So very different from the structured hierarchy of Riviere.

The only downside is the massive gleaming building on the hill that overlooks the city. My eyes seek it out even as I continue to make my way through the streets. Each city that's of Mineval's size or larger has a reigning Lord—or God. Another way for them to keep a watchful eye on their mortal cattle. I've been far too lucky to be able to live my life in the shadows and away from their watchful gazes. No doubt the Mortal Gods in the Academy have their lives scrutinized each second of every day.

I grimace. If I do decide to take on Ophelia's offer, then I'll have to come to terms with living under such a regime for weeks if not months. A job like this will no doubt take a long time. I understand what the client is thinking— whoever the target is, they're obviously not easy to get close to.

For me, merely infiltrating one of the Mortal Gods Academies will be risky by itself. Yet, the thought of receiving four million denza sits at the back of my mind as it has since the night before. No doubt Regis expects me to agree to the terms of the job despite the lack of information provided by the client, and I have to admit, it's still appealing.

I make my way through the early morning market crowd with ease. Without my cloak, I know I look less like a man, but people still avoid me as I'm not dressed like the regular town girls. A dress would only get caught up around my legs if I need to move fast.

As the sun rises into the sky and the heat beats down on my head, I reach back and gather my hair, yanking it up and tying it with a strip of leather from my wrist. Little wisps of baby hairs touch the base of my neck and around my temples, but without the heavy fall against my skin, new air washes over my otherwise sweat-soaked skin, granting me some relief.

The day etches closer and closer to noon as I meander down the streets, picking up a few things here and there. An apple to replace my uneaten breakfast and cure the headache throbbing against my skull. An extra flint rock to store in my bags. More leather twine. I'm about ready to turn and head back to the inn to see if Regis has woken from his late-night-to-early-morning rendezvous when a startled shout echoes up the too close buildings a split second before the scrape of wheels on stone and the groaning of metal reach my ears.

The crowd around me freezes and then they begin to move quickly. Half of them turn and dash away from the sounds of shouting and crying, while the other half—too curious for their own good—shuffle towards it.

It doesn't take long for me to contemplate what I intend to do. The more knowledge I possess, the better. Or rather, that's what I tell myself to hide the fact that I'm just fucking nosy as hell. Spinning on my heel, I head back towards the road, but instead of following the crowd, I catch sight of a ladder leaning against a wall inside the mouth of the alleyway. I take it, moving up the wooden pegs two rungs at a time, getting high enough to catch the underside of the roof's overhang. Locking my fingers onto the stone shingles, I heft my body onto the sun-warmed surface and roll to my feet before I sprint across it towards the next building, leaping across the opening to the following roof.

Below, more people begin to gather, all collecting on the sides of the road. A massive carriage that hadn't been there when I'd passed through several minutes before takes up the majority of space at the center of the market street. I scowl. *What fucking idiot would drive their carriage right into the market?* A carriage that's quite obviously too large to fit comfortably through the streets of Mineval. Almost as soon as I have that thought, it occurs to me. The carriage looks far more like the kinds that are popular in the God Cities. A grimace overtakes my face.

I scan in the direction of the shout and as I come up to

the edge of the second roof, I pause, dropping down onto my haunches to watch the scene unfold before me. The carriage door swings open and my scowl deepens. A God. Of course. Not just any God, though. This one isn't even attempting to mask their Divinity, but instead letting it all shine free. Golden trinkets adorn the long pale locks of hair that drape down past their feet, dragging behind them as they make their way down into the street.

"What is this commotion?" she demands, waving a crimson fan in front of her perfect face.

Even if I didn't already know who this God is, just seeing her would allow me to accurately guess what gives her the confidence to appear before the people of Mineval with such disdain.

This is Mineval's God. Talmatia. God of Vanity.

The morning sun glints off of her golden hair and tanned skin. The softness of her features, the rounded cheeks and button nose along with the slender curve of her breasts beneath the ornate gown she's wearing, is all an illusion to the true wickedness beyond the Goddess' shell. She's well known in these parts for being both extraordinarily self-obsessed—a trait from her powers of vanity, I suppose—as well as incredibly cruel.

If they know exactly what's about to happen, the other Gods—the ones that are hiding their Divinity—will quickly disperse into the crowd to make their getaway. It's an insult to hide one's Divinity as, according to the Upper Gods, it's nothing to be ashamed of. Lower, less powerful or wealthy Gods, however, prefer their invisibility over Divine expectation. Talmatia is not one of them. She turns to the crowd and waves her fingers expectantly.

"Well? Which of you is responsible for stopping my carriage?"

"M-my Goddess," an older man steps forward from where he stands in front of her gilded carriage. "We apologize, but your carriage, i-it nearly ran over my son. He's—"

My attention turns to the ground behind him where a small form is held, clutched in his mother's arms. Blood splatters soak into the road stones as she carefully rocks the crying child. There's no nearly about it—Talmatia's carriage had, in fact, run over the boy—and from the looks of things, he isn't long for this world. No doubt the man had softened his phrasing in the hopes of not placing the blame on the Goddess and earning her wrath, but the damage had already been done.

"Unacceptable!" Talmatia shrieks. "How dare you! Do you not know how to address me?"

A sinking *knowing* sits in my chest as I rise to my feet and step back, away from the edge of the roof. A few of the onlookers below note my shadow, but by the time they look back, I've already moved out of their line of sight. I blow out a breath, resting my back against the sun-warmed chimney at the top of the roof.

Disgusting. Vile. Unworthy. All things the Gods toss at us, humans. The last one is what hurts the worst. *Unworthy.* Unworthy of what? I've always wondered. Unworthy of pity? Of patience? Of love?

If we are so unworthy, then why did they come here to begin with?

I turn away from the sight and slide down the opposite slope of the roof. A cry rises up—a man's choked strangulation. I grit my teeth. *Ignore it, Kiera. There's nothing you can do for him.* I have my own skin to worry about.

When my feet are back on solid ground once more, I turn and glance at where the backs of the people are still gathered in the market square. The mouth of the alleyway is crowded with them. Above them, the sounds of Talmatia's shrieking reach my ears.

"—dungeons, at once! Daring to disobey your Gods, how blasphemous." My hands clench into fists. The weight of something familiar sits against my chest. Helplessness. Powerlessness. Rage.

"*Fuck it,*" I mutter, turning back to the square. Perhaps if I hide my face then— I don't get a chance to finish the thought.

The second I move for the crowd, a hard hand closes over my shoulder and jerks me back. "Don't even fucking think about it," Regis' dark voice hisses into my ear as he manhandles me away from the mouth of the alley and around the next corner.

With a growl, I slam my elbow back and down into his lower abdomen. He grunts and wheezes at the blow, loosening his grasp enough for me to spin out of his reach.

"Don't!" he snaps, his tone breathless as he places a hand over his stomach. "Kiera, it's not worth it."

Violence sings in my blood as I hear a woman's cries reach a new pitch. "No one else can help them," I snap.

He shakes his head. "And neither can you," he says. "You can't or you risk all of us in the Underworld." He's right. I know it well. The very first thing Ophelia should've done when I was brought to her was send me into the waiting arms of one of the Academies and the Gods themselves. She didn't, and because of that, I am not only beholden to them, I am at constant risk.

"Let it go. It's not our fucking business. If you're caught, you'll be dead." Regis rubs his hand over his stomach and takes a step closer to me. "I know you want to help them, but be smart about it." Emotion pours through me, flooding my system with the need to fight, but as he closes his arms around me—softer this time, gentler—it all flies away. "If you want to help them, then wait."

"They didn't do anything wrong," I say.

"I know, Kiera," he whispers. I duck my head against his shoulder and after a brief moment of hesitation, he lifts a palm to the back of my head, pressing it harder against him. Were he anyone else, I wouldn't even dare show this vulnerability, but he's not. He's Regis. My friend, my comrade. He's known me as long as I've been in the Underworld. "I know," he says the words again, his voice sharper and deeper than before. If anyone were to understand the incredibly unfair differences between mortals and Gods and the tyranny with which they rule the world, it would be Regis.

"They'll be taken to the dungeons," I say. "Probably the boy too." That's where he'll die. I know it, though I don't say as much. From the looks of it and the amount of blood, he'd needed immediate attention from a doctor—not to be carted off with his parents to dungeons for some perceived insult to the God of this city. Guilt weighs heavy in my veins.

Regis nods and pulls away from me. "Then we'll get them out," he says. "But not now. We cannot risk your existence being found out. Especially not now."

His meaning is not lost on me, but I know he's right. I hate it, but I allow myself to be led away by him. Each step feels like I'm striding across broken glass, and no matter how far away the cries become, they echo in my head.

Regis keeps his arm around my back, refusing to allow me to turn back.

"Tonight," I repeat, looking up at him as we finally make it back to the front of the inn. "Promise me."

He sighs and finally releases me to take a step back.

"You're a damn bleeding heart, Kiera," he states. "It's a fucking wonder you've lasted as an assassin, much less a good one."

"I only hurt my targets," I remind him. "If there's no money to be made, then there's no point."

It doesn't hurt that Ophelia had learned to only give me targets that I could convince myself deserved their deaths. Rapists. Murderers. People that destroyed the lives of others just because they could. I'd like to believe that humans were different from Gods, but that was one thing I'd become excruciatingly aware of in the last ten years—Gods. Humans. Mortal. Immortal. It didn't matter what blood ran through you. Everyone was capable of the worst.

"Fine," Regis huffs at me. "I promise. Tonight. We'll save them."

That's all I need. I don't care if he calls me a bleeding heart. Unlike the Gods who once abandoned us and the God parent I have who actually did as well, I can sleep at night knowing that at least I've got one.

CHAPTER 3

KIERA

The human child and his family were taken to the God Lord's castle. By twilight, all of Mineval knows this. For daring to stand up to the Lord—no, not even for standing up, but for failing to fall to Talmatia's feet the second she stepped out of her carriage and beg for forgiveness for an accident they had no hand in—they'll perish in the dungeons.

Or at least they will if something isn't done.

"In and out, Kiera," Regis says quietly as we stop alongside the back of the stone wall that circles the southern side of Talmatia's castle. "I don't care what you run across, we're just here to get the family and leave."

"Understood," I say through clenched teeth. I stare up the wall, eyeing the tight stone bricks with displeasure as I reach up and drop my cloak from my body. "We'll enter and exit here," I say, tossing my cloak onto a mound of dirt. I kick some grass and leaves over it—enough to cover its presence, but not so much that I won't be able to quickly find it when we return. It's a cooler night, but all that fabric will get in the way and we need to be quick about this.

Regis curses under his breath. "You're damn lucky I'm even helping you," he mutters. "If it were up to me, we wouldn't be getting involved at all."

"You're welcome to leave," I tell him, retrieving a few of the stilettos in my belt. I glance over the thin knives and think better of it, shoving them back into place, before I retrieve the thicker daggers strapped to my thighs. "I can handle this alone."

Regis scoffs and follows my actions—dropping his own cloak and removing his daggers as well. "There are three of them," he says. "The child will likely be unable to walk after the accident. No doubt the father was beaten by the guards." *If the child is still alive, that is.* It's a thought both of us, no doubt, have, but we keep it to ourselves out of sheer hope.

My lips curve down in a scowl and I shove the pointed end of my dagger right into the stones—wedging it between two loose bricks. "Then keep your thoughts to yourself, shut up, and let's get on with it," I toss back.

Jumping, I shove my second dagger a foot above and wedge the first one out to do the same once more. Using nothing but our upper body strength, Regis and I scale the wall to the top until we're able to swing our bodies onto the ledge and return our daggers to their rightful places.

"The dungeons should be in the lower regions," Regis whispers. He points one way and then the other. "You go that way and I'll go this way. If you need me—"

"The spiders will find you," I say.

He grimaces and a small shudder works its way through his system. "Yeah, fine," he says. "Just don't let those little fuckers touch me."

The small, offhand comment finally clears some of the rage from my mind. It'd probably be best not to tell him that my little spider mates do far more than touch him—they do me the favor of keeping an eye on him whenever I need them to.

Regis jumps off the ledge and disappears into the darkness of the courtyard below. A cloud of dust and dirt filters up from where he lands, and the sound of his footsteps fades quickly into the night. Crouching, I turn and run down the length of the wall's ledge—placing one foot in front of the other to keep my balance as I hurry along. It's like walking a tightrope, but thankfully the stone wall is well built and there aren't any crumbling parts at the top that might disrupt my speed.

I make it to the end and leap down with stealth, hurrying through the side lot, where I suspect the guards usually train, and into the outer corridors. The smell of smoking meat filters through the castle grounds and happy voices echo out from the primary public chambers. Servants of the Goddess, Talmatia, enjoying their evening and the efforts of serving such a supposedly great creature, all the while innocent civilians starve down below. It's disgusting. No doubt a few of the higher-ranking soldiers are Mortal Gods—my very own kind.

Mortal Gods are worse than Gods. Whereas Gods are their own entity—they have no notion of the plight of mortals—Mortal Gods are mortal themselves. Yet, both treat humans as little more than cattle to be ruled over and slaughtered.

I suck in a breath and push down my desire to let my fury reign free. Instead, I focus on finding a staircase leading down to the lower levels—the dungeons. The outer corridors disappear at my back the second I find what I'm looking for. A wooden door leading right into the basement of the castle. I crack it open and slip inside, flinching as hot putrid air hits me in the face.

Unwilling to waste time with discomfort, however, I hurry down the staircase—letting the few torches anchored into the walls light my way. The smell of rotting wood and mold filters through my nostrils, and with a grimace, I reach down and pull the scarf around my neck up over my mouth and nose to dull the scent.

The sound of weeping reaches my ears and I follow it into a darkened chamber, pausing when I see the narrow bars of metal lining one side of the small room. The woman from this morning—plump and middle-aged with round, albeit grimy cheeks—sits with her back against the wall, clutching a small form against her chest. She rocks it back and forth, though it doesn't stir.

In front of her, the man who'd attempted to defend her by standing up to Talmatia lays on his chest, facing the bars. He's unconscious with the half of his face that is visible bruised and bloodied, his gray hair matted to the side of his head. The woman, being the only one awake and aware, doesn't even react to me when I approach.

I pause in front of the door and bend down. "Ma'am."

Her head tips up at my voice and her eyes widen. "Please," she says quickly, holding the boy in her arms closer. "Please don't."

I look at the young one and my chest tightens. He's blue and white and stiff in her arms, faded marks of red lining his nose and mouth. His legs dangle past her skirts and from the tears in his clothes, I can see the wounds from the carriage. Long gashes up his legs and chest. My chest fills with remorse. Our assumption had been correct. He hadn't lived long after the accident—the wheels had obviously crushed his tiny form. Likely one of his lungs had been punctured by a broken rib or two. He'd died in pain, drowning in his own blood, unable to cry out or do anything to stop his soul from fading from this world. The tragedy steals my breath and causes pinpricks of hatred to stab at my flesh.

I swallow roughly. "I'm not here to take him away," I assure her quietly. "I'm here to get you out of here." I withdraw a few small instruments from one of the many pockets in my pants and set to work on the lock. It's primitive—obviously, Talmatia had not been concerned with a jailbreak. No one else would dare to pull a stunt like this.

Just as I hear a click, a small black creature crawls down one of the bars next to my head. I glance up and eye it. Staring into the spider's beady black eyes, I send it away with a mental push to hurry. Regis should be nearly finished with his own duty by now since he'll have determined that his side of the castle dungeons didn't hold our targets, but it's better to check the progress nonetheless.

"My boy," the woman sobs, "he can't walk."

I close my eyes and grip the door of the cell, letting it swing inward. "He can't do anything anymore," I say to her. Cruel, yes, but necessary. "I'm sorry." The apology I offer won't help, and won't erase what has already been done, but I say it anyway.

The woman cries harder, muffling her sobs against her dead child as she clutches him in her arms. I step into the cell and reach down for the man, pressing two fingers to his neck. Thankfully, there's still a pulse. I roll him to his side and then his back and feel a breath of relief leave me as his eyelashes flutter open and a groan rumbles up his chest.

"No..." He moans. "No ... Gods, have mercy."

I bite back another angry growl. *The Gods never have any mercy.* "Come on," I say, hefting him up into a sitting position. "Wake up, now. We must be quick if we're to get you out of here."

He blinks at me, his gaze full of pained confusion. "W-who..."

"Don't worry about who I am," I say with a shake of my head. "If you want to live, you'll let me get you out of here. You'll follow me and you won't ask any questions."

It's not a hard decision to make. The man nods and then slowly—with my assistance—crawls to his feet, shaking and trembling on, no doubt, sore legs. "My wife..." He turns to the woman, pausing at the sight of her clutching their child. His eyes water and he bites down on his lower lip until the scent of blood invades my nostrils. Then, in a careful voice, he moves away from the stability of my hold and reaches for her. "Irina, we need to go."

"No!" the woman—Irina—cries, shaking her head back and forth. "Henry can't—he's not able to walk. We can't leave him."

The man stands over her and it's clear that he's well aware the body his wife holds no longer contains the soul of his son. The child is long gone. Surprisingly, however, he doesn't say as much. He merely crouches next to her and nods. "You're right," he tells her, cupping her cheek gently. "Will you allow me to carry him, my love? Your arms must be tired from holding him for so long."

"You won't leave him here?" Irina asks.

"*Never.*" The man's reply is fierce. Despite the obvious pain he's in, with that one word and the harsh tone it's spoken with, it's clear he's willing to die rather than leave his son's body behind.

I stand back, stunned into silence as he quickly strips his shirt from his back—showing that he had, in fact, been beaten. There are several deep wounds in his skin—the color of bruised apples, dark and red. The imprints of fists. My attention lifts to his face, at the gaunt lines of both cheeks that speak of malnourishment and the gray-and-brown patchy beard that doesn't seem to know where it wants to grow. His eyes are lowered, shielding what I already know to be dark soil-rich eyes as he works his fingers against the dirty clothes in his grip. I bite my lower lip to keep from speaking a single word as he takes the fabric and begins to rend it into strips.

His arms tremble with the effort. It's only because it's taking so long, time we don't have, that I step forward and stop him. Pulling out a dagger from the sheath strapped to my forearm, I help him cut up the shirt. Using the strips, he and the woman place their child against the man's now naked back and tie him down. When the man stands, he wavers on his feet and I catch his shoulder.

"Will you be able to move with him on your back like that?" I ask. "I have a friend forming a distraction, but you'll still have to keep up."

The man sucks in a breath that expands his chest and he reaches up, locking one hand on the several straps that crisscross over his chest. "My wife carried my son for nine months to bring him into this world," he replies, holding his free hand back for her to take as his dark eyes lift to meet my gaze with stony confidence. "It is only fair that I carry him out of this world. I can make it."

The man's words penetrate me far deeper than anything has in a long time. They're sincere and solid. Despite the obvious shaking in his limbs and the white lines etched at the corners of his eyes and mouth from holding back what must be severe pain, he doesn't hesitate to speak them, and I know, without pressing, that even if I insisted on leaving the dead child behind, he wouldn't.

I swallow my words—no matter how well-meaning they'd be, I understand that there are some things a parent cannot do. Not these parents anyway. "Alright," I say instead, turning away from them. I hold my hand out onto the wall in front of the entrance to the chamber and wait patiently until a spider crawls onto my pinkie and down to my knuckle. I hold it up and close my eyes.

Just as I'd said, it appears that Regis has realized his section of the dungeons were empty and he's now proceeding to do what we discussed before coming here. In the eye of the spider's webs, I can see him gathering supplies into a small, darkened room. A flare burns bright orange and then slowly dwindles to an ember as he tosses something into a bale of hay before bending down and blowing on it.

The fire will begin small, but by the time we make our way outside, the smoke will have made its way through the castle's ducts and alerted someone. It's the perfect distraction.

"Come on," I say, putting my hand back to the wall and allowing the spider to crawl away to freedom. "Let's move. Stay behind me and stay close."

CHAPTER 4

KIERA

The sound of harsh panting breath is overly loud to my ears as we make our way out of the dungeons and back up the stairs I'd come down before. The man and his wife move slower than I need them to, their footsteps far louder than my own. To their credit, neither of them utter a word of complaint. I sniff the air, wondering how far the fire Regis started has spread and if the castle's residents have noticed it yet. We pause inside the wooden door that leads into the courtyard beyond and I turn back, placing a hand out to stop the man and woman's forward momentum.

"Stay here," I say quietly. "Wait for my signal."

The man places a hand on the wall, heaving and panting with the exertion of his movements, but he nods his assent. I slip into the corridor and push out my power of Divinity to sense the surroundings. Sensations assail me almost immediately. I imagine Gods must have this feeling constantly and it's a wonder how they bear it. They must tune it out. They'd have to or risk going mad. Every single sound slams into my ears—metal cups scraping against wood, loud and boisterous male laughter, crackling fires from the torches. The rustling of leaves in the trees. Footsteps...

Footsteps approaching. I turn towards the coming person and fade against the wall. Shadows cling to my limbs as I slide two daggers from their places pinned against my forearms and hold them loosely against my palms. I wait patiently. One second passes, two, and then ... Regis rounds the corner, barreling down the path with stomping feet that somehow hardly make a sound. If I weren't listening for the sound, if I weren't using my Divinity, I'd never have heard him. I don't know how he does it.

Regis doesn't notice my body as he passes by. I breathe a sigh of relief and drop the cast of Divinity in the next moment, sucking in breath after breath. Regis turns slightly and jerks back in shock as he catches sight of me out of the corner of his eye. A sword comes swinging towards me and I barely duck out of the way in time. The sharp end of his blade slams into the stone wall and sparks flash in front of my face, illuminating exactly who it is he just attempted to kill.

"Fuck—Kay!" Regis hisses at me in shock and irritation. "I could've beheaded you."

I stare back at him and swallow my irritation. "If you could kill me that easily then I'd have died long ago," I remind him, shaking my head.

He returns his blade to his sheath and steps closer. "I couldn't find the family," he says. "So, I did what we discussed and—"

"I know," I cut him off, striding past him back to the door. I open it and gesture inside for the man and woman to come out. "I've got them. Let's go."

The man is the first out of the stairwell and he pulls

back the second he sees Regis, suspicion and wariness in his gaze. "It's fine," I assure him, stopping him from his retreat. "He's with me."

Regis' sharp inhalation reaches my ears and I turn back, but his eyes aren't on me. They're on the small figure attached to the man's back. He shoots a look my way and I shake my head. Now is definitely not the time. I'm sure he understands that as well as anyone. We're still in enemy territory and our next goal should be getting out of here.

"The fire will lead the guards down to the lower chambers soon enough," he finally says, eyeing the man and woman. "They won't be able to climb, so we should take them to the messenger gate along the north wall."

I nod and gesture for him to go forth. "Lead the way."

He gives the couple another last look before doing just that. Together, the group of us move as quietly as possible as we slip through the courtyard and along the back wall. After several minutes, the sound of shouts and curses rise into the night sky. The woman whimpers quietly behind me and I glance back to see her clutching at her husband— silent tears trickling down her cheeks, washing through the dirt and grime in clear lines.

"They're going to catch us," she sobs.

"No, they're not," I assure her, pausing as I allow her and her husband to move forward. "Keep following my friend," I say. "If anything happens, I'll lead the guards away."

"Thank you," the man whispers, his voice tight and breathless. He's shocked me with how well he's managed so far, but I'm glad that Regis recommended the gate. There truly is no way he'd have been able to climb with his wounds.

The woman's feet begin to stumble along the path and

as the voices from the castle grow louder, I practically push her forward, forcing her to move faster and faster despite her obvious exhaustion.

Finally, a thin metal gate comes into view. Regis stops ahead and holds up a fist, telling the rest of us silently that it's time to make our escape. I push in front of the couple once more. "Stay here," I whisper to them as I approach Regis.

"What do you see?" he asks.

I scan the wall and up and down the sides of the gate. There are no guards, which could mean this is a forgotten entrance. However, we know better than to trust simple exits. I close my eyes and push out my Divinity once more, sensing the slow buzz that only I can recognize. It moves out in waves, lapping at each and every object surrounding me.

I can sense the bone-jarring emotions of the couple behind us and Regis' icy exterior. Beyond that, the warmth of the soil, and then ... there it is. The very thing we'd both been worried about. "The lock's enchanted," I say. "If we break it or pick it without the key then it'll send an alert to its owner."

"Just the lock?" Regis inquires.

I nod and he breathes a sigh that sounds like relief. "What are you thinking of?"

Instead of answering, Regis removes the pack on his back and slings back the top flap, reaching inside to pull out a thin leather case. "If we can't go through the gates, then all we need to do is simply remove one side."

I frown, confused. "What are you—"

"Stay here with the couple and keep watch," Regis cuts me off, handing me his pack. "I'll be right back."

A curse strangles in my throat as he moves away faster

than I can catch him and I'm left to follow his orders with nothing else. "Where's he going?" the man behind me asks quietly.

"He's checking the gate," I say, turning and eyeing him. "You look like you're going to pass out."

"Gordon?" Irina clutches his hand and looks up at him at my words. "Is Henry too heavy? Should I take him?"

He shakes his head and through the sweat covering his brow, he clenches his teeth. "No," he replies. "I can handle my son."

"You should at least sit down while we wait," I order. The man jerks his head to the side. I scowl. "It wasn't a suggestion," I say. "Sit down before I make you."

The man pales and then pushes himself up a little more, using the wall as leverage. "I can't," he replies.

"Why?" I demand.

He blanches and after a beat, he lowers his voice. "I don't think I could stand back up if I sit now."

I frown and move towards him. I touch his chest and smooth my fingers over his ribs as he breathes shallowly. Concern bites at my insides. If he's truly as bad as he seems, then it's a wonder he's even moving. "Does it hurt to breathe?" I ask.

He nods.

My gaze narrows on his expression. "Does it feel like stinging or burning?"

"Both." He hisses between his teeth.

Shit. Not good. I reach up and bite down on my thumbnail, considering my options. There's no telling how long it'll take Regis to finish what he's planning and I don't know how much longer this man can go without passing out. Neither Regis nor I could carry him and still make sure our hands are free to fight if we were to get caught. Trying would put us in too much danger. If he's to get out, he needs to walk out on his own two feet.

"Can you do anything?" the woman asks, her voice desperate. She looks at me with hope and watery eyes.

Damn it. I really wish she hadn't asked. Hope is a cruel thing for anyone in her position. I curse and turn away from both of them. I bite into my thumb *hard*, and my free hand goes to my pocket to withdraw a small vial of clean water. I hold my thumb over the opening and let a few droplets of my blood slip inside before the wound can close on its own. Where humans take a long time to heal, Mortal Gods don't.

As the blood drips into the small vial, the area on the back of my neck grows warm. I've never done this before despite my findings about the benefits of Divine Blood. The few books on Divine Blood and its abilities that I'd found and read in the Underworld and across Anatol's continent were murky on whether this would actually work. It'd been theorized and I'm sure it'd been tested before, but for some reason, no author ever wanted to say outright if a God's blood or a Mortal God's blood would truly heal a full-blooded mortal. I'm sure it will. I hope it will.

There's nothing in that tenuous blood bond at the back of my neck that suggests Ophelia would know what I'm doing save for that warmth. The brimstone always seems to react to any time I use my Divinity. As if it's heating up to prepare to repress my powers. Thankfully, as long as I don't take it too far or overuse my abilities, it doesn't keep me completely powerless and it doesn't stop me from killing whoever I need to.

By the time I turn back around, my thumb is free of the small tear I made with my teeth. I recap the vile and shake it before shoving it into the man's hand. "Drink this," I snap. "Quickly."

He takes the vial and eyes it with confusion. I can understand. It's no bigger than my pinkie. Even medicine vials are larger. "What is it?" Irina asks.

"Something that'll help your husband," I say. "The effects will allow you to breathe better and you'll be healed temporarily, but you'll still need to seek a doctor after we get out of here."

The man's eyes soften and he uncaps the vial. "I have a feeling finding a doctor will be the least of our worries after we escape this place," he says, "but you have my thanks, stranger. For everything."

With that, he tips his head back and swallows the vial's contents. For a moment, the feeling of guilt hits me. This man is far too trusting. Then again, why would someone rescue them and then try to kill them? Maybe I'm thinking too far into it and overcomplicating things. It wouldn't be the first time.

When the man is done, he hands me the now empty vial. I shove it back into my pocket and together, the three of us wait. Several seconds pass and I watch the man's progress with intent eyes. The consumption of God blood—or Mortal God blood—isn't well spread, but I'd learned that consuming Divine Blood can heal mortals to an extent. I have to hope that I have enough Divinity in my blood to help him and that the brimstone mark under my skin won't affect its potency.

After a few more tense moments, his breathing does seem to ease and color returns to his cheeks.

"Honey?" Irina touches her husband's bare chest, around the straps still anchoring their dead son to him.

"I'm fine," he assures her, somewhat wide-eyed and surprised as he sucks in a full breath. When he turns his gaze my way, I look down and move closer to the wall.

"Good," I grunt. "Then get ready to move—my friend should be back soon."

Silence and then, softly, the man responds, "Thank you."

I ignore the whisper and wait. When Regis returns, his eyes scan the three of us, stopping on the man. He narrows his gaze and then cuts a glare my way. I don't answer his unspoken accusation. Gordon already looks far better now that he's had a few droplets of my blood. The evidence of what I've done can be seen on the color that has returned to his cheeks even if only slightly.

"Is it ready?" I demand.

He continues to glare at me but answers regardless. "Yes. Follow my footsteps," he says. "Do not deviate from my path." His attention moves to the couple. "Do you understand?"

"Yes," Gordon replies.

Regis moves past me. "Then let's go."

Together, we track Regis, moving as he moves. Step by step as we head for the gate. Once there, he moves to the side of the long metal spokes welded together and then wiggles a few stones out of place. Taking a small tool in his hand he slams the blunt end up against the bolts on the top and bottom, knocking them out of place just enough for him to be able to swing the loosened side of the gate out a few feet.

"Alright," he says. "I'll go first. Kay?" Just as he hadn't earlier, Regis doesn't use my full name as he turns back to me and arches a brow. We know better than to do so in the midst of a job.

I nod. "Go, I'll follow after they're through."

That's all it takes. Regis slips through the opening he's created and the man pushes the woman forward. She clutches at him, but at the last second, she finally releases her husband's hand and slides her body between the rock and metal and onto the other side. Her plump body presses tight to both sides and she wiggles a bit, forcing her way out. The creaking of metal scratches at my ears and I look back anxiously, but we remain undiscovered.

I stop the man just before he moves forward. "You can't go through like that," I say, gesturing to the child on his back.

He reaches up and tightens his hold on the straps keeping the child in place. "I can't leave him."

"I know," I say. "But you'll have to remove him and go through on your own. I'll pass him through."

"You won't leave him?" the man demands.

I press my lips together. I want to tell him that his dead son can't feel it if they leave him now. That nothing would change if they left his body behind, but I don't. If anything, I respect them for their decision not to leave the child's corpse behind, but this is an instance where he needs to trust my judgment.

"I will pass him through to your arms," I repeat. "You have my word."

A beat passes and the man finally starts to untie the straps on his chest. I shake my head and unsheathe a dagger. "We need to move faster," I whisper absently as I start cutting away the straps, grabbing them before they can fall to the ground and stuffing them wherever I can. We can't leave them behind. Hiding our means of escape will buy the two of them time.

Behind me, I can hear the shouts from the castle. Smoke drifts into the air, filling my nostrils. *How big did the fire get?*

We get the child unlocked from his father's back before I ever get my answer and I tuck my blades back into place

41

quickly as he passes me his son's body. I hold the thin boy's frail corpse against my chest as the man turns and moves towards the opening Regis has provided for us. He looks back once, eyes crinkling with anguish. He meets my gaze and I nod, stepping after him.

It's an easier fit for the man as his back presses to the stones and he slips through. No metal shrieks and then his arms appear in the darkness, waiting. Carefully, I turn the child and pass him through the thin opening. Sweat collects at the top of my forehead and behind my neck, sliding down into my clothes. Air brushes over my flesh, sending several droplets skittering down my spine. It's just enough of a warning.

I drop the boy into his father's arms and turn, withdrawing one of my daggers from my leather arm sheath at the same second a man slams into my front. I don't even hesitate. The edge of my blade cuts over the man's eyes and blood squirts.

"*Fuck*!" Harsh, deep, and grunting, his voice slides over my ears as my back is pressed into the stone. Divine scent hits my nostrils, like fresh overturned soil and wisteria trees. Not a God, but a Mortal God. He'd moved fast enough to make me question it, though. So silent that I hadn't detected him until that last second.

Fingers grip at my throat, but I turn my blade from his face and slice through his wrist. A fist slams into my abdomen and air escapes my lungs. The fist cracks into my ribs and it's only because of my blood that I know I'll heal quickly. Even still, it fucking hurts. A wheezing breath leaves me, but I don't curse. I don't say anything. I can't. I've blinded him quickly enough that I doubt he's seen me, but the healing abilities of Mortal Gods differ—there's no telling how fast he'll heal from the wound.

A flash of raven hair flutters in front of my face, combined with a chiseled jaw and a straight nose. Of course —he's fucking gorgeous. Definitely Divine in some capacity.

"Quick bastard," the Mortal God snaps. "Did you really need to go for my damned eyes?" Despite the words, he doesn't sound especially angry—more shocked, almost impressed. His lips spread into a smile and pearly white teeth shine through the darkness. I feel like he's baring them as both a reward and a warning.

Yeah, dumbass, I really did. It was either that or risk him identifying me later. Silver hair and gray eyes may not be entirely uncommon, but put them together along with my youthful face, and well, it's not a risk I'm willing to take. That is ... if I don't kill him here and now.

Quick as a shot, I duck under his other arm, only to come to a slamming stop as he tackles me to the ground. Dirt fills my mouth, sliding across my tongue, and I rear back, spitting it out and coughing as my hair is gripped in a fist. "Ah. Ah. Ah."

The body pressed against mine is rock hard and cut like a warrior's. Wide shoulders press my back down, strong legs clamped on either side of mine. The sound of his voice, though, as he'd spoken was light and amused.

Is he fucking playing with me?

"Not so fast," he says against my ear.

Oh yes, that fast. It's hard not to reply to every word aloud, but I manage it. I can hear Regis on the other side of the gate along with the other two. Their shuffling footsteps are unsure. Fear tinges the whole area, permeating everything around us. Tossing back my elbow, I nail my attacker in the temple. He grunts but maintains his hold.

Stubborn fucker.

"I'm not going to kill you," he seethes, "but you'll pay for blinding me first."

What a little fucking baby. I roll my eyes. *He'll heal up soon enough anyway.*

I slam the point of my dagger into the ground ahead of me and use the anchor to drag myself out a little bit from his embrace, rolling and kicking against his stomach. His sword clanks at his hips, undrawn. Why?

Before I can figure it out, however, another dagger comes flying out of the darkness from somewhere behind me. It slams into the man's shoulder and his grip doesn't just loosen. One of his arms goes completely slack and another curse spits out of his lips.

Regis! I use the opening he gave me to slip out of my attacker's hold and sprint towards the gate's opening. I slide right through the too small space, my clothes catching on the metal, but I don't care. One sharp stone cuts against my thigh and I wince, smelling my own blood in the air. So much for not leaving any evidence, but it's too late now anyway.

A roar echoes at my back, but I don't let it give me pause. Already the human family ahead is rushing to escape. As soon as I'm on the other side, Regis shoves my cloak into my arms—he must have retrieved it while I was fighting—and grips my arm, yanking me after them. Our stronger bodies catch up with them quickly and Regis casts me a look. I know what he wants.

I head for the woman, tossing my cloak around her shoulders and then scooping her up in my arms as Regis heads for the man. Now that we're out of the God Lord's castle, all we need to do is put some distance between us and those dangers. If it weren't for my height, I might've taken the man myself—since we both know I'm the stronger of the two of us, but then again, carrying him as well as his son would likely give my Divinity away. It makes more sense for Regis to take on the bigger load of the two of us, if only to keep these two from finding out my secret.

Once they're both clasped in our arms our speed increases, and with the fire and shouts at our backs, we disappear into the darkened woods.

CHAPTER 5

THEOS

The wet slick sounds of the pussy slapping down on my lap numb my ears. I close my eyes, relaxing back against the silken cushions and pillows of the bed as Rahela rides upon my cock. Up and down, back and forth. Her moans increase in volume until they start to penetrate my mind with little pricks of annoyance. Why does she always have to be so fucking noisy? At first, I hadn't minded it. In fact, I'd relished in the vocal proof of my skill, but now...

What was intended to be a well-deserved break and reward for myself has quickly become worse than a bore—it's become a vexation.

Over me, Rahela shudders as she rides herself to completion. *Her* completion—not mine. I can tell when her insides suddenly clamp down on me and contract in little bursts of movements. Her lips open as she gasps for breath and then smiles at me all bleary-eyed as she bends forward. I turn my head as her mouth tries to fall upon mine.

"If you're done," I snap. "Get off."

Rahela squeaks out a shocked protest. "B-but, I just—"

Fresh irritation spins through me. My hand clamps over her mouth, cutting off her words as I roll on top of her, sliding one of her legs up and out and repositioning my cock at the opening of her pussy. With one single thrust, I seat myself to the hilt. Tight, inner walls wrap around my flesh. Yet, there's no sound from her. Yes. That's exactly what I wanted.

No more of her cries as I fuck her. Just blissful much-needed silence.

I begin to move, thrusting my cock into her channel. In and out. Rahela's inner muscles tighten and contract with each pass. I groan, squeezing her face harder. I refuse to remove my hand just yet. If she starts to moan or make noises again, I'm afraid I'll be left with yet another body to dispose of and no release of my own. Considering, though, that Rahela is a fellow Mortal God rather than human, I doubt it'd be looked upon well that I'd kill one of the stronger races. Besides, as a Mortal God, she should be able to take this level of violent fucking without breaking.

Once I take over, fucking into Rahela as if she's merely a hole for my use—which, at this moment, that's exactly what she is—my orgasm finally comes to me. It rushes forward, starting low at the base of my spine before shooting upward and out. My balls draw up tight and I still above the soft body beneath me. Her breasts heave up and down, flushed a bright pink color that darkens her nipples as she attempts to breathe around my harsh grip squeezing her cheeks. Her hands are locked on my wrists, eyes gazing up at me, almost pleadingly. No, I don't care what she wants.

With a grin, I withdraw my cock and then slam it into her again. Her eyes sharpen and her nails lengthen, stabbing into my flesh and drawing blood. Yes, just like that.

That's what I want. A little bit of fight. I fuck her harder through my release, dumping my seed into her channel with each pass until I swear she's sucked me dry.

When I'm finished, I pull out and roll away, releasing her just in time for her to gasp for breath. "You fucking asshole!" Rahela snaps as I crack my neck to the side and sit up, swinging my legs over the edge of the bed. "What the fuck was that?"

Frowning down at my quickly softening cock, I reach to the side and grab up the nearest thing—the silken blouse of the Academy's uniform she'd been wearing before. Using the fabric to wipe myself clean before standing up, I toss it back onto the girl's bed and then bend to find my own clothing.

"Theos, answer me!"

A groan unleashes from my throat as I finish tying up the laces of my trousers and find my shirt. "Gods, does your mouth ever stop screeching?" A pillow flies in my direction and I deftly dodge it as I slip my shirt on over my head.

"Never again, Theos, do you hear me! Ride your own cock from now on." Rahela seethes in fury on her bed, dragging the sheets up over her naked form as I spot my boots and grab those to tug on as well.

Once I'm finished, I turn back, offering her little more than a grin. "I'd wager I would do a better job of it than you did, Sweetling."

She growls and as I move for the door, a gust of wind slams into my back accompanied by a burst of water. It soaks my freshly donned clothes through and I pause with my hand on the knob.

"Get fucked, Theos," she snaps behind me. Were I one of my brothers, she'd be screaming in pain for mercy at this moment. Fortunately for her, I am not them. So, I leave her without a response, slamming the door on my way out into the corridor.

"Fucking cunt." I shake out the water in my boots.

"I suspect that's exactly what you did, brother. Fuck her cunt." I freeze as Ruen's deep baritone hits me. "Or was that not the point?"

"There a reason you've followed me here, Ruen?" I lift my gaze to his and lower my foot back to the ground.

Standing against the opposite wall from me, with his arms crossed over his chest, Ruen's face is shielded in shadow. He pushes away from the stone wall and moves forward, into the light. The glittering lamp swinging from the wall several paces away illuminates the jagged scar that severs the dark brow above his eye on the right side. The look of it is a cruel reminder—it takes a lot for a Mortal God, the son of a God, to maintain a scar into adulthood. That scar is a testament to Ruen's darkness.

"The Council has been called," he says.

My blood turns to ice in my veins. Though a God Council being called means nothing for us Demi-Gods or the other Mortal Gods, it means that the strongest and most powerful of the local God Lords will be descending upon the Mortal Gods of Riviere soon. This means that our father will be coming as well—the very creature that gave Ruen that scar.

"When?"

"Unknown," he replies. "I suspect it'll be at the term's end, after exams. It'll take that long for the lot of them to be reached and for them to crawl their way out of whatever hedonistic desires they've been saturating themselves in to arrive."

I nod sharply and turn down the hall. A few heartbeats later, I can hear the soft sound of Ruen's footsteps behind me. He doesn't speak and neither do I as he follows me back to our rooms.

By the time we reach the tower on the northern part of the dormitories and climb to the uppermost section—the rooms for male First Tiers and their Terra, the mortal servants hired to attend to our needs—I'm starting to feel the exhaustion of the day. Rahela had been constantly yapping at me until I'd finally given in and allowed her a fuck, but at what cost really? My fucking eardrums? The release I'd gotten from her cunt had been adequate at best, and at worst, pointless. Time to cut her loose, I should think. She was entertaining in the way she'd cut through all of the other Tier girls with her jealousy, but that had faded as she'd become more desperate and clingy—half expecting her little threats to not fuck me anymore to have weight, as if I care enough about the body I use to dull my senses.

The door swings open and Ruen and I march inside to see Kalix in his usual spot against the wall. He's staring through the arching windows that take up the entirety of the wall to the courtyard. He doesn't look back as we enter.

"You're back," I say. "How was Mineval?"

"Interesting," he responds. His eyes remain glued to the scenery outside as he speaks.

"Was it?" Ruen asks as he strides to the bar along the wall and lifts a decanter full of liquid ambrosia, pouring himself a hefty glass. "That's rare coming from you. I thought you despised Talmatia—it's part of the reason you were so resistant to her summons."

I wince at Ruen's words. Giving in to Rahela's licentious pleas had been partially to forget the fact that yet another of our father's friends was using her power to command us. No, it wasn't enough that she could fuck whoever she wished, but anyone who denied her, especially those of us who weren't Gods ourselves, had to contend with her temper tantrums and demands. She'd accepted Kalix this time, but next time, I have no doubt Talmatia or one of Azai's other copious God companions will call upon Ruen or me as well.

"She simply had me working as a guard for the duration of the break," Kalix replies. "It was either that or join her in bed, and I've already done so. I find her boring at this point. Whatever Divinity she has, it's certainly doing nothing for the dryness of her cunt."

Harsh but no doubt true. Talmatia is nothing but a God obsessed with herself. It makes sense that she'd be close to someone such as Azai since our father is not unaffected by his own appearance or strength.

"What made this trip so interesting?" I ask as I throw off my wet shirt. It plops onto the floor and I reach for the ties of my trousers to shed them as well. They get stuck on my boots and I toe the fuckers off before striding towards the wardrobe naked.

"A thief," he replies.

"Someone stole from a God?" I pause as I reach the wardrobe. "How did Talmatia kill them?" As vain as she is, no doubt her punishment had been cruel.

Kalix's voice, when he responds, is full of chortling amusement. "She didn't."

Ruen looks up from his station. "What? She let them live?" I agree with Ruen's confusion. Mercy isn't like a God, especially one known for her cruelty.

Kalix shakes his head. "No, the thief got away—stole a few humans right out of the dungeons and disappeared. Talmatia was in quite a rage."

"What did they steal?" I ask. What could be so important that a mortal would risk their lives for it?

"Nothing of consequence," Kalix replies with a wave of his hand. "Just a few prisoners set for death anyway."

"No doubt for a ridiculous reason," Ruen muses.

Kalix shrugs. "I suppose. Regardless, the thief got away and so did the mortals."

I release a slow whistle. "That man must have balls the size of a God's," I muse. "Even I avoid irritating Talmatia if I can help it."

"*If* it was a man," Kalix says.

"You don't think a woman would've defied the Gods, certainly not a God like Talmatia," I scoff. "There's no way."

Kalix shrugs. "The thief smelled far too good to be a man to me," he says.

"You got close enough to smell them and they still got away?" To say I'm surprised would be an understatement.

"They blinded me," Kalix replies. "As if they were hiding their identity—they went straight for my eyes the second I grabbed them. I haven't battled a human that could fight back so well. I hope to meet them again someday."

"If you meet them again and Talmatia finds out that you didn't inform her, she'll hang you from her castle with arrows in your eyes," Ruen warns.

Kalix sighs. "Ah, but it would be worth it, I think, for another battle with the thief."

"Careful," I warn him. "You might heal fast but pain is still pain." Regardless of whether he seems to like the agony, there's only so much even our bodies can take before it's too much. Ruen and I share a glance. The scars he bears should be a constant reminder of that fact.

Kalix hums in the back of his throat and then switches the topic. "I heard that we'll be getting a new Terra," he says.

"Oh?"

"Speaking of Terra, what happened to the boy we had?" Ruen suddenly asks, setting the decanter down. "Shouldn't he be here?"

I glance behind me as I pull out a fresh pair of pants. Kalix finally looks at us, his lips twitching in that unnerving way of his. "He won't be returning," is all Kalix says.

My hands are still on the opening of my new trousers and I growl. "Did you fuck or kill this one?" I demand. "We can't keep going through them like this, Kalix. What am I supposed to do? Clean my own room?" I finish yanking on my pants and point to the pile of soaked clothes and boots on the floor. "Since you're the reason our servant is gone, you can pick that shit up."

Kalix merely grins. "He was so tasty, brother. I couldn't help myself."

I scoff. "He was a fucking virgin who'd never set eyes on a Mortal God before arriving here," I snap. "He was from the outskirts. What about him was so intriguing?"

A light catches in his eyes, the faded green color glowing slightly as his face contorts in remembered pleasure. "He clung to me when I fucked his ass," he says. "So trusting, these little humans. Show them the slightest bit of kindness and they'll give you everything you ask for. With the two of you, he thought I was his fucking savior. It was quite the high, like ambrosia on my tongue ... or rather, my cock."

I wrinkle my nose in distaste. "I don't care who you fuck, Kalix," I snap. "But by the fucking Gods, themselves, at least leave whoever we get next alone. If I have to train another after this, I'll be shoving a broomstick up your ass and using you to sweep the room."

Instead of being insulted, Kalix chuckles and returns his gaze to the window. I finish dressing and take a seat on one end of the lounge in the center of our shared common room. Four doors are spaced out evenly along the wall— one to each of our rooms and one to the hallway. I have half a mind to stomp down to the level below ours where the Terra for this tower reside and grab ahold of one of the female servants to come and service me. Rahela's cunt did nothing to assuage my mood and Ruen's sudden announcement has only soured it further. I know, however, that if I were to do that, it'd invite Kalix to destroy yet another perfectly good servant.

With a groan, I rest my head back on the cushions. What fucking Mortal Gods we are.

Three broken savages hiding away in this fucking tower, imprisoned by the blood that runs through our veins. I glance down and watch the pulse in my wrist throb against my flesh. Sometimes … I think. Sometimes, I wonder how much good it would do the world if I simply sliced it open and let it all run out. Maybe then, I'd feel some sort of freedom from this curse we've been given.

There is no freedom from the Gods, though. So long as we exist in the same world, they hold the authority, and we are merely temporary borrowers of that authority.

A higher domination there has never been than that of the creatures that masquerade as benevolent, but fuck their way through the bodies of their worshipers to no end but pleasure and power.

CHAPTER 6

KIERA

The sound of rain resonates into the quiet interior of the horse-drawn carriage as Regis and I finally find our way into Riviere. The ride had been long and tedious. My backside is sore and my hair—the moonlight color of it dulled due to the grease and dirt and sweat buildup—is plastered to the side of my temple and the back of my neck. The capital of Anatol's continent is just as I distantly recall, luxurious as ever. Even under the dim gloom of rain and clouds, I can see that. I've been to a few of the other cities that house Mortal Gods Academies—three in total—but as the capital, this one is different.

The buildings in Riviere are taller here, stronger, built to house Divine Beings. The roofs are sloped and edged in expensive material. Gold and silver plaques line the streets. Some windows are colored and painted to depict stories from ancient days. The fairy tales of Gods lending aid to their human counterparts rather than reigning over them as the cruel overlords that they are. A more self-absorbed race I've never found.

The carriage's ride smooths out the very moment our

wheels hit the city's streets and we pass through the gate-way, pausing to show our identities—perfect fakes, cour-tesy of the Underworld and, I assume, our client. I've used many pseudonyms before to get into places I was required for other jobs, but this is the first time I've used one so close to my actual name and for such an extended period of time. Months if all goes well and possibly a year or more if it gets drawn out.

Across from me, Regis sits with his back against the wall, separating him from the driver, his hood pulled down low over his face. With the only light coming from the water-soaked windows, all I can see is the lower half of his face.

"Are you nervous?" he asks.

I scoff and shake my head. A nervous assassin. That's an oxymoron if I've ever heard one. I don't even think I was nervous when I made my first official kill—just annoyed. Then again, it's been so long that I feel like looking back on those memories colors them differently. Perhaps I was nervous, but now I'm not. Ophelia made sure I would be who I am today. Devoid of emotion when it comes to my kills.

This line of work is disgusting, I'll admit. It's shown me, more times than I care to count, all of the ways that people will take advantage of others. Unfortunately, it's also shown me that humans and Gods, no matter what the Divine Beings will have everyone believe, aren't nearly as different as they seem.

I take no pleasure in killing, but on occasion—when I see the people who could've died instead, at the hands of my own victims—it does make everything a little better. Or at least, it makes *me* feel better about it all.

"You'll get used to this job pretty fast," Regis assures me. "You're not changing your name much anyway."

"Just because I'm going by my first name, doesn't mean it won't take a godsdamned lifetime to make this work," I reply. "I'm not comfortable with the fact that even though I've decided to take on this job, the client still hasn't revealed the target."

Regis shrugs. "That's just the risk you take for that kind of money, I suppose."

"It has to be multiple targets, don't you think?" I ask.

He turns his head towards the window and the passing scenery. The golden-etched buildings with tall pillars soon grow smaller and smaller the farther we get into the city. The streets narrow and so, too, do the alleyways we pass. Divine Beings become the minority as we enter Riviere's second district, the human habitat. Still, though, to the village cities outside of Riviere, even the slums of this God City are rich comparatively.

"I try not to think too deeply about our clients' plans, Kiera," Regis finally answers. "I don't concern myself with what happens after I've shed blood, only on how to survive until the next day."

My gaze moves over him. Stoicism from Regis is rare, but it always seems to come about when he's surrounded by Divine Beings. Dimly, I recall the first day he'd realized what I was. It'd been the turning point in our strange friendship.

"Stop crying."

My muffled sob hiccups and I jerk my head up. "What?"

The boy's lean face twists in disgust as he looks at me. Bushy blond brows furrow and the hollowness of his cheeks seems to darken as his lips pinch. The greasy strands of hair that match his brows are longer at the top than at the sides. No wait, it's not grease but water. I blink and cast a curious look from the wet hair slicked back over his scalp to the smudges of dirt and other gray and brown grime left on the skin of his face and neck— streaked in an obvious attempt to remove it. I look up at him and wipe my sleeve under my nose. It comes away smeared with snot. His face wrinkles further and he even goes so far as to scoot away.

"No one here cares if you cry or not," he says. "They're all irritated by it—fuck, I'm irritated by it."

Did he just say ... fuck? Dad told me that was a bad word and it was liable to get some of that gross brown bar gunk from the market shoved in my mouth—the stuff that's supposed to be for washing not eating—as punishment.

"It hurts," I say, blinking as more tears cascade down my cheeks. My whole body hurts. From my back to my legs to my arms. I feel as if someone tied me to the back of a horse and slapped its rear end.

With a huff and an eye roll, the boy turns and fully looks at me. He leans down and appears to inspect me with his eyes. "Ya ain't on the verge of dying," he says finally with a nod. "If ya were, ya wouldn't be here. There ain't no parents to hold your hand here, kid. Tears are for people who care. You ain't gonna find no one like that in the Underworld."

"You're a kid too," I snap. "Don't say that like you're not."

The boy sighs. "I'm less of a kid than you are because I don't cry like one."

I hurriedly finish wiping my face with my other sleeve, clearing away the tracks of my tears. "Well, I'm not crying now," I say.

He arches a brow. "And? You'll probably cry some more in your bed tonight when it's lights out."

"I will not!"

He snickers and his hand comes down on the top of my head, scrubbing as if he were petting a particularly rowdy cat. I growl at him. I'm not a kept animal—I'm not like what that woman said.

"That's it, keep saying that, kid," the boy replies. "Maybe someday it'll be true. For your sake, I hope it is. Criers don't last long here."

I grumble and look away from him. Pulling my legs up from under me, I wrap my arms around my knees and set my head down on them. I should've never entertained him, I think. He's annoying.

Minutes go by and the boy's hand retracts. I think we've fallen into some sort of semi-considerate silence, but then, he speaks again. "What's your name, by the way?" he asks. "Mine's Regis."

I lift my head and turn to see him holding out his hand. With another sniff I reach out, pausing when he jerks his hand away and grimaces. "Don't shake my hand with the same one you rubbed your snot all over," he snaps.

Ugh, he's such a picky guy. I replace it with my other hand. "Kiera," I say. "My name's Kiera, but my dad used to call me Kiki."

"Is that so?" Regis drops my hand and tilts his head. "Where's your dad now? He sell ya?"

I shake my head. "No, my dad would never sell me," I said. He loved me. He always told me so, and my dad didn't lie.

"Then where is he?" Regis presses. For all his boasted maturity, he obviously doesn't pick up the clues when someone does not want to talk about something.

I sigh and tell him anyway—after all, it's not like giving him information about my dad will hurt me. "He's dead," I say. Just saying the words hurts more than whatever strange

Divine spell the weird lady who had bought me from the bandits did.

"Oh." Regis frowns. "Well, I'm glad he didn't sell you."

"Why would you even think that?" I shake my head.

"'Cause, it's not unusual for poor people," he says. "My dad sold me and my brother."

"Your brother?" I repeat, glancing around as if another carbon copy of this boy will somehow appear out of nowhere. No one does.

"Yup." Regis sniffs and scratches his nose. "But we got split up at the auction. Some pretty God bought Grell and now it's just me." He offers me a toothy smile and I notice that one of his front teeth wobbles a little bit, crooked and loose.

"A God?" I repeat.

His face squishes up and his smile fades. "Yeah." Regis turns away. A moment later, he mutters a curse under his breath. "Bitch."

That's a bad word, too, but I don't tell him that. I think he already knows and that's why he said it.

"So why are you here?" he asks. "How'd you end up in the Underworld?"

I shrug. "Some people kidnapped me and when they realized they could get in trouble for having me, they sold me to the lady here."

"Ophelia?" he clarifies.

I nod.

The frown he gives me deepens. "What do you mean, when they 'realized they could get in trouble for having you'?"

I shift uncomfortably where I sit. His stare doesn't let up. "I'm not supposed to say."

"Who told you so? Ophelia?"

"Yeah."

Regis' forehead pinches as he contemplates my answer. He's wondering if he should press or not, I can tell. A part of me wonders if him asking a second time would be a good thing or not. I've never told anyone else but my dad about the things I can do. Ophelia already knew because the bad guys who killed my dad and brought me to her told her what they'd seen. What would happen if my new friend knew too?

"I see," Regis says as he leans back against the wall.

I blink at him, surprised. "You're not going to ask?"

He shakes his head. "I shouldn't," he says. "If Ophelia finds out, I'd be in trouble. I don't want a whipping."

"What if I told you anyway?" I ask. "You could always say I gave you the information without you asking."

His eyes shoot to me, curiosity lingering in their depths as well as wariness. "If it's something you're not supposed to say, then you could get a whipping," he warns me.

I chuckle. "That's okay, I'll heal fast." That's one of the things I can do well—heal from any sort of punishment.

He snorts. "No one heals from a whipping that fast."

"I do."

Regis' amusement slowly dissolves as he looks back at me and his brows lower. "What do you mean?"

"Just what I said." I contemplate how to explain it to him, but it would likely be easier to show him than to say it in words. I shift my fingers over the hard ground and find a rock. "See, watch."

I strike the rock against the wall, sharpening the already pointed side, and then bring it down hard on my forearm as he watches on in confusion. The edge of the rock stabs into my arm and he gasps, reaching out and grabbing ahold of me. Regis slaps the rock out of my hand and lifts my arm with a scowl.

"What the fuck are you doing?" he demands.

"Look," I say, pointing down at the skin I've broken open. It stings, but the smear of blood lessens almost immediately and his

eyes widen as the skin knits itself back together. He rubs a thumb over where the cut was and finds smooth, unblemished skin. The remaining blood is all that tells of the wound that was once there.

"That's not ... possible," he says. "If you heal this fast then that would mean that you're a..."

Stunned eyes lift to meet mine. His hand grips onto my forearm tighter, to the point of pain. I flinch. "Hey, that hurts." I pull away and he releases me almost as if he's still surprised. I rub the area he'd been holding, soothing away the slight indentation of his grip as it dissipates.

"You're a Mortal God." It's not a question, but I nod anyway.

As soon as I do, however, his expression darkens. Regis' hand snaps out and circles my throat as he slams me up against the wall. "You fucking—"

"Hey!" One of the adults patrolling the hallway comes rushing over. "What are you doing? No fighting!"

Tears burn at the backs of my eyes. But Regis' earlier words remind me. This place is not one for criers. I'm not a baby. I hold them back but still struggle against him. "Let go!"

He leans closer. "You're a fucking Mortal God," he hisses. "Why the fuck would something like you be here?"

"I don't know what you mean." I flop against him, my breathing coming faster the tighter he squeezes. "You're hurting me."

"Hey!" the adult calls again. A hand lands on Regis' shoulder and pulls him back. He finally releases me. I cough out a breath and suck in another. "What the fuck did I say?" A hard hand cuffs Regis across his face and then again. Each strike following the man's words, "No. Fucking. Fighting."

Regis is unceremoniously tossed back against the wall and a finger is shoved in my face. "You too," the man snaps before storming away.

I feel along my throat as Regis shakes his head and scoots several feet away from me.

"Why did you hurt me?" I manage to ask after several minutes have passed.

"Because you don't belong here," he replies. Regis pulls his knees up to his chest and wraps his small arms around them. "You're the reason my brother's gone."

"I've never met your brother, though."

"Doesn't matter." He shakes his head. "You're just like the God that took him."

"No, I'm not."

"You are," he insists.

Anger pours through me. "No. I'm not!" I yell.

"Quiet!" the man from before barks from the end of the hallway. "One more fucking shout and you and your friend will be sleeping in the courtyard instead of getting a bed."

That threat has me shutting my mouth, but I shift towards Regis despite it. He shifts away. "Don't come near me," he hisses.

"I'm not bad," I tell him. "I didn't do anything to your brother. I promise."

Regis is quiet for a long time, so long, in fact, that I fear he's resolved to ignore my existence. Eventually, however, he speaks. "Mortal Gods shouldn't be here," he says without looking at me. "Mortal Gods are better than humans."

I frown at that. "Why would you think that?"

"Because it's true," he snaps. "You heal faster. You're smarter. You're stronger. It's why Grell went with that God—because we, humans, can't defy them."

"My dad said that humans and Gods are the same," I tell him.

"They're not."

I bite my tongue to keep myself from screaming at him. My dad's not a liar. He wouldn't have told me something that wasn't true. I sniffle and the sound makes me realize that the tears have returned. No matter how much I try to defy them, they run down my cheeks. Each wipe dries my skin only for it to be taken back over by the fresh saltiness of my own pain.

A sigh comes from the boy and I sense rather than see Regis' head turn towards me. "What did I say about crying?"

I hiccup. "My d-dad didn't lie," I say.

"What?"

I sniff again and rub my face hard with the dirty sleeve of my shirt. I rub until my skin feels raw. "My dad didn't lie," I repeat the words. "He said that humans and Gods are the same. He's not a liar."

Regis is quiet for a beat and then he shuffles closer. I look up. His face is twisted and full of guilt. "I'm not calling him a liar," he tells me. "But we are different. Gods have power and ... mortals don't."

"My dad was mortal and he was the strongest man I know," I say.

"Your dad's dead now, though," he replies. "Gods don't die."

I blink and sit up straighter. "Yes, they do." I straighten my shoulders. "My dad said that Gods can be killed, but only if their killer has Divinity of their own."

Regis' gaze widens and his lips part in shock. Suddenly, the look in his eyes changes. He stares at me for several long beats of silence, his face a mask of emotions—none of which I can place or understand as they pass over his features too quickly for me to catch them. Finally, he sits back against the wall and looks away.

"You're right," he says. "I forgot about that. I just ... I didn't think anyone with Divinity would ever try to kill a God."

I cross my arms over my chest. "Well, I'm going to," I snap.

"What?" His head pivots to face me again.

"I'm going to find the bad people who hurt my dad," I say. "I'm going to find the Gods who took my mom and I'm going to kill them."

Regis stares at me for longer this time. So long that I wonder if he's even seeing me or if he's fallen asleep with his eyes open. When his lips part and he sucks in a breath, I know he's still awake. His hand comes up and I flinch away from it, worried he's going to hit me for saying something that Ophelia had only laughed at. It's not funny. It's the truth. But Regis doesn't hit me, nor does he laugh.

Instead, he pats the top of my head with his dirty, grimy fingers. "That's a good goal, Kiera," he says. "A good goal indeed."

CHAPTER 7

KIERA

"We're here." The carriage stops and Regis gets out first, flipping up his hood to keep his head from getting drenched in the rain. He reaches back automatically and for a moment, I stare at his upturned palm. Then with a sharp look up at him, I deliberately ignore it and jump down the stairs to the ground myself. He curls his fingers back into his palm and lowers his hand with a smirk. "Alright then."

"You should know better," I tell him as I move towards the door of the building we've stopped in front of. "I'm not one of your bedmates."

"That's for damn sure," he mutters beneath his breath as he follows me inside.

Once the solid, windowless door shuts behind us, we pull down our hoods and shake the water from the ends of our cloaks. The inside of the shop is dark and musky, smelling heavily of herbs and firewood. The reason for the scent is obvious as there's a rather fierce fire burning in the brick hearth at the far back of the main room and all around us, dried herbs are hung from twine. I brush a few twigs aside to move farther inside, and behind me, Regis does the same.

"Hello?" I call out. A door slams open to my right, the rusty hinges screaming with the force as a short round woman appears. "Madam Brione?" The woman is older, with gray flyaways hanging in long curls around her surprisingly clean face. With the state of the shop, I'd expected her to be just as dirty and dust-smudged.

"Ah, you must be the girl from the Hinterlands," the woman says, quickly bustling into the room. Despite her stature and obvious limp as she lists heavily to one side, she is quite fast.

Regis and I exchange a look. Ophelia's contacts are always the most eclectic bunch. Nothing really surprises me anymore. Madam Brione moves behind a wide counter and casually lifts a book before slamming it down on a skittering bug. I don't jump, but my lips do pull back in a grimace. I'm simply thankful it wasn't a spider. While I realize that humans aren't particularly fond of the creatures, I certainly don't like seeing them squashed just for existing. They were likely here in this world long before humans and will remain long after them.

One glance at Regis' horrified expression brings me a small kernel of amusement, though. In fact, he's had a slowly brewing look of disgust since we entered the poorly maintained shop. If I had to hazard a guess, I'd say this whole place is simply for looks. There's no clear item for sale, just an eclectic mix of junk covered in thick layers of grime and dust—as if the dirt itself is a warding spell meant to scare off potential customers to keep them from looking too closely at a shop that can hardly be called that.

No, Madam Brione's carefully maintained image as that of a hoarder is likely little more than window dressing for a place meant as a rendezvous point. When Madam Brione lifts the book up and scoots away the smooshed bug as if it's little more than a piece of lint, I swear I can hear Regis gag a little at the green and brown goo that smears over the counter's wood. If Madam Brione notices or hears, though, she doesn't comment.

The book opens and Madam Brione leafs through the pages before stopping somewhere in the middle. She sets her palms down and looks back up at us. "So, is it both of you then?" she asks.

"No," I answer. "Just one, if you could."

"A new identity and a recommendation to the Academy?" she clarifies.

I nod.

She clucks her tongue and goes back to the book, flipping another page. "You want to keep your name and just change the surname then?"

"I don't have a surname," I tell her. My father never had one and I'd never known of my mother's actual name much less a surname. Did Gods even have them?

"Oh." She slaps the book closed. "That makes it easier then. I assume Ophelia erased your existence when you joined the Guild?"

There hadn't been anything to erase since my birth had never been recorded, but I nod anyway. The chill from the outside versus the heat of the shop is slowly catching up to me. Sweat collects at the back of my neck and slides down beneath my clothes. I reach up and tug at my collar. It's too hot.

"If you're from the Hinterlands, they won't accept you," Madam Brione says. "We'll give you a different background, I think. There a region you are particularly fond of?"

I shake my head. "Not really."

"Any surname you'd care to take?"

"Not real—"

Regis locks his hand on my shoulder, stopping my repeated answer as he leans forward. "Can she take Nezerac?" he asks.

I blink. "That would make it obvious that I'm a nomad," I point out. "It's not even a real last name." It would defeat the purpose, too, of hiding my Hinterlands origins since only nomads roam the outer borders of Anatol.

Regis glances down at me. "Nomads are stout," he says. "They last and it'll explain … well, if you're going to be there for a while, I doubt you'd manage to keep up the facade of a helpless little human for months on end."

A scowl twists my lips. "Are you suggesting that I can't do my job, Regis?"

He shakes his head. "Of course not, but we don't want to make this more complicated. A lot of your … mannerisms can be explained by the fact that you're a nomad."

"I can act," I say. "For a time."

"Not for months," he repeats. "Besides, the best lies are the ones that are still somewhat truthful."

"Nezerac is a good name for a nomad. They're rare in the God Cities, though," Madam Brione states. "It's a risk, considering how close nomads are to hinterland backgrounds."

"Won't we risk me not getting in at all?" I argue.

Regis meets my angry gaze. "The closer the lie is to the truth, the easier it is to maintain. You'll get in, I'm not too worried about that."

I cross my arms over my chest and lean back on my heels, eyeing him. "And why is that? Do you have more information you've yet to share?"

His gaze skitters away and his jaw clenches. "The

Academy of Riviere is opening its doors to more Terra sooner than usual, that should tell you that they're in desperate need of servants."

My irritation fades. He's not wrong. If they're opening their doors to the humans earlier, then that can only mean that they've either killed or run off the servants they had before. I turn back to the woman. "Fine," I snap. "Nezerac, then. I want that last name."

She twists her lips as if the decision displeases her but shrugs. "Have it your way," she says. "If we're going with that, then we need a recommendation. I can purchase one from a Lower God without issue, but I have to ask—have you ever actually served a God?"

I shake my head. She sighs and turns away, shuffling towards the cabinets built into the back wall. The doors clatter open as she bends over, her backside swaying with sharp jerking movements as she digs into the dark interior. A moment later, she pulls out another book and blows a layer of dust off of its surface before tossing it onto the counter towards me.

With a frown, I lift the book and read the title aloud. "*The Perfect Terra: Etiquette Required to Best Serve Our Divine Gods.*" This can't be real. I prop open the cover and then blow at the second layer of dust covering the pages inside before I continue reading. "'Always keep your eyes downcast unless you're called. Prepare your body in regular water baths and should your God ever call upon you for night service, you must always be ready to soothe their amorous desires.'"

Regis snorts and when I jerk my head back to glare at him, he quickly turns away and covers his mouth with the back of his hand as he fakes a cough. A poor cover-up. *Prick.*

Turning back to Madam Brione, I set the book back down. "I won't need this," I say, pushing it towards her.

Without batting an eyelash, she pushes it back at me. "If you've never been a Terra, then you will. This teaches the best ways to deal with and handle the Divine Beings as their servant."

"I'll take my chances," I snap, unwilling to pick up that offensive piece of literature again.

Madam Brione eyes me. "The Academy Terra are regularly punished for their God charges' offenses." It's clear that her words are a warning, but I don't care. Pain, I can handle. Even sex isn't something I'm adverse to. I've fucked to kill before and I'll do it again if the situation calls for it. It's just an action. It doesn't have to mean anything. But catering to pompous Divine creatures and licking their feet is something I won't do.

"I'll handle it," I tell her.

Regis reaches forward, however, and plucks the book off of the counter. "I'll convince her," he murmurs to Madam Brione with his usual playboy smile. "Thank you for the assistance."

Her expression doesn't inspire confidence, but I don't care. She's not the one that needs to be confident. I am. "Suit yourself," she finally says, nodding to Regis before casting a cutting look my way. "You wait right there. I'll be back."

Just like that, Madam Brione moves out from behind the counter and disappears through the door she'd come from earlier. I wait a few moments to ensure she's out of earshot before I whip around and face Regis. "I'm not taking that," I snap.

Regis rolls his eyes. "Stop it," he says, holding up his

free hand. "You don't need to bring it with you, but think of it as research. Give the contents a look through."

"It's insulting," I bite out.

"So?" He tilts his head. "We've done far worse, haven't we?"

I ... have no response to that. My shoulders droop. He's right. "Fine," I mutter. "I'll read through it." I fucking hate it when he's right.

"Good." He nods and passes the book over to me. I hold it in my grip for a moment, scowling down at the cover before I slide it into my bag and sigh heavily. I lean back against the counter and cross my arms again as I eye Regis and the contemplative look on his face.

"What?" I demand when minutes have passed and he hasn't spoken.

"I'll be staying in Riviere during the length of your mission," he says.

A twinge of irritation slithers through me. "Why? Does Ophelia not trust me with something this big?"

He shakes his head. "No, that's not it. You know she trusts you, Kiera, but this job is more than just dangerous to you. If you're found out..." His words trail off but he doesn't need to finish because I understand his meaning.

An undocumented Mortal God that's lasted as long as I have without being caught and reported can only mean one thing—helpers. If I'm found out now, I'll be tortured until I give up the people who knew my true identity, and the only punishment for a crime such as this is death. Ophelia, Regis, and likely everyone else I've ever come into contact with until this point will be found and slaughtered. It's not just my life on the line. It's the entire organization's. It's shocking that Ophelia would even allow me to take on a job like this in the first place. I suppose money makes people do crazy things, though. It's the only reason I'm here after all —that and the promise of freedom.

"I won't be found, and if I am, I will kill whoever discovers me." It's the only assurance I can offer Regis. Thankfully, my words hold truth. I've been trained for something like this. Ophelia made sure of that. Even if I'm taken, even if I'm found out—I'll be able to withstand torture. I'll keep my mouth shut or kill myself if I can't. She's nothing if not thorough. I offer my friend a slight smile. "You know me," I tell him. "I can take it."

Regis levels me with a serious look. "I know you can," he replies, "but that doesn't mean I wish pain upon you, Kiera."

"It'll be fine," I say, reaching up to rub against the sudden ache in my chest as if that'll make it go away. "I'll get into the Academy as a Terra and I'll find my target— once the client tells us who it is—I'll get close to them and then"—I draw a line across my throat—"I'll get out."

"That seems too easy," Regis huffs.

"The best plans are often the simplest," I remind him with a shrug.

"Regardless," he continues, "I'm staying in the area. The client still hasn't released the target's name. I'll be playing Ophelia's messenger until further notice."

"What about your own work?" I ask. "Or your personal matters? I thought you were still looking for Grell?"

Regis stiffens at the mention of his brother. "I'll do what I can from here," he says gruffly, looking away. It's a clear signal to drop the topic and I respect it. Instead of pressing, I allow silence to fill the space between us and become our third, invisible companion as we wait for the return of Madam Brione.

Minutes pass and the clock on the wall ticks past an

hour since her disappearance. It's not like we have anything else to accomplish today and we can't move forward with our plan until she delivers my papers. So, we wait.

The rain outside comes down harder on the roof. Dripping down the fireplace until the once roaring flames dull into embers. The warmth begins to dissipate and Regis takes it upon himself to move to the hearth to restock it. He finds long matches and lights the new blocks of wood he replaced in the interior and I watch as fresh flames erupt from his ministrations.

My thoughts are consumed by his words and the possibilities of the future. I've been to plenty of God Cities before for different jobs, but this will be the first time I'll stay in one place for so long. I haven't stayed in one location since I finished my training some eight years ago. I'll have to acclimate to the stationary life, but eventually, I know my mission will be done and I'll disappear as I have hundreds of times before back into the lifestyle I've grown accustomed to. Inns and taverns. Different cities and villages. Different faces and all of my possessions easily packed into a large bag that can be swung over the backside of a horse.

Some few hours later, the sound of footsteps alerts Regis and me that the madam has returned. As if she hadn't left the two of us in her shop without warning for how long she'd been gone, the woman appears in the mouth of the doorway with papers in hand.

"Alrighty then, kiddos," she announces. "All is completed." She wobbles towards me, leaning heavily on her bad leg until she comes to a standstill before me and hands me the papers. "A copy of your new identity and the letter of recommendation."

"Thank you," I say, nodding to her as I take the offered pages.

"Your application of servitude has been sent in as well. If you're selected, they'll send a notification to your address —which I've marked as the rooms above this shop."

"We're staying here?"

Madam Brione pushes past me back behind the counter and rummages around underneath it. "Well, of course, child," she huffs out as she continues to dig. "Did you think they'd accept someone staying at an inn or without an address at all? That reeks of desperation." She shakes her head. "No, we keep empty rooms above the shop for situations such as this. I've got keys here, just give me a—aha!" Her cry of triumph is followed by the appearance of what looks like a ring of keys, each one more rusted than the last. Red flakes drift down on top of the books still sitting before her. Not that she seems to notice. "Now then, which one..." She flips through the keys as her face pinches in thought. "I think I cleaned out a few just a month or so ago."

I glance around. Judging by the cleaning she's done in her shop, I can only imagine what the rooms will look like, but if it's a free room and I can save my earnings, then I suppose it's worth taking—dirt and all. I glance back to Regis whose face is wrinkled as he watches Madam Brione. I bite down on my lower lip as he seems focused on the dirt and flakes of rust coming away on her fingers. It took years for him to overcome his aversion to grime, but still, it's so amusing to see his past distaste reemerge.

"These should be the right ones," Madam Brione finally says as she slips off a key from the ring, and it takes me a moment to realize that it's actually two keys—fused together. She grips the bottom ends of them and grunts as they come apart, some sort of sticky residue breaking as she does so. Regis' face turns pale and I choke, turning away to stop from laughing out loud. "Here ya are!" Proud, Madam Brione offers up the keys.

"Thank you," I say with a smile as I reach out and take mine. Regis stares at the second key as if it's one of my spiders before gingerly reaching out and pinching it between two of his fingers in an effort to touch it as little as possible. For someone who's dealt in the blood and cum of others, he's just as squeamish as he was ten years ago.

"Just head through that doorway," she points to the same door she'd come from. "Up the stairs to the left. Yours will be the first room on the right." She turns to Regis. "Yours will be across from hers. Might as well head up now and settle in for the night. If you're hungry, you'll have to fend for yourselves, though. I'm not much for cooking."

"Is there a kitchen?" I ask. "We can cook for ourselves while we're here. That won't be an issue."

Madam Brione bobs her head. "Same doorway," she says. "'Cept instead of taking the stairs, you'll go straight back down the hallway. Now, head off, both of ya. I got some cleaning to do in here. I'll let you know if we get notice of your rejection or acceptance."

"Alright, thank you again, Madam," I say as I snag Regis' arm and pull him along behind me.

His sour face follows me through the doorway and up the staircase, but he waits until we're clear enough away from Madam Brione before speaking. "You're checking my room for any of your disgusting friends," he snaps. "I can handle a lot of things, but if I have to stay in filth then at the very least, I am not sleeping with your spiders."

I smother another laugh. "Didn't you hear her?" I ask. "She said she had to clean. Perhaps we simply caught her on a bad day."

"She said she last cleaned these rooms a month ago,

Keira," he whispers heatedly. "*A month!* Do you know how much dust accumulates in a month? Do you know how many vermin can sneak in during that same amount of time?"

I snort and use my key to unlock my room first before I hold my hand out for his. He hands it over without complaint, and I stride across the hall to his door and open it for him before stepping inside. I push a quick burst of power out, seeking out any untoward little creatures. Several small minds respond to my call and I silently urge them to disappear into the walls and floors so that Regis won't notice them.

"Well?" he asks as he steps up behind me and peeks into the room.

"You're good to go," I say. "No spiders."

"Great." His eyes scan over the interior of the room. It has a single slit for a window and what looks like a sagging bed pushed into the corner next to a desk and wardrobe. "Now all that's left is to clean out the mounds of dirt."

I finally let loose a chuckle and move back into the hall, leaving him behind as I go to my own room—a practical replica of his, dirt and all. "Whatever helps you sleep better at night, Regis," I call back before repeating it with another quiet laugh. "Whatever helps."

CHAPTER 8

RUEN

"Caedmon!"

Ahead of me, several paces down the long-walled corridor full of windows, the tall dark man dressed in a royal suit embroidered with gold filigree pauses at the call of his name and turns slightly back. The sun pouring in through the open glass panes glitters on the accents of gold that surround the man. Unlike most of the instructors in the Academy, Caedmon actually waits for me to catch up to him. The gold hoops pierced through both of his ears glimmer as the sun sets beyond the windows at my back, a stark contrast to his dark skin.

"Good evening, Ruen," Caedmon says as I approach, his voice smooth and even. "To what do I owe the honor of your presence?"

I come to a stop before him and breathe in through my nose and out through my mouth. Coldness seeps through my bones, etched into my veins as the reason I'd called out to him sits in the back of my mind. I wait a moment, and then a few more, as his gaze falls over me. He's an assessing male, the God of Prophecy. Despite knowing that I trust him more than I do most other Divine Beings, his brown eyes—that often turn a bit hazy and clouded as if he's looking into the very fabric of the world and seeing all of the threads of futures to come—keeps me cautious.

"Is it true the Council is being called?" The words come out, more demanding than I intend, but I don't apologize for that. Apologies mean nothing if you do not mean them.

Caedmon's face, once pleasant and open, closes quickly. Though he's not ostentatiously angry, the moment the Council is mentioned, his guard slams into place. My body tenses, half expecting a raging outburst. Nothing. Caedmon's dissatisfaction is a slow silent creeping thing. I'm far more accustomed to violence rather than silence, and even if I like this male, regardless of his standing as a Divine Being, my own body prepares for it. A lifetime and a childhood of having to do so cannot be erased in the span of a few years.

I likely should have eased into this conversation, I know, but my greed for information commands me and drives me. I inhale once more and stand taller as I wait for his answer. I tower over the God of Prophecy physically, but I know that if it were to come down to a true battle, I would not win. His power is far greater than mine.

A buzzing starts up under my skin as he tilts his head up at me. It's a warning, one that I'll ignore if it means earning even a modicum of the information that I seek. I stare back at him, meeting his gaze as I know few often do.

"You know that's none of your business, Ruen," Caedmon says, his voice quiet but firm. "Whether or not a God Council is called does not concern students."

I frown. "You mean Mortal Gods," I say.

"Considering that all students here are Mortal Gods," he replies, "then yes. That's exactly what I mean." Eyes equally as dark as his skin peer into mine. I know he's warned off plenty of curious students with that disquieting look of his. The God of Prophecy is feared and revered by Mortal Gods and Gods alike. I won't be cowed, though.

"Why do you wish to know?" he asks. "Is it perhaps because you worry that your father will return to Riviere?"

I stiffen. His gaze hadn't made me feel nearly as defensive as the mention of my sire does. I resist the urge to scowl, but still, the weight of my discomfort falls over me as I gaze back at the Divine Being before me. Were it any other God, I wouldn't even be here, but Caedmon treats all Mortal Gods as equals. A rather bizarre trait for someone of his position to be so kind and polite to those below him, but it's also what gave me leave to approach him. Therefore, I disregard my own discomfort and answer.

"Azai doesn't seem too concerned with his sons. Why would that bother me?" Ice drips from each word.

Caedmon's eyes soften at my words, and he takes a step towards me, reaching out with his free hand as his other keeps a book close to his chest. He closes his fingers around my arm and squeezes. My muscles bunch tight, but I don't pull away. "Azai might seem a large and intimidating figure, but he is just as much at the whims of the God King as the rest of us."

The God King. My chest hardens and my abdomen clenches. Though I've never met Tryphone, the effects of his power permeate every speck of my life and surroundings. This very Academy, as well as the whole of this mortal plane, are under his control as well as that of his closest Council of the Upper Gods. Upper Gods such as my father.

When Caedmon speaks again, his tone is gentle, almost reassuring. "*If* a Council happens, he will come if he's called."

Not before, though. Gods forbid the God of Strength pay attention to his bastards. That was fine with my brothers and me. His infrequent visits were not the blissful reunions of Mortals and their own offspring. He can play with the dozens of other Demi-Gods he's created over the years and leave us the fuck alone.

I nod once before I step back and away from his hold. Caedmon releases me with a wan smile. "I suggest you turn your focus to closer impending matters," he says. "The start of the new semester and the addition of new faces, perhaps?"

"You mean the incoming servants?" I frown. "We're due for a new Terra after the last one's departure, but I doubt whoever they are will last long. Kalix..." I let my words drift off. Asking about the Council is one thing, but discussing my brothers is another subject entirely. One I do not consider freely. No one can truly control Kalix's darkness, save for himself, and he refuses to so long as Theos and I are unharmed by his actions.

Caedmon's eyes glow unnaturally, the earthen color fading slightly and swirling with mist in that otherworldly way as his smile widens. "Yes, I did hear that Kalix and your last Terra did not end on the best of terms." That was putting the situation mildly. Kalix had used the human as little more than entertainment for when he was bored. That never ended well and it hadn't this time either.

I shook my head. "The Terra will not return," I say. "It's for the best."

Caedmon sighs. "Yes, well, I would not worry about your next one," he replies. "I suspect that this semester will see quite an intriguing change."

The way he phrases his words makes me think he's seen something in one of his visions. He so rarely shares them unless ordered by Tryphone that the mere fact that he's hinting at it to one such as me makes me curious.

"What do you mean?" I ask. *Is it about the mortals?* I have to wonder. Is that why he mentioned the new Terra? What could they do here in a school run by Gods and Mortal Gods?

He closes his eyes and shakes his head. As if he hears my inner thoughts, his response pricks at something deep inside of me. Something surrounded by walls of ice and thorns. My pride. "You'll see, Ruen," he muses. "I dare say, you'll see quite well what kind of mortals will soon enter your life."

That definitely sounds like a prophecy to me, but I know better than to push him to reveal more. No good ever comes from prodding for insights into the future—doing so, as Caedmon has taught, will inevitably alter it. The moment one learns what will befall them, it'll disappear like smoke into the wonders of the past, present, and future. It is better to go into the darkness of life without a clue and adapt as you proceed.

"I'll see you in class, Ruen," Caedmon says, bowing his head slightly as a nod of respect. "Have a good rest of the break."

As I watch him go, that prickle of unease blossoms into something more. As much as I respect Caedmon, I cannot help but feel a bit of pity for him. He's a grand instructor, well versed in all subjects from history to power control. Unlike other Gods, however, he is always found alone. Reading or musing to animals—creatures with lives shorter than even mortals.

It is truly mournful how a God as kind as he is isolated because of his abilities.

Knowing too much is as much of a burden as knowing too little, perhaps even more.

Still, I cannot help but wonder at the meaning behind his words.

I turn to the windows and look out as the sun sinks behind the southern wall of the Academy dormitories. Something is coming—that much Caedmon had made clear. Perhaps this *something* will find a way to ease the torment inside my heart. If not, perhaps it will simply end this unnatural life of mine.

Half mortal. Half God. A being caught between two worlds in which I fit neither.

One can only hope.

"I'm not wearing it."

"You must."

"No."

"Yes."

Regis shoves the damn overly long cloth at me for the hundredth time and I shove it right back, half tempted to ball it up and stuff it directly up his fucking ass. The stiff woolen fabric is a dark gray with long sleeves and skirts that would most likely cover the tops of my toes if I were to wear it. The dress is the same style as any middle-class mortal might wear, and though I know what Regis is trying to do, I find staring at it the same as staring a prison cell in the face.

"It's unnecessary," I snap, blowing the silvery strands of my hair out of my face.

He holds up the dress and shakes at me. "You *do* realize that most women your age wear dresses, correct? You are the anomaly. I'm sure Ophelia didn't miss this part of your training."

I ignore the dig about Ophelia. "If you love them so

much, why don't *you* put it on?" I finish lacing up my boots and then tuck the tail of my black tunic into the back of my trousers. My relationship with dresses is complicated. It's not necessarily that I mind the idea of wearing one, though I'm not entirely comfortable with them since I'm so used to wearing trousers. However, the idea of wearing a dress into the most dangerous place on the continent for a secret Mortal God like myself feels akin to binding my hands behind my back before walking into a lion's den.

Regis tosses the dress onto my bed with a sigh. "You don't want to mess this mission up before it's even begun, do you?" he demands. "You're lucky enough that they accepted your application, but you can't expect them to not look at you strangely if you—a *woman,* in case you've failed to recall your own gender—show up in the garments of a man. Terra in the Academy wear uniforms—*female* Terra wear dresses."

"You're the one who said that the best lie is the one that's closest to the truth," I remind him as I grab my coat and slip it on over my loose tunic. It's so old now that the fabric has grayed and worn through in some places. It's not like I have time now to go out and buy new clothing, though. Besides, like Regis stated, there will be uniforms to wear at the Academy.

"What assassin would walk so blatantly into the Academy standing out like a rotten thumb?"

He groans. "It's sore thumb," he corrects instinctively. "And you're exactly right—no assassin would ever do that!"

"So they won't expect it," I reply tartly. To stand out, in some instances, is also to blend in.

Throwing his hands up in frustration and hopefully defeat, Regis turns away from me and stomps towards the door only to pause at the last second and whip back around to face me. He points at my face and scowls. "You're wrecking your own chances at that four million denza," he snaps. "If they don't accept you then you have no one to blame but yourself."

"They already accepted me," I remind him blandly.

"That doesn't mean shit," he snaps. "They could very well take one look at you and kick you right out the gates and then where will you be? No closer to your freedom and our four million denza."

I pause for a moment as I consider his words. If I've learned anything in this life it's that if something seems too good to be true, it usually is. The four million denza ... it's a miracle offer. One I'm afraid to take, and yet, the desire— the greed—for freedom forced me to take it. One more mission and then, this will all be over. No more killing. No more Divine Beings. I can free myself from Ophelia's contract brand and leave the rest of the world behind.

The money itself means nothing to me. I don't care what it can buy, save for my freedom, my life back in the Hinterlands. Dimly, I wonder if the cabin I lived in with my father even remains. Okay, maybe I'd keep the money left over from the mission to fix it up if it is still there.

"Do you really want to risk the four million denza just because you don't want to wear a dress?" Regis asks, bringing me out of my thoughts and back to the present.

I shake my head. Wearing a damned dress won't make or break my mission. "If that's to be, then let it be," I say. "I'm not going to waltz in there dressed like a tavern barmaid."

He arches a brow. "I think you'd make a fine barmaid, Kay," he says. "I haven't seen the tits you hide under those man garments, but I'm sure—" I swing my fist before he finishes that statement. Just as expected of a fellow assassin raised under Ophelia's tutelage, Regis ducks the attack with a laugh and little effort.

"Keep your thoughts about my tits to yourself, Regis," I snap. "I'm there to placate annoying Mortal Gods and find a target. Nothing more."

"I hate to remind you, darling, but you *are* a Mortal God yourself."

"A fact no one will find out, I assure you—dress or no dress." I will slit my own throat first before I put him and the rest of the Underworld Guild in danger. Loyalty before dignity. The life of one isn't worth the risk of the lives of others, even if that one life is mine.

Regis groans, but knowing me as long as he has, there's no way he isn't aware of my complete and utter seriousness in this matter. "Fine," he grumbles. "Finish packing and I'll meet you outside. The carriage should be here to take us to the Academy any minute."

"You're going?"

He nods. "You're looking at your very loyal elder brother, darling," he says. "If I ever need to meet with you and we're spotted, we don't want it to look too suspicious. Besides, I hear plenty of families come to bid farewell to those who have been accepted as Terra. It would be odd if a Terra showed up with no one to wish them well." He knocks once on the wooden doorframe as he exits. "Hurry it up."

I sigh and return to my packing. Though there's not much to return to my bags, we've been staying in Madam Brione's shop rooms for a little over a week now and a few more little trinkets have appeared courtesy of her appreciation of our cooking. It's unnecessary, of course, but I don't mind the little extras—sprigs of herbs, a leather bracelet with a single flattened metal charm, and most preciously, a hair piece meant to stick through the hair in a knot that doubles as a weapon. I take the slender stick and make sure the sheath is on the blade appropriately before shoving it into my bag and then lifting the whole thing and tossing it over my shoulder.

Minutes later, I'm clomping down the stairs with Madam Brione nowhere in sight. I take one last lingering look at the dusty shop that she never actually cleaned and smile as I realize that Regis will likely continue staying here after I'm gone. The thought of him, alone, in a house full of dirt, brings me such unadulterated joy that I'm grinning as I exit the shop and meet him in the street.

Regis looks up as I step out and pulls back as he sees my face. "I don't like that expression," he says. "Stop smiling, it's creepy."

I roll my eyes. "You're playing the brother perfectly," I tell him, maintaining my grin.

"I'm serious, Kiera," he says. "That smile makes me think you're planning something—specifically something that has to do with me."

"Does it?" I ask lightly as I head for the waiting carriage door. Pausing outside, I unload my bag and toss it inside against the far wall. The carriages of the Gods usually have room at the back or on the roof to carry heavy bags, but unfortunately for us—we're not Gods. We have to content ourselves with the much narrower and rougher traveling carriages and cabs meant for lower-class citizens of Anatol.

I climb into the carriage and take a seat with my back to the driver. Regis follows shortly, taking the seat opposite me as the door behind him closes and the stairs are pushed back under the cab before the driver takes his position.

"Shall we talk about the plan?" he asks.

"Is there a need?" I lean against the wall next to the

door and blink at him. "It's simple. Get in. Kill the target. Get out."

Regis presses his lips together and rubs a hand over the top of his blond head. He tugs the leather tie binding the longer strands into a loop of hair at the back of his skull free as he does so. "The client is being less than forthcoming with information," he says as he gathers his hair into a fist and wraps the leather band around it, tightening the strap with clear frustration. "Ophelia is concerned that this is a trap."

"If she was that concerned, then she would've shown up or sent another message telling me to refuse the job," I point out. Is it dangerous? Yes, but so is every job we've ever done. I can't deny that this mission is more important because of the possibility that it could gain me my freedom. As ... useful as the Underworld Guild has been and my training as an assassin, with the promise of four million denza comes the realization that I could actually leave it all. I could stop. Anytime I wanted to. I wouldn't *have* to be an assassin purely for survival. Though, I can't imagine what else I would do, the mere fact that I'd have a choice is enough to leave me salivating with hope.

Regis' hands continue messing with the leather band as he pulls it flush against his neck. "You're not wrong, but that doesn't mean we shouldn't be ready for every eventuality." He finishes with his hair and then turns, reaching into his own satchel to pull a long scroll free. Unwinding it, he sets the paper on his lap for me to see.

I lean forward, curious and impressed by what he reveals. "Is that a map of the Academy?" I ask.

"Yes, cost a pretty denza too, but I thought it necessary for designating your escape routes, should you need them," he says.

I catch the edge of the page with one hand and smack his thigh with the other, urging him to scoot over so I can switch seats. He grunts and shuffles closer to the wall as I swap into the opening he leaves behind. It's a tight fit, but neither of us cares much as we pore over the map in our laps.

"Here, here, and here," he says, pointing to various points on the edges of a deeply inked line. Each point is marked with an X. "These are the main entrances and exits. Smaller Xs are servants only and, of course, the larger ones are for the Gods and Mortal Gods."

"This map doesn't take into consideration windows and other possibilities," I say. "If needed, I can get out through the sewers in an emergency." I'd prefer not to, but it's one thing I like about cities—added escape routes.

Regis grimaces but nods his agreement. "Let's hope it doesn't come to that."

"I doubt it will," I say as I look over the various other markings on the map and the names of the buildings. I point to a tower on the northern side—the one farthest from the other exits. "This is where the notice said I'm to report for duty," I say.

Regis curses. "Of course it did," he mutters. "As far from the normal escape routes as possible."

"It has to be that way for a reason," I say, considering the rounded portion of the wall that separates the Academy from the rest of the city. "What do we know about the Academy itself? Is there something on the northern side that prevents other escape routes? I don't see any gates there."

With a sigh, Regis rolls the map up and hands it to me. I take it willingly and stick it into my bag. "You'll see soon enough," he huffs, "but to answer your question, yes. The northern side of the Academy faces the ocean. There are a few pathways that lead up along the coast, but I did some investigating myself and they have a decent amount of foot traffic. There's a point here." He gestures to a place on the edge of the map that's nearly off the page. "They call it the Point of No Return. I advise you to stay away from there unless you're out of options because the only way out at that point is to scale down the cliffside."

"Cliffside?" I repeat. "Not docks?"

He shakes his head. "No docks can be put in that particular spot because it faces a massive cliff." He eyes me. "I suppose, with the right supplies, you could scale down the length of the cliff, but you're more likely to survive the sewers. I suspect the Gods built the Academy on the cliffside so they could put their spawn onto a pedestal for all of Riviere to see."

I arch a brow at Regis' comment. A pedestal? I highly doubt that. The Gods see their own offspring as little more than dangers to their own safety. If it weren't for the evolutionary aspect that slaughtering one's own children is taboo to all, I have no doubt they'd have done so long ago.

No, putting the Academy on the cliffside wasn't to show off the Mortal Gods—it was to ostracize them from mortals. To separate them and show them as better in some aspects and ... poorer in others. Mortals, at least, are underestimated by the Gods. It was how the Underworld Guild had come to be. Divine egos don't allow for them to consider mortals a threat. But Mortal Gods ... the Divine Beings are smart to keep their offspring under lock and key, considering that the only way a Divine Being can be killed is by one of their own or one of their children. They are doing what anyone would in their circumstances—keeping their enemies right under their thumbs.

I don't say anything in response as I move back to the seat across from him. The carriage continues on, the ground beneath it getting rougher as the cab sways back and forth, nearly knocking me into the wall several times as we hit a particularly rugged piece of land.

"How much fucking longer?" I demand after what feels like a solid hour. "Are we leaving Riviere?"

Regis shakes his head. "I think you forget how big the God Cities are, Kiera," he says with a sigh. "We're almost there, though. Look." He pulls back the curtains over the window and nods to the scenery outside.

Hesitantly, I lean forward and peer through the dirty glass. My lips part as I spot the big castle that sits high above the other buildings. It's a big, black behemoth of a creation with several dozen spires and towers circling the entire expanse. Even from where we are as we slowly climb the next street into the higher regions of Riviere, I can see the separations and stained glass windows.

Despite its grotesque sort of beauty, there is one thing that draws my attention more than anything else. The closer we get to the Academy, the fewer buildings there are that surround us. As if the Gods are being separated from their own children. Raised up from the common classes of mortals into a world all on their own, yet not quite far enough to touch their parents.

Mortal, but not human. Divine, but not Gods.

The carriage slows down and turns. Outside, I spot several more carriages and cabs, horse-drawn open-air carts too. Terra—new and old—making their trek to the illustrious Mortal Gods Academy of Riviere, the capital God City of Anatol, and the Academy that houses the most powerful of all the Mortal Gods.

I'm not entirely sure if this mission had sent me to one

of the other two Mortal Gods Academies whether I'd feel the same as I do right now. From what I've studied in books and learned of the continent of Anatol, the others, the only ones of their kind, places of darkness and fear, are spread far and wide. The God City of Perditia is housed farther east in mountains so tall, the tips can't be seen as they ascend into the skies themselves. I could have handled Perditia. I can handle Riviere. What I am thankful for, though, is that I was not forced to journey to the south. To Ortus.

Despite the warmer weather and the beautiful oceans that surround the first and oldest of the Mortal Gods Academies, there sits a memory in the back of my mind from long ago. A memory of a hand holding mine. Young. So fucking young. Barely old enough to toddle after the one clutching my fingers.

The castle that housed the first Mortal Gods that had walked the continent had been built just off the coast of the God City of Ortus. I remember seeing it before just once. It'd been the closest one to the Hinterlands, and I recall how it had glimmered amidst rock and frothy blue-and-green seas. Opaque. Like a mirror facing the rest of the world or a mountain cracked open. An ancient structure made of onyx, glassy clawing hands reaching up and outward. A blackened crown atop that tiny island. More a prison than an Academy. Cut off even more so than the one we're currently heading towards. Even if the Mortal Gods Academy of Riviere is set outside of the actual city upon a cliffside that could collapse at any moment, at least it's still a part of the mainland. Separate ... but not so treacherously remote.

I'm not entirely sure if it's still useable considering its age, but there'd been people standing atop it—Mortal Gods and Gods alike. Young and old. That was only fifteen years ago, so it probably still is an Academy. I'm thankful that

Ortus is not my destination, that ... *that* place is not my destination.

A chill dances down my spine at the old memory. Regis, either sensing my unease or seeing the evidence of it on my face before I can draw up my careful mask, reaches out and touches my knee. "Just treat this like any other job," he advises. "Once we have the target name, I'll send it by bird and then we'll work on your escape plan. Kiera Nezerac will be burned and gone into the night and you'll be able to buy a whole new identity with the denza you'll receive."

I nod, though my attention is fixed squarely on the quickly approaching gates. Now that I'm about to step into a world full of Divine Beings and Mortal Gods, I'm reminded of the singular Mortal God I've ever actually met and known long enough to hold a conversation with. Unlike the Mortal God I'd fought in Mineval, the one I'd killed years ago had been far more haughty and wicked—more Divine than mortal in mannerisms. Cocky and arrogant and cruel. It'd been the last time Ophelia had come with me on a mission. Killing someone who held abilities just like me had been the ultimate test.

I didn't regret killing him—not when I knew the things he'd done to humans simply because they were powerless against him. Now, I'll be faced with more of them. The spiteful spawn of the Divine. Crueler, somehow, for their hatred of mortals when they, themselves, were born out of such beings.

"New Terra are often tasked with the worst Mortal Gods," Regis tells me, pulling back. My eyes remain on the window and the castle. "If need be, don't hesitate to make yourself appear weak—too weak to be of consequence. The less you're noticed, the better."

I notice a figure standing atop the gates as our carriage

pulls under it into a courtyard. The air in the cab changes, growing tense and tight. "Whatever you do, Kiera," Regis says, "don't"—his voice catches in his throat and draws my attention to his pinched face—"get yourself killed. Don't become a tragedy to me, darling. I have few platonic friends in this life and I'd really prefer not to start over from scratch."

My lips twitch at the platonic comment, but I can't help the response that comes.

"The Gods are amused by tragedy," I say absently. I can feel his eyes steady on my face, burning into my cheek. The words come anyway. "They revel in the sorrow of our lives and the control they wield. Do you think they came down from the Divine realm out of goodwill?" The question is rhetorical, but still, I laugh at the mere thought. "Think again. They came down so that they could sit in the front row to our terribly pathetic little attempts to fight against them. They got tired of watching the play from the outside and decided they would become part of it even if it meant they had to portray the villains." I lift my fingers to the windowpane. "They'll never return to the Divine realm. They love their positions too much for that. They enjoy the power they hold over us all and they don't care if it's unjust or cruel. At the end of the day, Gods are not human. There can be nothing humane about them because they lack the core essence of what it entails."

The Gods will always be cruel wicked creatures playing with the toys they've created.

A beat passes and then the carriage pulls to a stop. It sways as the driver climbs down from the roof. "Remember that, Kiera," Regis says. "Everything you just said, no matter what you see in there. No matter what you experience. I want you to remember what you just told me."

I lift my gaze to his and realize that his brows are pinched. "Even if they don't kill you, I don't want to lose you in other ways." Though I'm sure it's only a heartbeat, it feels like it takes my mind a long time to catch up with his meaning.

I shake my head as the driver appears outside the door. I reach down for my bag and lift it back over my shoulder. "Don't worry, Regis," I say as the driver props the door open and takes down the steps. "The Gods are responsible for a lot of evil in this world—if anyone remembers that, I do. Whatever blood runs through my veins. I'm mortal. Just like you."

A Mortal God is still *mortal* after all, even if the others of my kind refuse to acknowledge that fact.

CHAPTER 10

KIERA

One by one, the incoming Terra gather in the front courtyard of the Mortal Gods Academy of Riviere. I assemble with the rest of them, watching as more and more cabs and carriages and open carts arrive to drop off their friends and family members. The faces of those departing appear both relieved and concerned—as they often glance back to those that are left behind.

From what I understand, being accepted as a Terra to this Academy is a thing of praise—likely because of the income it brings per household. As for mine, I know it'll go into a safe account with my pseudonym as the sole proprietor. How amusing, I think. That I'm getting doubly paid as an assassin. Not that I'm confident that account won't be seized the moment I disappear, but it's still an amusing thought.

It takes several hours for the last of the servants to arrive and their family and friends to leave. Twilight is upon us before the gates have even closed and by the time they do, the sun is all but a distant memory. The chill of the night air has settled over us all and the only sweat that remains is cold and fearful.

"Excuse me. Pardon me. If you will just—oh, thank you!" A squeaky boy's voice echoes from somewhere far back in the crowd, moving forward with each sentence until the person from which it comes finally stops at my side. His frizzy mousy brown hair is a little longer than is popular, curving behind his ears and down to the back of his neck as he sets the bag he's brought with him on the ground and adjusts his cloak. It appears too big and heavy for a man of his size, but he manages to fix it so that it's half tossed back over his shoulders and the front of his body is visible, giving him just enough room to lift his bag back into his hands and turn towards the front of the crowd.

"Exciting, isn't it?" he asks absently, almost as if he can't keep the words down but he's not too concerned with whom he's talking to.

I hum in the back of my throat as a response and feel the burn of his stare on my face until I turn and meet his gaze. "You're an odd-looking one, aren't you?"

I blink. "Excuse me?"

Red stains across his cheeks and he quickly looks away. "I-I'm sorry, I didn't realize I-I'd said that aloud."

A frown steals across my face. "What do you mean, you didn't realize you'd said that aloud?"

He dips his head further, practically shoving his chin into his chest. "I-I'm not quite—I mean, there's nothing—I didn't mean anything by it. Just that your hair is quite ... unique."

Reaching up, I finger the silver strands. It's only slightly lighter than blonde. Should I have dyed it, I wonder, but no, that would've required constant upkeep and if I'm going to be here for the next few months, the fewer lies I tell—visual or physical ones—the easier it'll be to blend in.

"I-I'm sorry, I sometimes don't realize I've said something until it's already out," the boy explains, seeming nervous as his eyes keep bouncing up to my face and back down to the ground.

"It's fine," I say, unbothered. "You're right. Silver hair—it's not common." An oversight on my part, for sure. Too late now, though, I suppose.

"It's pretty, though," he says almost hurriedly as if he's afraid he's offended me despite my words. Then again, anyone else would've been.

"Thank you."

The boy shoves his hand out, fingers straight. "I'm Niall."

"Kiera." I take his hand.

"Are you a returner?" he asks. "I haven't been here before."

"No," I answer. "I'm new as well—new to here anyways. I used to work as a servant in a Lower God's house, but never anywhere as infamous as one of the Academies." The lie slips out easily.

The relief on his face is amusing. The tension in his shoulders melts away and he reaches up, releasing my hand as he adjusts the worn cravat tied at his throat. There's a shadow of hair under his jaw and along his upper lip, but it's not dark enough to actually be considered facial hair—just the mere hint of something to come. My lips twitch. How cute and also how sad. He's too young, in my opinion, to be somewhere as dangerous as here.

"When I received the letter of my acceptance, my family was overjoyed," he continues, sputtering as the words spill out of his mouth. "We never thought I'd be chosen. I mean, so many people apply but only a certain number are accepted each year."

"Oh?" I arch a brow. "Why is that?"

He blinks. "W-why is what?"

"Why do you think so many people apply?" I ask.

"Well, of course it's because we'll be able to make our families proud and raise our status by serving such Divine Masters."

Masters. The very word makes a dark, gloomy feeling arise within me. Poor Niall can't understand what that word actually means to someone like me, but I force a smile on my face.

"I'm sure you'll be a wonderful addition."

His responding grin is bright and full of straight white teeth. Yes, it's clear he's worked for a God before. Only humans who've had to be around Gods for so many years would be so well-kept. No doubt, they accepted him because he's pretty. Gods do seem to adore pretty things. In fact, a quick glance around tells me that most of the waiting servants are humans of great beauty. Perhaps keeping my silver hair natural will be beneficial.

A loud clap rings out over the crowd and the soft lull of conversation ceases almost immediately as the attention of those gathered within the courtyard turns to the stone steps where a man and a woman stand. The woman is obviously human. She's beautiful, but her age is somewhere between her early to late forties, and Divine Beings rarely look as though they've aged past thirty.

She stands ready, at attention, with her dimpled hands clasped before her long skirts as the man at her side steps up and calls out over the crowd. "Welcome to the Mortal Gods Academy of Riviere! We're proud to welcome the new crop of Terra to our most Divine of institutes."

I glance around. Crop is right—it feels as though each and every person here has been harvested simply for the matter of being stepping stools for the Mortal Gods beyond those doors.

"The lot of you have been specially chosen to serve the next generation of Gods," the man continues, carefully smoothing the thin brown locks of hair back over the tops of his ears, the strands barely long enough to cover them. His bony face is gaunt in the cheeks, which is only made severe by the bright plastered smile he presents. His lips are stretched impossibly wide as he smiles down on us.

"As many of you are aware, the Gods came down from their Divine realm hundreds of years ago to live among us"—he spreads his arms wide—"their children and servants. It is the duty and pleasure of each and every mortal here to love and respect their Gods. For the next four months, each of you will be assigned to a room that may house anywhere from one to three Mortal Gods—or as we like to refer to them here, our very own Mortal Gods."

My neck cranes back as I listen to the man's spiel. His voice is amiable in tone, but his words sound regurgitated. Worshipful. It grates along my nerves. Still, I remain stationary, watching him with focus and keeping the sole of my attention trained ahead so as not to appear disinterested.

"For those of you who are new here, we simply have three rules," the man states as he holds up three fingers. "We welcome all of you and will provide you with your uniforms, meals, and boarding, but anyone who disrespects the future of our great races—Divine and Mortal alike— will suffer the consequences." He pauses, his smile slipping a bit as his expression turns more serious. Then, after a beat, he lowers his hand and looks to the woman at his side. "Ms. Dauphine?"

The woman nods to him and steps forward as he moves back. "As my partner, Mr. Hael, stated—there are only three rules which you are to treat as your life's motto in this institution. Number one," she holds up a singular finger, "Gods are the most blessed of creatures and their word is law. You shall treat their children as a higher authority unless otherwise disrupted by a Divine Being. No human may contradict a God's command."

It's a fight to keep my expression placid, especially when—out of the corner of my eye—I notice Niall's enthralled face as he clasps his hands together and leans forward. The reverence in his expression is mirrored by those of the faces around me and, somehow, I manage to keep it from making me physically sick.

"Second," Ms. Dauphine says, holding up a second finger to join the first, "you may not, at any point, over the course of your employment and service here to the Gods and their children, leave the Academy grounds without permission. Permission may not be granted by your charges. You may come to either myself or Mr. Hael if you have such a request."

"Who would even want to leave?" I hear Niall mutter to himself.

Oh Gods, he really has no clue. I shake my head slightly and refocus on Ms. Dauphine as she gears up to unleash her final rule. She holds up a third finger and gazes out over the crowd. Her eyes pause on me for a brief moment and I blink, startled by the sudden attention. My spine stiffens and I straighten my shoulders as I meet her eyes. She arches one brow and then speaks.

"This final rule was recently applied," she explains. "Once you've been assigned your charges, there will be no changing. All Terra are required to live in the same buildings as their charges within the servants' quarters, regardless of gender. We recommend making sure that you please your Mortal God charges or else the next four months will be quite long and strenuous for each of you. Any displeasure with your charges is unacceptable. You are Terra—mortals graced with the opportunity to exist in the same world as those that could smite you but have chosen to be accepting and loving."

My insides roil with disgust at her sickeningly sweet words. Lies. All of it. I've seen the so-called love that Gods share with their mortal counterparts. The memory of the family from the dungeon in Talmatia's region remains a constant in my mind. Though the man and woman had survived long enough to be spirited away to the Hinter-lands—where I hope they live long lives—a small child had been brutally murdered by the callousness of a God. The care they give isn't care at all—it's tyranny. A domination that we all must somehow find a way to survive.

"Here at Mortal Gods Academy, we do not throw out unworthy creatures." She lowers her hand back to her front and weaves her fingers together before offering a smile that scrunches her eyes. The most terrifying smile I've seen yet. If it were just the smile, I might not be so bothered. However, as Ms. Dauphine says her next words, she focuses on me again and her expression combined with the final note of the rule sends a chill down my spine. "Anyone caught breaking the rules will not be returned to their families. Instead, they will be graciously sent into the loving arms of the Divine realm. We hope that you're ready to stay here, though, as our benevolent Divine Beings wish to continue to support all who have come to worship and serve them."

My jaw drops. All around me, however, claps ensue. Even Niall applauds Ms. Dauphine's final words as the excitement of the humans surrounding me expands outward. My heart pounds inside my chest. Dauphine just threatened their lives should they dare contradict the Gods or leave the school, and no one has seemed to notice. No, instead, they seem to see the thought of being "sent into the loving arms of the Divine realm" as a blessing. Lifting my hands, I give a begrudging few quiet claps to keep up the pretense and then put them back down the second the applause fades.

The massive etched double doors behind Dauphine and Hael open, creaking under the heavy weight. "Now!" Hael calls out. "Ladies will follow Ms. Dauphine and men will follow me as we lead the group of you to be fitted for your uniforms and then assigned your charges."

In one big wave, everyone moves forward, crowding towards the steps as they align behind each of the senior Terra. I pass a glance to the side at Niall as he offers me a slight blushing smile and picks up his bag.

As I watch him follow the other men, I have a most disturbing thought. How many Terra actually leave the Academy? If they're constantly on the search for new ones like Niall and me, what happened to the others before us? Dauphine said no one was thrown out, so does that mean they left willingly, or worse?

Chest tight and emotions wary, I adjust my own bag and move forward. I don't know why—I just met the kid, but still, in my heart ... I hope he's not one of the unfortunate ones sent to the Divine realm. I hope like fuck they don't kill him.

CHAPTER II

KIERA

The inside of the Academy—the halls with vaulted ceilings and arched windows and even the Terra's workspace—is the most opulent place I've ever seen outside of the wealthy mansions of the Gods. I'd only been in a few—Lower Gods' mostly, as they were more apt to end up on a kill list than the Upper Gods, considering the cost of killing an Upper God and the special circumstances as such is practically impossible. Ophelia had revealed to me that though mortals know that one needs Divine Blood to kill a God, there were rumors of poor Lower Gods and mortal sympathizers who were willing to take on kill contracts. Rumors she used to continue to hide my existence. A distant thought occurs to me—perhaps one reason the client has been so secretive about my current target is that it involves an Upper God within the Academy.

I've never killed an Upper God, but if that were the case … I hope I can manage it.

"—depictions are of the various Gods' ancient stories," a voice explains from ahead of the long line. "Each

Academy specifically depicts the Gods that are in residence —the instructors."

I glance up at the girl Dauphine had introduced to the mass of us as Liana when we'd entered after we retrieved our assignment papers and our uniforms. She's at least two decades younger than Dauphine with long thick dark brown hair draped down her back, and she's obviously quite well versed in the Academy's infrastructure and expectations.

Now that we're all gathered into smaller groups, I can also see the boy from earlier—Niall. He lifts a hand, awkwardly struggling to hold all of his things as well as his new supplies as he does so. I smile at him.

"That, there, is Caedmon," Liana says, stopping below a particularly dark painting as she points with a freckled hand. "Lord Caedmon is the God of Prophecy," she explains excitedly. "He's the kindest God I've ever met, myself. Perhaps, if you're lucky, a few of you might be able to attend classes with a few of your charges and get to sit in on one of his lectures."

Shock slaps me in the face. "We'll be allowed to attend classes?" The question pops out of my mouth before I can stop it. Several heads turn my way and Liana, thankfully, simply smiles and nods.

"Of course," she says. "You'll be expected to follow any of your charges should they require your assistance. Many Mortal Gods ask that their servants carry their supplies for them as they attend classes."

I arch a brow. "They don't have bags?"

Several paces away, Niall's eyes widen at my question and he ducks his head as if preparing for an outburst. Liana's once pleasant expression creases and she frowns.

"Of course they do," she says. "All of our charges are provided with anything they might need—bags included."

"Then why don't they carry their own supplies in them?"

Someone in the crowd snickers and Liana's head snaps to the side as if she's seeking out who would laugh at something like that. The truly humorous thing, however, is the fact that she's acting as if Mortal Gods can't possibly carry their own things. If anything, humans are far weaker in strength.

Liana's lips press into a straight line as she returns her attention to me, obviously frustrated by not being able to find the giggler—and perhaps at my question itself.

"What is your name?" she demands.

Damn it. The question was too much. I shuffle on my feet, mimicking discomfort and worry. "Kiera," I reply. "Kiera Nezerac."

Her eyes widen in surprise the second my surname escapes. "Ah, I see," she says with a decisive nod. "No wonder you're unaware. With a name like that, you must be from outside the cities."

Hold it in, Kiera, I order myself. *Don't do it. Don't fucking make a face. Don't even show an ounce of irritation. Just nod along like a dumb little servant. Smile and blink, Kiera. Smile and fucking blink.*

"Oh, yes, I am." I dip my head in subservience and plaster a fake polite smile onto my face. "I meant no disrespect, of course."

Liana strides forward and the small group parts to allow her access as she approaches me and puts a soft hand on my shoulder. She gives me an understanding smile. "No, no, you would never disrespect our Gods," she says. "You wouldn't have been accepted here if you were so blasphemous."

I grit my teeth behind my smile. I'm getting the sneaking suspicion that Madam Brione had managed to work some sort of Divinity herself. I knew my papers were forged, but what the fuck had she put down?

"We are here to serve our Masters," Liana continues, offering me another delicate squeeze—as if she's comforting me—before turning back to the rest of the group and rejoining those at the front. "They are capable of great things and what they carry is our society, our very lives, on their shoulders. It is the least we can do to follow their example and carry the minor things for them."

Several eyes glance from her to me and back again. It's taken years of practice, but I manage to keep my serene smile in place. I hope that whoever I'm left to trail behind is not nearly as self-absorbed as the senior Terra of the Academy seem to want them to be. It would be just my luck, though.

Liana claps her hands, recalling everyone's attention to herself. "Now, let's head this way, ladies and gentlemen," she announces. "I'll show you the dining hall meant for Terra and then we'll direct you to your rooms to allow you enough time to settle in. Tomorrow, your duties begin in earnest and you'll meet your charges."

The group of us fall in line, trailing behind her as she continues to rattle off facts and point out paintings and portraits as we pass by them. I slow my gait as we walk, however, lingering more towards the back as I ignore her words and instead, choose to take in all of the hallways and small little alcoves. The corridors are littered with unshuttered windows. The walls are thick, made of strong stone, but there are more than enough exits, should an unforeseen emergency arise.

"It's a grand place, isn't it?" Turning my head, I meet Niall's gaze.

"It's quite something," I hedge.

He withdraws a pair of spectacles from his pocket and then rubs them clean before perching them on his nose. Once they're in place, he lifts his papers from his hands and glances over them as we walk. Reading glasses, I realize. He must be from a more affluent human family if he's able to afford those—or perhaps things are different in the cities. Perhaps even the impoverished of the God Cities are graced with their basic needs.

"I have one charge," he says. "A Second Tier Mortal God."

I hum in the back of my throat and his words incite my own curiosity. I lift my papers, leafing through them until I find my assignment. "I have three charges," I say. "Looks like a trio of brothers." They all have the same last name. Darkhaven. How fascinating. I didn't know Mortal Gods were given surnames.

"What Tier are they?" Niall inquires, his gaze moving to the pages in my hand as we continue forward behind the rest of the group.

I glance back at the sheet. "First Tier," I answer.

"They must be powerful then," he says.

"Oh, are the Tiers meant to differentiate them?" Despite the fact that I've already guessed the answer, it couldn't hurt to appear as fascinated with the children of the Gods as the others are.

Niall shoves his glasses up his nose and nods briskly. "Oh yes," he answers. "There are Mortal Gods within the Academy that are several generations removed—as in they might have perhaps had a grandmother or grandfather as their God ancestor. First Tiers are as close to pure-blooded as possible. They are the true half-Gods. They are also usually the most powerful. The Tiers are set to power dynamics. Those who show the most Divine talent are First Tiers. I'm not entirely sure how they decide who gets put in which Tier. From my understanding, all Mortal Gods are tested once when they begin to show signs of Divinity and then again when they enter the Academies."

I glance over the names on my paper.

Ruen. Theos. Kalix. Three First Tier God sons. I wonder who their father must have been. The further I read, the more I realize how close they are all in age. Whoever the God was, he had certainly been a busy man. Siring three sons within the same year.

Before I'm finished reading through the rest of my papers, Liana stops the group and we're introduced to the Terra amenities within the Academy grounds. It would seem that eating and sleeping near humans is something the Gods and their children want to avoid. A clear line has been drawn in the invisible sand. Terra have their own cafeteria, their own sleeping quarters—often close, but never on the same level, as their charges—as well as their own infirmary.

"Time off is rare, I'm sure the orientation included that rule. If you require a visit off the Academy grounds, you'll need to request permission from Mr. Hael or Ms. Dauphine," Liana states. "If you're granted the privilege, they'll let you know. If, while you are serving our Mortal Gods, you fall ill, please see to it that you visit the human infirmary posthaste. There's too much to do to allow yourselves time off for something so mundane as sickness and appearing before the Gods and their children in any state of disease is frowned upon."

My brow pinches down as I force back the scowl that threatens to break free of my careful mask. *As if humans* plan *to be ill.* My invisible scowl is followed by an invisible eye roll as well. It seems that the Gods and their children view ailment as little more than an inconvenience to their pampered existence. I'm sure it is. Though I haven't experienced it myself, I've seen the devastation of illness and disease on human lives in the outskirts of the cities. I keep my mouth shut, though, and simply nod along with the rest of the sheep.

We finish going through the rest of the servant amenities before we're finally dismissed with our room assignments. I check mine and am directed to the northernmost tower of the dormitories for male First Tiers. As time has passed, my bag has steadily grown heavier and heavier and I adjust it, swapping it to my opposite shoulder as I follow the basic map I'd been given during orientation.

It's a wonder, though, that any of the other servants manage to find their places with the damn thing. The layout is confusing and often incorrect. Thankfully, I recall the more detailed map that Regis had given me. I don't take it out of my bag, though, and simply use what I can recall to find my way to the correct tower and climb the stairs up to the floor just below the uppermost one.

Using the key I'd been given as well, I open the door to the Terra quarters and hurry inside, slamming it at my back and sagging against the worn wood. To say I'm exhausted by the day is an understatement. I take a look at the surroundings of the room and am unsurprised to find that it's a narrow closet-like space. A singular slit of a window sporting a crisscrossed grate covering it hovers between two sagging beds where there is barely enough space for a person to stand. The window is big enough that should anything occur, I'd be able to escape from it.

Unlike other rooms, I'd guess, however, the second bed is empty. I must have the room to myself. Another thing to be thankful for. Before heading to the bed, I assess the access points. The window might be small, however, it will not only allow for a second escape route but also a way for Regis' messenger birds to drop off notes. There's virtually no place to hide things, though. The floor is bare and creaking with each step. I could try to pry up one of the panels and hide my extra weapons there—I will if I can't figure something else out. The bed ... I'd prefer to move it, but considering the closet-sized space surrounding me, there's nowhere else for it to go. I drop my stuff onto the second bed and collapse onto the other.

Tomorrow, I think, *it begins.* Tomorrow will be the first day of many that will either be the start of my downfall and insanity or proof that I have what it takes to kill a true God. Because the longer I contemplate the client and the ridiculous amount of money being offered, the more I'm coming to understand, beyond a shadow of a doubt, that my target must be powerful. And it's too late to back out now.

CHAPTER 12
KALIX

Metal collides against metal, sending sparks flying into my sweat-drenched face. The hot embers dance along my cheeks. The pain only invigorates me. I still remember the burn of the thief's blade across my eyes, slicing through my sight and stealing it from me in mere moments. The need to train that weakness away burns in my gut. Across from me, Theos growls, and I grin because I know the angrier he grows, the easier it is to lead him exactly where I want him. Turning to the side as he dives forward, I pause and watch him fly past and spin back to me with a reddening face.

"Stop playing with me, Kalix," Theos snaps. "Fight like you fucking mean it!"

"I always mean it, brother," I reply easily as his sword clashes with mine. More sparks dance before my eyes as the jarring weight of his assault forces me back a step. "I just happen to be in a wonderful mood and you are a fucking grouch."

Along the side of the sparring grounds, Ruen looks up, his cool eyes roving over me, assessing as always. It doesn't bother me. He can look and scrutinize me as much or as long as he wishes. Even though he's been doing it for years, he has yet to figure out the inner workings of my mind the way he seems to have done for everyone else. Even I can't tell him what is missing. Sometimes, I'm caught up in the wave of euphoria that life has to offer—with all of the sex and pain a man could want—and sometimes, it evaporates, dropping me into the worst of nightmares.

It all depends on the day.

"What has gotten you into this mood of yours?" Theos asks as he parries the next thrust of my blade and then delivers his own attack. "Enlighten us—and give me a hint as to how I can take you down."

I skid out of the way of the next slash of his sword, my booted feet sliding sideways through the dirt as I narrowly miss being cut. "The new Terra have gone through their orientations," I answer. "Ours will appear in the morning."

Theos' face twists. "Don't break this one," he warns before stabbing at me with the end of his blade.

I laugh as it slices across my bicep just as I dodge and round towards his back. It's never my intention to break the little humans. I only wish to play with them. It's not necessarily my fault, either, that they get wounded so damn easily. Theos doesn't give me a chance to say as much, though, as he dives headfirst into a series of attacks that I'm forced to ward off.

Back and forth, the two of us move. Our blades clash, metal scraping against metal. Unlike playing with the other Tiers, sparring with my brothers is always a game of chance. Sometimes, I win. Sometimes, they do. And sometimes, like today it seems, we're drawn into a deadlock and neither of us can claim victory. They truly are the only ones who keep me guessing.

"Alright," Theos says nearly an hour later as he stands back. "I've had enough. It's a draw."

Wiping the sweat from my brow with the back of my hand, my chest rises and falls with the heaviness of my breathing. All over I can feel the tingles of my skin working to fix and heal the wounds I sustained while fighting with him. I lick my lips, my tongue coming back tasting of salt and blood.

"It was a good session," Ruen comments.

"I want our Terra now," I say distractedly as I look to where the old one used to stand. "I'm too excited to wait." Will they be male? Female? The Gods have only given us males for the last couple of years—they seem to last longer, if only marginally. Doesn't bother me, though. The males have tight holes ready for fucking just as much as the females.

Theos and Ruen exchange a look—one I recognize. It's taken several years, but I've finally come to understand what the raised brows and pursed lips mean. Exasperation and concern. Sometimes irritation when I really press them. I wait, curious to know if they'll deny me my fun and I'll have to sneak in on my own or if they'll help.

"Do you promise not to do anything to the new one?" Theos asks as he strides to the side and tosses his sword into the pile that will be later collected by Terra and cleaned before being returned the next morning.

"I just want to greet them," I say, following him and doing the same. It isn't a lie per se. My greetings are still greetings after all.

Out of the corner of my eye, a male Terra appears carrying an armful of towels. He marches right towards us with strong confident strides, but the second he spots our faces I see the way he pauses and ducks his head. I bet he's wishing he'd have checked which Mortal Gods were using this training courtyard before he came here.

He's a cute little thing with big eyes that flicker up at me as I reach out and take a towel from his hands before he recalls his place and looks back down. A fresh hunger awakens, and within my trousers, I can feel my cock stiffen.

It's amusing to watch how he trembles ever so slightly the longer I remain near him, patting the sweat and blood from my already healed wounds with the towel. I have no doubt he would scuttle away and back into the building if it weren't for the fact that he hasn't been dismissed. Without a word from any of us, he's incapable of leaving on his own and I do so love to watch the humans fight their instincts. Fear. Nervousness. *Curiosity.* That last one always gets them, and eventually, me too.

The Terra is a skinny little creature with narrow shoulders that look as if they belong on a girl. I know he's of age, though. Only adult servants are allowed within the Academy. Too many 'accidents' and too many wandering eyes and hands—from Mortal Gods and Gods alike. Neither I nor my brothers would be here if that wasn't the case. Normally, I'd prefer someone with a bit more confidence— though there was a tiny bit of it before he realized which Mortal Gods he was serving. I'd never had one, not with the way the mortals worship our kind, but I imagine I'd truly enjoy a human that bites back, giving me just enough pain to relish in the agony of the battle between us.

To fuck or be fucked—that is the question. The answer lies in this male's downward gaze. Oh yes, he would like to be fucked.

Ruen sighs as he stands. "We are not calling them just yet," he says. "You can wait until tomorrow to meet the new Terra."

With a grin, I finish mopping up my blood and sweat from my face, neck, and chest. "You are ruining my fun," I say.

Noticing my interest in the human, Theos and Ruen both move towards me. Theos hands the now used towel to the servant who dips his head once more and thanks him. "I'm sure you can find another way to entertain yourself," Ruen replies, arching a brow my way. "We'll be in the rooms when you're done."

"Perhaps you could find some entertainment yourself!" I call after them. "Or at least someone to pull that sword from your ass."

Theos chuckles, but Ruen doesn't reply. Instead, the two of them exit the sparring ring and private courtyard, leaving no one else but me and the servant.

"Sir?" The male's head tips back as I graze the bunched towel in my fist over my bare chest and abdomen.

I hum in the back of my throat. "What is your name, human?" I ask.

"A-Adam, sir."

He stutters. *How precious.* I drop the towel to the ground between us and without hesitation, he bends to pick it up. My hand drops on his head and he freezes. My groin tightens further before the words even escape my lips.

"Get on your knees, Adam," I order. "I have need of service."

His head tips back and those wide, luminous eyes of his gaze up at me. A pink little tongue comes out and licks across his lower lip. My cock hardens further. I wait a beat, wondering if he—like the rest of these indoctrinated little mortals—will cave to my demands. It is both a relief and a disappointment when he quietly consents and sets aside his towels to follow my order. He slides to his knees before me, uncaring of the dirt that coats his once clean clothes.

I cup the back of his skull, rubbing my fingers through the curly locks. "Is your mouth trained?" I ask.

He nods. "I am here to serve, Master," he replies breathily. "All of me is trained." Just what I wanted to hear.

"Good." I untie the band holding my training trousers closed with one hand. "Then open your mouth and take my cock. Suck it well. I want to know the effects of your *training*."

That's all it takes. A hiss escapes me as the male leans forward, parting his lips as he takes the head of my shaft into the wet interior of his mouth. I'd almost feel bad for them, these humans, if they weren't so prone to such temptations. My brothers aren't nearly as understanding of the human way. They hate our father—and in turn, the Gods—but they don't hold nearly as much respect for those of the mortal classes even as they bend to our every whim and offer their holes up for usage. They are truly a blessing.

My hand on the back of his head firms as I drag him closer, pushing my shaft deeper. He chokes, the sound filtering through my ears. Soon, I think, we'll have our very own Terra again and I can do this to them. I'll fuck their throat and think of that creature from Mineval. The thief that blinded me, if only for a moment. How exciting it was to have someone best me. Escape me.

My other hand moves to the back of the male's head, meeting my own as I weave my fingers together against his curls. My grip tightens as I imagine the thief before me rather than this servant. Hunger takes hold within my groin. I can feel my cock throb against the wet tongue stroking it. "Fuck." I gasp as he takes me deeper, that expert tongue of his lashing against the underside of my cock.

"Yes, lick it just like that." Whoever trained him did well if he's able to draw my thoughts away from the thief from Mineval.

I close my eyes as I sink past the human's lips once more and the head of my dick penetrates his throat. Little puffs of air linger on the top of my cock as he breathes heavily through his nose. I hold him down against the base of my shaft for several long seconds, counting down to see how long it takes him to fight back. They so rarely do. I've even managed to fuck a few of the servants so hard that they passed out from lack of oxygen. Never once did they curse me or struggle until they truly thought they would die.

Come on, I urge silently. *Resist me*. I bet the thief would. Though I couldn't be entirely sure if they'd been male or female, I imagined the thief to be female. Their body had been slim—like a girl's. A pretty woman she would be, with striking features and a scowling mouth. I picture long hair I could twist into braids and wrap around my hands as I used them like handholds to power deep into her throat. She would most assuredly fight back. Nails would scrape my thighs, blood would slip out from the wounds. My chest rumbles with a barely repressed moan. My sack tightens and draws up as I continue to fuck the waiting mouth in front of me.

The thief I encountered in Mineval would never simply *let* me do this. I'd have to force my way past resistance and the battle she would give me would no doubt be legendary. For a change, I might actually have to work to get my dick wet. I find that I quite like that idea. Even the imaginary challenge does more to heighten my pleasure and arousal than the actual hole swallowing my cock. I close my eyes and instead of the willing servant on his knees before me, I continue to picture the shadowy figure from Talmatia's castle.

More seconds tick down. Despite his discomfort, the man never resists. His head works back and forth as he swallows against the invader pummeling the inside of his throat.

With a disappointed sigh, I withdraw, allowing him a moment to take a breath and then I cup the back of his head once more and thrust back inside. My head cranes back as I force my cock inside, too harshly out of my own disappointment. Back and forth. Into his throat and out again. He chokes. He coughs. He never tells me to stop.

Every once in a while, I'll look down to see those worshipful eyes gazing up at me in wonder. Even as tears streak his face and red splotches stain his cheeks, turning him into a filthy whore-like mess, he still keeps his lips stretched, placatingly around my shaft, practically begging for the honor of swallowing my seed.

A sigh slips free. Had I considered them a blessing? Perhaps that thought was only reserved for feisty humans such as the thief. This one seems pathetic.

My cock jerks and I release a groan as a spurt of precum juts out of me and into the waiting mouth of the servant. He moans his pleasure, sucking it down. A hot tongue swipes down the underside of my shaft before curling around the head.

More. I desire more.

My thrusts increase in pace. Harder. Faster. I arch over the human, using my hold upon his head as an anchor. I grip him and shove him down, fucking into him as if his mouth is another's pussy. She would fight me, I expect— that thief. More than fight, she would draw blood, scar me with her resistance. She would wound me and then ... in the end, she would mount me and ride my cock to completion. Hers as well as my own.

The push and pull of blood and violence and physical demands is what makes me truly uncomprehending of my father and the other Gods. Overly willing bodies are nice enough for a time, but at the end of the day, a fight makes for a delicious orgasm. Exerting effort and coercing an evasive body to give in? The headiness is such a release.

It does not matter to me who wins. She or I. So long as the struggle gives me the sweet taste of satisfaction of having worked for it.

The very thought of that shadowy figure tossing a leg over my hips and taking my cock between her legs, slamming her soaking wet pussy down over my lap, makes me unleash my cum. I come to a stuttering halt in my thrusts, holding down the skull in my hand until the boy's nose is buried into the thatch of hair at my groin. I release myself into him, groaning as it erupts. My cum pours from me, sliding down his throat and into his belly.

As I pull out, finally freed of my imagined partner, he quietly takes my cock in hand and licks up the underside. With a smirk, I watch him clean off the last remaining vestiges of my orgasm. He closes his lips around my head, his tongue dipping into the slit there and I have to pull sharply back to keep him from giving me yet another erection. I've already made my brothers wait long enough, it would take at least an hour more to enjoy this boy's backside, and after having gotten my release, I don't want to have to listen to their scolding any more than I no doubt already will.

"That will be all," I say, lifting my trousers back up and retying them.

"You were pleased, Master?" He glances up at me, lips shining wet and his face a red mess.

I smile down at him and swipe my thumb over his lower lip before lifting it to my mouth and sucking off the last droplet of my own release. "Quite pleased," I tell him, knowing that it's only a half lie. "The service of your mouth was gratifying."

His expression blossoms. "If ever you have need of me," he says. "I am happy to provide this service and ... others."

"Duly noted," I say, pulling away from him as I finish doing up my pants and turn away. "You may continue your duties here."

With that, I leave the human on his knees, belly full of my cum, and head for the chambers at the top of the northern tower.

CHAPTER 13

KIERA

Morning comes with a dusky awakening sky and silence. If there are birds on the Academy grounds, they're either asleep or dead. It's unusual to wake to the sound of nothing and it does not put me at ease for my first day masquerading as a servant within the Mortal Gods Academy.

The spiders within the walls and floorboards bring with them information. Lying in the piece-of-shit bed that I crashed into the night before, I let them crawl out from between the stones in the walls and make their way over me. The second their hairy little legs touch my skin, I'm catapulted into their tiny minds and the last views that they've collected to bring to me.

Three Mortal Gods appear in my mind's eye. All of them tall and stacked with muscle. Are these the Darkhaven brothers I'm to be in charge of? The images change, swapping as I'm presented with a scene from an outside courtyard. My lips part in shock as I watch one of them with a male Terra. The Mortal God seems vaguely familiar, though I can't quite place him. His hair is slightly longer than average, hanging in dark waves around his shadowed face. I watch as he thrusts the long length of his cock into the mouth of the young man on his knees.

The memory is obviously one from the day before if the daylight is anything to go by. I watch in commingled fascination and disgust as the Mortal God jerks his head back, his body trembling in the throes of his release as he buries the smaller man's face in his crotch—and his cock down the male's throat.

This is what is to be expected, I realize. When the senior Terra say that we're meant to serve the Mortal Gods—it's more than just to carry their books to classes. My brow pinches and I shake off the particular spider that brought me that information before I realize what I'm doing. After a beat, I reach out and ensure that the spider is alright, but it's already crawling away from me, returning to one of the holes in the wall.

My guilt fades as I sigh and take in the next scene. The other two are just as tall as the first—though as different as night and day in looks. Whereas one of them appears to have a golden halo of hair around his head with equally golden eyes, the other is as dark as his brother is light. There's no telling which of them is which—Ruen, Theos, or Kalix. What I can say, however, is that I should be particularly cautious around the one with longer hair. He seems to have no qualms about using Terra as his whores.

It's not like I haven't fucked for a job before. It's just sex. The first time had been the worst, which Ophelia told me was normal for a woman, but every time thereafter ... well, I learned fast to separate emotions from the act and it's easier when you've done it without any actual connection.

Sitting up, I shake off those ugly memories and lift my hand to set the spider that brought me the second scene onto the windowsill. I look outside as I get out of bed and the sky brightens further as I find my uniform among the packages I was given before being released to my room yesterday. Inside is a single flat white tunic and black jacket with a matching skirt. It appears much the same as the uniforms the other Terra that had led the orientation had worn. Almost as if the clothes are meant to help us blend into the background, to be seen and not heard by the Divine Beings around us. They didn't even bother to add extra, as if they expect all Terra to wear the same exact outfit day after day.

I lift the skirt with a scowl. Worse, if all I have is a skirt then there's no way I'm going to fit in as I want. A small part of me says I should just suck it up, but another, far louder and far more cautious part of me says that to wear a skirt or dress would be a death sentence. How would I move? How would I run if need be?

I should've requested a male's uniform. I contemplate putting it on and just leaving it for the day, but the rising tide of apprehension makes me decide against it. My pants from the day before are black enough to match the top portion of the uniform. It'll be fine until I can get a change.

I dress quickly, fitting the tunic under my jacket and tucking it into the waistband of my trousers, tightening the bindings of the belt so that it doesn't slip out even as I lift my arms, allowing room for movement. I snatch up my boots and tug them on, doing them up quickly before making my way out into the corridor. The papers I'd been given the day before had detailed exactly what was expected of me. Terra, especially those that are marked to serve the Mortal Gods or Gods themselves at the Academy, are expected to act independently, reporting for duty to their charges immediately upon rising and waiting for further instructions. So, I do just that, climbing the wide stone stairs at the end of the hall to the top floor of the northern dormitory tower.

There's only one door at this level. Another thing I'd memorized from the map. This is the only tower that only has one set of rooms on the top floor. Suspicious, but it could be because these three Mortal Gods are brothers and they share their chambers. I move forward and reach out, ready to knock, when it opens suddenly and I come to an abrupt halt, fist raised. The blond from the spider's memories stands there, without a shirt, grinning as he looks me over. I take a step back, my hand lowering back to my side, and bow my head.

"Good morning, Master." The words flow easily from my lips, and though I nearly stumble over the 'master' bit, I manage to keep going, ignoring the near blunder. "I am Kiera Nezerac, your new Terra. I am reporting for duty." The damned book Madam Brione had given me and Regis had forced upon me had made sure I knew this protocol. Head down. Body lax. Calm and polite tone. I hope I exemplify the perfect Terra posture and respect.

"Hmmmm." The hum that escapes him is low and vibrating. I don't lift my head to meet his sunshine-colored gaze and instead, wait for his response. "They sent a female," he says, the sound of his tone lilting with amusement. "I can't tell if the senior Terra are as sadistic as the Gods or simply stupid."

Finally, I lift my head, and my brow puckers. "I'm not sure what you mean," I say. "It's an honor to be accepted into this most prestigious institution." A fine display of fake admiration, if I do say so myself.

The blond Mortal God's grin turns into a scowl and he shakes his head. He turns away, stepping back into the chambers beyond, leaving the door open. Under his breath, I hear the muttered phrase, "Another insipid worshiper," before in a louder voice he calls back to me, "I suppose it doesn't matter." He lifts two fingers and makes a come-hither gesture. "Enter."

My fingers itch to tighten into fists, but I resist the urge. I step forward cautiously, one foot in front of the other as I stare at the wide expanse of his back. Golden muscles contract as he lifts his arms over his head and stretches onto his toes. My gaze spans down over the silken smooth skin that leads straight to his ass encased in dark trousers. "You must be new to the Academy and not just us as your Masters," he says, glancing back over his shoulder as I follow him into the room. His scowl disappears as I let the door close at my back. His gaze moves to it and he smirks. "Definitely new," he surmises, repeating his assessment. "Or else you wouldn't have closed off your only escape route."

I'm not supposed to, I know it, but for a brief moment, I let my gaze meet his at that comment. It's almost a warning from him, but the fact is that the door is not my only escape route. There are three large windows at his back and in front of them a spiral staircase, though I suppose he knows a human wouldn't survive a fall from the top of this tower.

I'm not human, though. Not completely.

"I'm afraid I don't know what you're—" A door slams open above our heads, cutting off my response, and my whole body goes stiff as the man from the other memory—the one with dark hair hanging into his face—comes barreling down the staircase. He sets his hands on the railing and casually leaps over once he's reached halfway down. Booted feet slam into the floor and he straightens.

My eyes alight on him and the dark brown leather

trousers like the kind I had worn many times during training cover his lower half. My gaze crawls up from there over the broad chest just as ripped as the first male's. A defined abdomen with a V at his hips that points down directly too— I glance to the wash of dark fabric in his hand. He holds the black tunic loosely, his muscled forearm tightening as he lifts it and tosses it over one shoulder. I trail the tan skin revealed by his lack of donned shirt up further to the face of the man himself, made of stone and the essence of masculine beauty.

The golden-haired man turns and gestures to me. "She's here, Kalix," he announces. "Remember what we said—don't break this one. I'm not cleaning my own room."

Cold invades my chest as this 'Kalix' turns his gaze on me. His eyes are pure green, full of nature and moss, but deeper than the color, I see something more disturbing. I've seen eyes like his before. They are the eyes of men locked behind cell doors—wild and untamed. Minds full of disturbing desires and the lack of impulse control to curb those desires. What had the first one said? Don't break this one? Don't break *me*?

Inside, I curse. Yes, of course, luck would not be as graceful as to allow me easy charges. No. I must somehow cater to these spoiled Mortal Gods, at least one of them with a mind of madness. Without knowing, too, when my client will unveil my intended target, there's no telling how long I'll be subjected to their presence.

I bow once more, gritting my teeth through my second greeting. "Hello, I am Kiera Nezerac. Your Terra, reporting for duty."

Footsteps echo across the room and stop right in front of me. A hand finds my chin and tilts my face up. Emerald eyes rove over my face and then down further, stopping when he gets to my attire. "You're out of uniform?" Kalix doesn't appear angry. Instead, his brow creases with confusion.

"I was given the wrong one," I lie.

"But..." His hand leaves my face and touches the jacket I'm wearing. "You're wearing the top part." His chest is so damn close, but I ignore it. Or at least, I try to.

"I wasn't given pants," I state.

He snorts. "No, of course not. You're a woman. You should be wearing the skirt of the uniform for servants," he says. "How else is a man to flip them over your back and take you when he has his needs?"

"The same way he takes a man, I suppose." The tart reply comes before I can stop it. *Fuck.*

For just a breath, the room is silent and I fear my own lack of impulse control has ruined me, but then there's a laugh. Deep and echoing. I look up and am surprised to find it's not Kalix, though those daunting eyes of his dance with mirth. I turn to look at the blond, but he's also not the one laughing. Instead, his eyes are widened with surprise and turned towards the corner. Concern marks his brow, pressing a line into the pristine flesh in the center of his forehead.

"Ruen?" the blond calls—giving me the final piece of the puzzle to decipher which of them is which. If the green-eyed monster is Kalix, and the third and last Darkhaven brother in the corner is Ruen, then the blond must be Theos.

Shaking my head and pulling myself away from Kalix's grip, I turn and look to the corner where a rather large man is stretched out along a cushioned lounge with a book opened over his chest that rises and falls with laughter.

"Amused, brother?" Kalix asks, his voice ripe with the obvious desire to laugh himself.

Booted feet hit the ground as Ruen sits up from his reclining position. The book on his chest slips down and he catches it, snapping it shut and setting it to the side before it can fall to the floor. Theos tears his gaze from his brother and fixes me with a dark, almost violent look; one I can't possibly understand.

Ruen's laughter subsides as he stands and strides across the room. Unable to give my back to an enemy without a weapon in my hand, I pivot my body—angling myself so that I'm facing all three of the Mortal Gods. I stiffen as he approaches me, and despite the fact that he's the only one wearing a tunic, somehow that makes the open gap at his collar that reveals smooth, cool-toned flesh that much more eye-catching. He doesn't stop until he's before me, so close that I can see the flecks of red and gold in his irises and the slight dimple in his right cheek.

"Are you going to greet me, human?" he asks, leaning forward.

Intimidation. These men have it in spades. Too bad for them, I am not one to be easily intimidated. They don't know that, though, and I still need to act the part if I'm to remain here to find my target.

I force a little stutter into my tone once more as I greet him, repeating my earlier words. "H-hello. I am Kiera Nezerac. Your Terra, reporting for duty."

Ruen continues to stare at me. There's a thin line, slightly paler than the rest of his skin, that divides his right eyebrow. It's long enough that it nearly reaches his eye. It's old, that much is for sure, but that's not the odd part of the scar. The fact is—this man is a Mortal God and at the rate he should be able to heal, it would take a lot to permanently scar his face like that. Perhaps brimstone? That's the only mortal object that's been known to wound a Divine Being, and unfortunately, I know about its effects all too well. But then, who would be allowed to scar a God child like Ruen Darkhaven?

Unlike Kalix, his attention doesn't creep along my skin. Instead, he makes me nervous in a new way. It's as if he can see deep into my mind, pick apart the thoughts that even I'm not aware of.

Are there abilities like that? I suddenly worry. Gods and Mortal Gods that can read minds? If that's true, then it's too late for me. There's no doubt he'll find out everything if he can, in fact, see into my thoughts. I hold my breath, waiting for that inevitable moment where I'm about to be told that I have some godsforsaken nerve to try and sneak in here to kill one of their own.

A minute passes, a second, and then a third. He doesn't speak for the longest time and with each pass of the clock, my heart beats faster. My head is swimming, but I refuse to release first. Not until I know for certain whether or not I've been caught before I've ever had a chance to begin.

Finally, after weighted eons, he straightens away from me and turns his head back to his brothers. "I give her a week," he states.

I blink. A week? How little does he think of Terra then? Or ... how badly do they treat theirs? I force myself not to react. Instead, I keep my expression passive and unbothered.

Theos seems to contemplate his brother's words as his body relaxes. "Is that generous by your standards?" he asks. "Or stingy?"

"Generous," Ruen replies before stealing a glance back at me. "She's a bare wisp of a creature." He shakes his head as if he almost feels pity for me. "They should know better than to send someone so ... small and weak."

Don't, I order myself even as I start to feel my muscles tighten and my senses bristle. I'm fine with being underestimated. Truly, I am. It makes my job easier. Somehow, though, the way he says it awakens sensibilities and pride I thought I'd long since tossed away.

"I will do my best to serve you," I say in response.

Kalix is the first, and most eager, to respond. "I'm sure you will," he says as he finally removes the tunic from his shoulder and slips it on over his head. "I, for one, look forward to your service." I blink as his chest disappears from view and he rolls up the sleeves while maintaining that ever-present disturbing grin of his.

"Breakable, Kalix," Theos reminds him. "Very breakable. Should we make a bet of it?"

"I'm sorry?" I frown. "A bet?"

Theos ignores me as Kalix seems to consider his brother's words. He turns to Ruen and lifts four fingers. "Four weeks," he says.

"A month?" Ruen replies, sounding rather surprised.

"If she can last that long, what do I get?" Kalix asks.

"Are you planning on keeping your hands off of her for four weeks?" Theos asks.

My understanding of their conversation deepens. The three of them are placing bets to see how long I'll last and from the sound of it, Kalix is the decider of such things. The sexual innuendos riding off of his words come as almost a second language that isn't too hard to understand even if it does disgust me.

"Of course not," he chuckles, "but"—his eyes cut back to me, narrowing as he roves from the bottom of my booted feet up to my face—"I have a good feeling about this one."

"Fine, then," Theos says. "I'll take that bet. I say two weeks at most."

Ruen shakes his head. "One week. No more."

The more they discuss my possible expulsion or perhaps my own willingness to leave their service, the more it rankles me. A sensation I thought I was above now, after all of my training. It would be smarter to keep my mouth shut. That much I know for sure, yet somehow, that logical part of my mind doesn't seem keen on overtaking the illogical part and I find myself opening my mouth.

"What do I get if I last longer than any of you say I will?" I ask.

All three pairs of eyes fall on me in an instant. Silence fills the room. I wait with my spine straight and my shoulders thrown back, showing the trio of them that I'm not afraid of their words or assumptions.

Theos is the first to crack a smile. It spreads slowly, deepening until it crosses his entire face. "Does the little mortal girl wish to play with the Gods?"

"Are you Gods?" I find myself asking. "I was under the impression that I would be serving their children. My apologies, oh Divine Ones." I bow slightly at the waist once more. "I have come to the wrong rooms then."

A bark of laughter escapes Kalix. "Oh, she's a feisty one. I like that. We don't have those here."

"I think I've changed my mind," Ruen says.

"More or less?" I ask, curious enough to lift my head and meet his gaze. Blue eyes striking like the midnight hours glitter dangerously.

"Less," he answers.

I offer him a smile. "Then I look forward to exceeding your expectations. I'm sure if you think so little of me, they won't be difficult to beat."

Ruen tilts his head to the side. "I've never met such a combative mortal," he comments. "Perhaps it served you well outside of the Academy, but here"—he steps closer, moving until the heat of him is damn near searing my flesh even through my clothes—"things are a bit different."

"I'm well aware that the status within the Academy is different for mortals," I state. "I came here despite knowing that fact."

"Did you?" he inquires. His hand lifts, almost the same size as a bear's paw as he touches a strand of my hair resting upon my shoulder. I keep my chin up, needing the advantage to keep his eyes locked with mine as he stares at me. "Poor little mortal," he says, lifting that silver strand to his mouth.

I watch as he brushes the feathery tips of the end of my hair across his lower lip. "You have no idea what's in store for you."

Somehow, it's his words and not those of his brothers that strike me deep. It isn't the conversation they'd had as if I weren't standing before them, well aware that their topic of ridicule was me. It isn't the overtly carnal gaze of his brother, Kalix, or the obvious hints that he'd somehow been responsible for the loss of many of their Terra before, but the vague threatening promise of Ruen Darkhaven.

Regardless, I keep my gaze up. I've experienced torture. I've lived through loss. I've been burned, scalded, half drowned, starved, beaten, and more. I truly believe, deep in my soul, there is nothing the three of them can throw at me that I wouldn't be able to handle.

If anything, I look forward to seeing them handle *me*. My lips form a smirk as Ruen continues to stare at me as if waiting for me to realize my mistake and back away. That won't happen. If anything, my response solidifies that I am not leaving. This is my chance to attain my freedom and even if it means I have to put up with three spoiled Mortal Gods for the foreseeable future, so be it.

I continue to smile as I offer my response, "May the best woman win."

CHAPTER 14
KIERA

Three pairs of scrutinizing eyes watch me with mistrust and curiosity. Mistrust, I understand. Curiosity … well, you know what they say. Curiosity killed the cat—three cats in this instance, if they hinder my progress. I force my shoulders down and my muscles to remain lax. Their gazes and attention are not something I'm accustomed to. I'm far more familiar with hiding in the shadows. Hiding in plain sight is a different skill set. One that Regis is far more suited to than I. But there's no turning back now.

"Careful with your words, mortal." Theos' tone is a warning. "We love a good challenge and we have no intentions of losing."

What a coincidence, I think. *Neither do I.* Instead of saying as much, though, I tip my head up, looking back at him, and smile. "Of course not, Master Theos."

"Yet, you still wish to play with us?" The question is accompanied by the golden glow of his irises darkening and his lips twitching. The pulse of excitement within him is palpable. Kalix practically vibrates at his side.

"Depending on the reward for lasting longer than any of you seem to give me credit for, I'm fully prepared to win this bet of yours," I inform them.

"Mortals do not take part in our bets," Theos says.

"Is that because they are too frightened or is there some rule against it?" I ask, reaching up and tapping a finger against my chin in the way I'd seen small children do when purposefully pretending to be clueless.

The scar that cuts through Ruen's brow tightens as his face reacts. "They are too frightened," he answers, stepping away from me. "*Usually.*"

His brows draw down low over his expression and he continues to stare as if he half expects me to sprout a second head. I can understand his perplexity. No doubt the Terra they've experienced were a bit more reserved. A part of me is raging in caution, telling me that I should back off and apologize for my disrespectful attitude. A different part of me, however, is dancing with glee, with anticipation.

This particular mission is a rarity. I have to wonder if it's even real, or if it's something else entirely—perhaps a test set about by Ophelia. Yes, that would make the most sense. Why else would she even consider sending me into the lion's den? She knows me. She knows what I'm capable of. Still, there's a small ember of hope that swells within my breast, reminding me of all I could have if this job is, in fact, real. If it is, and I do manage to get that four million denza, then I can walk away from this life. I can leave assassination behind and be myself again. I can leave people entirely and live in peace in the Hinterlands.

The yearning for freedom is poignant. It's irresistible to someone like me. I grit my teeth and shake my head as I rid myself of those worldly desires. What I need to do now is focus on the men in front of me. I've already let my mouth take control. It's pointless now to act the part of the subservient worshiper. Besides, I've learned from experience that keeping one's mouth shut is only for certain occasions. I can't let these men think I'll be easy to get rid of, not if I'm going to find my target—if there is one—and buy back my freedom.

"Then feel free to consider me *unusual*," I say with a polite smile.

"What is your name, Terra?"

I stiffen, but return my attention to Theos at his question. "Are you usually forgetful, Master Theos?" I ask. "Should I make a note to remind you of your schedule as well?" There's a fine line between careless words and subversive insults and I walk it with confidence.

A puckered V develops between his brows as if he's confused by my question. If I had to guess, I expect it isn't so much that he's forgotten, but more so that none of them had been paying attention in the first place.

I sigh. "My name is Kiera Nezerac," I repeat.

"Nezerac?" Ruen repeats the surname. "A nomad?"

I look back at him. "Yes. I was." It's a simple answer, one that offers no other explanation and no apology. His brow furrows further.

"You wish to take part in the bet, little human?" The green-eyed Mortal God moves forward, bypassing his golden-haired brother who stiffens and sways forward as if he means to stop him. Interesting. Is it concern for me or for his brother? A beat passes before Theos grits his teeth and falls back on the soles of his feet once more without stopping him, though his eyes continue to track his brother across the room as Kalix approaches me.

For some reason, as I stare into the glowing mossy color

of his irises, I have the distinct feeling that I'm meeting the same eyes of a vicious and deceptive snake. The outside may appear human, his face may be cut into a beauty that is purely Divine, but his pupils are narrow, shaped almost like slits. Inside this man, there lies, with cunning patience, a venomous creature ready to swallow me whole, and I have to be very careful not to become his prey.

Kalix towers over me in height, covering me in his shadow. He smiles, his upper lip pulling back to reveal sharp canines. I blink, swearing for a moment that they seem longer than normal, but when I look again, they don't appear any different from anyone else's. There's an air of tension in the room. Ruen and Theos say nothing, but I can sense their rapt attention on their brother.

I can be contentious as a person. I know that, but have I made a mistake in assuming these three would walk all over someone with a more submissive personality? My heart beats wildly in my chest and I swear they can hear it —that he, Kalix, can hear it and he's pleased by the sudden shift in the room.

"If I'm the reason for the bet, then why not?" I offer and my mouth tastes of dust as I force the words to sound calm.

The answer must incite him if his growing smile is anything to judge by. "I think we should let her," he says, directing his words to the others, though his gaze never leaves my face. "It's been so long since I've been this intrigued."

The rapid pulse of my heart slows until it nearly stops. My blood rushes through my ears. Too late, I realize that intriguing this man is probably a bad idea. Appearing weak, though, doesn't seem like a better option. To the three of them, I am a mouse caught in a lion's trap and the only way to get out without being eaten or scarred by their claws is to do that very thing—heighten their intrigue.

Theos groans. "The last time you were intrigued, you made a Terra go insane."

My eyes cut to Theos. That comment would scare me— it *would* if I didn't already know that sometimes being insane is the only way you can survive. I do not pity the deranged. I understand them. "If you order me not to, I wouldn't dare take part in your bet, Masters," I say.

"If we order you not to?" Bright golden eyes settle on me. Theos looks as if he's swallowed a lemon whole and the damn fruit has peeled itself open in his gut, scouring his insides with its acidity.

I offer a smile in response. "Of course." I nod. "I understand that it would be disgraceful for a Terra such as myself to challenge her Mortal God Masters. It was inconsiderate and presumptuous of me to insert myself. I beg for your forgiveness."

Eyebrows raise all around. Kalix's expression turns to one of absolute glee. "You think yourself a challenge?" he asks. "So sure you'll win?"

I blink, feigning innocence. "Master, it would be disrespectful of me not to consider all of the options. While I do say you three have much higher chances than I of winning this game as you are its creators, it would be the height of arrogance to assume that anyone—Mortal God or mortal alike—has absolutely zero chance of winning." Like dancing on a fucking tightrope, I scan their faces, waiting for their response. Ruen's face is all shadow and darkness. A telltale twitch pulses in Theos' forehead. "I wouldn't want to tread on that territory if making bets with mortals is too risky," I finish in my feigned polite tone.

Three sets of eyes, one gold, one green, and one blue, settle on me. It takes considerable effort not to smirk. I honestly don't know how I manage to withhold it. Regis has always warned me that my mouth will get me into trouble someday. That day just might be today.

Apparently, using that Divine pride of theirs proves to be the perfect tactic, though. "Fine then," Theos growls. "Let the little Terra play. Perhaps once she's lost we can borrow a Terra or two from the others to clean our rooms. It'll be far more amusing to watch this one break."

"Enough that I can do as I please?" Kalix asks, excitement clear in his tone as the corners of his lips turn up further. Were I truly mortal, fear would no doubt be skittering through me. That smile of his is unsettling. What pleases others no doubt has little effect on him, and something tells me the grotesque is what he enjoys. It is, after all, a good thing for a mortal to have their fight-or-flight reflexes. Right now, that half of me is screaming to *run*.

As much as I don't want to ignore it, I do. There's no leaving now. I've already passed the point of no return. Already they must sense the difference in me. I resist the urge to cup the back of my neck where the shard of brimstone rests beneath my skin. The spot there tingles as if in response to my thoughts, an illusion likely. Whenever I think about it, I feel as if the stone comes alive, a creature shrouding me from all prying eyes as much as it ties me to one person in particular. Another reason Ophelia had forced it upon me—it mutes Divinity not just in strength but in the eyes of those who would figure out what I am just by looking at me.

"Within reason," Ruen snaps before Theos can respond, shaking me from my internal thoughts. "No killing."

I look at Kalix at that statement. I grind my teeth to keep myself from reacting. No doubt, Ruen isn't telling me that. He likely believes me incapable of such an act, but it also makes me wonder. I doubt they truly care about the lives of those they deem beneath them. So, why the no killing rule then? It's a curiosity that might just stay a mystery.

Kalix doesn't seem too put out by Ruen's demand. In fact, his eyes flick back to me and sharpen, glittering with intensity. "That's fine," he replies. "Killing her would mean this game ends far too soon."

"Are there any other stipulations?" I inquire, keeping my tone even and unbothered. Theos stares at me. There's a bubble of something in my stomach that lights up when I think of how easy and amusing it'll be to prove these bastards wrong. It's been a long damn time since I've let myself have a little fun. Deep down, I know I should retract my interest in this game of theirs and take several steps back, but I find that I can't. They aren't the only ones intrigued, and perhaps this will reveal the real Academy rules more so than the Terra orientation ever could. There's bound to be a difference between what's written into law and what is actually enforced.

If I'm going to be forced to remain in this place for an undetermined amount of time with no target, I need something to keep me occupied. Let it be these three. I have no expectations that they will treat me fairly. It can't hurt to show a few Mortal Gods their place, could it?

"Just ... no killing," Ruen finally says, answering my question. "That's it." Deep cold blue eyes steal over my face. Were I an insect, I have no doubt he'd have me pinned under glass and picked apart in less time than it takes for me to inhale. "*Everything* else is fair game." What is most assuredly a warning sounds like the ringing of a battle bell in my ears.

I smile wider as I lower myself into a bow before the three of them, feigning the perfect Terra reverence. "As my Masters' command."

CHAPTER 15

KIERA

L ike the rest of Anatol, the Mortal Gods Academy of Riviere is plagued by the current of classist egoism that inhabits the rest of the world. It permeates the grounds and those who live within its walls. It doesn't take me long to figure out the hierarchy of Mortal Gods Academy. Just as the Gods are divided into their own sections—Upper Gods and Lower Gods—Mortal Gods are the same.

First Tier Mortal Gods have the most power. Second Tier Mortal Gods often have power, but whatever their specialty may be, it is either weak or not a combative ability. Third Tiers are merely a step above mortals. Their powers are either incredibly feeble or they have proven to have God blood but individual abilities have yet to manifest.

Gods aren't the only ones to enable the segregation of those with and without powerful abilities. Terra do too. I've already seen it—from orientation to meeting the Dark-haven brothers. The indoctrination is strong here, perhaps more so than in the Hinterlands and outskirt cities and towns since Gods aren't as common in those parts of the world. Here at the Mortal Gods Academy, the gazes of new and returning Terra are ripe with worship. The casual expectation of such from the Mortal Gods, themselves, is another reinforcement of the idea that they've reaped the benefits of their birth without regard for anyone else.

I stand just inside the doorway of the Terra dining hall, a long stretch of a room with few windows and high ceilings. Despite the mass of people that fill the space, the room is still chilled with how wide and tall it is. It's a monstrosity, almost too big for a place meant for mortals. I watch in both curiosity and disgust as the senior Terra practically shove the newer, less experienced ones out of the way in their haste to grab their food, scarf it down, and sprint off to their next destination. It's a waste of space in my opinion. If all they're going to do is snatch and go, then what is the point of the multiple long wooden tables scattered throughout the room?

A familiar face catches my attention in the crowd several paces away. His mousy brown head turns as if seeking something and then when he spots me—hovering just inside the doorway—his face lights up and he gestures for me to hurry over. The excitement and welcome in his expression almost make me feel guilty. If I want to fit into this place then I'll have to at least make it look like I'm approachable to the other Terra. To look approachable, I have to make 'friends' and Niall is, so far, one of the only ones to offer himself up, however unknowing, for the role.

I trace the room, working my way along the outer edges as I watch Niall shoulder his way out of the crowd that surrounds the food tables until he breaks free.

"Kiera!" he calls out. If it weren't for the fact that he's

now holding two plates in his hands, I'd suspect he'd be waving. As it stands, he can't seem to not wave so instead he wiggles his chicken-like arms up and down in excitement, elbows out. I bite my tongue to keep myself from laughing at the sight.

Niall hurries towards me with a face-splitting grin as he holds up his plates like they're blocks of gold. "I managed to get you some as well," he boasts. "It's a madhouse over there."

Unable to stop the chuckle that slips free, I lean forward and take one of the plates off his hands. "Thanks," I say.

He blinks at me for a moment, eyes focused on my mouth before darting up to my eyes. "Erm ... right, shall we sit?"

I nod and follow him to one of the tables towards the back of the hall, away from the rabble still yelling and fighting over the food. We take our seats at the end of a table with a small group of Terra at the opposite side. Strangely enough, when they look up and see me, their eyes widen and within seconds, they're collecting their half-eaten plates and trays of food before they quickly leave. I frown as I lift a fork set over the top of the plate from the food and watch them go.

"Don't worry about them," Niall says quickly, distracting me from the other Terra's odd behavior. "I'm sure everything will work out fine."

"I'm sorry?" I direct my gaze to him as he shovels in a mouthful of dried potatoes and begins chewing. "What exactly will work out?"

He stops chewing and then gulps down the food in his mouth before tilting his head at me, the fuzzy curls at the ends of his locks shifting with the moment. "You ... don't know?"

"What am I supposed to know?" I ask, perplexed.

"I just thought you would have—I mean, I assume you've met your Masters by now." Niall dips his head in embarrassment.

My fingers close around the fork much like they would the handle of a knife at the reminder of my 'meeting' with them. "I have," I state. "What about them?"

Niall scoops up another forkful of his food, but instead of immediately shoveling it into his mouth, he tips the utensil over and lets it spill back onto the plate.

I sigh. "I'm not going to be mad," I say, hoping I didn't just tell another lie. "Just tell me what that was all about." I stab my fork into a glob of what looks like softened meat.

"Well, it's because it's … *them*—the Darkhaven brothers," Niall says, dropping his voice into a whisper as he says their name. "The senior Terra gave the rest of us a warning about which of the Mortal Gods to avoid and it seems … well, what I mean to say is—"

"Let me guess," I say, cutting him off. "I'm tasked with the worst of the worst?" That would be in line with how my luck has always gone. Enter one of the most dangerous places in the world for someone like me and it's a given I'll be slapped with the shit end of the stick.

A hint of pink steals across Niall's slender cheeks. "Yes, th-that does seem to be the case. I-it was after the orientation, but I didn't see you so I assumed someone had passed along the information."

"No." I shake my head. Perhaps Liana had liked me even less than I thought. I spear the strange meat with my fork again. "I assume that means no one wants to associate with me to avoid contact with *them*." I look towards the fleeing Terra. There goes my ability to make 'friends.'

"I-I'm sure that once everyone gets settled, it'll be easier," Niall tries to assure me. His kindness almost hurts to hear and it definitely doesn't do anything for the guilt still lingering within me. I pass him a smile as I shovel a few bites of food into my mouth to let him know I don't blame him for this turn of events.

If it's fear keeping the other Terra away then that's not really anything I can help right away. They'd likely react the same way had the Darkhaven brothers gotten a different Terra. My sudden and unfortunate luck does seem a curious thing, though. As I spear more food into my mouth, chewing and swallowing without tasting a damn thing, I wonder if perhaps Ophelia's client had anything to do with this. If this isn't a test but a real mission—and I need to treat it as such in the event that my earlier suspicion is wrong—then I need to consider my placement as one of intent rather than coincidence. Madam Brione had assisted me in gaining entrance to the Academy, but the client had to know that one of the new Terra was the assassin they'd hired.

Had I been unintentionally discovered? No, if I had, they likely would've come for me already. Or ... would they? If their end goal was to have me kill a God or Mortal God, they'd want to keep their involvement as secret as possible. Ophelia had taken quite a long time to train me so even if I am discovered here, I'm confident in my ability to escape.

Still ... things can always go awry—the best-laid plans are, after all, ones you survive long enough to see in hindsight.

I resolve to contact Ophelia via Regis later to follow up on the Terra assignments as I quickly finish my plate, polishing it clean in under five minutes. Niall watches in a mixture of horror and confusion as the food on my plate rapidly disappears and he still sits with the remainder of his meal.

"Thank you for helping me get food," I say, wiping the back of my mouth with the edge of my sleeve. "And for that information, I'll be sure to return the favor."

"You don't have to—Where are you going?" Niall asks abruptly as his head snaps back and I stand up from the table.

"Classes should be starting soon and I need to find the right building," I say. "Good luck on your first day."

The clatter of his fork, as he drops it on the edge of his plate, pierces my ears as he reaches forward and snags my jacket sleeve. "Wait!"

I pause, looking down at him—pointedly staring at his fingers locked onto the fabric of my uniform until he gets the point and releases me. "C-can you wait for me?" he asks hesitantly as he dips his head. "I'll finish fast, I was just h-hoping we could walk to the classroom building together."

I consider his request. No doubt he's nervous for his own first day and he did, after all, give me information about why the Terra were avoiding me on top of procuring my breakfast for me. "I suppose so," I answer rather lamely after a moment.

If Niall is put off by the pause before my answer, he certainly doesn't show it. In fact, before I even speak, as if he's anticipating my denial, he hurriedly scoops up several mouthfuls of food, shoveling them into his mouth until his cheeks bulge out like a squirrel's. I watch, giving him just enough time to finish his meal as I hover nearby.

Choking down the food still in his mouth, Niall jerks up from the table, snatching his plate and stealing mine from my hands before hurrying off to where they're supposed to be left after we're done with them. I contemplate taking the opportunity to sneak away despite my acquiescence to walk to class with him, but I remain in place until he returns with a flushed face and relief etched into his expression.

"Oh good, you didn't leave." He sighs and then gestures for me to step ahead of him towards the exit.

"You asked me to stay," I remind him, peering at him curiously as we start walking.

Niall ducks his head but peers at me out of his periphery as we stride for the exit and head from the Terra amenities to our next destination. "A lot of Terra don't seem to be too welcoming of newbies," he replies. "So, I figured we newcomers should stick together."

"Ah," I crane my head back and release a light laugh. "That explains it."

Curls swish over his ears as he turns to look at me. "Explains what?"

"Why you're being so friendly with me," I say.

"Is there anything wrong with that?" he asks.

My smile hardens a bit as it falls into place, held there with no little effort. The only friend I've ever had is Regis. He's someone I don't have to lie to, someone who knows my reality from my bloodline to my trade. A friendship built on lies is nothing but a crumbling house, and here is a boy so readily offering it despite the fact that he's already been warned that I'm in a position that could be dangerous to him. It feels a bit too easy, and anything too easy is never good.

Instead of answering, though, I simply keep walking, my long legs eating up the distance. Behind me, I hear the telltale sounds of Niall's breathlessness as he huffs and hurries to keep pace with me. It's clear that, despite his tall frame, his lankiness is due to malnourishment and inactivity. He's definitely going to have to increase his stamina if he's going to keep up. Maybe staying in the Academy will be good for him. At least he'll have his meals provided for him; they won't allow him to starve.

"So, what are they like?" Niall asks abruptly, revealing the real reason he asked to walk with me. I chuckle and don't even attempt to not know who he means.

"They're Mortal Gods," I say with a shrug. "They're just like the others, I guess." I cut a path out of the building and head down a set of stone stairs into a barren courtyard. Unlike the courtyards meant for Gods and Mortal Gods, with lush greenery and cloth tents to protect frolickers from the burning sun, the courtyards of the Terra buildings are merely a formality. The stone statues are meant to remind us who we're here to serve and worship. Plaques with each God's name etched into the bottoms of their likenesses.

"I told you that my charge was a Second Tier," Niall chatters on. "Her name is Maeryn. She's quite kind—far kinder than I expected. Maybe that's because she's a Second Tier. I'd heard from some of the Terra that Mortal Gods could be cruel, but obviously not all of them are if she's so sweet. She even thanked me. Can you believe it? A Divine child *thanking* me?"

Niall's words run together. "She even showed me some of her powers. Apparently, we'll be learning about Mortal Gods and their abilities in some of their classes. Her mother is a Lower God of Music, but Maeryn doesn't have the same abilities as her. I had a gash on the back of my arm from moving some boxes and she noticed, so she offered to..."

His words fade as my footsteps slow in front of a particularly large statue. It's bigger than the rest and stationed in a place that seems more noticeable than the others within the circular courtyard. At my side, the buzzing sound of

Niall's voice remains a constant—though I'm no longer listening. My entire attention is fixed on this statue.

The man it depicts is barrel-chested with a long beard that reaches the center of his wide pecs. He looks like the lumberjacks of the Hinterlands that chop wood for sale in the smaller towns. Big, muscular, gruff. His upper body remains naked and the lower half is covered by draping clothes. None of that sets me on edge. The thing that does, is the circlet adorning his head. It's not ornate nor is it large. It's a rather simple band, the stone version crafted perfectly to not flatten his hair as it might if he were real. None of the other God statues have the same circlet.

It's just a statue, I tell myself, but the expression on the God's face is incensing. Almost as if this inanimate object is looking down upon me and everyone that passes by. It's impossible, I know, but I swear the longer I stare, the wider his wicked grin grows.

"Kiera?" Niall's voice sounds distant—far away. I want to respond, but I can't. I'm held captive in this space as I stare at the man.

He's just a man. But that's not true. He's not just a man. He's a Divine Being. Is he watching me now through the statue's gaze? Is that possible?

"Oh wow, would you look at that..." I finally break through my reverie and peer over at my companion. Niall gapes up wondrously at the statue.

"Who is he?" I ask.

"You don't know?" Though his tone isn't condescending, the shock of it rubs me the wrong way. As if it's positively preposterous that anyone in the world would not know who this man is by the sight of his face. What I know is that Gods have many faces and almost all of them are lies.

"No."

"That's Tryphone!" He grabs onto my arm in excitement. I turn and look at Niall as he leans forward, eyes focused on the plaque beneath the statue. "This is the God King—a rendition of, course. No human has ever actually seen him, save for the humans who were here when the Gods first came down. How lucky are we to have an idol of him?"

Lucky? Is that what he thinks? Is that what the whole of the human race thinks?

No. They don't. If they did then there would be no Underworld Guild. No Regis. No Ophelia. And certainly no Mortal God assassin.

Shaking away the deterring thoughts, I move away from the statue and keep walking. "I'm happy that your Mortal God is so nice," I say, responding to Niall's earlier commentary to quickly change the subject. "But I suggest you stay away from mine. They're not nearly as sweet or tenderhearted. If you can avoid them, you should do so."

"Are they truly that awful?" Niall, in his steadfastness, follows.

Awful? Maybe not. Dangerous, though? Yes. They would rip poor naive Niall apart with their bare hands and laugh as he bled out over the toes of their boots.

"Yes." And he would do well to remember that he'd likely gotten lucky with his own charge—or she's simply easing him into things before she rips him to shreds.

I've seen it far too often in the outskirts—Gods of all levels playing with humans like toys. This place is no different. The Academy is like anywhere else. Everyone is out for themselves and it's survival of the fittest.

I cast a glance at Niall as he walks at my side. Watching him get ripped apart by the animals that are the Mortal

Gods is a sight I don't wish to see. Just the thought of it makes my stomach cramp. The other Terra were smart to avoid me. Any involvement with the Terra of three First Tier Mortal Gods might risk their own safety. I don't blame them.

CHAPTER 16
KIERA

Niall and I head across the Academy grounds, pausing and bowing our heads respectfully as Mortal Gods and Gods stride by. Their gazes, however, always remain up and focused, uncaring of the lesser beings they bypass to their next destinations. Niall is enthralled by it all, turning his head at each passing God in wonder once he's done his Terra duty of kowtowing to them.

The heavy weight of this mission is wrapped around my neck, clinging like a dying bird. It's growing in both size and burden as it remains. If, by some miracle, this isn't just a test schemed up by Ophelia and it's really an actual job, I just wish the client's target is revealed soon. Then I can find them, kill them, and move on. Being around this much Divinity is a new thing for me and not something I'm comfortable with, especially not with the ever-present responsibility I have to not just myself but everyone who knows my identity in the Underworld Guild.

"Terra!" The word is shouted from down a long corridor. A split second later, the soft whoosh of an object sailing towards me reaches my ears. Instinctively, I put my hand out, grabbing hold of the back of Niall's shirt, loose fitting as it is, and yanking him out of the way as I stop both him and I from being struck by the bag that comes flying past my face. The bag sails towards another Terra who is too slow to react, sending both the skinny girl and her companion—another Terra of similar stature—down to the floor in a heap and cries of sudden pain. Had I not stopped and pulled Niall back, that would have most certainly been us.

"Awww, why'd you make me miss?" Turning my head at the playful, yet annoyed voice, I spot a rather tall, beefy-looking Mortal God making his way down the hall, heading straight towards us with a disappointed frown marring his otherwise perfect features. He's tall, though not as tall as the Darkhavens. What he lacks in height, however, he makes up for in sheer width.

Everything about him is broad. From the wide expanse of his chest and shoulders to the bulging muscles of his biceps and the trunks of his thighs as he strides down the hallway, through the throng of others. The light pouring in through the doors and windows glints across the short russet strands of his hair with each step.

Niall makes a choked sound in his throat. "Th-that's Malachi," he stutters, his voice dropping likely in the hopes that the Mortal God won't hear him. "Rumor has it that he's the Messenger God's son, but his abilities are closer to that of the God of Strength."

The Mortal God stops before us, smirking down at me before looking at Niall and jerking his head to the side. "Get lost," he snaps.

Niall hesitates. It's sweet, truly. He's so skinny and frag-ile-looking, but the fact that he doesn't immediately scamper off is telling. He's not an average kid, but likely one who's been beaten all his life and has still somehow managed to maintain his kindness. I should hate people like that. They're weak-willed and frustratingly kind even when it will damage them to be so. I can't seem to hate Niall, though, not even when he frustrates me by not looking after himself.

"You heard him, Niall," I say, releasing his shirt. "Follow his orders."

Niall's eyes widen as he jerks his attention from me to the man before finally nodding and hurrying away. With him now gone, I direct the full weight of my attention to the creature before me.

"I don't believe we've met," I say before executing a bow. "I am Kiera Nezerac, Terra to the Darkhaven brothers. How can I help you, sir?"

"Oh, I know exactly who you are," Malachi states, grinning wickedly as I stand up from my bow. "Theos told me all about you."

I tilt my head to the side. "Did he?" Curious. Very curious.

As if mentioning a Darkhaven's name conjures them, Theos, Ruen, and Kalix appear at the mouth of the hallway several paces behind Malachi. Over the Mortal God's shoulder, I see Theos grin my way before giving me a distinctive wink.

I see. So, this is the first test. How juvenile. I repress the urge to roll my eyes as my attention returns to Malachi. I suppose I shouldn't fail their expectations. "Is there something I can do for you, sir?" I ask, forcing a polite smile as I clasp my hands behind me like a well-trained soldier ready to do anything and everything ordered of them.

"Yeah, sure is." He grins, crossing his arms over his

chest. "You can take off those clothes and bend over for me right now. It's been a long time since I've had fresh Terra pussy. Theos has given me leave to enjoy you."

My smile tightens ever so slightly as my gaze cuts to the Darkhaven brothers over his shoulder a second time.

Conniving, I think. *How so very conniving.*

It's almost pathetic that this was the route they chose to take. Sex? Did they really think that would break me? I look Malachi up and down before glancing around us, where a fairly sizable crowd has gathered. One option would simply be to accept Malachi's demands since Terra are all well aware that to deny a Mortal God or Divine Being anything would be subject to punishment.

Crowd or not, Mortal God or not, being fucked in front of these people won't stop me from completing my mission, but it would likely hinder me. To accept this would ensure that I'd be branded as a Terra whore, free for the taking. Even if it's well known that many Terra already fuck their Masters and whoever they're ordered to, doing so behind closed doors allows Terra to at least maintain some sort of dignity. This is a trick by Theos—and his brothers—to rid me of that dignity.

How, then, will I be able to get out of being fucked by this thick-headed brute on my first day?

"I'm happy to remove my clothing and service you," I say slowly, letting my smile drop away as I peer up at him with a concerned expression. "But are you sure that's wise?"

His smirk fades, and a line forms between his brows. "What do you mean?" His eyes cut to the side as he grows increasingly aware of the crowd he's drawn on purpose and the fact that I've yet to undress and bend over.

Turning my head, I scan those surrounding us—not the

least of which include the damned Darkhaven brothers. Standing just behind Kalix and Theos, Ruen's expression appears rather bored with the scene, as if he's just there because his brothers are. Still, he doesn't leave. He must be curious as well. I'm nothing if not obliging.

Sensing weakness, I take a step closer to Malachi and look up into his face, my brows pinching together as my lashes lower once and then lift again. "I'm sure you know that as the Darkhavens' Terra, I'm more than aware of their desires," I say.

Unease flickers across Malachi's face and his muscles bunch. "So?" he demands, his voice turning defensive.

My smile widens. I release my hands from my back and twist them in front of me instead. "I don't wish to embarrass a Mortal God of your skill and renown." It's a lie, especially considering I've never even heard of him before today. Unfortunately for him, though, he strikes me as the type that's so overconfident, it's implausible that anyone would *not* know of him, and I'm usually right about my instincts.

His dark brown eyes narrow on my upturned face. "Why the fuck do you think you'd be able to embarrass *me*, Terra?" he sneers.

I blink up at him, eyes wide and feigning innocence. "Oh no, sir," I reply. "Not *I*—but my Masters ... well ... I'm sure you're aware that they wouldn't ask you to fuck their Terra in front of such a large crowd if they didn't want to cause *someone* embarrassment, and it wouldn't be me, since bowing to your graciousness is nothing but a glorious pleasure for one as lowly as myself." The words come easier and easier. Tricky, tricky, little liar. That's what I am. I'd almost feel bad for the meathead if I didn't know that he'd absolutely strip me bare in front of all of these people and fuck me just for fun, for a dare.

I lift my hand and carefully set it upon his massive chest. His heart beats faster, the sound and reverberation against the center of my palm. I delicately swipe my tongue over my lower lip and cast my eyes up through my lashes. "My Masters desire amusement, sir," I tell him. "If you're willing to play the part then I will do my best to satisfy you. I just hate the thought of them attempting to make a fool out of someone so strong and great."

Shock crosses his features a split second before realization dawns at what I'm insinuating. "I am no one's fucking fool!" Took him long enough. He turns abruptly and stares down the hall towards Theos, Ruen, and Kalix. "Theos! You bastard!"

Theos blinks and steps forward, glancing between Malachi and me before settling on Malachi. "The fuck are you talking about?"

My lips twitch, but I repress the smile that threatens to form. The seed of doubt I've sewn into Malachi's mind has already taken root. "You think you can play me? You think you can humiliate me by tricking me?" Malachi snaps. "I'll have your head for this in sword training later."

A second passes and then another and another. Theos' once self-satisfied expression is now a pleasant one of surprise and bewilderment. My tongue rolls against my inner cheek as I continue to battle my own amusement and smugness. I wait, patient now that I know I've won this round, until finally Malachi curses again, and then holds out his hand.

"Pick up my fucking bag, Terra." His command is ripe with anger and confusion.

Still smiling, I bend. "Of course." I lift the bag and hold it up for him, but of course he doesn't take it.

"Terra!" Malachi's overly loud bark makes several Terra

in the vicinity jump, even the two who'd been knocked over yet stayed out of curiosity. Finally, after a beat, one of the smaller, newer Terra squirms his way out of the crowd, hurrying forward. It almost seems a cruelty to give a boy so young and small to a man like Malachi.

It seems, too, that Malachi uses the servant's status as a calling card rather than actually learning individual names. With a sigh, I turn and hand Malachi's bag to the round-faced boy. His cheeks are sweaty and flushed, but he takes his Master's belongings and quickly follows him when Malachi curses and turns away, stomping off.

The threat of shame and humiliation works wonders on all races.

Slowly, I pivot back to face the Darkhavens. As those around us disperse and head towards their classes, I bow slightly with my own pleased smile as I spot the shock in Theos' expression, of forced indifference on Ruen's, and excitement in Kalix's eyes.

They'll have to try harder to make my life worse than anything I've experienced thus far.

As if sensing my thoughts, Theos' shock turns to irritation and he turns, striding away. His long legs eat up the distance as people—students and Terra—quickly hustle to get out of his way. Kalix laughs and follows, using the open path caused by Theos' anger to his advantage. Then it's just Ruen and me. With a sigh, he points towards the end of the corridor.

"Come," he demands. "Class is about to start and you're required to be there."

"Of course, Master Ruen." I take a step towards him, pausing only when he holds up a hand.

"Don't," he growls.

I blink. "I'm sorry? Don't what?"

"Don't call me Master," he commands.

My chest tightens. Is it because of me? Is my distaste and hatred for the word obvious?

Licking suddenly dry lips, I swallow roughly. "Have I done something offensive?" I inquire, forcing my voice to remain calm.

He shakes his head. "No, I just ... hate it. Don't call me that. Just Ruen."

That's a surprise to me, but I don't let it show. Instead, I nod my acquiescence. If he doesn't want me to call him Master and I don't want to anyway, then there's no point in arguing.

Clouded sky eyes stretched over canvas, with lines of every midnight shade pulling towards his blackened pupils, Ruen glares at me for several long moments. The muscle in his jaw bunches and releases, making me curious about what he's thinking. I don't ask, though. I simply wait. Until, finally, he turns back and starts walking, leaving me to trail behind him—the image of the perfect servant.

I wonder now, how my insolence in undermining Theos' attempt to thwart our bet will go. There's really only one way to find out and that's to remain at their sides, no matter what plans they concoct in the future.

Ruen and I pause in front of a wide arching doorway, and he lifts the latch, swinging the panel of wood inward to allow us access. I scan the room, taking in the design. Academy classrooms are built like miniature amphitheaters. I assume the doors to the corridors are meant only for students as they're angled at the back of each room so attendees must descend to the seats of their choice. There's another door at the bottom near the darkened board with scribbles written in chalk over its surface. I catch sight of

Niall, again stationed against the farthest wall. He leans away and gives me a half-hearted wave.

Despite one of the selling points of humans serving Mortal Gods in order to gain access to the classes, it's obvious Terra aren't treated as real students but are relegated to staff that stand along the outer edges of the rooms, waiting for when they're needed. They might be in the same space, they might hear the same lessons, but they are far from equal.

When Ruen and I enter, I pause alongside the other Terra as he moves down to a center aisle and takes a seat next to his brothers. Several heads turn at his entrance, both Mortal God and Terra alike.

The Darkhavens, it appears, are quite infamous if the attention they garner is anything to go by. Is it because they're rare First Tiers? Or is it something else? I'll have to do more research into their backgrounds.

The singular door at the bottom of the classroom blasts open, slamming against the wall behind it as a tall woman in long dark robes appears in the entryway. I hurry to station myself against the back wall with my hands clasped tightly behind my back and my head trained forward. The Goddess has the appearance of a bird with a rather large nose. Despite that, however, her skin is unmarked and shining with an internal light that I know all too well.

I clench my hands into fists at the small of my back. Mortal Gods aside, I haven't yet seen one of the Divine Beings since entering the Academy grounds. The distant memory of Talmatia in Mineval slips through my mind, and I grind my teeth.

"Texts," the Goddess barks, and as soon as she does, several Terra move forward, removing books from the bags they're holding and setting them in front of the appropriate Mortal God. Without a bag or texts, I remain silent and still.

None of my charges look back at me. In fact, Kalix even goes so far as to yawn and arch his back, slipping his booted feet onto the table in front of him. The Goddess doesn't turn around and instead, writes out a series of words onto the board, including her name: Narelle.

I search the information in the back of my mind, but I don't recognize the name. A Lower God then, I guess. That would make sense. From what I understand, there are only a few Upper Gods that take positions within the Academies.

Narelle finally pivots to face her students and scowls when she spots Ruen, Kalix, and Theos—all sitting front and center. "Where are your texts?" she demands.

Theos shrugs. "Didn't bring 'em."

The scowl on her perfect face deepens and she directs her gaze upward. "I know you three have been given a new Terra, which of these is yours?" the Goddess asks.

Ruen leans back and glances over his shoulder—directly at me. Fuck.

"You!" Narelle points one long finger at me and then turns her hand upside down before curling it towards her. "Come here."

An invisible pull catches around my throat and tugs me forward. I curse internally as I stumble away from the wall and find my legs moving of their own accord. This is the danger of the Divine. Their ability to enter and coerce. Only by the grace of something un-Divine are most Mortal Gods incapable of using it. The feeling of another's Divinity crawling over me and through me makes the hairs on the back of my neck stand on end.

My legs don't stop until I'm standing right before the

grand Goddess. "You are responsible for bringing the supplies of your charges," she snaps. "Where are they?"

"I was given nothing, Your Divinity." My words cut through my lips with the utmost politeness. All the while my fingers itch for a blade.

"Excuses. A punishment is required." Without another word to me, she flicks her finger through the air and my body spins to face the students. Theos leans forward, propping his elbows on the table in front of him and clasping his hands together to set the bottom of his chin on his steepled fingers.

Narelle scoffs and I feel air on the backs of my legs. "An unusual uniform too," she chastises. "How impertinent." I stiffen and have to force myself to relax. Whatever the pain is, it'll be that much worse if I tighten my muscles.

Standing there before dozens of eyes—all ranging from curious to amused to pitying—I bite down on my tongue as the God, Narelle, delivers her punishment. The first strike leaves me breathless. The second sends vibrations of pain up my calves. By the third, the fabric of my pants is yanked up further by the same invisible force this Goddess seems to possess.

My lips part and fire lashes over the backs of my calves. I nearly go down onto my knees as the intensity only increases. Pain sears over my flesh. Another lash. Skin splits. Blood leaks down the backs of my ankles.

Violence pours through me, sealing itself within my blood. The need for retribution sets at the edge of my teeth, waiting with drooling desire to sink into Divine flesh and rip it free from bone. Another strike and then two more. I close my eyes, sinking into my head and praying to some unknown entity—certainly not anything Divine—for this to be over quickly lest my healing takes over and reveals my secret. I'm cursing myself for not foreseeing something like this.

The assaults come to a halt and I crack my eyes open. The first thing I see when I turn my head is Niall's face—horrified and full of concern. Too kind for his own good, truly. The loosened fabric of my pants legs falls down, sticking to my wounded flesh and exacerbating the pain.

"You may return to your station, Terra," the Goddess snaps. "Hurry it up—you've already interrupted my class more than enough."

"Yes, Your Divinity." I straighten and walk stiffly up the stairs, well aware that heads turn. I ignore them all, save for the three responsible. As I pass by their seats, I cut a look their way. Unable to stop myself, I silently promise my vengeance. Theos tilts his head but offers no smile or other sign of amusement. Kalix yawns, completely missing my glare. Ruen ... avoids my gaze altogether and stoically stares towards the blackboard at the front.

Cowards.

By the end of the class, my legs are a mass of fire and I taste vomit in the back of my throat. As Terra trail their Mortal Gods from the room, I turn and stumble into a pair of thick arms. Looking up into a familiar pair of blue eyes, I rip myself free and take a bow.

"If you'll tell me where the texts for the rest of your classes are," I hiss through clenched teeth, "I'll go retrieve them."

Ruen says nothing. Instead, he takes my arm and hauls me out into the corridor. The wounded skin of my calves stretches with each stride. I bite down on my tongue to keep from making a sound. Ruen doesn't stop until we're out of the building and at the very edge of the open court-yard farthest from the entrance.

With a scowl, he points—gesturing towards the northern tower. "Get yourself cleaned up," he snaps, "and don't return today."

"But—"

"Dismissed." That's it. Ruen doesn't stay to see if I'll follow his order. He turns on his heel and stomps back to the building's entrance, the doors hanging open as both Theos and Kalix wait on either side of the open pathway.

I close my eyes and suck in a deep breath. As if I could refuse his order here or now. The pain in my legs reaches its crescendo as I make my way back to the northern tower and the tingles of my own ability move over the shredded flesh. A curse slips from my lips as I slam into my room and shut the door at my back.

No doubt it'll seem odd if I'm not limping or at least flinching for the next few days. With gritted teeth, I do the only thing I know to do. I reach into the minimalistic sack I brought with me and remove a carefully hidden dagger as I take a seat on the creaking bed. Dragging my pants legs up my caves, I place the handle between my teeth and bite down as I roll the fabric all the way up to my knees.

It's hard to see with such little light, but even beyond the rivers of red that are quickly drying on my skin, I can feel the split and raised flesh. I'm half tempted to wonder if the Goddess held back at all because a true human likely wouldn't have been able to make it back to their rooms without help as I have. Yet, she'd not spared me a single glance once she was done with me.

Removing the hilt of the dagger from my teeth, I set the sharp edge to my flesh and swipe several lines across the skin that's already in the process of knitting itself back together. Breath rushes out of me as my stomach cramps. I quickly perform the same to my other leg before dropping the dagger and bending in half, stuffing my head between my knees as I huff and pant through the pain.

The light poison on the blade's sharpened edge will do the task. It'll slow down the healing long enough for it to be feasible that I'm nothing more than an unfortunate mortal tasked with three of the worst Mortal Gods in the Mortal Gods Academy.

Heat fills my mouth and with it, my saliva. Still, I fight back the urge to puke. Whether they had meant to or not, the irony of failing to humiliate me only to have an unintentional shame and punishment brought about by the Gods themselves is not lost on me. It's almost worse than if I had simply bent over the corridor and let Malachi fuck me as he and Theos had wanted.

Hissing through the pain, I clutch at the edge of my mattress. Dizziness assails me. It grows and spirals through my mind until positioning my head down between my legs isn't enough. Sitting up, I flop down, my back to the bed as the wooden beams above me spin and spin.

I close my eyes. The poison works its way through my system, all too fucking familiar.

CHAPTER 17

KIERA

"This is a game of endurance." Ophelia's words filter through my mind as my muscles jump and twitch beneath the surface of my flesh. The rotten taste of decay sits on my tongue, choking me with each breath I wheeze out. "If you are caught, you will be tortured for information. Who helped you? Who knew of your existence? Where were you born? Who is your father? Who is your mother? What are their names?"

Everything from the back of my throat to the front coating of my teeth feels bone dry. My vision has long since blurred and the only thing I can even feel is the abundance of pain. The flesh that's been ripped clean from my arms only to grow back minutes later hangs like ribbons over the sides of the chair I'm currently tied down to.

No amount of relief could put the fire of my body out. I am nothing but a smoking pile of cinders, unaware that I've already died. And because there's still one pinprick of light left, Ophelia focuses on it, bringing it back to life over and over again, only to snuff it out in the cruelest of ways.

If she wanted information, I would give it. If she wanted my *death, I would slit my own throat. If she wanted anything, I would make it happen. Whatever it took to stop the agony that rends my flesh from my bones and leaks the blood from my veins. But she doesn't.*

The burns along my spine flaking away the deadened skin to reveal a new, unmarred surface underneath. That more than anything—the healing—was what broke me. It feels like hours, days ago that I finally cried until I had nothing left but dust in my eyes. Dust and rot. I gave all I had to give her. My tears. My pleas. My promises. My undying devotion. All of it in vain because the faster I heal, the faster I'm pressed back deep within the quagmire of agony.

All the while, Ophelia circles me. Around and around, she goes. Like some sick twisted nursery rhyme meant for children's play. Not that I know what that is anymore. I haven't been a child since the night I was brought here. Since the night she bought me.

Hunger stabs at my gut, a vicious spinning blade ripping through my insides. The rumbling sound my intestines make forces me to close my eyes again in preparation. The cane falls down across my bare back, right over the burned flesh from the fiery brand of the last session that's only half done knitting itself back together. I bite down on my tongue hard enough to draw blood and my mouth fills with blessed liquid—tasting of rot and rust.

"Control your urges." Easier said than done. Ophelia continues. "Your existence risks more than just yourself," she says. "It risks me and the entire Guild. You know I'm only doing this because I must." A soft hand settles at the top of my head and I resist the urge to jerk away. Not out of fear or pain but because she's right. I need to control my urges and the first way to start is to be completely still. No matter that even her gentle touch now makes me feel as if every inch of my flesh is covered in

170

biting little insects. I want to vomit up what is left in my guts—which is nothing but hopelessness and bile.

"Good, you're learning." Ophelia's praise falls on deaf ears. I don't care for it any longer. We've been at this for so long that I've forgotten what time means anymore. If I've learned anything from the torture, it's that she's a master of it. Positive reinforcement. Gaining the target's trust. Getting them to drop their guard so that they give you all the answers you want.

The difference between true torture and this is that ... Ophelia already has all of the answers that I could possibly give her. There's nothing I can do to stop it, no amount of begging or offering desired information I could give until she decides I've learned the lesson.

My pain is nothing compared to the lives that are at risk just by hiding my existence.

"Sink somewhere deep," I hear her say as my mind fades away from reality, back into the darkest recesses of my personal oblivion. Her hand moves over the top of my head, through my hair. "Don't let them fool you. The Gods are not your friends. Not even if they offer to find your God parent and bring her to you. They are tricksters. Liars. All they want is to destroy you and control you."

So do you, I think. I bite the words back, reminding myself that if I let her break through to me now, I'll have wasted all of this time bearing her 'lessons' for nothing.

The sharp drag of a blade runs over my skin. Blood flows down my arm. I fade faster, pulling further and further away. The pain doesn't stop, but my reactions slow down until it's like I'm not reacting at all. Nothing will stop this. It's all at her will. No answers. No begging. No pleading can end it all. The Gods will be worse.

Fingers grip my wrist, lifting and not minding the strap holding it down. Red-hot liquid fire burns up my arm as it's snapped back. I want to scream as the pain jolts me back into the real world. More blood fills my lips, chasing the sound down my throat until it chokes me.

Breathless, I want to sob but find there's nothing left inside of me—no air or sound in my vocal cords to do so. I just want it to stop. I want it all to stop. I never wanted to be this. Not a Mortal God. Not a cursed existence.

"You're lucky." Ophelia's tone is indifferent as she speaks, her words shooting past all of my barriers like poisoned arrows. "Humans wouldn't be able to heal as you do. With you, I don't have to worry about damaging you beyond repair. You'll still be able to perform your duties as an assassin even after I'm done with you—perhaps even better. You'll know, personally, what hurts your target. What will incapacitate them, render them defenseless with their pain. Use that knowledge to manipulate your targets the same way the Gods manipulate the rest of the human race, Kiera. Feed on it."

More than hunger. More than pain. More than relief. I want to know ... why any of this is necessary. Why must I be the one to feel it at all? Is there a point? And if so, why was I born without knowing it?

If Gods are so awful, then why did one lay with my father? Why did they give birth to me?

It's long since past the time I knew how to cry. I stopped when I realized that no one cared, no one would comfort a crying child who had nothing to give. Who had nothing but the curse of her own blood flowing through her veins.

Regis had been right. No one in the Underworld concerns themselves with crying children, and besides, I'm not a child anymore. Children have parents. Children have hopes and dreams. All I have is ... this.

I am a weapon now. An assassin. Those who take lives don't deserve to weep. So, even as Ophelia's lessons continue, not a single tear falls. Instead, it's me who falls—deeper and deeper into the dark.

THE INCESSANT *TAPTAPTAP* of something pecking at the glass of my window jolts me out of the old memory and half-dream. With a groan, I sit up and wince at the stretch of my flesh at the backs of my legs. At least one thing is going my way today—the poison, even if it's working its way out of my system, worked long enough to form scabs over the wounds. I quickly wrap them and jerk my pants legs down over the bandages. It's not so bad now that a few hours have passed.

Taptaptap.

The noise starts up again and I twist my head to spot a dark bird with its beak glistening in the dim light outside flapping its wings on the opposite side of the glass. Quickly leveraging up off the bed, I head to the window and open the pane. With the mesh of crossed wrought iron bars placed over the window, the bird has nowhere to perch but the metal itself. So, with its claw-like feet wrapped around one of the bars, it flaps its wings again and emits a soft *caw*.

Just above the sharpness of its claws, I spot a tiny scroll no longer than my pinkie attached to the bird's foot. Weaving my fingers through the bars, I carefully remove the twine holding the scroll to the bird's leg and unfold it.

TARGET REMAINS UNKNOWN. *Deposit fulfilled. Await further orders.* — R

. . .

MOTHERFUCKER. In my anger, I crumple the paper into my fist before I can think better of it. Once I've realized what I've done, though, I sigh and drop it into the metal plate beneath the candle on my nightstand. It only takes a moment to find the matchsticks and light both the candle and the paper, erasing the evidence of Regis and, therefore, Ophelia's message.

There is at least one good thing about Regis' message coming now, though. If the deposit is fulfilled, then that means at least half of the four million denza is waiting for me upon the completion of this mission. Still, though, if the client has already handed over half of the reward, why is there no more information on the target?

As that thought percolates in my mind, I quickly scribble a note back to Regis, requesting a new poison, and attach it to the bird's leg before tapping the end of its beak twice to let it know that its duty is fulfilled. Punishments like the one I suffered today will likely continue to happen so long as the Darkhavens' ridiculous bet remains. As much as I hate the idea of weakening myself, I'll take every precaution necessary to ensure that my identity remains a secret. After all, my life isn't the only one at stake and even if an assassin often works alone, I can't betray those who've allowed me to live this long.

All I need to do is make it past a few weeks, but until then, making sure I actually maintain the wounds the same way a human would is imperative.

Once the bird is well on its way, I quickly change into the only other pair of pants I have, a dull black pair that's faded into an off-gray over time. Now that my legs have been bandaged, even with the poison flushing out of my system, it's easier to move. Since I doubt having shredded calves is excuse enough not to finish my duties, I head up to the chambers of the Darkhaven brothers and set about finishing the tasks I was informed of during orientation.

Entering the Mortal Gods' rooms without the owners present feels eerily similar to my training exercises as a child—sneaking into shops and other buildings for reconnaissance. I ignore the warning signs and take my chance to snoop. The initial room is circular in size, stone walls darkened further with ornate paintings and swooping drapes and tapestries.

Unlike my closet of a room, the open shared space between the brothers is wide with three arching claw-like windows that begin at wide bases and stretch up towards a narrowed ceiling, getting smaller and smaller until they come to a point. Stained glass blurs the image of the outside world on the two side windows, highlighting the clarity of the center one. I stride towards the windows and the set of spiral stairs that cling to the wall crossing over the upper part of the glass and head for the second floor.

There are two doors on the second floor. The first leads into a bathing chamber, complete with a bronze claw-foot tub facing a round window overlooking the ocean and sky. It's a luxury I've only seen in similar places—rooms and mansions possessed by the Divine. The second leads into a bedroom—Kalix's, I presume.

Standing in the doorway, I take it in. Various weapons hang from the walls. Several swords—some long, some short—daggers, crossbows, arrows, and axes. The types are endless. I stride farther into the darkened interior, past the plush bed that is much larger than the entirety of the room I was given and topped with fur-lined blankets and pillows.

The room is quiet, too quiet. There's not even a scurry of mice within the walls. I close my eyes as I reach the center and push out a bit of my power, seeking out the spiders I know linger everywhere. Only, I find none. Reopening my eyes, I glance around and find myself strangely alone. None of my little friends reside within these walls. I've never been in a place—house or not—that didn't have at least a few of them.

The feeling of emptiness leaves me unsettled, so I quickly go about my tasks—making the bed, sweeping the floors, and collecting the tossed clothes to be laundered later before departing. Though it was curiosity and wariness that led me to his room first, I find myself suffering with a strange prickling sensation at the nape of my neck as I work. As if I'm being watched.

That prickling grows fiercer and fiercer the longer I linger. As I leave, I know that if Kalix Darkhaven's name comes back to me as my target, I'll have no choice but to return, but for now, I'd like to escape his inner sanctuary as quickly as possible. I don't care for the sensation of being watched. Not in the past and not now.

As I make my way down the stairs, the door to the shared space opens. I pause on the last step, turning my head as Ruen steps inside. I expect him to be followed by Theos and Kalix, but he only kicks the door shut and quickly removes his uniform jacket before tossing it across the space onto the back of one of the lounges. Though I'm sure he's well aware of my presence, he ignores me and strides across the room towards the same darkened corner he'd been in when I'd first caught a glimpse of him.

I debate my options. Do I ignore him and continue with my Terra duties? I'll have to put my investigation of both his and Theos' rooms on hold while he's present. That won't be a problem, though, since I expect to be here for quite some time.

Gingerly, I take a step off of the last stair and make my

way across the room, feigning a light limp to avoid suspicion. It doesn't take much acting, my calves are, after all, on fucking fire. I get about halfway when his voice calls me to a halt. "I thought I told you to clean yourself up?"

With my back still to him, I reply. "I did, Sir Ruen."

"I don't recall telling you to continue with your duties when I sent you away," he states.

Slowly, I pivot my body to face him. "I apologize for the inconvenience," I say. "Would you like me to come back later?"

Ruen drops into a chair and lifts his booted feet to a table set at the perfect distance for him to plant his heels, crossing one over the other. Still, he doesn't look at me. "Are you here to clean?" he asks.

"It's one of my duties."

The deep baritone of his hum rumbles throughout the room as he lifts a book from the arm of the chair where it'd been placed haphazardly before, its pages split open to some unseen story. "Duty, huh?" he mumbles. "What are the duties of Terra again?"

I blink at him. He can't be serious. I wait a beat, sure he's going to laugh and wave me off, but no. He's quiet, and when I don't offer an answer, he lifts his ice-coated gaze to mine. "Well, Terra?" he prompts me once more. "Recite your duties to me."

"It is a Terra's duty to foresee any need or desire from their Masters. We are to clean and provide a comfortable living space for our assigned Mortal Gods as well as to attend to their needs in whatever fashion they wish." As much as I hadn't wanted to take the book that Madam Brione had given, it had proven more useful than I'd initially thought and I relay the information he's requested like a well-trained worshiper of the Gods.

"Correct." He snaps the book shut with a loud thwack. It takes me a moment to realize that I should've feigned a jolt as any human would, but by the time I think of it, the time has passed. Ruen's eyes narrow on me. "It is a Terra's duty to attend to our needs."

I nod slowly. "Do you have need of me, sir?" Surely, he's not going to be like that other Mortal God and demand I strip down and service him. I can't quite say why, but Ruen Darkhaven strikes me as a conservative sort. He wouldn't be the type of man to fuck a woman in a shared space like this. No. He'd want her all to himself in a private chamber. No doubt where he could pour all of the subtle darkness I sense deep within him into her and release it. Then again, he is a Mortal God and I've been wrong before. Rarely. But it's possible.

"Yes," he snaps. "What I need from you is simple."

"I'll make it my utmost priority, sir," I reply. "If you'll just give me your command."

"I need you to get the fuck out."

My lips part. "What?"

"Get out," he snaps again. "And this time, don't fucking return. They'll send someone better next time. Someone stronger. Perhaps a male, but you—well, it doesn't matter that you outsmarted Malachi. Anyone with half a brain, mortal or not, could do that. You might have surprised Theos but not me. You strike me as a female of decent intelligence. So, do yourself a favor and leave while you still have life and limb to. I won't take responsibility if my brothers rip you apart in their ever-fervent quest to seek amusement."

Perhaps it hadn't been stoicism that I'd seen on his face after the classroom incident but guilt. Odd. I'm a Mortal God and I've felt more than my fair share of it, I have to admit—even if it's only to myself—so they must all be capable of the same emotions as me.

A burning sensation forms in my chest. Something like the dying embers of a fire illuminated after too long in the cold. I inhale a breath through my nose and then quietly blow it out through my mouth. As if he's satisfied that he's effectively scared me off, Ruen lifts the book back into his hand and splits it open once more.

"Do I scare you?"

The silence following my question is palpable. Slowly, Ruen raises his head and fixes me with a stare so intense it could only be described as fatally dark. "*Excuse me?*"

There's no point in pretending like he didn't hear me the first time, but I repeat it anyway. "Do I scare you?"

The book in his hand lowers to his lap. Quiet stretches around the room, wrapping around it several times before the string breaks and Ruen speaks. "In what way do you think a mortal such as yourself is capable of scaring me?" Though his voice is deep, riddled with anger and insult, his eyes remain on mine, unmoving and unchanging.

"Everyone feels fear," I say. "Even Mortal Gods."

He stands but doesn't move towards me. Blue eyes darken at the edges as they glare at me. "If you refuse to leave then I suppose I'll have to do it for you."

My body tenses. I open my mouth—to say what, I'll never know, because before I can utter a single word, a wave of air sweeps through me so intensely that I flinch back. My eyes shut and when they open again, I'm standing in the corridor at the stairwell with the feeling of Divinity sliding over my flesh like a breeze.

I turn and gape at the now closed door to the Darkhavens' chambers. What ... just happened? An ability? Space manipulation? I'd never experienced something so strong ...

or dangerous. As my eyes settle on the scarred wood leading into the private rooms of the Darkhaven brothers, I realize something.

It's not just Kalix that I need to be concerned with. If my target is any one of the Darkhaven brothers, I might be in for more trouble than I can handle.

CHAPTER 18

KIERA

One thing I have to say about Mortal Gods Academy over the following weeks is that it's a strange combination of lavish playground and prison for those inside. After my initial thwarting of their attempt to make me regret taking part in the Darkhavens' little bet, they seem to lose interest in tormenting me, to lose interest in the bet altogether. I'm just fine with that. After all, it was only because of my need to rebel against anyone who tries to squash me that led me to make that ridiculous decision. If they're to forget all about it, then it's no longer an issue.

I follow the Darkhaven brothers to their classes in the mornings after my breakfast and carry their supplies—which mysteriously appeared on the table of their common room the morning following the first day. If Ruen is angry that I've refused his offer to escape, he doesn't let on. Instead, he chooses to ignore my presence as much as he can. That, too, I'm fine with. Being an object with little to no animation suits my purposes quite well.

I watch as they yawn and half sleep through lessons on

Divine history and Divine lineage but never fighting. It's the fighting that confuses me. All Mortal Gods, regardless of Tiers, are taught—and with great concentration, I might add—to hone their individual abilities and use them in battle. Swords. Archery. Hand to hand. Even the weaker of the Tiers—third-class students within these walls—are given the same strict guidelines to better themselves.

And the only thing I can wonder is ... why?

For as long as I've known why my blood makes me so dangerous, I've known Gods to fear death. If the only thing that can kill a Divine Being is one with Divine Blood flowing through their veins, shouldn't they want their children to be weak and unable to fight back? One might think so.

Instead, the Mortal Gods who fail at training their bodies and developing their Divine skills are ridiculed and scolded. Becoming a Terra versus a student was a far better choice as it allows me to stand back and see it all. I am, for all intents and purposes, invisible until I'm needed and that's just fine by me.

A rushing oomph escapes the female Mortal God as she's tossed from the ring of her training class. At my side, Niall winces as the poor thing slams into the dirt, her head smacking against the solid ground with a loud crack. Her opponent, however, doesn't stop. Instead, she dives over her, driving a fist straight into her face. The crunch of cartilage breaking under the assault reaches my ears, reminding me of my childhood.

"Don't." The warning comes out of my mouth before Niall can dive forward and assist the fallen Mortal God.

His wide puppy-dog eyes lift to me. "But she might need—"

I shake my head, cutting him off. "No one has called for

you," I remind him. "If you step away from the wall now, you'll be punished. Trust me, you don't want that."

And just like that, my words do the trick. He settles back into position. Though I'd hated it at the time, it appears that my example on the first day of classes was enough for the rest of the new Terra to understand what happens when they displease their Masters or the faculty of the Academy. Despite that, though, Niall is one of few with a particularly soft heart. Even if the girl is currently being pummeled by her red-faced and grinning opponent, he can't step in to help her.

"Alright, that's enough!" All heads turn at the call of the God in charge of today's training class. Standing more than a head taller than anyone else in the nearby area, Axlan, God of Victory, leans against the staff at his side as the sounds of fighting diminish.

The Mortal God duo that Niall and I had been watching separate and the girl that rises to her feet blinks past the blood coating her face. Call it curiosity, but my attention moves past her to my own charges.

Theos, Kalix, and Ruen stand several paces away, but none of them have been fighting with the others in the class. Instead, they take turns battling it out with each other in their own ring. The first time I'd noticed they didn't interact with anyone else in this class, I'd expected the God in charge to demand they change opponents, but it never happened. Which can only mean one thing—they've already fought everyone in this class and have beaten them all. That, in turn, begs another question. Why have they been placed here if they're too good for anyone else?

The answer, I realize, is something I'm about to get.

"Theos," Axlan calls out, and gestures for him to step forward. Theos moves through the students until he stands before the God. The two could not be more different. Where Theos is light-haired and pale-skinned, Axlan has the ruddy complexion of a man who spends a great deal of time beneath the sun. Where Theos is slender and wiry, Axlan is broad. "What do you think?" Axlan demands.

Theos places his hands behind him, curling them into fists at the small of his back in much the same way I had during my days of training when both Regis and I had been lined up along with many other recruits—forced to run miles into the night, sweat through blood and tears, as we were screamed at to keep going. The similarity makes me curl my lips back in disgust. I dislike the comparison even though it was mine to make.

"Enid is ready for advancement," Theos announces.

Axlan seems to consider this and turns his head. "Enid, approach." The girl that had pummeled the face of the Mortal God Niall had been watching moves through the crowd proudly, her head tossed back and her shoulders straight. She doesn't stop until she's stationed side by side with Theos.

She's only a few inches shorter than Theos, but unlike many of the other students in this class, she's got the solid build of someone well-versed in fighting. Her sandy blonde hair is pulled back and up out of her face. I realize that my charges have not been placed in this class for training at all, but to pick out those who are ready to move forward. Interesting.

"This is your choice?" Axlan asks Theos who nods. "Fine then. Ruen?"

Without moving forward, Ruen responds. "I recommend Darius for advanced placement."

I'm so focused on the girl that it takes me a moment to notice the way Theos stiffens at her side. When I do, however, I turn my attention to him and the rather shocked expression that sweeps over his face a moment before he suppresses it in favor of a look that's more enigmatic. It's fast, unnoticed by most, I suspect, but not by me.

Axlan turns and points to a tall boy farther behind where we're standing. Darius, I assume. He's big and broad, like the God himself with a mane of red hair that hangs to his shoulders, wet with sweat. "Alright then. Enid and Darius will be moving to advanced placement. The rest of you will continue to train," Axlan announces.

My brow creases. Along the ring where Ruen still stands, Kalix rocks back and forth on his heels. If he was asked to be in this class, why was he not also asked for a recommended student? As if he can sense my attention, Kalix turns his head and meets my gaze. His grin is predatory. I straighten my spine but otherwise don't change my expression. There'd be no point anyway. No doubt he'd take that as a challenge.

"Class dismissed."

The moment those two words are called out over the dirt training field, the air of tension that seemed to linger disperses. Bloody faces are cleaned up and Terra move away from their positions against the long wall that surrounds the sides of the arena as they're called to their Masters. Across the field, Kalix lifts a finger and curls it in.

I repress a curse as I sway away from the wall. "Good luck," Niall offers as he bows his head and scurries towards his charge.

Luck. I'm not entirely sure if my entire life has been one fucking battle with it or not. On one hand, I'm still alive. And on the other, I'm always on the edge of discovery and subsequently death. What kind of life is one where you're constantly worried about it ending?

I make my way across the field, moving quickly around both Terra and Mortal Gods until I'm finally standing before Kalix and Ruen. "You called for me?"

Kalix grins and moves forward, turning to face his brother as he swings an arm over my shoulders. "Sure did. What do you say we have some fun tonight?"

Ruen's expression sours. "Don't play your stupid games, Kalix," he growls. "You remember what Theos and I warned you of."

"What?" Kalix blinks with seemingly feigned innocence. Though, for some reason, I don't think it's feigned. Perhaps he truly thinks his actions are fun and game-like. As much as I'd watched him over the course of the last few weeks, picking up on even the smallest hints in his attitude and changes, I've noticed that he appears to be more unaware of the expectations of others. He doesn't get insulted by comments that would enrage others. He seeks pleasure when he can—fucking any willing Mortal God or Terra that catches his eye—even if that pleasure has pain mixed in.

The only reason I haven't gotten caught up in his recreational activities as of yet, I suspect, is because of the other two. Footsteps prick at my ears and I turn and bow as Theos approaches, his booted feet scuffing the dirt out of his way.

"Master Theos," I greet politely. Golden eyes move over me before ultimately, he appears to decide to ignore me in favor of his brothers.

"Darius?" He sets his eyes on Ruen.

"He's ready," Ruen replies.

Theos grits his teeth and a low growl erupts from his throat. "He has the brawn but not the prowess. They'll eat him alive in advanced placement."

"Then he'll learn how to develop the prowess, Theos,"

Ruen says. "You can't protect him forever."

Placing his hands on his hips, Theos glowers at his brother. "I'm not protecting him, damn it."

Ruen doesn't back down. "He's your friend."

Moments of tense silence pass between them. Theos neither refutes Ruen's words nor does Ruen recant them. It breaks with a muttered curse and Theos turning away to kick at the dirt. "Axlan thinks we should move up with Enid and Darius," Theos states.

Ruen nods as if he'd been expecting as much. "We've done our job of inspecting the class," he says. "I doubt we'll see any improvement with the rest of them until next semester."

"Does that mean more fun?" Kalix inquires, jostling me against him as he bends slightly and tilts his head to the side. My insides contract and release as I repress the urge to fling his arm off of me and slug him in his face. I didn't realize how much I disliked being touched without consent until someone was *constantly* doing it.

"It means a schedule change," Theos answers. "Our new training class will be shifted to a more advanced time." Finally, he turns and looks at me. "You won't be required to attend, Terra."

Though a part of me is relieved to find out that I won't have to stand at the sidelines of yet another of their classes, another part of me is curious as to the reason. "Am I bothering you, Master Theos?"

I don't know if it's the sound of his name or his status that irritates him, but whatever the case, once the question is past my lips, his entire face contorts. Theos scowls at me, his golden gaze darkening at the edges. "Terra don't ask questions," he barks. "They follow orders. Nothing more."

Kalix snickers and leans into me even harder, forcing

me to plant my feet and widen my stance on the ground to keep upright. "He's still bitter about you thwarting his plot to embarrass you with Malachi," Kalix half whispers, half chuckles. He's making it incredibly obvious that he has no intention of hiding his words from his brother and is in fact using them to anger him further.

"Keep your mouth shut, Kalix," Theos snaps. "I didn't see you offering any solution anyway."

Green eyes alight on me. "No, I don't wish to run this one off just yet," he says. His words are coated in charm and if I've learned anything in my life, it's that charming men are often the most dangerous. Prickles of awareness spread over the back of my neck.

Sensing someone's eyes, I turn slightly and peer over my shoulder. A girl with hair blacker than a raven's wing pulled taut enough to make the sides of her face appear higher than is natural glares across the arena. Thick eyelashes lower and crystalline blue eyes glower right at me. Her full lips are twisted and scowling, turning her expression into one of both rage and disgust. A dreadful feeling blossoms in my lower belly. Somehow, I know that I should avoid that one at all costs.

"Enid and Darius might be able to match each other in battle, but the rest of this group is practically hopeless," Ruen comments, drawing my attention back to him.

Theos blows out a breath. "Agreed. They're in for a sore awakening once they reach their upper years," he says. "End-of-semester one-on-ones will be a bloodbath."

Kalix laughs, throwing his head back with great amusement. "It always is!" he crows.

My curiosity gets the better of me. "May I ask what you're referring to?"

All gazes fall on me. Kalix smirks. Theos frowns, but it's

Ruen who answers. "All of us are required to hold our own against another of our same status," he says. "We're tested on the usage of our ability and fighting skills at the end of every semester in one-on-one battles."

"The Third Tiers always come out with their bodies ravaged," Kalix says jovially, as if the thought of someone's pain is amusing to him. Who am I kidding? It is. The psychopath.

Theos sighs and reaches up, scrubbing a hand down his face. "God Axlan asked us to attend his lower classes for a few weeks to pick out the best students to be moved up," he admits. "But even with Enid's and Darius' skills, I suspect they'll have a rough time during the battles."

"Will you also be fighting?" I ask.

Ruen and Theos exchange a look before nodding. "All Tiers are required to fight, no exceptions," Ruen replies.

It's an interesting piece of information. "What's the reason?"

That question, though simply and innocently put for mere curiosity, causes quite the stir between the three of them. Or rather, for Ruen and Theos, who bow their heads and clench their fists. Kalix is the only one among them that doesn't appear bothered by it.

"Power, obviously," he says.

"Power?" I repeat, still not understanding.

"Of course." With his arm still around my shoulders, Kalix turns me and begins walking, forcing me to keep pace with him. A quick glance back tells me that, though Ruen and Theos both appear irritated, they follow. "What is the most frightening thing for a God?" Kalix asks.

"Loss of power?" I guess.

"Close but not quite," he says. "It's death."

My eyes widen a split second before I twist my head

around. The arena, however, has now been cleared out and we appear to be the only ones left even as we make our way to the exit. How could he say something so unabashedly out loud in such a public setting? Even if no one else but the four of us are here. It's still dangerous. He can't truly be that unconcerned, can he?

But he is, I realize, because he's not done talking. "Gods can only be killed by other Gods or those with Divine power. You know who else has Divine power aside from a God?" He doesn't need to answer what I already know, but he does regardless. Kalix jerks his free hand to himself and points right at his chest. "We are."

"Should you be talking about this here?" I demand as we approach the double black doors that will lead us from the outside arena back into the building.

"She's right, Kalix," Ruen speaks up. "Lower your tone."

Kalix glances back. "Why? Everyone knows it."

"Just because everyone knows doesn't mean it should be said," Theos snaps.

For my entire life, I've only ever focused on how Gods treated humans. It had never occurred to me that they might have treated Mortal Gods in a similar fashion, considering Mortal Gods are, ultimately, direct descendants of themselves. Just as powerful if not as long-lasting.

They are aware of their own status. Or at least, these three are. It's ugly and often cruel, but someone always gets shit on and unfortunately for Mortal Gods, they're just not as perfect as their godly parents.

We enter the corridor and Kalix removes his arm from around my shoulders, pushing me to the side as he turns to his brothers. "Why are you so bothered by it?" he demands. "We're the strongest anyway. We can kill anyone we want." He laughs.

Neither Ruen nor Theos respond. Instead, Theos merely storms past Kalix, shoving him into the nearby stone wall as he stomps away. And not for the first time, unfortunately, I find myself filled with an almost exhaustive empathy that I don't want to feel.

"Hey, fucker!" Kalix shouts as he rights himself and starts off in the same direction as Theos, only to have Ruen quickly grab hold of him and halt his movement.

"Let him go," Ruen orders. "You've pushed him enough today."

"I only said the truth," Kalix snaps back.

Ruen shakes his head. "Sometimes that's all you need to say to hurt someone."

A truer statement I never expected from a spoiled Mortal God raised within the gilded walls of one of the Mortal Gods Academies. The pang in my chest spreads wide, and instinctively I reach up to rub where it began, right between my breasts.

No. I shouldn't feel so bad for them. After all, they've enjoyed more luxuries than most mortals ever will in their entire lives. Mortal Gods are as bad as their Divine betters in the way they treat humans.

Even if a few of them hate the idea of killing others, they'll continue to do so for their own survival. I admit, it's clever of the Gods. Separating their children out and pitting them against one another. I can see it clearly—their reasoning for why they take their half-mortal children and place them within this very structured system. It all becomes clear why each one, regardless of power or Tier, is forced to train. Keeping them so focused on fighting each other prevents any of them from fighting those who have put them here.

I'd find it all amusing if it wasn't so godsdamned tragic.

CHAPTER 19

KIERA

Anger, I've found, is more useful than any other emotion. It's better than sorrow, than hurt, than guilt. I think that's why as I watch the Darkhaven brothers over the course of the next fortnight, I come to understand them a bit better.

In the end, they're all boys. Just boys. Bound to the walls of the Academy unless called upon by other Gods. If life had been different, I might have been in much the same position as them. If—whoever she may be—my God parent, my mother, had decided to take me with her when she abandoned my father, if she had, perhaps, reported my existence to the Council of Gods ... I would be here just like them. Locked in this Academy with nothing more for entertainment than lessons by the Gods and the torment of humans.

It's no wonder they use their volatile emotions as a barrier. Not that I will forgive them for taking out their problems on me and the other Terra. I'm not that magnanimous. I prefer vengeance.

Dirt clings to the underside of my nails as I dig a small

hole alongside the three-tiered fountain in the center of a courtyard on the east side of the Academy. Sometime in the night, I'd been awoken by the whispering responses of the spiders I'd sent out far and wide across the Academy grounds and what they'd told me had led me right here the moment I'd woken. The early morning is cool with a gentle breeze that blows through the empty area. It's the singular day of the week in which not only are students of the Academy free to do as they wish instead of attending classes or physical training but so are Terra.

Laundering bedsheets and cleaning up blood from fights that both Theos and Kalix get into regularly can wait until tomorrow. I need a fucking break.

I'd love nothing more than to sit on the ledge of the fountain in the center of the grassy courtyard at the south side of the campus, tilt my face up to the morning sunrays, and luxuriate in the quiet. For weeks, I've been locked in this hell. Surrounded by Mortal Gods and worshiping mortals. For weeks, I've been waiting for the notice that my client has finally revealed the target they expect me to get rid of. For weeks, I've felt nothing but frustration and disappointment.

I'm starting to wonder if the client will ever reveal their target or if Ophelia will call the whole thing off and order me back to headquarters. As far as Regis knows, and thus relays via bird messenger, neither have happened. Waiting is the hardest part of the job. So many new recruits often assume being part of the Underworld is constant action and danger when the opposite is true. More than half of being an assassin is simply sitting and waiting for the right moment. It's excruciatingly boring.

That's not my concern now, though. I can handle the boredom. What I struggle with is the constant anxiety. It's practically unheard of for a client to go quiet for this long unless they're dead.

I hope whoever they are, they're still very well alive and kicking. That four million denza won't pay itself if they've up and croaked on me and that money is the key to everything. Which is why I now find myself here, wrist deep in dirt, looking for—

"Found you!" Relief pours through my veins as I seek what I knew was here all along. Not only had my other little familiars alerted me to this precious species, but I'd definitely had the buzzing inkling that I'd find something helpful in this courtyard.

A spider's burrow. Not just any spider, though. A rare one. *Euoplos dignitas.*

Ever since I'd become aware of my instinctive call over the creatures, they had become more than just my familiars, but an unerring fascination. The *Euoplos dignitas* is a spider I've only ever read about in the dusty old books Ophelia collected back at the Guild hall and, if I'm lucky, it'll be helpful to my current predicament in controlling the thousands of smaller spiders within the Academy. Trying to keep track of so many is overwhelming and I can't count the number of times I've woken to a handful crawling over me in my sleep. Just as I am curious about them, they, too, seem to be mesmerized by me.

I slide my fingers beneath the arachnid's fuzzy little striped legs and carefully extract him from his burrow, mentally apologizing for interrupting what I'm sure for him was a very good nap. Pressing some of my Divine power into my fingertips, I inhale sharply as the spider reacts immediately. His little legs spasm and his head twitters. The baby fangs beyond his mouth stick out and for a moment, I worry I've angered him, but after a moment he settles.

Though I can sense the direction of a spider's thoughts, I can't exactly read them considering they speak no human language and therefore don't think in such black-and-white terms. Instead, I can only garner a sense of their emotions as they pass through them. *Euoplos dignitas* are rare, but it's even rarer for a spider—or any other creature—to be able to handle Divine energy being poured into them without dying.

The little creature in my hand sits firmly in the middle at just under two inches long. It's warm from its time underground and though I'm particularly regretful to pull it from its serenity—I wouldn't like it either if someone ripped me out of my bed with no warning—I need it. Lifting the creature and nudging them with a finger to turn and face me, I lift my head and peer around, ensuring there's no one nearby before I send another wave of Divinity into the spider's mind.

Once we connect, a wave of nausea overwhelms me. The world tilts and I shut my eyes immediately, cutting off my own sight as the spider's vision enters my mind. The Divinity swelling up within me disperses and the brimstone embedded in the back of my neck, right beneath my blood contract mark, heats up, not quite enough to hurt, but it's definitely uncomfortable. I exhale slowly as I get used to the feeling of a new mind connected to my own.

It's exhausting to control so many familiars, to keep track of them, and to give them my orders. My new friend, however, twitches its legs against my palm. With him, it'll be easier. Just as I'm about to send my thoughts and intentions to the spider, a sudden and familiar voice penetrates the quiet serenity of the courtyard.

"Kiera!"

My eyes shoot open and for some reason, I stare down at the spider in my palm as if it'll somehow have a clue what to do next. Of course, it doesn't. So, as the padding footsteps of Niall get closer and closer, I decide to quickly put the little creature back into its burrow and turn around to face the incoming trouble.

I spot Niall coming towards me at a fast clip. His brows are drawn down and his lips are pinched as he hurries. "Good morning, Niall," I say, forcing a pleasant note into my voice.

"You can't be here," he says instead of a greeting.

My eyes widen. "What?"

He grabs ahold of my arm and proceeds to try and pull me away from the fountain's ledge. I don't move. "You can't be here," he repeats, lowering his voice to a hushed whisper, despite the fact that there's no one around us. "This isn't a Terra courtyard."

Carefully, I put my free hand on his and retract my arm from his grip. "There's no one else here," I say. "It's just a courtyard. Why does it matter if I'm here or not?" Even as the words of assurance come out of my mouth, my eyes dart up and around to, once again, make sure I'm right in assuming that we're alone here.

I hadn't known this was a Mortal God only area, but it doesn't surprise me that there are places like that on Academy grounds. As far as the Gods and their offspring are concerned, mortals are lesser beings who have no right to their things.

Niall's eyes practically bulge. "Please, Kiera," he begs. "We must go!"

If I were just here, then I'd very much take him at his word and leave, but the problem now stands: I *can't* leave. I have to finish the contract I've made with my new familiar. If I don't do it immediately, the creature may decide that these grounds are too noisy for his taste and disappear. If it leaves the grounds, then the trouble I went to in order to find the damn thing will all be for naught and I'll still be stuck with the problem of managing the amount of spiders in the Academy as my eyes and ears. Only certain spiders of size and nature are able to take on the role of a King Arachnid. This is one of those few.

"It's just an empty courtyard," I tell Niall. "I don't know why you're so concerned. If you're that worried, you should go."

Yes, I think. *Go*. Please. Then I can finish what I came here to do and be on my way.

"No, you don't understand." Niall's face is upturned. His eyes are big and round as he stares at me. He's practically in tears. His whole body trembles as he blinks rapidly and once again tugs on the sleeve of my shirt. "One of the First Tiers frequents this courtyard and I've heard she had a relationship with one of your—I mean with one of the Darkhavens. There're already bad rumors about her. If she sees you here *alone*, without one of them—"

Just the mention of the Darkhavens makes my upper lip curl back in distaste. This damn job wouldn't be nearly so fucking bad if it weren't for those three. "I don't need *their* protection," I snap, cutting him off. Irritation causes me to be sharper than I intend.

"W-what are you saying?" Niall's horrified expression burns into me as guilt blossoms. "I-if she catches you here and no one is around, then sh-she'll ... sh-she'll—"

I sigh and crack my neck to the side, cupping one hand around my throat as I do so. Inside, I'm anxious to get a move on. The longer he lingers, the longer it'll take for me to completely finish the contract with the *Euoplos dignitas*. "I know you dedicate your life to serving," I say, "but I'm just here for the money." For some reason, Niall's innocence makes me feel worse for saying it, but it's technically not a lie and it'd be far more dangerous for him if he knew the truth. "You worry about you and I'll worry about me. I appreciate it, but you don't need to look out for me."

"No." Niall shakes his head as if he can't believe what he's hearing. The flop of dull brown hair at the top of his forehead sways back and forth with the movement. "No. No. No. Please, Kiera." His begging is sad. How frightened must he be of Mortal Gods and Gods to be worrying himself stupid over someone like me? I don't understand it. He's been kind enough to eat with me and talk with me and ensure I'm not a complete outcast, but we're not friends. If he stays and we're caught, he'll be in trouble too. Regardless, this is getting neither of us anywhere.

Looking back at the stone edge of the bubbling fountain and then down further where the spider's fuzzy brown head peeks out, I debate my options. Perhaps, I can just...

Go. I try. Pushing the order into the spider's mind now that we're connected, I send a general layout of the route back to my room in the north tower. It's a chance. The spider isn't technically contracted yet. It doesn't necessarily have to see me as its master and it could scramble away, disappearing forever.

Niall tugs on my arm once more, distracting me enough to look back at him. "Hold on..." I say, pushing the repeated order back into the spider's mind to get a move on. The spider doesn't yet move and I curse internally. Stubborn damn creature. So willful. *Why do I even like them?* Perhaps because they remind me of myself.

I turn back to Niall with a sigh. I really have to get him

out of here. For a brief moment, Niall's face clears and turns hopeful when I meet his eyes. I cup my hand over one of his shoulders. "Niall," I say, settling my gaze on his, "they're just people. Sure, they might have abilities and powers that mortals don't, but you forget, they're half mortal too. If you're truly that worried, then please get out of here. I'll finish ... erm. I was just—I mean—" A believable excuse escapes me. I sigh again and tighten my grip on his shoulders, leveling him with a serious look. "I'll leave soon, *I promise.*"

Before Niall can summon a response, his pinched face practically squinting at me as he fights back tears, a gust of ice-cold air slams into my side a split second before water does. It covers both of us, drenching our bodies down past our clothes. My hand falls away from Niall's shoulder as the suddenness of the attack sends the two of us to the ground in a heap. Niall gasps and fumbles, coughing up water onto the grass and dirt.

For a single moment, I'm frozen. Both enraged and shocked that I'd been so focused on Niall, I hadn't been paying attention to our surroundings. A bloody stupid mistake on my part. Jerking up to my knees, I press against the ground and clamber back to my feet. Red-hot anger pounds through me, and slowly—with searing intention—I turn towards the sudden onslaught of water. *There,* standing across the courtyard with a scowl on her face and a rather large hovering bulb of water over her hand, is the same Mortal God I'd seen at the fighting classes two weeks previously.

Double. Fucking. Shit.

As if it senses what's about to come next, the spider I'd tried to command scurries away, and as much as I want to dive for it and keep it here, I can't give away what I'd been doing. If it's going to escape, then so be it. Right now, I have more important things to face—such as the bitter fury of the Mortal God coming closer to both Niall and me.

Her black hair is free and flutters around her face and down to her shoulders, but the look of disgust and rage remains. At this point, I wonder if it's just the way her face is rather than genuine emotion. Her blue eyes flash and I recognize the note of glee behind them. It doesn't take a genius to realize that she's more than happy to have caught me here in a Mortal God only courtyard. This must be the girl Niall had been trying to warn me about.

I feel his hands lock onto the fabric of my wet pants legs as he crawls back to standing, using me as his prop. "Are you alright?" I ask without looking back.

"I-I—" He coughs again and latches onto the back of my shirt so hard I can feel him trembling.

"If you know what's good for you," the girl begins, her voice ripe with revulsion, "you'll get on your knees and beg for forgiveness."

Niall immediately releases me and gets to his knees. "I-I'm so sorry, Miss Rahela," he stutters out.

It takes only a moment to debate following his example. I don't want this to turn into a problem, but it's clear from her eyes that no matter what I do, there will be no forgiveness. *What would be the point in begging now?* To keep up the facade. That's all it is.

My fingers clench into fists as I direct my gaze to the dirt and grass before us. I can feel my heartbeat pulse in my throat. Each beat is a reminder—of where I am and what I'm meant to be and do. Even if I don't want to, even if I'd rather flay my own skin off of my bones than bow to this bitch, I am—for all intents and purposes—beneath her here. So, with gritted teeth, I go onto bended knee. Just one.

"I apologize for any offense, Miss Rahela," I say, repeating the name Niall had called her. My words are halting, and as much as it heats my blood further, I do my best to ensure my voice sounds monotone, hiding my anger. Air wafts over my soaked shoulders and dripping face.

A beat of silence passes and at my side, Niall's chattering teeth and trembling limbs make my own body wind tighter and tighter in anticipation of her response. Her footsteps are soft as she approaches, slow but steady. A shadow falls over where I kneel on the hard ground. She doesn't speak for the longest time and the stretch of silence passes until I have the distinct impression that she's waiting for me.

Tilting my face up, I meet stone-cold eyes. Her lips twist into a smirk and she leans down, closer and closer, as the water she commands hovers over her fingertips. "Apology. *Rejected.*"

I inhale sharply and a moment later, I'm thankful I did because a ball of water comes careening towards me. The force of her Divine ability slams into me, lifting my body from the ground and surrounding me in the liquid. I bite down, grinding my teeth as a curse threatens to spill out. I resist, keeping the air in my lungs.

The prison of water bites into my flesh, swaying me this way and that. I'm completely off-balance and I know the only way out would be to use my own Divinity. The back of my neck heats again. I close my eyes. *I can't.* Even if she's trying to kill me, revealing my abilities puts more than me at risk. I peer through the murky water as Niall's head jerks up and through the warped liquid, I can make out his expression of horror.

Fuck. He really is too kind. Worried about me when he should realize that this girl has lost her mind and he could be next. My head turns back to her. Rahela's face splits into a huge grin as she throws her head back and laughs at the sight of me. She waves her hand through the air, and the water swirls, spinning me around, head over ass until I almost release the breath trapped inside as vomit threatens to come up.

She has complete control over both gravity and the water as she suspends me above the courtyard, carrying me up and over the fountain. *Fuck. Fuck. Fuck.* I fight through the water, waving my arms as I try to swim to the edge. As soon as I get there, however, the annoyingly grating sound of Rahela's laughter follows and the water bubble turns, tipping me over and over again. I cup my hand over my lips, forcing the air to stay in.

Though I know it's not the spider's fault, I can't help but silently curse the creature as well. Had he only followed my commands then perhaps Niall and I could've left the courtyard with no one else the wiser. Now, though, that's obviously not going to happen. I lift my head and glare at my assailant. I had made a rather arrogant mistake, I admit if only to myself. I should've waited until after dark, perhaps even hidden my face in case I was discovered. But no, I'd been too excited at the prospect of gaining a King Arachnid as a familiar.

Behind Rahela, Niall's horrified expression wavers through the water bubbles that float around me as he gets to his feet and stumbles back. *Go!* I practically beg him with my eyes. I don't necessarily consider him a friend, but that doesn't mean I want to see him hurt either, and there's no doubt in my mind that once Rahela is finished with me, he'll be her next target. If he remains, then there's even less I can do.

Rahela doesn't seem that concerned with Niall. The

entirety of her focus is on me, something I manage to be thankful for as he stumbles back another step and another and another until his head turns as if he hears something. Without another backward glance, Niall finally spins around completely and flees the courtyard. If I could breathe, I'd sigh in relief the moment I see the back of his head disappear around the corner.

Now, it's just her and me.

CHAPTER 20

KIERA

K icking my legs, I try to force my body in any direction, but the water follows me, keeping me securely confined. A rather powerful ability. No wonder she's considered a First Tier.

Despite my treatment over the past few weeks, I'd forgotten one key element of differences from this position versus any one I'd had before: Mortal Gods don't care if they kill out in the open like this. Maybe it's because I've never been in one place for a mission for so long—going on a few weeks now at least—nor have I been subjected to being so close to so many Divine Beings and their offspring, but I hadn't expected this level of animosity.

I close my eyes and gather my energy, feel it spread outward from my chest down my limbs and to the tips of my fingers and toes. The water around me ripples and pulls, sloshing against my body. It grows colder and colder and when I reopen my eyes, I see bits of ice have formed inside. No wonder it feels as if the temperature is dropping.

Rahela flicks her fingers, bringing the water closer to her. She leans forward, the thin wall of her Divine water prison the only thing separating us. "This is what you deserve, mortal *whore*," she hisses. Her voice is muffled by the water in my ears, sounding deeper and farther away, but I still hear her.

There isn't really much I can do in my current position and certainly nothing to stop her from killing me without revealing my secrets. For a moment, I think about it. There's no one else in the courtyard now. I could burst her bubble —quite literally—and end this farce right now. Almost as if the mere thought brings back the memory of my training, phantom pains shoot up my back and down my arms and legs. I squeeze my eyes shut and grit my teeth through the agony.

Your life is never the only one in danger, Ophelia's voice echoes in my mind. *Remember that. If you reveal who you are, you risk all of us. Your life is not worth everyone else's.*

My eyes open once more as the pain subsides. Spots of black and white dance in front of my vision. I've been holding my breath for far too long. I might be stronger and more durable than a true mortal, but I'm far from infallible. If this keeps up, I will pass out and I doubt that will make her release her spell.

So, in a burst of anger at my own inadequacy, I jerk my head back and stare at the Mortal God's expression of smug satisfaction. I open my mouth and blow out a bubble before grinning at her and lifting my hand, fighting through the weight of the water, until I pass my palm in front of her face. I turn it around and close my fingers into a fist right before I lift the middle one.

Attack me all you like, bitch, I think to myself. I won't beg for my life like a fucking dog and I certainly won't give her the satisfaction of seeing me struggle for it.

Her sharp angled face slackens with shock. Almost

instantly, I feel the weight of the water lift—the press of it against my flesh breaking for an instant before it comes down harder than ever. A silent curse slips through my mind as my arm is snapped to my side. Peering through the waves of liquid that flutter in front of my face, I watch as Rahela opens her mouth and unleashes a scream of feminine fury that would have me rolling my eyes if I had the strength.

As it stands, however, I'm using up the bulk of my Divine energy by maintaining the air in my lungs. Any other mortal, at this point, would have likely passed out. Not that Rahela seems to realize that—she's far too outraged by my insult to do anything but scream and stomp her feet as she reaches up, clenching her fist until a dark red liquid drips from her knuckles.

Blood. Fuck. That explains why the crush of the water became so tight all of a sudden. It's difficult to turn my head, much less fight the pressure that slams into me from every side all at once. Her rage might be a blessing, though. With anger comes ineptitude. Mistakes. All I need is one good spurt of energy. Even if I've never trained the same way she and the other Mortal Gods have, I know how to harness my own Divinity and use it to my advantage. How to do it, though, without her realizing...

As I contemplate my options—or lack thereof—I feel my mind rolling as more black-and-white dots dance in front of my vision, growing wider and wider with each passing second. My throat squeezes. My chest burns. It's been too long since I had fresh air. I need to figure out a plan and I need to figure it the fuck out *now*.

Just as that thought rolls through me, however, the water bubble surrounding me bursts and I fall to the ground. My side clips the edge of the fountain as my lips burst open and I gasp for breath. The sound of harsh voices reaches my ears as familiar hands grab ahold of my shoulders and roll me to face the sky.

Niall's face appears above mine. The ends of his hair drip forward, still wet, though this time I'm not sure if it's because of actual water or sweat. He's heaving for air just as much as I am, his normally pale face flushed pink with exertion.

"It's okay," he says. "Breathe, Kiera. It's okay."

I blink and cough and gulp down breath after breath. My insides seize and each lungful of air burns the inside of my mouth and throat. Reaching up with shaking hands, I wipe away the water still clinging to my eyelashes and face to clear my view. "What"—I gulp down more air— "happened?"

Before Niall can answer, a high-pitched voice full of anger snaps out.

"—do this!"

"That little rat offended me and I'll damn well do what I please, Second Tier!" Rahela squawks. The sound makes my head throb.

"Don't even think of it!"

I lift my head, turning it to find a red-haired Mortal God moving to block Rahela's path as she attempts to descend upon where I'm crouched down on the ground. Crimson curls sway with the wind as she stands between Rahela and Niall and me. Despite how much shorter she is than Rahela, I have to hand it to her. She's got guts to face that cunt when the two of them are on completely different levels—a First Tier and Second.

"Caedmon is on his way and he'll be quite upset by this," the redhead snaps. "You know you're not supposed to

207

use your abilities like this and especially on Terra that aren't yours."

"Of course you would go to him," Rahela scoffs. "What? Can't face off against me yourself? Is your Divinity that worthless?" Rahela twirls her finger and water lifts away from the ground around me—sucked out of the grass and stone at her behest.

"I'm warning you, Rahela," the red-haired girl snaps. "*Back. Off.*"

"Perhaps you have more mortal blood in you than any of the rest of us, Maeryn," Rahela growls. "Otherwise, you wouldn't feel the need to defend them so much."

"You're half mortal too," Maeryn replies. "Don't forget that."

Niall scoops his arm underneath my shoulder blades and I let him help me to my feet even though now that I've caught my breath I feel much better. *Caedmon.* The name rings a bell. He's a God here within the Academy. An Upper God at that. I know the name as well as his appearance since the Darkhavens attend classes taught by the Divine Being.

I grit my teeth. If one of the Gods in charge of the Academy is on his way here then that cannot bode well for me.

"Are you alright?" Niall whispers. I jerk my head down and nod. He seems to take it and then discreetly gestures to the red-haired girl. "That's my Master," he tells me. "I didn't know who else to go to and I heard her calling for me when you were in the water. I thought I could get her to help."

I shake my head. "No, you did the right thing. Thank you." I say the last two words and mean them. Had Niall not gone and gotten someone to break this up, I might have been forced to do something I'd immensely regret and all because of my own hubris. As it stands right now, I appear every inch the victim that was nearly drowned by a raging psycho of a Mortal God out for blood. Why, though? I still don't understand. "I'm sorry I didn't listen to you originally," I mutter.

Niall pats my back in response.

"You should've kept your nose out of my business, Maeryn," Rahela spits at Maeryn, her irritation not subsiding even in the face of the news that a God will be with us soon.

"You shouldn't have started this in the first place," Maeryn replies.

Despite the confidence in her tone, I spot the jump of muscle at the back of her arm. The hand at her side trembles ever so slightly and she turns it, gripping the fabric of her uniform skirt. She's not as brave as she acts. It makes me almost want to repent for antagonizing Rahela in the first place. To be fair, though, I wasn't sure if I'd be able to get free myself, and if I were going to die at the hands of a Mortal God like her, I was going to go with no small amount of fury of my own.

Were it just me and the First Tier girl, there's no doubt in my mind who'd win. She might have been trained in the Academy, but I'd been out in the real world and I wasn't afraid to kill. I'd done it before and I'd damn well do it again if I needed to—that is, if I could get away with it without revealing my identity.

"This is nothing but a jealous fit of rage, Rahela," Maeryn scoffs. "You need to get over it. Theos won't care even if you harm his Terra. He never has before."

My upper lip curls back. *Theos?* This was all about Theos? Is she fucking serious? I straighten and brush off

Niall's worried hands. I step forward just behind Maeryn. Rahela's gaze moves to me and darkens.

"If you have something to say to my Master," I say, my voice slightly rough but clear, "I'm happy to relay a message."

Maeryn whirls on me and I'm suddenly struck by the petite beauty of a face that looks almost catlike. "No—" she says as Rahela interrupts.

"Yes."

Maeryn glares at Rahela who, in turn, ignores her as she narrows her eyes on me. "You can tell your *Master*," she spits the word, "that if his Terra is caught in any place she's not supposed to be again, I'll *end* you. Rules be damned."

"Duly noted," I say in response. And definitely not something I'll ever relay to Theos or any of the Darkhavens. I don't want to find out what kind of punishment they'll exact on their own if they get irritated by this instance. I can't forget their stupid bet either. Even if I've lasted this long, I don't want them teaming up with this bitch to try and get me kicked out.

I have no doubt that if they smell blood or weakness, they'll go seeking it out like a pack of hinterland wolves on the hunt.

"I suppose that wraps things up, then." All four of us— Niall, Maeryn, Rahela, and even myself—jump at the sudden appearance of a new figure. Our heads jerk towards the tall, dark man walking across the courtyard grass towards us.

The Divine Being comes to a slow stop between Rahela and Maeryn, his shoulders straight and his arms clasped casually in front of himself. He turns his head, dark gaze falling on me. My entire body freezes. Though his facial features are youthful, there, in the depths of his deep soil-rich eyes, is endless time. Ageless knowing.

This is Caedmon. The God of Prophecy.

Rahela and Maeryn immediately lower their heads as does Niall. But not me. I can't seem to even though I know I should. I *want* to. I'm entrapped by his attention. The eerie glow in his brown eyes flickers and then his expression lightens, his lips curving upward. I suck in a deep breath and am somehow released from whatever hold he had over me to lower my head as well.

"Rahela, it's beneath you to go around tormenting the servants of the Academy," Caedmon says lightly. The chastisement is clear despite his polite tone. "I understand you have a temperamental nature but please try to refrain. As a First Tier student, you must exemplify self-composure and dignity."

In my periphery, I see her head dip down even further. "Yes, sir." Rahela's response is admitted through clenched teeth.

"Good, I'll choose not to punish you this time," Caedmon says, "but keep in mind that one instance of leniency does not guarantee two."

The look Rahela sends me is full of venom and retribution. As far as Caedmon's words go, they don't appear to sway her at all. I resolve to keep my eyes open and to steer clear of her if I can manage it. It would be my most mindful option at this point.

"Good. You may go then." Caedmon turns away, effectively dismissing her, and Rahela straightens, flashing me another look that promises this won't be the last I see of her.

"Maeryn, I believe your Terra is quite shocked by the

circumstances. Perhaps you should escort him to the Terra infirmary."

I turn and glance at Niall at those words. It's true he appears quite faint as he wobbles back and forth on his feet, gripping my soaking wet sleeve. Perhaps it's the drop in his adrenaline now that Rahela is gone. Maeryn, too, pivots and gasps as she spots Niall. Quickly bypassing me, she takes him by the arm and gently urges him to lean on her. I eye her warily but clench my fists to keep them at my sides, to keep from reaching out to drag him back to me for safety.

I've never seen a Mortal God treat a Terra that way. No wonder Niall felt comfortable running to her in a time of need. My chest tightens. A good, kind Mortal God—the realization of it almost makes me feel like I've been in the presence of a mystical being from legend rather than an actual living, breathing person.

"Thank you, Caedmon. I'll take him there," Maeryn agrees, flashing an apologetic look at him before offering me a small smile.

Caedmon nods and then steps to the side as Maeryn urges Niall past the two of us. I watch the girl warily, but her face never reveals anything other than concern as she leads Niall away. Once they're out of the courtyard, though, I have no other option than to face the God in front of me. My heartbeat races against my rib cage as I realize my new situation.

I'm left all alone with a pure-blooded God and those dangerous eyes of his, and I'm not exactly sure what to expect.

"Follow me." Caedmon doesn't say anything more as he turns around and begins walking in the opposite direction. For a brief second, I contemplate whether following him would be a smart idea, but if he wanted to … he could make me. Mortal God or not, Divine powers or not, he's a God.

So, with little other recourse, I put one foot in front of the other and follow after the Divine Being that just saved me from the wrath of another. I don't know if he can hear the rapid beating of my heart as we walk, but I practice every trick I know. Quietly inhaling and exhaling in slow even breaths. Counting the steps I take. Gradually, it works. My racing heart calms and I gain back the control over my own body—or most of it.

As we enter one of the stone buildings, the slight warmth from the sun drops dramatically. Water drips from the ends of my hair and my clothes. I repress the shivers, keeping my gaze trained before me like a criminal being led to the gallows. Eyes always forward in case Caedmon glances back even as I focus on my peripheral vision to pick up any signs of interlopers.

There's no way he can know ... is there? Despite my slowed heart rate, my thoughts clamber over each other. Anxiety. Fear. Rage. If Caedmon suspects me, he certainly isn't acting like it. In fact, during the entire journey from the courtyard to a solid oak door that he unlocks using a slender iron key from his pocket, never once does he turn his face back towards me. It's a natural inclination for any living being to be wary of an enemy at your back—but Gods are different. Perhaps, even if he does suspect me, he doesn't fear me as an enemy.

As we step into the unlocked chamber, my eyes immediately go to the massive desk piled high with papers and volumes of texts that look far older than myself. There are plants everywhere. Framing the door to my back are large palms that look as though they have more business in the middle of a desert than near frigid waters. Stacks of various flora in potted form are set next to books, tables, oversized chairs, and everywhere in between save for the center of the room that leads straight from the door to that desk.

To the back of the room is a rather large stained glass window with lines etched through the colors to depict a woman. Her long hair is a shock of white, whereas her body is coated in royal purples and indigos. Webs of cracks that seem purposefully placed descend from her fingertips to the ground and her eyes are straight black.

The image is as disturbing as it's beautiful. Caedmon strides into the room with familiarity and veers to the left to a glass cabinet with several decanters and crystal cups next to a rather large, spiked fern. Uncapping one of the decanters with dark liquid inside, he pours himself a hefty amount and sniffs it with a pleased sigh. Instead of drinking it straight, however, he shuffles to the side and pours it into a tea kettle I hadn't noticed.

Once he's done, he grabs ahold of the kettle by its weighted handle and carries it across the room to a large gray-brick fireplace. He sets it on a hook before lighting the fire himself. All the while, I stand there, feeling very much out of place, watching.

It isn't until Caedmon goes to his desk and takes a seat that he gestures for me to approach. Though I'm curious, I don't ask why he didn't order me—as a servant of the Academy—to attend to the little spectacle of his tea-making. I take my stance before his desk like a soldier preparing for battle with my hands clasped together behind my back and my gaze forward.

Caedmon's expression turns rueful. "Thank you for following me back to my office, Miss..." he begins, pausing with a raised brow.

Pressing my lips together momentarily, I frown before answering. "Kiera," I say. "Kiera Nezerac."

He nods but does not comment on my pseudo-surname. "Yes, thank you, Miss Kiera. I do hope you don't take Rahela's animosity to heart. Many students at the Academy have not been allowed outside of its walls and therefore, are often stinted in their social awareness."

Thank yous? From a God? Hopes? What the fuck is this?

"I wouldn't dare presume anything, Your Divinity," I reply tersely. "I am sure she was simply attempting to teach one such as myself a valuable lesson."

Caedmon snorts before covering his mouth and nose, eyes widened as if he, too, is surprised by the sound. Before he can say anything more, though, the whistling of his tea kettle sounds into the room and he quickly stands up. Once again, instead of ordering me to attend to it, I'm left to watch as he, himself, finds a small rag to pull the kettle off the fire and walks back over to his glass cabinet.

I watch as he pours the now steaming tea into his crystal glass before setting the still hot kettle on an over-turned empty pot next to the glass cabinet. Once done, Caedmon faces me and gestures for me to move towards the two wingback chairs surrounded by more plants next to the fireplace.

"Take a seat," he orders.

I'd really rather remain on my feet, especially when I have no clue what he wants nor what he expects, but there's no possibility of being able to refuse a God. So, I simply follow his command and ease myself gingerly into the smaller of the two chairs. My unease quickly turns to shock as he strides over to me and hands me the warm glass of tea.

I take it with two hands, staring into the strange mixture, blinking when I notice a small petal lift itself up from the bottom, floating to the surface of the rather muddy-looking liquid. "Um ... sir?" I raise my gaze from the glass in my hand to Caedmon as he takes a seat in the other chair across from me.

He waves one long-fingered hand to the drink. "Don't worry," he says with a light chuckle. "It's not poisoned."

I stiffen.

Caedmon leans back against the cushions of his seat and sighs. "I'm sure your throat is feeling rather sore from holding your breath for so long within Rahela's water prison. This tea is supposed to help that," he says. His brown eyes flash as if daring me to counter his concern. No mortal would. The fact that my throat hasn't been ravaged by being underwater for so long is a testament to my bloodline.

Carefully, I lift the glass to my lips. A tart, fruity taste floods my tongue a split second before a flora scent invades my nostrils. The tea is still scalding, but the sweetness of it coats the walls of my throat like honey as it goes down. Several moments of silence pass between us as I sip the tea given to me by the God, and he, in turn, watches me. Once the cup is completely empty, I lick the remainder of the sweetened taste from my lips before setting it down on the table before me.

"Your Divinity," I begin, "I hope you don't take offense to this question..."

"Feel free to speak your mind with me, Kiera," he says as my words dry up with my hesitation.

With what I know is a puckered brow, I lift my gaze to his. "Why are you treating me so kindly?" I ask.

"I'm afraid I don't know what you mean," Caedmon says. "In what way have I treated you with kindness?"

He doesn't know? Seriously? I gesture to the glass sitting between us. "A God such as yourself should have servants," I say by way of answer. "You could have had me do that myself."

"Ah." Caedmon nods as if he understands before stroking a hand down his smooth, unblemished face. The light shadow of hair above his upper lip does nothing to detract from his beauty or his deceptive appearance of youth. "I like doing things for myself."

I blink. "You do?"

His lips turn up at the edges. "Is that so hard to believe?" he asks.

Realizing my mistake, I dip my head. "I apologize, Your Divinity. I meant no disrespect."

"No, no, I wasn't chastising you, Kiera." A wary emotion rolls through me each time he says my name. There is a power in naming something and I normally don't like using my real one for missions like this, but going under pseudonyms for long periods of time is also a risk. *Too long as someone else and you start to forget yourself,* Ophelia had taught Regis and me. Sometimes, when an assassin is under an alias for weeks, months, even years, they start to become the people they act as. It's risky. *As killers, as those who've committed the most heinous of deeds, we must never forget who we truly are.*

"You look me in the eyes." Caedmon's sudden sentence has me lifting my head once more. Confusion is ripe within me.

"I don't understand ... should I not?" I ask.

He shakes his head. "No, what I mean to say is that I wanted to do something for one brave enough to meet my gaze."

"Brave enough?" I still have no clue what he means.

Caedmon taps his free hand on the end of one of the armrests of his chair. "Do you know what my specialty is, Kiera?" he asks.

Yes. "You're the God of Prophecy."

He nods. "Do you know why I find it so unique that you look me in the eyes even knowing that?"

I shake my head, and his smile widens, though only slightly.

"Gods and mortals alike fear the unknown," he says, turning his head. His eyes seem to fixate on the depiction of the woman in the stained glass. "Prophecy is a useful specialty as much as it's damning. It is both a blessing and a curse to know the future. Though many understand that I may have no hand in deciding fate, simply knowing it is a fearful matter in and of itself. It is a rare individual, I find, that is able to meet my gaze without fear of what they may see in my eyes."

Caedmon turns back to me and this time, as the brown irises of his gaze swirls, it changes. "What do you see, Kiera, when you look into my eyes?"

All of the breath I'd recaptured evaporates from my lungs. My shoulders sink down as an invisible weight settles around them. The brown of his gaze folds in on itself, leaving only darkness. Never-ending. Immaculate. Pure ebony. There's no light. None at all. My lashes flicker as I stare into the chasm that he shows me.

Tingles prick at my flesh, like the tiny legs of spiders crawling all over me. Familiar. Awakening. Perhaps this is a void he is showing me, but for some reason, I don't think it's empty. That abyss that I stare into ... somehow, I feel as if it's staring back at me.

I blink and the vision is cut off. I lean back, feeling a fresh coating of sweat all over me, lingering against my skin beneath my clothes. Clothes that have long since dried, I find. How long was I staring into his eyes for?

"Kiera?"

I jump at the sound of Caedmon's voice. "I-I'm sorry," I quickly say. "I didn't..."

"Can you tell me what you saw?"

Slowly, with great effort, I inch my head up and meet Caedmon's gaze once more—half worried at what I might find there. The chasm is gone now, though, and all that remains is the warm soil richness of his kind brown eyes. I release a breath I hadn't realized I'd been holding.

"Nothing," I answer him.

"What?" His brow puckers as his forehead scrunches.

"I saw nothing," I tell him. "Just ... darkness."

The effects of my earlier efforts to calm my racing heart have faded. The damn thing practically pounds against the inside of my rib cage, trembling with an emotion I can't name. It's not one I think I've ever felt before. It feels stronger than fear and yet more powerful than anger.

"Interesting..." Caedmon's response leaves much to be desired. I don't know what to say nor what to ask. In fact, there isn't a single question that formulates in my mind despite the mass of disorientation that has taken up residence in my head. "Very interesting."

Caedmon stares at me for a moment longer before dragging in a breath himself. Finally, he stands from his chair. Quickly following the movement, I, too, stand and then waver back and forth on my feet, unsure of what to do next.

"You should head back to the north tower," Caedmon says, turning away from me as he makes his way back to the desk that's piled high with books and papers. The light outside of the stained glass window has waned, a clear indication that much time has passed. "I'm sure your wards are searching for you by now."

"I..." How do I respond to that? "Thank you for your care," I finally gather the air to say.

The reverberation of Caedmon's chuckle makes the muscles across the backs of my shoulders bunch and jump. I see, now, why he had said people were fearful of him. Why they wouldn't look into his eyes. Now that I know of his abilities, it sets me on edge. If a God of Prophecy knows fate, then there's no doubt in my mind that he must know more about me than he lets on.

Why? Is it because he can't take part in the future? The present? What must that be like—to know things and yet be unable to speak of them? A bubble of sympathy rises in my chest. The life of this God—as different as he is from my expectation—is no life at all if he can't involve himself in anything. It's a half-life, a true curse as he said.

"If you need anything, you're always welcome to call on me, Your Divinity." The words escape my lips before I can think better of them. They're hypocritical and as soon as they reach my ears, I wish I could snap my hands out and grab them back, stuffing them back down my throat.

Caedmon leans back in his chair before spinning it around to face the window once more. His head tips back and he focuses on the woman surrounded by webs. "Caedmon, Kiera," he replies. "Please call me by my given name, and though I appreciate the offer, little one, you'll soon have your hands full. Don't concern yourself with me. You should only come back should you need to know more from that darkness you saw."

Not on my life. Though Caedmon seems kind, he is still everything I've learned to hate. Divine. Powerful. If anything, his benevolence is more terrifying than any anger he might have shown. The dark of the chasm inside of his eyes—whatever that abyss might have been trying to hint at—is not one I want to know. Prophecy be damned, fate is something I've chosen for myself and it's something I'll continue to choose.

My chest tightens, breath escaping my lungs. Be it darkness or light, the unknown and the future walk hand in hand and I fear both equally.

Lowering myself into a respectful bow, I clasp my hands in front of me. "I'll be going then ... Caedmon." The God's name tastes foreign on my tongue, but unlike I expected, it doesn't leave the lingering taste of something odious.

No. This whole conversation has left me with something else entirely. The only problem is that I can't identify it or whether or not it'll either help or harm me in the future.

CHAPTER 22
RUEN

The clashing of swords clang in the near distance. Sparks fly off the edges of the blades as both Enid and Darius separate only to come crashing back into each other. Each time it happens, the quick flare of metal scraping against metal lights up their faces, illuminating the cut of their darkened expressions and glistening off of the sweat clinging to their flesh.

Had it been a mistake for me to recommend Darius for advancement? I hadn't thought so at first, but now Theos' mounting worry is grating on my nerves. Though I'd already planned to help train Darius to prepare him for the battles, it is because of Theos that we're here on the training grounds, still at it hours after the others have gone to bed.

Night has long since fallen and now the arena is lit only by the flaming torches that circle the area. The fires flicker, causing shadows to dance upon the dirt ground as the sounds of grunting and curses fill the air.

"You're being too heavy-footed," Theos calls out, directing the comment to Darius as Enid forces the taller and wider man back. Despite her smaller stature, she is more skilled with her footwork. She's faster and she knows exactly how to use her speed. She'd been a damn good choice for Theos to choose, and for Darius she's just as good of a sparring partner. As long as the two of them keep up this level of intensity, whenever the Gods deign to announce their battles, they'll both have more than a fighting chance.

"Lighten your stance and use her speed against her, Darius," I call out. Both Theos and I keep several paces back as we watch our respective chosen ones fight it out.

The Gods, for all of their planning and scheming, appear to enjoy the randomness of when they announce their battles. There's no telling when it'll happen. It could be tomorrow or a month from now. Every moment with Darius and Enid counts. Every moment to train them and ensure that they will survive it.

Behind Theos and me, Kalix sits against the wall of the arena with one leg drawn up and bent towards his chest and the other straightened out. His groan of boredom sounds for the fifth time in the last half hour. Turning slightly to glare at him, I frown.

"If you wish to leave, you're welcome to," I snap.

He groans again. "What I *wish* for, you won't let me do!" he replies.

Theos turns as well and scowls at our brother. "We're training them not attempting to kill them," he growls.

Kalix sinks one hand into a mound of dirt at his side and flings it at Theos in childish annoyance. The mass of it doesn't even make it to the halfway point between the two. "If you'd let me call the Terra for some entertainment," he huffs, "I wouldn't be so godsdamned bored."

His fascination with the silver-haired beauty that's had

the unfortunate luck of becoming our Terra is getting on my last nerve. Though I have to admit she's impressed me with her reserve and ability to handle my brothers, at the end of the day, she's still mortal and therefore, breakable.

"No," I snap. "Now drop it."

"Ugh!" Kalix lets his head drop back against the wall hard enough for an audible thump to reach my ears. "Then let me fight," he insists. "I'll be careful. I won't kill them, but you have to admit that merely training them like this won't do much for them in the long run. You have to challenge them if you want them to survive the battles."

Theos' expression darkens further and he returns his gaze to the two battling it out several paces away. I'm starting to regret my decision to recommend Darius for advancement. I know how Theos feels about him. Of the few Mortal Gods we align ourselves with, even fewer can be considered friends, and for Theos, Darius is one of those rarities.

Taking a step forward, I halt the fight with a raised hand. "Enid, pass me your blade." I can feel the heat of Theos' gaze on my back as I stride away from him and towards the two. Blinking with curious, dull brown eyes, Enid doesn't fight it as I take her sword from her and gesture for her to take up a stance at the edge of the arena.

I turn to Darius and take a deep breath. "Darius, do you believe I made a mistake in choosing you for advancement?" I ask.

He stiffens, wide shoulders tightening. "No," he grits out. "I'm ready."

"If you're ready," I say, widening my own stance and settling down into my thighs. "Then show me."

That's all the encouragement he needs. His sword clashes with mine, sliding down the flat end as I twist it and spin out of his control and reach. My body, similar in both size and weight to his, appears to have a better effect on his mind as he watches my movements. He counters faster when I drive him back and then dodges at just the right moments.

All the while, the searing mixture of Theos' anxiety and anger lingers over the space of the arena. Thrust. Dodge. Counter. Strike. Around and around we go, Darius and I. Little beads of sweat pop up along my spine. Training with someone other than my brothers will usually ensure that my own Divine abilities are repressed, but this is different. Darius is Theos' friend and as such, he'll need to learn to fight with his abilities and against those of others.

A breath hisses from my teeth as his sword clips my shoulder, cutting through the fabric and into my flesh. A moment later, though, with a rush of Divinity, I appear behind him and flip my sword so that the hilt is what slams into the side of his back, right over one of his kidneys instead of the sharp end. With a pained grunt, he goes down to one knee.

I could stop there. In fact, I contemplate it. But it's not enough. He hasn't reacted fast enough and the battles are quickly approaching. I lock my hand onto the back of his neck and allow the Divinity collecting beneath my palm to spread outward. The sharp tingles of my power stab forth and the scream of agony that echoes out of Darius' lips, arching up towards the night sky, is met with shocked silence.

"Ruen!" Theos' angry yell has me pulling my hand back immediately as Darius collapses the rest of the way to the ground. Theos jogs up, hurrying to put himself between us as I take a step back and allow it. "What the fuck were you thinking?" he demands, looking from Darius to me.

"I was thinking he needs to be better if he's going to survive the battles," I reply.

"You're not Kalix," Theos snaps back. "That's not how we do things."

"Perhaps training with Kalix will better prepare him than training with you."

Theos rounds on me, rage flashing in his eyes and darkening the golden hue into near blackness for a brief second. "What *the fuck* is that supposed to mean?"

The sound of boots scraping against the ground reaches my ears and I already know that Kalix is on his way. I blow out a breath and close my eyes for a moment before reopening and fixing my attention on Theos. "You're going too easy on him," I say. "I know Darius is your friend, but this is serious. He'll need to get used to others using their abilities in the ring and figure out a way to counteract it. Not only does he need to be physically faster, but he needs to be mentally a step ahead."

"Theos..." When Darius gets to his feet and turns to face both of us, I lift my gaze to his. A small part of me feels a twinge of guilt at the pallor of his skin and the way his hand trembles when he grabs ahold of Theos' arm. "He's right."

"No." Theos shakes him off. "No, this was ridiculous. You need to tell Axlan that you were wrong to advance him. He's not ready for—"

"Theos!" Darius' voice deepens and Theos finally stops glaring at me to look at his friend. The second he does, Darius' face softens and he changes tactics, reaching up and cupping a hand over Theos' shoulder. "I can handle this. Ruen is right. I've got the strength and control over my abilities now. I just need to put what we've learned into action. Trust me. I've got this."

Before Theos can formulate a response, twin arms come up and round both my shoulders and Theos' in the same instant. Kalix dives his head forward with a grin and fixes his intense look on Darius. "Then do you think you can take me on too?" he asks, excitement dripping from his tone.

Darius' expression goes from placating to nervous, but instead of backing away as I would expect any sane person to when propositioned by Kalix, he draws in a breath, drops his hand from Theos' shoulder, and nods. "Yeah, bring it on."

I nod. "I think that's a good idea." Jerking my chin back, I wave Enid forward. "Darius, you and Enid should try to take Kalix on using your abilities. If you can land one hit on him then you can call it a night."

That perks him right up and I hear Enid's footsteps pick up the pace as soon as those words are out of my mouth. The two of them have been out here for hours, so of course the thought of a break from more training is something that'll motivate them.

Kalix whoops and dives forward, swinging an arm around Darius and leading him away as Enid quickly rushes past Theos and me, taking the sword I hold out for her on her way. A moment of silence passes and then another and another. Neither Theos nor I say a single word until we're sure Kalix has led the other two far enough away and distracted them to keep our conversation as private as it can be here.

Turning on me, Theos shoots me a look full of venom. He opens his mouth, no doubt to lay into me, but I stop him before it starts. "You know I'm right about him," I say. "You're too easy on him."

"At least I don't try to fucking kill him in the name of training," Theos spits back.

I sigh. "You know I'm not trying to kill him. If I wanted him dead, he would be." That's a simple fact. At Darius' current level, he couldn't hold his own against me even if he tried. The three of us—Kalix, Theos, and I—were entrusted with advancing others for a reason and it's because we've gone through our own battles multiple times.

"He will get better," I continue. "He couldn't stay in the lower classes forever, you and I both know that. This would've been his third time being passed up for advancement. One more and he would've been required to move up regardless of whether he was ready or not."

Theos bares his teeth and turns away from me, anchoring his hands on his hips as he takes two steps and then stops. "We could've had more time at least, damn it."

"Why are you so concerned about the timing?" I ask. "Most of the Gods who preside over the battles don't demand the death battles."

"*Most*," Theos bites out the word, repeating it as he looks back at me. "Not all."

I lean back on my heels, reaching up and fingering the open slit over my shoulder where Darius' blade had actually managed to pierce me. Despite the blood lingering on the fabric, the wound has already healed. "I think you're scared," I reply. "You care for him and I understand that, but you should know as well as I do that anyone too weak to win their own battles will never last—not here and certainly not around us."

"You think you know me so fucking well, do you?" Theos turns completely and drops his hands from his hips as he strides forward. I don't move as he walks right up to me, not stopping until our chests brush against one another. "You and I both know that misfortune strikes not when you least expect it, but when you've become arrogant enough to think it will never touch you." His words pierce me as his upper lip pulls back in a sneer. "Your arrogance is showing, brother."

With that, he pushes away, turns, and calls out to the others. Loathe as I am to admit it, even if he is right, there's nothing either of us can do now. Darius will either pass these battles with the wounds of hard-fought lessons or he won't ... I dread the day we find out. Because if the former happens, I fear Theos may never be the same.

CHAPTER 23
KIERA

To my surprise, the *Euoplos dignitas* appears in my room a few days after the events that took place between first Rahela and I and then Caedmon. Though I can't truly talk to the creature, I can sense that it seems curious about me if not still feeling me out, but at least it follows my summons.

The *Euoplos dignitas* is like no other familiar I've ever had. It appears when it wants and where it wants. Sometimes, I'll find it resting on my pillow on my bed as if it's a slumbering dog waiting for its owner to come back from a long day at work. Other times, it disappears and when it returns, it acts as if nothing has changed.

With the creature firmly under my purview, I'm thankful that I no longer have to directly control the sheer amount of spiders within the Academy. I can pass along orders to the *Euoplos dignitas* and it'll see to it that the other spiders act accordingly. It'd been worth it to sneak into the courtyard and dig it up.

Though time has passed since my initial meeting with Caedmon, the memory of the darkness in his eyes remains an ever constant in my mind. Some nights, as I lay beneath the thin sheets on my bed, closing my eyes only brings it all back. It doesn't matter how many of my little friends I call to me, even the venomous bite of a spider can't always pull me out of my thoughts.

There's a sudden urgency within me, a need to find my client and therefore, my target, and get this job over with. I want to be free. I want to leave the Mortal Gods Academy and, the universe willing, I'd like to never fucking return.

Taptaptap.

The sound of a bird's beak clipping against the glass of my window has me up and out of bed in an instant. It's not as though I was sleeping anyway—sleep is an ever-elusive beast now and in its place, a strange anxiousness has appeared. I quickly unlock the window and swing it open to allow the bird to stick its clawed leg between the metal mesh.

I unravel the little note tied to its foot and read the contents.

MEETING REQUESTED. *Riviere shop. — R*

THERE'S no date and no time, but Regis knows better than to expect me to be able to sneak out at any given time. Only by the fact that we've known each other for the last decade do I expect that he'll be waiting around Madam Brione's shop for however long it takes me to get out of the Academy and meet him.

Turning away from the bird, I grab a matchbook set next to my bedside, light it and the candle there, before holding the thin piece of parchment over its flame. I watch until the last of the page's ashes have disintegrated into the cool metal bowl beneath the candlestick.

The bird flutters off, no need for a return message. Regis and I have an understanding. He doesn't request meetings unless there's actually a need for one. I'll be there when I can, and I hope whatever he has to tell me concerns our client and target. I don't know how much longer I can bear to be locked within these walls with no purpose. *Soon.*

I close the window just as the sun crests over the mountainous horizon. Not seconds after I've shut the window and relatched it, however, a bell chimes in the near distance.

I freeze. It tolls ominously. One, two, three times—each one seeming to grow louder as if its echo is infused with someone's Divinity. The sound is low as it reverberates through the stone walls of the north tower. It's signaling something, that much is for sure. Whatever it is, there's only one way to find out.

Without wasting time, I quickly slip into my uniform, sliding a fresh tunic over my head and tucking it into the pants that others have finally grown accustomed to seeing me in despite my gender. I braid my hair back so that it swings behind my shoulders, away from my face save for the short tendrils at the front of my forehead and the sides of my temples. Once I'm done getting ready for the day, instead of heading to the Terra dining hall, I go up to the Darkhaven quarters.

I knock a quick barrage against their door before opening it and stepping inside without being called. To my surprise, I find the three of them already in their shared space, all of them facing the overarching window as the last vestiges of the bells toll. They stand several paces away from each other, with Ruen by his books, Theos opposite him, and Kalix right by the stairs and closest to the window. Each of them has an expression of anticipation on their faces, but only Kalix appears even marginally excited by whatever this sound means. Ruen and Theos appear very much disturbed by it, and it burns me that I do not know.

"Good morning, Masters." My voice appears to do the trick of bringing the three of them out of their reverie and in sync, they turn towards me.

"Terra!" Kalix bounds across the room and I tense, keeping my hands at my sides as he throws himself at me, grabs me around the waist, and lifts me into the air. "Did you hear the bells? Do you know what this means?"

He spins me in a circle and it takes every ounce of my self-restraint not to bash him over the head and free myself from his grip before he sets me back down with a bright face. "I'm afraid I don't, Master Kalix."

His grin is boyish and charming, reminding me instantly of Regis when he's trying to woo an unsuspecting barmaid. It's almost enough to make me forget what I've seen him do in his training classes—*almost*. As it stands, Kalix has something about him that sets me on edge. I haven't been back in his room other than to do my hurried cleaning since that first day, but every time I intrude into his private spaces, I have the distinct feeling that something continuously watches me. He may seem jovial and pleasant at first glance, but there's a deep twinge of lunacy in his rich green eyes.

I don't trust this sudden excitement from him.

"It's the mid-term battles announcement," Ruen says, his voice strained and quiet as he answers my unspoken question.

I lift my head and glance his way before swapping to

Theos who turns away from all of us and stomps across the room into one of the bedchambers. The slam of the door vibrates up the wall and despite the stone outline, several paintings shake at the force of his irritation.

"Ignore them," Kalix insists, throwing his arm around my shoulders and sending me off-kilter as I stumble under the abrupt weight. "They're just worried about Theos' friend."

"And you're not?" The question escapes my mouth before I can stop it.

Kalix laughs, though, without offense, and shakes his head. He shrugs. "The boy will either win or he'll lose," he says. "No use worrying about something we can't change."

How easy must life be to go through it without any sort of concern? It's truly amazing. Reaching up, I grip his hand and carefully pluck it off my shoulder before lowering it back down between us. Men like him are an effort in futility to try to understand. There's no use in bothering. Instead, I turn to the only one of the brothers remaining.

"Is there anything I need to do to help you prepare?" I inquire, directing the question to where Ruen still stands, his gaze centered squarely on Theos' door.

A beat passes and then he blows out a breath. "No," he says. "We likely won't be called to fight. You'll just need to come to the arena and stand with the other Terra—"

"Awwww, come on, why can't she sit with us?" Kalix whines and just as if he's completely forgotten that I've already removed his arm from my shoulders once, he replaces it, and I stiffen with repressed rage. He leans into me, rubbing the side of his face over the top of my head like an overgrown animal.

Yes, an overgrown animal—that's exactly what he is. I peer at him with new eyes. He'd probably look quite at home with a leash and collar. The image that brings up in my mind forces my lips to twitch in amusement. It doesn't slip his notice.

"See!" Kalix exclaims. "She likes the idea!"

The twitching immediately stops.

"Fine, I don't care." Ruen sighs and waves his hand at the two of us absently. "Go do ... whatever it is you normally do this time of day. You won't need to return for classes; they'll be canceled in preparation for the battles. Meet us at the arena just before noon. Battles will start then."

Despite Kalix's sour expression at Ruen's words, I'm more than happy to do that. I quickly lift Kalix's arm back off of my shoulders once more, bow, and escape into the corridor. My feet eat up the distance between the north tower and the Terra dining hall. What little the Darkhavens had managed to gift me in terms of information would need to be expanded and there was one person I knew well enough for the task.

Unfortunately, when I make it to the Terra dining hall, I find it strangely void of people. There are a few newer Terra scattered about, all of whom have paused their meals to look around in confusion. The one person I was hoping to find—Niall—isn't there. Why had Ruen told me to go off and continue my schedule as normal when it's clear from the lack of Terra available that a normal schedule on a day when battles are to commence isn't usual at all?

With a defeated breath, I grab an apple from one of the carts and head back to the north tower. There's no point in going to search for Niall when it's clear he won't be where I expect and I'd rather avoid running into Rahela or any of the other Mortal Gods that could make my life here within the Academy even more atrocious than it already is.

I've already done far too much wrong as it is in drawing

attention to myself. Perhaps it's my poor luck, but I've found that being in charge of the Darkhaven brothers— though an adequate barrier between myself and most of the other Terra—only leads to disruptions and trouble with the students. On my days off, now, as few and infrequent as they are, I avoid the majority of the student body while maintaining an appropriate level of reconnaissance.

In fact, now, as I bite into the flesh of my apple and chew thoughtfully, I peer up at the spires arching across the Academy's rooftops. It's been so long since I've exercised. Terra are usually too busy to do anything more than work, eat, and sleep only to wake up and do it all again the next day. It's a wonder they haven't reared up and demanded better treatment. Then again, I suppose that's the true power of the Gods—to make those beneath them believe in their benevolence even as they stand on their backs to hoist themselves up.

A scowl overtakes my face at that reminder.

Finishing my apple, I dump the core into one of the garden beds lining the walkway and kick dirt over it before turning and heading in the opposite direction of my initial goal. Instead of heading back to the north tower, I think it might be better to check out the battle arena and find out just what to expect.

I FIND THE ARENA, and to my surprise, the missing Terra. They are all hard at work, sweeping the stands, hanging banners over the edges of the arena walls with depictions of various Gods, and raking the dirt to level the ground. Several elder Terra shout to the younger ones and I dip back, sliding into the shadows of the tunnel entrance I decided to use versus the doors on the other side. I spot Dauphine towards the head of the stands where she directs several Terra to set up a black tent to block the sun's rays.

There's so much noise and work going on that it's easy to duck my head and blend in with a passing group of Terra, all hurrying towards a staircase leading towards the upper stands with their hands full of cushions. I follow them in silence until they reach the top of the staircase and then quickly slide away from their line and into the shadows once more—taking care to keep my back to the walls as I observe the goings on.

A buzzing of anxiousness and urgency permeates every Terra that passes me, heads bent and eyes focused, as they go about their tasks. After several minutes of searching the arena, I finally spot what I've been looking for. Relief hits me as the top of Niall's fuzzy brunette head comes close enough to nearly pass where I stand against the wall.

Snagging his arm, I quickly slap a palm over his mouth, halting the shout that tries to emerge from him before it can even begin. His eyes widen when he looks back and sees that I'm the culprit who's interrupted his duties.

"Kiera!" He brightens. "Oh, it's good to see you. Are you here for the preparations?"

"Uh ... sort of." I glance around once, ensuring that no one has noticed the two of us before I drag him after me, down the nearby stairwell and back into the darkened tunnel entrance. "Actually, I came for something else," I admit once we're alone.

Niall blinks his innocent eyes up at me as his brow furrows in confusion. Guilt pangs in my chest at having dragged him into my plans. Sure, it's just information seeking, but if he gets into trouble because of me, then it'll only work against me in the long run. Seeking out attention is not good, but from the way everyone—from the Dark-havens to the Terra—is acting, then these battles are a rather important part of the Academy and it's strange enough that Regis hadn't informed me.

"Are you feeling sick?" Niall asks. "Is that why you've just arrived?"

I shake my head. "No, I'm not sick," I tell him. "I'm confused—what's going on?"

This time, when Niall blinks at me it's out of surprise. "You weren't informed about the battles?" he asks. "Maeryn told me to expect them. I'd assumed your Masters had told you."

"No, they didn't," I say. But of course, it shouldn't come as any surprise. If it's something they're responsible for telling me, they don't. Just like they hadn't given me their class supplies until *after* I'd been caned in front of their class.

"Oh dear." Niall lifts one hand to his mouth and bites down on his thumbnail as he looks to the ground before lifting his gaze back to me. He drops his hand once more and sighs. "Apparently, the Mortal God students in advanced classes are required to participate in one-on-one battles once a semester," he explains. "All students and Terra are required to attend unless they've been given special permission."

"Is it such a big deal?" I ask. "And why did no one inform the new Terra?"

"Well, there was a meeting with Dauphine and Hael after the first day of classes ... erm, I remember you weren't there," Niall says hesitantly. Of course I hadn't been. The first day of classes had ended as abruptly for me as it'd begun and I'd slinked back to my room in the north tower after being caned by that pompous bitchy Goddess. If the head Terra had called a meeting, then there's no way I'd been informed. "It wasn't a big meeting, but just the newest Terra were called. We were informed about the battles and a few other things concerning the exams of the students and then we were dismissed. Perhaps, they forgot to inform you since you weren't found in the infirmary."

A curse lingers on the tip of my tongue. This lack of information couldn't be a coincidence, could it? Maybe it's because they know I'm an assassin masquerading as a worshipful Terra, but it feels very suspicious. Had I decided not to go to the Darkhavens and then seek out Niall, where would I be now? Would I even have known enough to come to the arena?

"What happens to Terra who don't show up to watch the battles?" I ask, curious.

Niall's eyes widen and his lips part with a sharp inhalation. "Oh no, please don't try anything, Kiera," he says, mistaking my question for one of intent. "I heard that even Mortal Gods are heavily punished if they have no reason for not being here. I can't bear to think of what they'll do to a Terra."

I hold up a hand as his words come out in a rush and he reaches for me. "I wasn't asking because I don't plan on coming," I assure him. "It was just curiosity." And now, more than a suspicion. I clap Niall on the shoulder and force a pleasant smile. "Don't worry about it. Of course I'll be there."

He holds his hands between us, cupping one over the other in an almost prayer-like gesture. "You swear it?" he presses.

"Yes," I say readily with a nod. "I swear. Now, I've taken enough of your time." I turn him towards the end of the tunnel and gently nudge him forward. "Go on with your duties and I'll attend to mine."

Niall takes a couple of steps under my urging but pauses and looks back. His lips are pinched and his gaze visibly mistrusting. I smile wider and wave to reassure him. Though he doesn't say anything, Niall continues to peer back every few feet until he's completely out of sight and only then do I drop the pretense.

Turning away from the direction Niall had gone, I lean back against the tunnel wall and cross my arms over my chest. If Dauphine and Hael were in charge of informing all newbie Terra of the battles, it is entirely possible they'd merely overlooked my absence due to the injury I'd sustained on that first day. However, it's also possible that I'd been left out on purpose to ensure I'd be punished further. The only thing missing from these assumptions is motivation. Why would they do that? Why me?

Whatever the case, I'll have to be even more wary of the people in this Academy—more than just the Mortal God and Gods themselves, but now even mortals pose a threat. All around me, I sense nothing but enemies. When will it ever stop?

CHAPTER 24

KIERA

The Darkhaven brothers show up at noon on the dot, but before they do, at least ninety percent of the Academy populace has already arrived and taken their seats. There's a buzzing of excitement that pulses between the short, stinted silences that echo through the arena as the last of the Terra hurry to finish their duties and get into place.

Turning my head, I scan the crowd noting that Mortal Gods and Divine Beings are separated into their own stands. Instructors—the Gods that aren't presiding over the arena—are collected under a lavish tent with cushions. There are Terra holding bubbly drinks in crystal glasses upon trays. It's as if they're ancient nobles attending a theatrical play versus Gods watching their children getting ready to kill each other.

"Terra." Ruen's sharp bark has me righting my posture as he steps past me out of the entrance at the top of a staircase where I've been waiting since I spotted them enter below.

"Your seats are this way," I reply, pivoting to lead them

towards a row at the very top of the stands across from the Divine Beings' tents. Kalix bounds past me, his long legs eating up the distance with obvious enthusiasm.

There are cushions placed across the stone benches for Mortal Gods and there are Terra that stand at the edges of each one, at the ready for any command. Unlike the Gods, all of whom are pleasantly chattering and placing bets on who will be taking part in today's battles, there are more than a few Mortal Gods who are noticeably agitated and nervous for the start of the event.

Theos is one of them. He's unusually quiet as he bypasses me and takes a seat at the very end of the stone benches alongside his brothers. Ruen sits back and crosses his arms over his massive chest, and I peer down, noticing the small white scars that dot his flesh as his shirtsleeves ride up. Interesting. What must it have taken for a Mortal God of his descent to have maintained those scars considering that anyone with Divine Blood should be able to heal nearly instantaneously? I store that piece of information in the back of my mind for later. Any knowledge is good knowledge. After all, there's no telling, yet, who my actual target could be. For all I know, it very well could be one or all of them. They certainly have the attitudes to make someone crave their deaths, in my opinion.

"Who's presiding?" Kalix leans forward, head lifted up and pointed at the opposite end of the arena where the Gods sit. He doesn't have to squint to see the woman who steps forward at the edge of a stone railing covered in a bright royal green tapestry. His face falls and with a groan, he sits back and sighs. "Ugh, her? That's not fair."

At his side, however, both Theos and Ruen appear to relax. "It's Maladesia," Theos practically breathes out the Goddess' name in relief. I scan the crowd and settle on the

Goddess. She's tall, taller than any woman I've ever met—even more so than Ophelia. Her height is countered by the willowy frame of her body, cloaked in thin sheer white robes. With the sun beating down, shining over the top of her ebony hair, braided in long ropes all around her head, she appears almost like a queen of old. Or she would have, had she been wearing a crown.

Maladesia. I rack my brain for the Goddess, but there are so many. I have no recollection of reading or hearing about her.

"Who is that?" I don't mean to say the question aloud, but somehow it manages to slip free.

Ruen is the one to answer. "Goddess of Praise," he says, keeping his voice low. "She's usually in charge of the younger Mortal Gods. She's instructed most of the students here at some point or another. That combined with her natural inclination for praise will at least ensure that these don't end in death matches."

"It's boring," Kalix complains.

Theos grits his teeth and shoots daggers at his brother through his eyes. I sigh. These three, I swear. They might look like hulking behemoths and have the capacity for murder and slaughtering like any Divine Being, but at the end of the day, I often feel as though I've been put in charge of three fledglings.

Now that the presiding God has been announced, Theos and Ruen appear more excited for the battles. It's as if the black cloud of fear for their friend has been washed way. I watch them out of the corner of my eye as Theos cranes his neck, peering around the stands until he pauses. I follow his gaze, spotting his friend, Darius, and the girl he recommended for advancement as well, Enid, sitting in the lower half of the stands along the left side of the arena. They appear jostled with excitement themselves, talking animatedly to one another. I'm surprised they aren't more concerned.

"Will your recommendations for advancement be in the battles today?" I inquire, curious.

Theos nods sharply. "Yes. All new advancements are required to perform in battles," he answers.

"Is it just the new advancements?" With my hands clasped at the small of my back, I glance over Darius and Enid, trying to spot any nervous Mortal Gods and pick out the ones that already know they'll be fighting today. It's not difficult—at least, for me it's not. I can smell the added bit of excitement and agitation a mile away. Across the arena, seated in a section reserved for the lower Tiers, I spot the girl Niall serves. Her red hair makes her stand out even when it's pulled back sharply away from her face and tied up. I scan her surroundings and find Niall hurrying down the stairs, carrying a tray of drinks.

"No," Theos replies, distracting me. "The Gods don't like boring things, so they'll select previous champions at random and throw them into the ring at will."

"That might not be so true with Maladesia in charge today," Ruen says. "She's more interested in draws and clear winners—the more praise those around her receive, the higher her power."

"The higher her power?" I peer down at him, meeting the midnight color of his eyes as he looks up at me.

"Gods often gain a bit of power from those around them. Strength. Praise. Sex. Axlan is the God of Victory, therefore he feels a bit of an increase in energy when his students win matches—even in class. Demia, the Goddess of Birds, usually has one with her at all times. They are addicts to their own abilities and the longer they feed their need for them, the stronger they are."

My lips part in surprise. How fascinating. Who knew there were still things I didn't yet know about the Gods? I turn my eyes to the arena with a newfound interest. "Then why were you so surprised that the Goddess of Praise would be presiding over the battles today?" I ask.

"Because she's not bloodthirsty," Kalix mutters.

"Not bloodthirsty?" I repeat.

"Battles usually call forth the Gods who prefer to see blood and damage," Theos says. "God of Victory, God of Battle, God of War, God of Pain, God of Strategy—we expected any of them. Not the Goddess of Praise."

I consider that for a moment. It makes sense, I suppose. The less violent Gods likely would have no interest in watching their children fight each other. Then again, I wonder if there is a God who lacks any sort of violence. There must be a God out there whose power stems from peace or tranquility. Would they be here, though? On this mortal plane where everything is chaos? Doubtful.

A pity, I suppose. Mortals could use more peace and tranquility. Perhaps even the Mortal Gods could use it too.

A horn sounds, echoing across the arena and silencing the chattering crowd in an instant. "It's starting," Theos mutters, leaning forward, his gaze fixed across the arena on his friend. As if instinctively influenced by those around me, my heart rate speeds up and I, too, find myself locked onto both Darius and the Goddess that stands at the helm of the arena. We wait with bated breath.

"Greetings, students!" Maladesia calls across the arena, her voice ringing out with clarity despite the distance. There must be some sort of Divine artifact she's using to do so. "Welcome to this semester's battle arena!"

A cheer echoes up from the students with hands and fists being thrown into the air. The Goddess smiles and allows the interruption for a moment before once again, holding up her hands and silencing them.

"As all of our newly advanced students make their way to the arena, we will have a word from our Academy's dean, Dolos."

As she speaks, a shadow at her back moves forward, slithering to the front of the railing that separates the presiding Gods from the rest. A man steps from that shadow and takes her place. Maladesia bows slightly at the waist and shuffles to the side for him to address the crowd now held enrapt by his sudden presence. I stiffen, my chest growing tight as I swallow against a lump in my throat.

"Shit." Theos' quiet curse tells me all I need to know. This God is not well-liked.

"Welcome all," Dolos announces. His face is sharp, almost skeletal. His eyes are sunken back into his head with shadows that stroke down the sides of his face, strengthening the image of a skeleton covered in the thinnest of skin. Blood rushes through my ears. My breathing comes faster. "It's such a pleasure to see you all here," Dolos continues.

A heavy weight falls upon my shoulders and back and several beads of sweat pop up along my spine. The sound of his voice fades into the background as my blood rushes faster and faster and my heartbeat takes over. Ice slips over my limbs. Vomit threatens to spill forth. I swallow and swallow again, tasting rot and bile. *What. The. Fuck.*

Fingers latch onto my wrist, burning hot. "Calm down." I hear the command but I can't follow it. My stomach churns, threatening to expel everything it contains—including the organ itself.

Distantly, I can hear the God still talking, but whatever words he is saying never reach my ears. The hand on my wrist is like a manacle and yet, a soft thumb strokes over my racing pulse. "Almost done," the deeply masculine voice says. "Hold it in a bit more."

I'm going to pass out. Shit. I've not done that since I was a fledgling would-be assassin, and even then, it was only after days of harsh training. One breath. Two. Three. I keep breathing, focusing on the action to keep myself from running. Invisible chains wrap around my body, choking me.

Then, as quickly as the strange sensations had come, they disappear. I blink and realize I'm on the ground with my knees pressed into the stone steps. Sweat pours down my forehead and temples. Blinking furiously, I lift my head and peer around. Shockingly enough, many Mortal Gods appear uncomfortable, their faces leached of all color, and more than a few Terra who've passed out.

"You handled that surprisingly well." The voice comes from the one sitting at my side whose fingers still grip my wrist.

I lift my head to find that Ruen and Theos have switched places. Ruen's eyes, the same color of the night sky, meet mine briefly and I'm held spellbound, captive in both his gaze and his grip. Quickly yanking my hand away, he surprises me further by releasing me immediately. "What..." I try to catch my breath. "What *was* that?"

"That"—Ruen turns back to the arena—"was Dolos, God of Imprisonment."

God of Imprisonment? What the fuck was that power? I gasp for more air, but no matter how much I breathe, I feel as though I can't get enough.

"It's normal," Ruen says, answering my unspoken question on why the fuck I'm feeling as if I've been weighted down by heavy chains until they nearly crushed me.

I glance at him sharply and his lips twitch. Is that amusement? From *him*? A shocker.

"To feel like I'm choking to death?" I demand.

He bites down on his lip and I narrow my eyes. I swear to the Gods, if he smiles right now...

I don't finish the thought. "Yes," he replies. "Dolos carries a heavy curse with his abilities. He's usually seen shrouded in his own shadow to keep those around him from falling to their knees, but his ability pertains to imprisonment. Anyone in his presence feels as though they've been chained up and bound by him. He rarely shows himself."

"I can see why." Once again the words slip free before I can think better of it. Of course a God of Imprisonment would be a dean at one of the Mortal Gods Academies since this is little more than a prison to watch the spawn of the Divine Beings. How obvious of them.

"I would be careful about what you say," Ruen says quietly, looking around pointedly as I finally climb back to my shaking legs. It irritates me that he doesn't seem that impressed by Dolos' ability.

"Why don't you feel it?" I demand.

Ruen arches a brow at me. "Who said I don't?"

My upper lip pulls back. "You don't seem to."

He shrugs and gestures to Theos and Kalix, both of whom also seem unaffected. In fact, the two appear rather bored as Maladesia retakes her place and continues with her speech. "We've met him a time or two," Ruen says. "The more you're exposed to his power, the less it takes effect. You get used to the feeling of being restrained when that's all you've ever known."

His words give me pause. I turn towards him and narrow my gaze. It hadn't really occurred to me before now that they would understand their own restrictions, but perhaps I was wrong. Ruen doesn't return my attention and refocuses on the arena as the first fighters are announced.

"So..." I hedge, "you seem unaffected because you're experienced?"

Still, he doesn't look at me, even as he responds. "We've all been down there at one point or another," he says. "And we've all met Dolos. The Gods have made our standing among them quite clear." He gestures to the arena. "After all, it's not like you'll see one of *them* down there, fighting for their lives."

The bitterness that encompasses that 'them' comment doesn't go unnoticed. "Fighting for their lives?" I repeat.

"What happens to the fighters—regardless of whether or not they win—is ultimately up to the God presiding. If it's Maladesia, then it's likely they're not going to die. Were it a different God ... however..." He lets the statement fall off, but it doesn't matter. I understand what he means.

The Darkhavens seem viscerally aware of their standing amongst the Gods and the fact that they're prisoners to their whims just like mortals. While Kalix might seem to take joy in the blood of battle, the other two understand that they can't always be in control, and that, more than anything, pisses them off.

I was under the impression these three were simply spoiled assholes, but from this, I catch a glimpse of more than I ever expected. They care more about their fellow Mortal Gods than they let on. Well, Ruen and Theos do, at least.

We've all been down there at one point or another. Ruen's

statement resonates inside my head. Does that also mean, at one point or another, they've all had to kill to survive?

The question leaves me feeling a strange sense of unease in my chest. I reach up and press my palm between my breasts, rubbing at the sore spot. If that's true then that means the three of them are far more like me than I care to admit.

I don't like it. Not at all.

I ronically, the battles remind me of home. Or what home has been to me for the last decade. Opponents are given weapons—swords, bows and arrows, daggers—whatever their specialty seems to be, and then pushed into the center of the arena to fight.

Even if Maladesia isn't as bloodthirsty as the Mortal Gods had expected of the presiding God, she doesn't stop the fights from turning into real battles. Arrows fly—stabbing into guts and arms and sometimes even eyes. The warrior-like cries of those in the ring echo up to the stands, inciting the masses to scream in encouragement as students and Gods alike place bets on who will win.

There's a hollow emptiness in my stomach as I watch. It's almost as if seeing the Mortal Gods go after each other with the same intensity of weary assassins in training becomes tedious to me. I stand on my platform, hands clasped behind my back as the Darkhavens watch in near silence. The only one who makes any sort of noise is Kalix, who yells and hollers like an annoyed animal when fighters falter or slip or drop their weapons.

All around the arena, Terra stand at the ready, some with trays of drinks and others just watching the fights. Once again, I catch a glimpse of Niall standing alongside the girl from several days ago—his Mortal God, Maeryn. I blink as I finally realize the clothes she's wearing. Gone is the ultra-feminine princess-like lady from before, and in her place sits a neutral-faced woman, dressed in a sea foam green tunic and dark trousers that mold to her lower frame.

Why? Almost as soon as I ask myself the question, I understand. She's dressed that way in case she's called upon to fight. That realization slams into me and causes me to jerk my head up, roving over the crowd of Mortal Gods seated in the arena. All of them, every single one, are dressed similarly. In trousers. In tunics. In clothes that will be easier to fight in. The frown that twitches at my lips is one of reluctant sympathy.

Every once in a while, Niall will flinch at something that happens within the arena—an arm getting sliced off or a spurt of blood from a fighter's abdomen—and Maeryn will lean towards him, gently patting his hand in a way I don't expect. He should be grateful. Of all the Mortal Gods, Niall managed to get one that seems closer to that of a mortal sympathizer than a true God's daughter.

A horn blares, announcing the end of the latest battle, and two Terra jog out onto the now bloodied field, lifting the losing Mortal God who groans as blood pours from the open wounds on his leg and shoulder. They half carry, half drag the body away, struggling under the weight of the big-boned Mortal God. The winner, a lithe Enid, stands and holds her hands up, sword and all, with joy.

"She did well," Ruen murmurs absently.

Without turning my head, I glance towards him out of my periphery. His brow is scrunched inward, but he blows out a breath that seems relieved. "She got lucky," Theos replies. "Her footwork was simply better than his."

"At least she didn't have to kill," Ruen reminds him.

Not this time, I silently amend. I have to admit, as much as I despise the Gods, they are clever beings. These battles are madness incarnate, but there is a method to it.

Separating their children and pitting them against one another. I can see it clearly—their reasoning for taking their half-mortal children and placing them within this very structured system. Gods develop these Mortal Gods to their specifications and allow for no outside interventions to interrupt their careful training. Then they put them into the ring and watch as their own children fight for survival.

Cruelty—thy name is Divinity.

"Terra," Kalix calls, distracting me momentarily.

I lean forward. "Yes?"

"Get me a drink," he says, waving a hand. "I'm bored."

I repress my irritation and give him a smile. "Of course." Turning towards the back of the stands, I walk up the staircase to the spread that several Terra are currently standing alongside. I grab a crystal glass from one of the Terra holding trays, offering them a bittersweet smile of sympathy at their plight. Unlike the Mortal Gods and Gods, we, the Terra, have been on our feet for hours.

When I return to the Darkhavens, I bend and offer the glass to Kalix. Instead of taking it, however, he shoves my hand away and leans forward, his eyes lighting up in a way they haven't since the battles started.

"Sir?"

"Fuck." Ruen's dark curse has me jerking my head to the side as I see Maladesia turned and talking to someone behind her—someone shadowed. I stiffen immediately. Dolos?

"They're changing the presiding Gods," Kalix's tone is ripe with frenzied excitement and I can see why. He's right.

I watch as Maladesia says something and then bows her head, stepping back and allowing for Dolos to step forward. This time, however, he doesn't release his shadow—a blessing I hate to view as such, but I don't know if I could handle the pressure of his unshadowed presence again so soon. The glass in my hand lowers to my side, but before it can reach my hips, Theos' hand reaches out and snatches it from my grip.

Startled, I release it to his grasp and stare in disbelief as he puts the rim to his lips and downs the liquid in a sharp swallow. "Kalix Darkhaven." The sound of Dolos' deep baritone echoes across the arena and then a second name. "Deva Carlona."

"Yes!" Kalix practically leaps from his seat.

Theos squeezes the glass in his hand as it slowly lowers back to his side until the damn thing cracks. "They've never switched in the middle of the battles before," he snaps, turning to glare at Ruen.

Ruen is silent, but from the hard expression on his face, he is just as caught off guard by this sudden turn of events. Kalix shoves people out of his way as he practically crawls over the seats in front of him to make his way to the stairs, bounding down instead of taking the circular route at the top. Once he reaches the very bottom, he grips the tapestry-covered railings and heaves himself up and over, dropping down onto the blood-soaked dirt below.

The Divine Beings across the arena lean forward with interest. "Is there a problem?" I ask the two remaining Darkhavens. "I thought you said you'd all participated in these battles before?"

"We have," Ruen snaps. "Kalix will be fine—he enjoys them after all—but now that they've changed Gods..."

I see his meaning almost immediately. With Dolos now the presiding God, things are likely to take a quick change. "They called on him for a reason," Theos growls. "Kalix is a monster in the arena. Anyone left to fight will be fighting death battles."

And Darius has yet to go.

I straighten my back. More and more, I'm finding that these Mortal Gods are little more than better prey for the predators known as Gods. This is all a facade. The Academy is nothing more than a prison for these Divine children. Mortal Gods are just enough of a threat to the Gods for them to take advantage of them. This place is little more than an asylum of pseudo-education. At the top, the Gods reign supreme, and at the bottom, humans are left to pick up the scraps they leave behind.

THE NOISE amidst the stands is deafening as Kalix takes center stage—striding across the ground until he reaches the middle and stops. Dolos maintains the shroud of shadows that keep his ability repressed enough for the rest of us in the arena to watch the proceedings. The one called Deva steps forward—a particularly buff woman, wide all around with a masculine face. Only her name and the slight curve of her breasts as they press against her leather tunic reveal her to be female.

At my side, both Theos and Ruen recline back—unbothered by the fact that their brother is in the arena for a death match. It doesn't take long to find out why. The battle begins without Kalix holding a single weapon. Instead, he crouches into a stance I find familiar. He should be holding a sword of some sort. Instead, he merely tips his head back and grins at his opponent. A wicked light enters his green eyes, blurring the color as the two begin to circle each other. I'm locked upon him, unable to pull my attention away.

In the crowd, hands exchange paper denza. Cries and demands rise up from both Mortal Gods and Gods alike. Kalix's green eyes morph, shifting to red and back. Over and over again, as he circles his enemy. For her own part, Deva appears wary of him. Smart. I would be too if a man such as him entered an arena for a death match weaponless and yet still maintained that same confident air about him.

I blink as something out of the corner of my eye moves. I jerk my head to the side, fixating my gaze on the ground at Kalix's feet. It moves. No, it moves *again*. That was what had caught my attention. The dirt pushes up and then depresses as if something beneath it is crawling under the surface.

Deva releases a war cry and dives for Kalix, wielding a massive sword that requires two hands just to lift it. Metal glints as the sun shines off the smooth surface of the side of the blade. A ray of light slams into my eyes, and I flinch back, momentarily distracted.

When the sudden light leaves and I return my attention to the field, Kalix has deftly maneuvered out of Deva's path of destruction. In fact, he's standing with his hands on his hips, laughing as she screams and whirls about to face him once more. It's as if he's a great big animal who's captured a tiny little mouse and he's playing with her before he kills her. The brutal delight on his face makes me shudder.

I want to look away, but I can't. All else blurs around me as I fixate directly on the man standing in the center of everything. And as if he senses my thoughts, Kalix's head turns ever so slightly and his green eyes meet mine. His lips part and as he smiles, his twin canines extend downward in a way I've never seen before. The black of his pupils cut into slits. Just as the ground beneath his feet had moved, something beneath his flesh does as well.

Scales glimmer on his cheek and down his throat. A warning. The last one.

This time as Deva dives for him, Kalix doesn't move. His arms snap out, both at the same time. One grips her wrist and the other wraps around her thick throat. Without even a second between, Kalix jerks the hand around her wrist down and snaps it cleanly—the break echoing off the stone walls of the arena as the crowd hushes.

Deva screams again, only this scream is filled with pain rather than the rage of battle. It's ghostly in my ears, vibrating along the inner walls of my head. He's going to kill her. Even if he had a choice not to, the look in his eyes as he stares back at me tells me he would do it still.

Why? I want to ask him. She's just like him. A Mortal God. Should they not be on the same side? Should he not at least show some remorse for being forced to end someone else's life?

I've learned to hide my remorse—or at the very least bury it in a place that I can rarely reach. That was by necessity. For Kalix, though, it doesn't seem to exist at all.

His smirk remains in place as the sword falls from his enemy's hand. He drops her and as she clutches her broken limb to her chest, Kalix bends down and lifts the heavy broadsword. One hand, a sign of strength. The crowd roars, going wild.

"Damn it," Theos mutters. "He's going to end it too soon. The Gods won't be pleased."

"He's too excited," Ruen agrees.

"Why?" I can't stop the question even if I wanted to. It makes no sense. Ripping my gaze from the arena, I turn to face them. "Why does he enjoy it so much?"

Theos presses his lips together for a moment. "Why does anyone enjoy anything?" he snaps, a clear non-answer.

"Does it have anything to do with your God parent?" The second I ask the question, I know I've made a mistake. Ruen yanks his head to the side and fixes me with a scowl so dark and thunderous that I feel my chest tighten in response—almost as if he's using an ability similar to that of Dolos.

Before he can say anything, however, Theos reaches over and grabs ahold of his arm. "Don't," he warns, "cause a scene."

With a growl, Ruen rips himself free of Theos' grip and stands abruptly. He shoves past me and I'm left gaping after him in a mixture of shock and annoyance. Ruen's stride is short and clipped, but as he stomps off I note several Terra practically tripping over themselves to get out of his way.

Once Ruen is gone, Theos sighs and gestures for me to sit alongside him. I blink and stare at the cushion before dragging my gaze back up and looking around at all of the Terra standing. None are sitting. Theos' shoulders drop and he fixes me with an irritated look.

"Either sit or kneel," he snaps.

"I'd rather kneel," I say. At least, that way, it won't be nearly as attention-drawing as being on the same level as the other Mortal Gods.

He points at his side and I go to one knee alongside the stone benches. Carefully, Theos leans forward and drops his voice. "If you know what's good for you, Terra," he says, "you won't ask about our God parent again."

My lips part, another response and question on my tongue. Before it breaks free, several Mortal Gods jerk to their feet, shouting in glee, and I, too, find myself standing abruptly, my eyes fixed back on the arena.

Kalix stands there, coated in a spray of blood that extends from his throat down his tunic. He holds the head of Deva by the hair as blood drips in long strings to the ground beneath him. The remains of his opponent's body are sprawled across the ground, the severed part of her spine clearly visible through the gore as it sticks out of her cleanly sliced neck.

I sigh. The sound of Terra vomiting reaches my ears. I don't look over at Niall, but I hope he's turned his eyes away from the sight below.

"This," Theos says, calling me to turn my head towards him again, "is what you can expect from the Academy." The eyes he settles on his brother are both deadened and tormented. "He is violent entertainment and the Gods love him for it."

"They love him because he'll kill at their behest?"

"They love him because they *think* he'll kill at their behest," Theos clarifies. "And he feeds on it."

A hum settles in my throat as I face forward once more to watch as Kalix carries the head of Deva to the tent of the Gods. He holds it up for them, prompting many to smile and cheer. Several others, no doubt anti-betters, grumble. Kalix tosses the head upward and then catches it, like a cat playing with a toy.

"The winner is Kalix Darkhaven," Dolos announces. "Next fighters, take your places. Corillo Irritas and Darius Moxbane."

Darius. The newly announced name has me glancing at Theos' expression as it hardens into one that could've been carved from stone. He touches his jawline, the lightest tremor shaking his fingers as he leans back and crosses his legs. Even as Kalix leaves the arena—walking out of the tunnel beneath the Gods instead of returning the same way he dropped below—the savagery of the crowd doesn't diminish.

As the body of Deva is dragged out to make way for the next fight, the arena rumbles with noise in such a way that makes it feel as if the stone beneath us is shaking. Even if I don't particularly care for these Darkhavens, I know that I would not be any different than Theos were I in his position and Regis in Darius'.

It would have been easier for us both if we weren't so intrinsically aware that death is easy to come by when you're surrounded by the fervor of Divine violence.

CHAPTER 26

THEOS

The cries and cheers of the crowd fade from my hearing as the sole of my attention fixates on the man who steps out of the tunnel. Darius stands tall, a sleeveless leather tunic strapped to his chest and back. The muscles in his arms bulge with each stride and he lifts his head, turning it from side to side, eyes focused on the stands. He's searching for me.

I grit my teeth and force myself to remain still. I don't lift my eyes to the Gods across from me and I don't call Darius' attention to me. At my side, I can sense the Terra's curiosity. Fuck, I wish that Kalix hadn't been called down there. The ground is bathed in Deva's blood and even if it'll quickly dry under the heat of the sun, the stench is no doubt prickling at Darius' senses.

I clasp my hands in front of myself and drop them down between my spread knees. Maladesia was the perfect presider, but she was a red herring. I should have known. Finally, after what feels like a lifetime, I raise my head and peer across the arena to the tents shading the Gods watching this unholy performance.

It's an unholy display of power—one they revel in. I can pick out several of them who are grinning as Darius lifts his arms and several of our classmates—his friends—cheer. The stupid lot of them are so spellbound by their own blood that they think of this farce as an honor. My spine straightens and I sit up taller as a shadow reappears behind the Terra. Ruen stands on the platform with a dark look on his face—Kiera's earlier curiosity forgotten.

I'm half surprised he's returned so quickly, but thankful regardless as he takes a seat back at my side. "He'll be fine." Ruen's words are ones that I want to hear, but they don't ring with the same confidence I'm used to from him.

"I should've let you train him more," I mutter, cursing my own arrogance.

"He's strong," Ruen replies. It's not a confirmation, but it may as well be one.

We both know that between us, Ruen is the better teacher. The only reason I even insisted was because of who Darius is. I close my eyes again. If he dies...

The rising tide of my emotions gives way to power. It crackles along my spine and flows in my blood. Something shifts beneath the surface of my skin, like lightning coming alive and given a physical body. A hard, too warm hand settles on my shoulder. It should hurt. With just that singular touch, Ruen should feel the effects of my Divinity coursing through him and shattering apart his defenses.

But Ruen doesn't react to it. His knowledge of pain allows him to suck it all up and swallow it into himself, negating the reaction that should occur. "Don't let them see." His whisper is practically nonexistent. It's spoken so low that the next wave of the crowd's screams as the second opponent makes their way into the arena nearly makes it impossible to hear.

I don't have to ask who he's referring to. We're always aware of our *Masters*. Always watching. Always waiting. The muscles over my back ache and stretch from past reminders of our disobedience. Before me, Darius lifts his sword from the sheath on his back, his naturally slitted and narrow eyes growing ever more hooded as he circles Corillo Irritas—the one he'll have to kill if he wants to make it out alive.

Corillo has already killed. He's been in this arena at least once before. Were this training, I'd say he'd be a good match for Darius. But this is not training. For the two of them, this is life and death and Corillo already knows what's at stake in the most visceral way.

The scene before me fades, growing farther and farther away as I'm cast backward in time, to the very moment I realized that we—my brothers and I—found the inevitability of our existence.

"What is it?"

"Alive, I think."

"That's not what I meant, dumbass."

The voices fade in and out, growing louder one moment and then so quiet that I start to wonder if they're a figment of my imagination. That would be just the thing, wouldn't it? Alone for so long, locked in this dark place, and somehow mad with the yearning for something—someone—else to join me.

No one wants to be alone in the dark.

The door to my prison creaks open and a light penetrates the shadows. After so long, the adjustment it takes is painful. Unfortunately for me, even a dim light is too much of a kindness. No, instead, this light is blinding and the only thing that blocks it are the two figures that stand in the doorway.

"Did you know he was here?"

"The Gods knew," someone else says, but otherwise there's no answer to the first question that sounds as if it comes from a boy my age.

"Of course they knew, but this facility is only for the God children that don't present with powers. He obviously—" There's a grunt as if someone punched the speaker and stopped them from continuing. The only sound after is that of shifting bodies. A shrug? A shake of a head? Perhaps. I blink against the blinding light, trying to see the ones who've found me.

A hand hovers in front of my face, waving back and forth. "Hey, can you hear me?" Before I can answer, the boy asks another question. "Can you talk?"

Lifting my head back away from the knees that are drawn up to my scrawny chest, I stare blearily as a third figure joins the first two. The head of the newcomer finally blocks out the worst of the light, leaning between the others' frames.

My eyes slowly adjust to the light after several seconds and I peer at the ones who've discovered me. Sunken eyes but a bright smile. Long neck and even longer, wild hair cast all around his face, the third and final boy before me reaches between the other two and goes onto his knees in front of me.

"Hey, are you okay?"

Can you hear me? Can you talk? What's wrong with you? Why are you so useless? What's the point of spawn if they don't show talent or promise? All of those questions, I've been asked. Never before has anyone asked if I was okay, though.

My eyes burn and I dip my head back to my knees as trembling overtakes me. "No." I choke the word out. "No, I'm not."

My response is met with silence, long and aching. Finally, the boy's warmth grows closer and I feel arms close around me. "It's okay," he says. "You don't have to be."

Softness. Kindness. Gentleness. These are not things I know well, but I recognize them instantly. Even if the arms circling me are skinny and young, it doesn't matter. The fact that someone would let me be not okay, that someone would hug me to their body, sharing their warmth and existence after so long ... it brings all of the emotions buried inside to the forefront. It shatters the barrier I've built for as long as I've been stuck in this hovel of a room.

I cry and I cry hard. The tears come, and yet, the boy never lets go. He merely hugs me tighter, trying to put as much strength in his little arms as he can. As if just by will alone he could keep me from shattering apart. His care is so sweet, so unusual to me, that I don't have the heart to tell him he's hugging an already broken person. For fear that he'll stop if I don't respond, I find myself hugging him back and burying my face in his shoulder.

After an eternity of tears and sniffling, the boy finally pulls back and I glance away from him to the two still standing sentinel outside the doorway. They've turned their bodies to shield me from the light, and for some reason—as the taller of the two peers back—I have a feeling it was also for another reason. One just as kind as the hug I received.

"Are you better now?" the boy in front of me asks as he pulls back and stares down into my face.

I'm not, but I don't want to disappoint him. I nod. "I-I'm sorry."

His smile is easy. "Don't be," he says, shaking his head.

The two others turn back to us. "I don't mean to interrupt, but we need to know if we have the right kid," the taller says. "What's your name?"

"Th-Theos." My name is a croak. It's been so long since I've had anyone to talk to besides myself that my voice is nearly nonexistent.

The boys still standing exchange a look. The one in front of me sits back on his heels. "Do you know who your God parent is?"

Something foul fills my mouth with a horrid taste. Bile. My stomach churns and the face of my father is ever present in my mind. I nod and then turn my gaze to the hard floor. It's covered in dust and grime; the only changes come from the semi-clean scrapes in the dust where trays of food were shoved beneath the door and then retracted on a string.

The tall boy kneels next to the third. "I'm sorry to ask if it brings up bad memories, but we need to know," he says. "Who is your God parent?"

"Azai." The name brings with it a host of unwelcome emotions. Vile, cruel emotions. Anger. Hate. Fear.

There's a brief moment of silence and the first boy, the one with naturally slitted eyes, sighs. "He's yours then," he says.

"Whose?" I glance between them, but neither of them answers. Instead, the answer comes from the final boy.

"You're ours," he says, green eyes glittering down as he stands over us. Unlike the other two, his face is void of emotion. In fact, he looks almost bored—as if he could be anywhere else in the world and it wouldn't matter to him. "You're the one we've been looking for. Azai's called you. We're going to the Academy now. It's time to leave this place."

"Leave?" I repeat the word. I'll be allowed out? "Even if I'm not powerful?" I ask.

The kid snorts. "Not powerful? What makes you think that?"

I scowl at him and point to the area around me. "Non-talents are put here," I say. If he's like me then he should know that. God children without powers are little more than stupid mortals.

"Yeah, well, there was a mistake," the green-eyed kid replies. "You aren't a non-talent."

Why would he say that? A fresh wave of anger pours through me. Does he not know how long I've wished to be powerful, to have Divinity? If I had that then I wouldn't have been locked up here in the first place.

Placing one hand on the wall of the small closet-like room I've known for too long, I struggle to stand up on my own feet and find myself at the same height as him. The anger consumes me from the soles of my feet to the tips of my fingers, but all this bastard does is smile at me.

"You're a liar!" I scream at him. Why is he trying to give me false hope? What could he gain from tormenting me like that?

"No, he's not." The second boy stands to his full height, towering over us both. Eyes like black night with only a hint of the deepest ocean stare down at me. "We've come for you because we felt you, Theos. You're not lacking in power. You've been calling to us in our dreams."

"Your dreams?" What could he mean by that? All of my dreams were fantasies. Calling nameless and faceless friends to keep me company in this dark place. They weren't real.

"Yes, Theos." The first boy moves forward and offers a wan smile. Now that I've revealed my name and my father's name, he doesn't seem as warm, but he still tries to maintain a pleasant smile on his face. "You're one of Azai's sons and so are they. By God law, you'll be transferred to the Academy where Mortal Gods like us will be taught to control our abilities."

"They are?" I look over at the green- and blue-eyed boys before turning back to the one in front of me. "You are my brothers?"

He stiffens before shaking his head. "Sorry, not me. Just them."

I frown. Then why is he here?

As if he senses my thoughts, the boy gives another, feeble smile. "You called me into your dreams too," he answers. "We *weren't sure—and neither were the Gods—if you would belong to them or me."*

"Why would I belong to you?" I ask. If we weren't related then how could I possibly have called him from my dreams?

"We share abilities," he says. "Not blood."

"Dreams?" I clarify.

He nods. "Bloodline doesn't distinguish abilities," he says. "I'd hoped that we could ... I don't have any siblings, but..." His head dips and the feeling of disappointment wafts from him as if it were an actual scent I could inhale.

"This is a good thing," the green-eyed boy says suddenly. "It means you'll be stronger than him."

"Kalix." The blue-eyed one snaps the boy's name, his tone ripe with irritation and chastisement.

"What?" Kalix demands with a shrug. "It's true. No offense, Darius."

Darius—the one who hugged me—chuckles slightly. "It's fine." He shakes his head and then proceeds to hold his hand out for me. "We might not be blood brothers, but we can be friends."

I take his hand. "Friends?" I've never had friends before. Not real ones, anyway.

His expression softens and he closes his fingers over mine, tugging me out of the prison room I've been in and into the light. The fresh scent of cool air slaps me in the face. "Yeah," he says, "friends."

"THEOS!" Ruen's sharp tone jerks me out of the old memory of the day I'd been freed from the prison of failed God children. My eyes refocus on the scene before me and I find that I've missed at least half of the battle.

Darius is covered in bleeding wounds and weaponless as he races away from his opponent, diving down as a dagger comes flying at him from behind, he slides into the dirt and turns, jumping up before he can be pinned. My heart thunders in my chest. Where is his sword? I search the grounds for it and spot the handle sticking out where the blade is piercing a crack in the stone walls of the arena.

Kalix and Ruen had never been as close to Darius as I'd remained to him when we'd entered the Academy, but the tightness of Ruen's frame next to mine speaks of his own concern. My hands clench into fists as I lean forward, unable to stop myself from becoming enrapt by the scene before us.

Darius turns and faces his enemy, releasing a howl that's more animal than man. He dives forward, ducking down and narrowly missing the slice of another dagger. Instead, he and his enemy go into the dirt, Darius taking the lead as he grips Corillo's wrist and snaps it back. A shout follows, Darius quickly and deftly plucking the dagger from Corillo's grip.

He sets it to the Mortal God's throat and slices through. I'm shaking, the sounds of the crowd coming back to me all at once louder than ever before. Vomit threatens to spill forth.

He won. Oh, thank the ... well, not the fucking Gods. They're the ones who put him there, but the relief coursing through my veins, filling my bones, is so heavy I could collapse under the weight of it.

"*Wait.*"

I jerk my head back as Kiera steps off the platform beside our seats. Her gaze is heavily focused on the fight with a pinch in her lips as she frowns. Her eyes are squinted. Whatever food remains in my stomach from this morning curdles and turns sour as I jerk my head back to the arena.

No. I see it before it happens. Darius arms are wide, his face lit with triumph. The Mortal God beneath him holds his throat, blood pouring between his fingers—his face tight with pain and rage. I jump to my feet.

"Darius!" The scream comes too late. Fire erupts from the Mortal God's fingers and shoots upward, searing a path up Darius' body and right through his head.

The cheers halt and the crowd goes silent. Ruen curses and grabs hold of me, but it's too late. Darius' body jerks, goes still, and a moment later, he slumps over. Even from here, though, I can see the wide hole at the back of his head, seared at the edges of his charcoal colored hair. Blood. Brains. Lifeless. Limp. The winner chokes out one last breath and then he, too, collapses back against the ground, shaking once, twice, three times before a wheeze of breath escapes him.

Dead.

They're *both* dead.

"Shit." My head turns as if on a pike to see Kalix now standing a few feet behind Kiera, staring down the stands into the arena as a few Terra jog across the ground to take away the bodies of the fallen. "I never expected that."

No. None of us had. Numbly, I turn to look at Kiera. Her expression collapses into emptiness as she turns and meets my gaze.

How did she?

CHAPTER 27

KIERA

There is a hunger inside of me following the death of the Mortal God known as Darius. A hunger for knowledge and understanding. For retribution. Though I didn't know the Mortal God, just as I felt the sense of injustice for the family back in Mineval, the same emotion swarms me. The wrongness of this action cannot be denied, and yet ... it is.

I'm confused by my own emotions. As I'd watched the battle, my heart had raced in my chest. I'd found myself leaning forward, silently critiquing his skills and unwittingly praying for his safety. Turning my head, I scan the arena, starting with the students. There's an air of tension that I recall similarly from that market in Mineval. It's filled with a slow, quiet seething of malfeasance.

Curiously, I set my sights on the tents of the Gods. Several are laughing and chattering away. Few are actually watching the arena now as the bodies of Darius and Corillo are dragged out of sight. I want to ask what happens to them after this, but now is certainly not the time.

It did not—certainly could not—escape my notice that

he meant something to the Darkhaven brothers, especially Theos. As he and his opponent's bodies are dragged out of the arena by red-faced and struggling Terra, Ruen gently urges Theos back down into his seat. Kalix steps past me and takes his position at Theos' side—as if there is a silent connection between the three of them and Kalix knows that, despite his win, he needs to be mindful of his siblings.

I've never known what it's like to have siblings, but Regis comes to mind as my only example. It's clear from the pallor of Theos' skin and the faraway look in his eyes as he faces forward once more that he's distraught. Loss. Grief. It rolls off of him in painful, silent waves. Regis once said I was a bleeding heart, and now I think he was right. I never expected to feel sorry, to feel empathy for another of my kind, but that's exactly what this is. Understanding. Sorrow. Repressed rage and, as much as I wish I could deny it, compassion.

From that moment on, the rest of the day's battles pass in a blur of furious action, some cheering, and many more deaths. Over and over again. Mortal Gods are placed before each other, pitted against one another like animals fighting for survival, and this more than anything thus far makes me realize the truth of it all. They *are* animals fighting for survival.

Neither Ruen nor Theos is called upon to fight, and thus the two of them, plus Kalix, stay silent and watch the following fights with stoic and unbothered expressions. Even Kalix's earlier excitement has waned. He seems more bored than before. Tired, even. A yawn stretches his mouth wide as the final battle is called to an end when one Mortal God slices through her opponent's neck with a sharp sword, decapitating the man in a spray of blood.

Night falls and sconces have been lit all around,

throwing hideous shadows across the stained ground and the stone walls by the time the Gods call a halt to the battles. Dolos steps back and allows Maladesia to take to the platform once again. Her words are drowned out by the thumping pulse of my blood as I turn my gaze to my wards.

The Darkhavens have their eyes fixed on a point far away, and they don't react or even move a muscle until the beings around them begin to rise from their seats. Only when that happens do they seem to come back to themselves.

Theos stands up from his seat and shoves past Ruen, nearly crashing into me in his haste to leave. He doesn't look back. Quickly stepping to the side, I narrowly miss colliding with others as they part to make way for him—as if they can all sense the cloud of darkness that now surrounds him. I stare after him and I'm not the only one.

The silence from his absence is loud, echoing all around us. His brothers ... and me.

All around me, the children of the Gods slowly make their way out of the stands, giving the remaining Darkhavens a wide berth. All around me, I hear their voices, some softer and some louder than others. They are not human. They are not Gods. Yet, they are ... alive. They exist in a place between the two and, suddenly, they have my sympathy. They are not immune to emotion or loss because of the privilege in which they were raised the way I once assumed.

Loathe as I am to admit it, they are far more like me than I ever wanted to see. If I am able to feel pain and sorrow and hope, then, no doubt, they do too. For Theos ... I wonder what this loss will mean to him.

Already, I know it's an important one. Perhaps something, too, that will change the course of his life. I don't know what Darius meant to him, but it's clear his brothers do and their silence speaks volumes.

Pity, it seems, comes in many different flavors, and right now, it has the familiar taste of mourning.

"What do we do now?" Kalix asks, directing his attention to Ruen.

Ruen's gaze follows after Theos, a deep yearning in his eyes. Unfortunately, it is also one that I recognize. I've seen looks like that many times over the last ten years, usually in the mirror. Now, it makes me uncomfortable enough to see it reflected in someone else's expression that I turn away from him and lower my gaze to the ground at my feet.

"Let him go," Ruen finally decides. "We should find something else to occupy our time with tonight. No doubt he'll be drinking himself into a stupor."

Confused as well as surprised, I lift my head and turn my attention to Ruen. To say that I'm shocked by his choice of dealing with this would be putting it mildly.

"What about her?" Kalix jerks his chin towards me and Ruen blinks as if reminded, suddenly, of my presence. That's unlike him—to forget. Over the past few weeks, I've observed him. He's struck me as one of the most aware people I've ever had the misfortune of meeting. He sees too much, in my opinion, and the worry of him finding out my true objective here at the Academy has hung over my head like a sword of damage suspended from a singular spider's thread. Now, he's even forgetting my existence when I'm right next to him?

Ah, I see. It hits me then that despite his words and calm expression, Ruen Darkhaven is just as affected by Darius' death as Theos. He simply expresses it in a different way. His grief is quiet, buried deep within himself. The emotion in his eyes shudders as he gazes across the space, his attention settling on the floor of the battle arena where blood-stains still soak into the dirt below.

If these three know each other as well as I think they do, then Ruen's choice to not return to their rooms, to follow after Theos, must mean that he knows how his brother would prefer to mourn. Or perhaps, it's just that he has his own way of mourning, whether that be by distraction or something else.

Bowing slightly at the waist, "No need to worry," I say. "I shall take my leave if you permit it and leave the two of you for the night."

After a moment, Ruen replies, his voice tighter than I've ever heard it. "*Go.*" That's it. A single word and yet, within it, the meaning is that much deeper. He doesn't sound angry or full of expected sorrow. Instead, he sounds tired. Exhausted. As if the entire weight of the world rests upon his shoulders and he's become aware of it once more.

His dismissal is enough to get me moving. I don't wait around for him to change his mind. Despite the aftermath of the arena battles, I still have things to take care of. Regis' note from this morning still hasn't slipped my memory and I need to request permission to leave the Academy grounds from Dauphine and Hael.

My feet eat up the distance to the arena's exit. Because the battles had lasted until after nightfall, there are still several students, and subsequently Terra, in the corridors of the Academy. It takes more effort for me to get through them unnoticed. As much as I wish I could call upon my Divine abilities, I fear running the risk of discovery. So, instead, I rely completely on my normal skills—ducking my head when I pass the students, keeping my attention down, and my face shielded in the shadows.

Like the Terra dining hall, the offices of the senior Terra

are located in a different building than the rest of the Academy. Crossing through the Terra courtyard, I hang a right and duck behind a low stone wall, pausing when voices echo back to me. I wait, slipping further into the darkness, as a pair of Terra pass by chattering away.

I wait another few beats until I'm sure they're long gone and then make my way into the Terra office building that doubles as a separate residence for the senior Terra. Where the rooms for sleeping are built above the Terra dining hall, the offices are to the back and down a set of stairs that are as narrow as the ones in the north tower.

Once I reach the bottom, I spot the offices with dusty wood plaques outside their doors. Unlike the offices of the Gods, these hallways are narrow and dark. I pause in the doorway to the Terra I've been searching for and take a look inside. The room is slightly wider and longer than a normal office with a small slit of a fireplace and wooden beams overhead. It's certainly not as lavish as Caedmon's had been, but they are more spacious than my own room in the north tower.

The man standing by the fireplace, tossing crumpled pages into the flames every few seconds, straightens as the last one leaves his bony fingertips. I part my lips as he turns, but my words are immediately swallowed by the startled shout he unleashes. Hael jerks back, slamming his spine into the ridge that surrounds the fireplace with his hand rising to his chest. The thin strings of his dark brown hair hang limply around his thin face. His patchy salt-and-pepper beard is a bit fuller since I last saw him.

I freeze. "Um ... Mr. Hael?"

"D-dear Gods..." he murmurs, his eyes wide as he gapes at me. "When ... how long..." The elder Terra breathes heavily, his white face even paler at the fright of my presence. A beat passes and then another and another.

"I'm sorry for startling you, sir," I say.

"Y-yes, well, y-you're quite soft on your feet, aren't you?" Hael stutters out as he gradually steps away from the fireplace. With careful footsteps and eyes that quickly cut back and forth from me to his path and back again, he makes his way across the threadbare red rug that covers the cold stone floor to the thick dust and book covered desk in the center of the small room. "Can I help you, young one?"

My lips twitch at the endearment. It seems, away from Dauphine, the man is far more human than he appeared in front of the masses at orientation. No doubt, he can't recall my name. That's fine by me.

I step forward. "I was wondering if it'd be possible to request a day off this coming weekend," I begin.

"All Terra get one day off a week," he responds quickly, slowly lowering himself into the chair behind his desk. The creak of wood echoes up to the rafters, loud enough that I half expect the chair to disintegrate and fall apart as he settles his weight—no matter how slight—upon the seat of it. Surprisingly, however, it doesn't.

"Yes, I know. I was wondering if I may take some time from that day to visit my family in Riviere."

Hael's sharp eyes snap to my face. "You want to leave the grounds?"

I nod.

He hums in the back of his throat, steepling his fingers together on the lip of his desk. "We normally do not allow Terra to leave the grounds, especially not so soon after entering."

I lift my chin. Despite his words, I don't hear a 'no' and

so, I push forward. "I understand and I know it's unlikely, but I humbly request it still."

"Why?" Hael settles his eyes on me.

The why doesn't matter. That much is clear. Though he lacks the decisive 'no' that would end this conversation, it's clear to me that he wants information. That's not something I can give. Carefully stepping farther into the room, I turn and close the door at my back.

"What are you doing?" Hael's chair scrapes across the ground as I turn the lock.

There is no one else here in the room and though I could sneak out of the Academy grounds, I'd much rather do things the easy way. I pivot to face Hael whose pale face is quickly reddening with indignation and anger.

Pulling from my inner core of Divine power, I stare back at him and let it fill my tone. "Sit down."

His face goes slack in an instant and he drops back into his chair. I move towards him, not stopping until I'm stationed across from him. Hael's expression has lost the color of anger and now appears distant and dreamlike. My tongue swipes across my teeth nervously. I rarely use this ability as I've seen it too much. Seduction. Persuasion. The very reason Gods control everything is because of this—their power over mortals that convinces them to follow their every word.

"You will give me permission to leave the Academy grounds on my off day this coming weekend," I state.

Hael's head dips down and then jolts back up as if his skull is attached to an invisible string being plucked over and over again. "Should anyone ask," I continue, "you decided to allow me exit and entry for this one day due to a sick relative." He continues to nod with that glassy-eyed dull look. "You will forget this exchange ever happened and remember only that you agreed to this request." I can't risk him recalling the power in my voice. "Speak if you understand."

"I understand." Hael's dry tone is untouched by emotion.

"Good." I reach for a piece of paper on his desk and slide it towards him. "Write the permission and sign it."

In jolting, puppet-like movements, Hael takes the paper from my hands. He picks up a quill and begins to write. Dark ink splotches drip along the edge of the parchment, but once he's done, he signs the bottom before rolling the permission and sealing it with a wax circle pressed to hold it in shape.

I take it from him. "Thank you," I say. "You may return to your duties, Mr. Hael."

"Yes, I must return to my duties..."

I blanch as his head sways from side to side. It'll take a few moments for compulsion to wear off and I have no plans to be around when he comes to his senses—even if he won't remember my usage of it. Quickly returning to the door, I unlock it and step into the hallway, leaving the door as I'd found it—wide open—and head back the same way I'd come.

It takes me less time than usual to return to my room in the north tower. I cut across the courtyards used only by Mortal Gods and scale the short stone wall separating the tower from the rest of the grounds instead of climbing the outer stairs. Once inside, I hurry up the stairwell, find my own door, and slam into the room before shutting and locking myself inside.

The *Euoplos dignitas* is there, and it peeks one eye open curiously from where it's resting amidst my bedsheets. A breath of relief escapes from my lips as I sag against the old solid wood. The parchment in my hand crinkles, reminding me that I'll need to prepare for my departure in the morning. Striding to the nightstand alongside my bed, I lay the permission paper on the surface and drop down onto the creaking mattress. The second I do, however, a sharp sound of glass shattering reaches my ears, followed by a sudden and rapid *thud thud thud*.

My spider king shoots up onto his legs and skitters across the bed, dropping down over the side and disappearing from sight. I blow out a breath and let my head drop back on my neck as I glare up at the ceiling. The sound of furniture either scraping across the floor or being thrown shakes the wooden beams. Dust rains down and I close my eyes.

Godsdamn it. Ruen said that Theos would be drinking himself into a stupor tonight. It appears that's not all he's doing. I press my lips together as a roar echoes down into my room. With a groan, I collapse back against the mattress and reopen my eyes.

Above me, the sounds continue. A vicious creature screaming out their pain as they throw and destroy everything around them. Theos sounds like a petulant child, and yet, at the same time, knowing why he's doing it gives rise to the bubble of sympathy that wells up inside of me. Cupping a hand over my face, I groan again.

No. I don't want to fucking understand them. I don't want to sympathize.

It doesn't seem to matter what I want, though. The longer I lay here, listening to the pained cries in the chambers above mine, the more they seep into my head. For several long moments, I contemplate leaving to meet Regis tonight. No doubt, I could *persuade* Hael to rewrite the permission, though I already feel disgusting enough for using that ability.

Seconds pass and the chaotic noises coming from the Darkhavens' chambers lessen. The violent bashing, I could understand. The breaking of glass, I could forgive even if I know I'll be the one forced to clean it all up later. The silence that follows, though ... that is just too much.

I arch up out of bed and stomp towards the door, unlocking it just as quickly as I'd locked it, and slam out into the corridor before turning and taking the stairs two steps at a time until I reach the top. Pausing outside the chamber door, I notice it's open. Not thrown open, but cracked—allowing a mere sliver of sight into the interior. And what a sight it is.

Chairs overturned. Books and pages tossed here and there. Paintings and tapestries ripped from the stone walls. It looks as if a savage storm had ripped the place to shreds. I press one palm to the door and push lightly, frowning when it doesn't immediately creak open. Pushing harder, I manage to get the door to open about a foot more—just enough for me to squeeze in through the opening.

Fuck. It's worse than I thought.

I want to believe that there's no way Ruen could have known that this would happen. Otherwise, he's far more foolish than I originally thought when it became clear he wouldn't be here to keep his brother company.

"Get out!" Theos' yell is quickly followed by a book flying through the air. I dodge to the left and stand straighter. Considering that Theos is currently sitting in a chair facing away from me, I'm actually quite impressed by his keen aim.

I pick my way through the glass and broken furniture, grabbing a table—the thing that had kept me from opening the door all of the way—and setting it back onto its legs. The door shuts and though a part of me wishes I were on the other side of it, something keeps me in here.

The room's exterior paints a path of violence and an old memory climbs up into my mind—wild and unwelcome, but there regardless. Even if I wanted to deny it, my own history refuses to allow me even that small kindness.

Theos may be hurting now. He may be angry and saddened by the loss of his friend, but once long ago ... I felt the same burning rage of pain. And just like him now, I was alone then too. That, more than anything, keeps me from turning around and walking right back through the door. As if there are invisible chains wrapped around my arms and legs, I find myself walking through the destruction of the room towards him. Each step louder than the next.

Fuck me, but I do *feel sorry for him.* Now that I know that, there's no running from it any further.

CHAPTER 28

KIERA

The bite of ice under my nails, combined with the tears that blur my vision but refuse to fall, consume me. The house I once lived in, the home I knew, burns in the near distance. A raging inferno takes it all from me as the remainder filters down through the barren trees of the woods alongside it where I lay.

I claw at the snow, struggling to get up from beneath the creature sitting on my small frame, but it's useless. The black dog doesn't budge. It merely growls above me and settles itself even more firmly on my back, squeezing the last vestiges of air from my lungs until I want to scream, but there's no room for it left.

I didn't know pain could feel like this. Before this night, pain was caused by an accidental fall. A scraped knee. A tiny cut from chopping the root vegetables Father brought home from the market too close to my skin. Never by a swarm of dark-cloaked figures in the night who broke into my home and ripped me and my father from our beds before burning our home to the ground.

Across the small opening of the white-covered grounds, two of those figures hold my still struggling father on his knees. He fights and claws his way out of their grip, only to be wrestled back into place. His eyes are wild, like that of the feral wolves that often creep through these trees.

"Daddy!" I finally find my voice and scream for him. The dog above me grumbles out another low growl, but I ignore it. It's a stupid beast. "Daddy! I'm here! Help me!"

My father, a big man even compared to the blacksmith in the local village, jerks his head back and sends the figure behind him sprawling out onto the ground as the back of his skull connects with the man's face. A spray of blood decorates the snow from the man's nostrils. With a vicious roar, he attacks the men holding him. I've never seen my father fight a day in my life, but watching now, I realize ... there are some things I didn't know about him. Like the fact that he's a good fighter. Better than good; he's monstrous in his strength and size and he knows just how to use his abilities to his advantage.

In the blink of an eye, my father has seized one of the figures by their throats and—from the startled gurgled sound that erupts from them, I assume—crushed it, before flinging their form to the snow. He moves onto the next, attacking one after another until those gathered around me begin to shift in unease. They follow after their comrades, heading towards my rampaging father to curb his violence with their sheer numbers.

Hope swells within my chest. I begin to crawl on the ground beneath the big beast sitting on me. It growls and snaps, but doesn't harm me. Angry, I turn on it and start to push against its snout.

"Get off!" I command, pushing as much of my power into my voice as I can. The animal freezes and begins to whine, but still, it doesn't move. With a growl of my own, I push harder. "I said, get off of me!"

An invisible force pushes out from my chest and the beast whines louder, beginning to tremble as it rolls off of my once prone body. My throat burns and tingles from that strange core *within me that Daddy always warned me against using. This is an emergency, though. I have to. A nearby figure gives a startled shout.*

"What the fuck? Grover? Get back on her!" *a man's voice commands the animal, but I glare the creature down as I scramble to my feet and it shrinks back from me. The fire of my house rages in the nearby distance as I slowly raise my gaze to the cloaked figure.*

I can feel my anger begin to build, hotter than I've ever felt before.

Always control your emotions, Kiera, *my father once told me. I knew he said it as more than a way to teach me to be kind and have empathy for others, because it's dangerous for me to reveal these abilities.*

They're tethered to my emotions—raging and growing more unrestrained the more I'm unable to tamper my anger.

"My Gods ... you're a Mortal God," *the man utters.*

I frown at him and take a step back, half intent on running to my father's aid when he suddenly jerks forward and latches onto me. A gloved hand latches onto my wrist and holds tight. I scream in shock when something pierces through me—an agony I've never felt before—and I fall to my knees.

Panting and gasping, my chest squeezes tight as the pain recedes, but not enough for me to climb back to my feet. "What the fuck would a hunter be doing with a Mortal God child?" *The man's question doesn't seem directed at me, but more musing and confused than anything else.*

My pulse speeds up and I search the man's arm where he's still holding on to me for whatever caused the pain. When he pulls back, I see it—a thin metal bracelet locked around my wrist. Where it rests against my skin, I can feel a heat from inside it. At first, it had hurt so badly, but now it's a dull throb—

a prickling sensation, if any. It's uncomfortable. I try to remove it, but it doesn't come off.

"What..." I grip the little bracelet and yank hard. Still, nothing. "Get this off me!" I scream. More power is pushed into my voice, but it disappears almost instantly and the second it does, a wave of nausea and dizziness assails me.

"Honestly, I never thought I'd need to use this out here," the man mutters, "but don't try anything funny anymore. That bracelet will suck up all your Divinity."

"My what?" I shake my head, trying to clear it of a sudden pain-filled fog.

The man scowls down at me before pointing to the manacles. "That right there is brimstone-made, mutt," he sneers. "It's the only thing that can control a being such as you. Don't even think about fighting us now, 'cause you'll only lose."

My lashes flutter. I hate the prickling sensation crawling beneath my flesh where it touches me. It feels heavier than anything I've held before. I don't understand. "W-what's brimstone?" I slur out.

Eyes wide, the man stares down at me for a moment before he bursts out laughing. The sound is too loud and it echoes up to the tops of the barren branches of the trees around us. When he finally settles and his gaze returns to me, it's with a twisted expression. He leans down and grabs ahold of my face, holding me in his wide meaty fist.

"Let me give you a lesson, kid," he says, dropping his voice low as he speaks. "Brimstone is the only weapon mortals have against your kind. With this here"—he taps the bracelet, causing me to wince—"those abilities you've had so far are rendered useless."

He's not lying. I can feel it. The helpless emptiness of my powers, of the tether my emotions have to that strange place inside of me that's always allowed me to do things my father never could. Horror descends at the realization. I'm well and truly trapped. I rip my head from his grasp, ignoring the pain, and towards where the rest of the man's companions are subduing my father.

"Daddy!" I scream out, louder than I ever have before. Tears burn into my eyes and trail down my face. "Daddy!"

There's no response, though. Or if there is, I don't hear it because in the next moment, the man's hand comes down hard on the back of my neck. The world winks out of existence and I'm surrounded by nothing but darkness.

CHAPTER 29

KIERA

I pick through the overturned furniture, moving it piece by piece out of my way. Slowly, Theos' head raises over the chair he's slumped in. Golden eyes turn towards me, glittering with barely repressed rage. I shouldn't find that so amusing, but I do. He's usually playful, cunning, and manipulative. Now, he's little more than a wounded animal with a thorn in its paw.

I get it. I really fucking do. Nothing is fair in the realm of the Divine, not even for their offspring.

"I said *get out*," he snaps, lowering his voice.

I blink back at him as the familiar pulse of persuasion moves over me. I ignore it. "I heard you the first time," I say.

"Then what the fuck are you still doing here?" he demands, frowning as he realizes that his powers aren't working.

It's a risk, I have to admit, but I notice the mostly empty bottle turned over at the foot of his chair and hope he's had enough by now to equate my non-response to his own abilities failing. If necessary, I'll use my own powers of persuasion on him the same way I had Hael. A drunken Mortal God is far easier to control, after all, than a sober one.

"Cleaning," I answer calmly.

Dangerous. This whole fucking mission has been nothing but dangerous since I stepped foot on Riviere's Mortal Gods Academy grounds. With each passing week, I find myself more and more wrapped up in the daily lives of these Mortal Gods. Since day one I've had this nagging sensation in the back of my mind. The longer I'm here without an actual target to take out, the more I wonder again if this isn't a test from Ophelia.

I thought I'd proved myself to her time and time again. From my first kill to my last one. But Ophelia is nothing if not cautious. She's never been married and more than once swore that she trusted no one to be her partner because at the end of the day, humans and Gods alike are immoral creatures. Liars. Devious backstabbers. I guess it's difficult to run an assassination Guild like the Underworld and still believe in people. It wouldn't surprise me if this turned out to be another one of her trials.

Still, though, I don't leave the Darkhaven chambers and instead begin cleaning up the space. I pile shattered wood into a spot by the fireplace and pick up discarded books, stacking them on the table near Ruen's usual spot.

"Why do you never fucking listen to me?" Theos groans as he slumps back into his chair, his voice slurring slightly. In this entire room, the sole thing that isn't damaged is the cabinet across the space that contains the alcohol. It hangs open, but the glasses are unbroken, and the bottles are still in their spaces save for the ones that have been drunk.

I circle Theos' chair and stare down at him for a moment. He tips his head back, a singular lock of his pale hair falling over the side of his forehead. It makes him seem younger than I know him to be. Perhaps other Terra don't investigate their wards, but I'm not them. I'm not a real Terra at all.

"Because I am not your friend, Master Theos. Don't make the mistake of thinking I am here because I want to listen to your problems, especially when you fail to realize that you are not alone and everyone around you has problems, too, that they must face."

He rears out of the seat he's in so harshly that it sends the piece of furniture tipping back onto the floor. The loud noise of it clatters against the wood and echoes throughout the room as he advances on me. I don't move save to tilt my chin up and meet his eyes as he comes to a dead halt mere inches from my body.

"*No*," he grits out. "You are *not* my friend. I do not *have* friends. I have allies and I have enemies."

He doesn't have friends? Is that what he's telling himself after Darius' death? I meet his eyes. "And whose choice was that?" I ask.

He steps forward and I take a step back, the two of us moving in sync until I feel stone against my spine and stop with him hovering over me. Golden eyes narrow on my face, darkening at the edges. "You think it was *my* choice?"

Even if I can understand his hurt and pain at losing a friend, he has to know how that makes him seem to the Gods who orchestrated Darius' death as an act of entertainment for their own sick amusement. "You act like you don't have choices, Master Theos, when the truth is, you have plenty of them." *Far more than I was ever given.*

"And the choice of my birth?" he counters. "I didn't choose to be a fucking God's son!" His fist drives into the wall at my back, causing a rain of dust and stone chips to fall over my face and shoulder. I don't flinch, and after a beat, once his actions have caught up with him, his eyes widen.

"Perhaps," I reply, "but you sure have reaped the benefits being a God's son gives you. You relished in them."

"Oh no." He shakes his finger at me as he bares his teeth, forgetting the lack of reaction I'm sure he's accustomed to receiving from other Terra. "No, you don't get to judge me, little fucking human." *Oh, if he only knew.* "I would not have relished—as you say—in the benefits of my God blood and status if I didn't need to distract myself from *the fucking pain it brings me!*"

By the end of his words, he's screaming in my face. Spittle flies from his lips as the pale flesh over his cheeks grows redder with each passing breath. He blinks as if realizing his perpetuated loss of control and after a moment, he takes a step back. When he speaks again, his voice is back to its normal tone.

"I drown it out," he admits quietly. "With sex and drugs and liquor. I numb myself, Kiera ... but don't think that I don't hate my own existence. Don't think I do not crave the things humans have even if I have so much more." He laughs, though the sound is devoid of any real amusement. "Gods are greedy creatures," he says, "and their children are no different."

That, I believe, is the first thing he's ever said that I wholly agree with—myself included, though he wouldn't know it.

Theos turns away and his head dips towards his chest before he lifts it and moves. He strides back across the room and reaches the chair lying on the floor. With a swift hand gripping the solid back of it, he lifts it into place, turns, and sinks into it once more. His head bows backward and his white hair, just a few shades lighter than mine—with far less gray in it too—parts down the center to either side of his forehead. His eyes are open but unseeing as they squint into the shadows—past me, past the walls, and perhaps even past the truth that he just confessed to me.

A beat follows the silence and then another, and when the only movement from him is the slow slide of his booted foot drifting outward, laying stretched across the floor as he collapses even deeper into the chair and whatever depression has taken hold of his mind, I decide enough is enough. With a sigh, I move across the room towards the cabinets of liquor sitting in the corner with their doors wide open.

"You're not allowed to move unless I give you permission," he says tiredly, as if the words are drawn out of him unconsciously rather than by any will of his own.

"Then," I say as I find a full bottle of amber-colored rum and pull it down from the shelves, "I suggest you either give me permission or have me whipped because I have no intention of stopping."

The sole of his boot hits the floor behind me, but I don't hear the creaking of the chair that would tell me he's stood up, so I keep going. I grab a glass and pull that down as well and then uncap the bottle, pouring a hefty amount inside.

"You think I won't do it?"

"What?" I ask. "Have me whipped? No, I'm sure you would if you really wanted to." I recap the liquor bottle when the glass is nearly tipping over with fullness and then replace it in the cabinet.

"You don't seem that concerned about the idea," he comments. His tone is ripe with confusion, as if he can't quite understand my motive. To be honest, I'm losing my own reasoning too. As much as I don't want to, I'm feeling a kinship with Theos Darkhaven. I understand the hatred that dwells within him. The fear. The anger.

I am violent. Angry. But I was not born this way. No little girl is. I learned to be these things out of necessity and the same can be said for the Darkhaven brothers.

I respond to Theos' words and close the cabinet door before turning towards him. "I'm not." I was right—he's still in the chair, only now his leg is propped up again instead of stretched out. I stride towards him and circle the chair before holding out the glass.

Gold eyes flash to my face. "What's this?"

"Liquor," I deadpan.

He waves his hand as if ordering me to take it away. "I've already got a…" He drifts off as he tries to reach down only to come back up with an empty bottle. Theos' sunlight-colored eyes blink blearily at the clear glass over and over again until, with a sigh, I take it from him and lower it back to the floor.

I hold out the glass of amber liquid again. "Take it," I order. "It helps ease the burden of pain."

"Yes," he says. "*Physical* pain usually."

"Take it regardless," I say. "Alcohol poured on wounds helps physical pain, but the kind you drink helps the pain inside."

"I really will have you whipped," he threatens.

I shrug and continue to hold out the glass. "You'll do what you must. Now, drink."

He scoffs and finally reaches forward, snagging the glass from my grip. A little bit of the rum sloshes over the rim and hits my fingers as he drags it to his lips. I lift my hand and lick the remains. It's a nice spiced rum. The glass pauses right before it reaches his mouth.

"You're a strange one," he says.

"So I've often heard." They had said as much when I'd

challenged him and his brothers over their seemingly forgotten bet from my very first day here.

"You don't do what you're told here and if others find out about that, it won't just be me threatening to have you whipped. It will be someone who has no intention of letting you survive a whipping."

"Is that caution I hear?" I ask, bemused. "From my great Master and the magnanimous God son, Theos Darkhaven?"

His face pinches tight and he puts the glass to his lips. He sucks back a long draw of liquor, draining a good half of the glass in under a few seconds. When he releases the rim, he shoots me a dark look. "Don't call me that," he orders.

"What? Your name?"

"No." His voice is hollow as he speaks and it grows deeper, more ... intimate as he keeps talking. "Master or ... God son. You're not allowed to call me by my titles or status. To you, I am just Theos."

A blanket of silence descends between us. I'm not sure what to say, so I opt to say nothing at all and instead, respond with action rather than words. I reach out, grasping the glass in his fist and gently pry it from him. Tipping my head back, I meet his eyes as I put the same place his lips had touched on the glass to my own and drink. The rest of the liquid runs into my throat, burning a path into my stomach as I down all of it in several gulps.

"I do believe," I say when I finally come up for air, "that might have been a good step towards making friends rather than allies or enemies."

His gaze focuses on me for several beats and I watch as the curve of his full lips curl at the edges to form a smile. Theos rolls his tongue into one cheek as he turns his head and his attention falls to my throat and then further down before moving back to my face. "You don't take orders well," he repeats.

"Agreed." I shrug. "Not only do I not take orders well, I hardly take suggestions well either. Unfortunately, I don't see that changing much in the near future."

He snorts, turning his cheek as his hand comes up to cover his lips—as if he can't believe he made that sound. He shakes his head. "You'll need to learn to hide it, at the very least," he says. "Or risk death." Theos heaves a great breath and at the mention of death, his head dips and his shoulders lower. "It's up to you, I suppose, but it does make a man wonder why you're even in a place such as the Academy when you obviously don't belong. Not when you could be anywhere else in the world."

I detect a note of envy in that last statement, but out of respect for already pushing him to some sort of invisible limit, I ignore it.

"So long as I'm in need of money, everywhere is the same," I reply. It's not a lie, though, of course, but it is a bit misleading.

"Ah." He nods as if he understands. "So, it's the money, then, that brought you to the Academy. I always thought humans simply wanted to worship their Gods and Masters, but that makes sense for you." His eyes move to me and then away again. "You do seem more the logical type."

I smirk and reach out, cupping my hand over the top of the back of the chair. Theos' head whips towards me as I lean down into his face. My braid flutters against my skin, the soft strands a minor sensory itch to the increasing awareness of my position. "Why are you so concerned about it?" I ask. "Do you want there to be another reason?"

Those golden eyes of his flash pitch black before returning to their original color. It happens so quickly that I blink and wonder if I didn't imagine it. *Have my eyes ever done that?* I wonder. I've never had anyone to ask and those that might've noticed have never mentioned something such as that.

"Do not play games with me, mortal girl," he warns, voice deepening into a growl. A hand grazes my hip and I glance down at the movement just as he locks it around my side and yanks me suddenly into his embrace.

The glass flies out of my other hand and shatters against the floor as I'm thrust upon his lap, my legs encasing either side of his. I move to stand back up immediately, but he anchors me to him with his other hand, holding my waist tight enough that I flinch at the pressure. He doesn't even realize that any ordinary human girl would walk away from this encounter with bruises, or worse, broken bones.

"You tempt me, Kiera Nezerac," he whispers, the heat of his breath mere inches from my face. He smells of rum and spice. "I think you do it on purpose."

I meet his gaze, but I can't tell him the truth. That I am, in fact, tempting him on purpose. Sex is easy. Physical bodies colliding to offer release and pleasure. I've long since gotten rid of any notion of it meaning more. I've had to—or risk losing my mind to sleepless or nightmare-filled nights over those I'd seduced and killed.

For a moment, I contemplate pulling away and stopping this before it goes too far. Just once, though, I want to do what I want, and I find ... that I really fucking want to kiss Theos Darkhaven.

So, for the first time in a long time, I let myself do it. I let myself do something that I *want* to do and not necessarily something I have to. I lean forward, my braid slipping off my shoulder and swinging between us until it slaps his chest. I dip my head until the heat of my breath mingles with his. This is risky, I know, but it's been so long since I had something for myself.

I'm not like Regis. I can't just fuck to forget all of the kills. I don't fuck for any other reason than because it's necessary. This, I know, is not necessary. In fact, doing this is taking a step down a treacherous path. Somehow, I find myself unable to withstand the desire.

Theos lifts his lashes. His eyes watch me with fire burning in their depths. "If you are intent on tormenting me, Kiera," he murmurs against lips that have not yet touched his, "you are doing a splendid fucking job of it."

My mouth curves into a smile. Even if he doesn't realize it, in this moment, he's forgotten the reason for his anger and pain. "Good to know," I murmur.

I'm hesitating. No matter that I want this, there still lies, in the furthest recesses of my mind, all of the reasons that I shouldn't touch my lips to his. All the reminders of why I should not kiss him, the least of which being that he is like me. Half mortal. Half God.

Theos takes the last step, erasing that hesitation as he leans up. His hand comes around the back of my neck and drags me down that minuscule last inch that keeps us separated. His mouth takes mine in a heated fusion of lips and tongue. Fire licks along my flesh as I close my eyes and sink into it.

My groin moves down against his as his tongue explores. He kisses as if he means to steal the last of my sanity. Soft, but masculine lips move across my mouth, devouring everything in their path. My breasts swell against his chest and when a sound escapes me—a blasted whimper as I feel the tips of my nipples scrape his hard chest through our clothes—embarrassment pours through my mind. I attempt to move away, but he stops me.

Ripping his mouth from mine, Theos tightens his hold on the back of my neck and instead uses that grip to yank me closer. He presses my breasts flush against him until there can be no doubt whether or not he senses the hardness of my nipples. Glowing, golden eyes gaze at me, hooded only slightly by his lowered lids.

His tongue peeks out, the very tongue that had been inside my mouth only a moment before, and then licks across his already wet lips as if he can taste me there. Panting, flushed, I struggle not to grind my lap down against his. I can feel the state of his cock, hard and pressing against my covered pussy. It's another temptation I don't need.

"Don't pull away from me now, *Dea*," he says. "It's too late to regret this. If you're going to take things this far and torment me, I suggest you simply take the reins and actually follow through with all of your silent threats."

"Threats?" My breath comes out in a rush as I repeat his last word, confusion spiraling through me.

"Yes, threats." He nuzzles against the side of my face, moving downward until his next words are spoken against the racing pulse in my throat. "Every move you make, every reckless comment, every fucking look you've given me since the moment you arrived here, has been a threat, Kiera. I am all too happy to be the sacrifice to them. Now..." His other hand finds my hip and he jerks me down harder against the ridge of his erection.

My neck bows back as I feel the hot rush of wetness flood my insides as he rubs right over the bundle of nerves above my cunt. Fuck, it feels so good. It's sending me into perilous territory. My stomach churns and my mind fogs over with the pleasure it brings.

"Take me," he growls as he sets his teeth to my neck, biting down lightly and then harder until I cry out. Frustration eats away at me. I want to ride him. I want to pull him free of his trousers and remove my own before taking him into my innermost depths. I want to feel how hot and hard he actually is inside the walls of my pussy.

"Find your pleasure," Theos insists. The hand at my hip moves to my lower back and he begins to urge me to grind. Up and down, back and forth. His breaths puff across my quickly flushing skin. "More."

My fingers sink into the fabric of the back of the chair, my nails biting into the surface, creating indents as I try to fight the sensations flooding me. Hunger. Fervor. Desire. It's been so long since it's been this *real*.

"You feel so perfect," Theos whispers. "I can smell how wet you are for me, how much you want me."

His words are sinful as much as they are unsafe. Too much and I know I'll lose myself in a way I never have. Sure, I've taken pleasure in the act before, but it's always been tainted by the knowledge that I was meant to kill my target. For now, at least, this act remains unsullied by such knowledge.

So, ride him, I do. I move my hips at his urging and I rock against his erection. Each movement causing more and more wetness to soak my pussy until I can feel it dripping down my thighs inside my pants.

Unable to stop myself, I reach out and grab ahold of a large chunk of Theos' hair and yank his head back. The action startles him, I know because his eyes widen as he looks up at me. I don't care. I dive down and take his lower lip into my mouth, I suck on it before biting down lightly—dragging my teeth over the sensitive flesh until he moans.

"Fuck," he hisses when I pull away. "You are like an uncontrollable flame," he says.

He has no idea. None of them do. I am far worse than a flame that could burn him. I am a shadow deceiving the lot of them. A sword hanging in the darkness just waiting to end their existence. I should not allow this. It is cruel. But now that we've started, there is no stopping it.

I kiss him again, desperate—even if only for a moment—to forget who I am. To forget who *he* is. All I want is for us to find pleasure together. I bite down upon his lower lip again, harder this time, until I draw blood and then when I lick it off, I feel his cock pulse between my legs.

A groan releases from him as he holds me tighter, closer. Theos brings me down upon his lap hard and sparks dance behind my eyes as I feel my insides flutter, contracting as they seek out the hardness of a male and find none. That is the only part of this that is disappointing.

I shudder as he forces me to ride him through his own orgasm, the two of us coming in our trousers like youths in ways I'd never before experienced. Hot wicked flames flash across my skin. I want more. Tears prick my eyes and his grip turns into iron.

Finally, the two of us are left soaked in our own sweat and panting for all we're worth. I close my eyes as I rest my forehead against his shoulder.

I hope it's not him, I think to myself. I really hope I don't have to kill Theos Darkhaven.

CHAPTER 30
KIERA

"I hope you don't think that's the end." I don't get even a moment of reprieve it seems before Theos' sudden words are followed by the even more abrupt movement of him standing up from the chair with me still in his arms.

As he hefts me higher, I blink lazily as I lean back and wrap my legs around his hips to keep from falling. The grin I'm met with on his face has cleared away all of the earlier agony. For this moment, he seems to have forgotten his sorrow and I don't want to remind him.

"No," I say, circling my arms around his neck and shoulders. "It's not." For once, I want to be someone's solace and not their demise. Forcing a smile to my own lips at the reminder of what I've been to so many others, I allow Theos to carry me across the space to the open doorway of his bedroom. "Are you going to show me what else you're capable of, Theos Darkhaven?" I challenge him.

A lock of pale hair slides over his forehead as he shakes his head. "You are a dangerous creature, *Dea*, but yes, I'm going to show you exactly what I'm capable of."

The place between my thighs twinges with discomfort. The wetness from before isn't drying at all, not with the way he brushes against me—his quickly rehardening cock rubbing against my pussy through our clothes—with each damnable step he takes.

Theos moves into the room and turns, the door swinging shut behind us, and then I find myself with my back pressed against it. My insides cramp and jolt, tightening and releasing in anticipation. When was the last time I did this? Have I *ever* done this without there being an ulterior motive? I'm sure I have, but I can't think of it right now. I can't think of anything but the man in front of me.

Slowly—with almost painful increments—Theos lowers his head. Down and down further still, his golden eyes locked onto mine as if daring me to look away. I don't. Soft lips touch my flesh and finally, the spell of his gaze is broken. I arch up against him, pushing my hips out and down against him as I crane my neck. The back of my skull bumps into the wood of the door as Theos kisses the rapid beating pulse in my throat.

Breath after breath sears the inside of my mouth, coming up in hot panting waves. His tongue grazes my skin, moving up and licking the salty sweat that clings to me. I want to do the same to him too. Will he let me? I wonder. Only one way to find out.

Jerking my head down fast enough that he's forced to pull away, I ignore the glower on his face and reach around the back of his head, fisting a handful of his hair the same way I had before. I bring him closer still and then kiss him. This kiss is anything but kind. It's demanding, provoking, and—I hope—enough of what he needs to remember that I'm not the type of woman to be kept waiting.

I nip his lower lip, sinking my teeth into his Mortal God

flesh and biting down to the point just before drawing blood once again. Deranged as Theos is, all that does is make him smile against me, wider and wider still. "So vicious," he muses. "You're more like a wild animal than a Divine worshiping Terra. Are you seeking pain or pleasure, *Dea*?"

"Both," I say, releasing his lip. "And I won't stand for you denying me either." I rub myself against him, using the muscles in my hips and abdomen to undulate into his groin and the evidence of his own renewed arousal there. "You promised it wouldn't be the end. So, what are you waiting for?"

"You should know what you're getting into," he replies, golden eyes darkening ever so slightly as his face grows serious.

I tilt my head to the side. "What do you mean?"

"You got out of fucking Malachi," he reminds me.

My eyes roll. "Is this about your stupid little bet?" I ask. "It's been weeks, so I assumed you and your brothers had forgotten it—or at least that you didn't want to be reminded that you'd been bested by a *mere Terra*." The last two words come out sharper than I intended, perhaps inflamed by my own internal irritation at the subjugation I've been under since I arrived here.

Theos shakes his head once more. "That's not what *this* is about," he says, nodding down between us where our bodies are practically fused together. At least, as much as they can be without his cock in my cunt. "What you are, though, will affect you. If it becomes known that you've fucked me—"

The irony of his statement—what I am? It's laughable, but with it, the memory of Rahela's rage and my near drowning in one of the courtyards specifically for Mortal

Gods comes back to me. "There are those who already assume I'm fucking you," I tell him. There are likely many others who assume I'm fucking all of them. "What does it matter if I actually do it or not?" In fact, if I'm going to be accused of something and attacked for it the way Rahela had, then I'd much rather at least get the pleasure of actually doing it.

I've never known another man presented with sex to talk so damned much. Theos, despite his reputation around the Academy—and from what I've garnered from Niall's impressive ability to befriend literally everyone and therefore pick up tidbits of information, it is a very notorious and salacious reputation—is a chatterbox. It makes me want to lower my legs, yank him over to the four-poster bed I see behind him, push him down, and rip his clothes off so that I can fuck myself on what I know will be an impressive cock, so I can at least find pleasure in his body if I must be forced to listen to this.

"You are intentionally misunderstanding me," Theos growls, his voice deepening. One hand snaps up and grips me around my throat. My breath catches for a singular moment and my body locks down as I fight back the training that urges me to free myself from the hold. To my shock, however, as I let Theos hold me in such a way, embers of anticipatory pleasure flame to life within my body, spreading from my chest down to my pussy. Never knew I'd be so aroused by a man's hand around my throat, but here we are.

I arch against him once more. "And *you* are stalling," I snap back. "If you don't want to fuck me, fine. Let me go so I can go find someone else to take care of this ache."

Glimmering gold eyes flash black in an instant. Theos' entire body stills and grows so rigid that I don't even feel him breathe, but he must be because he's still able to speak. "What the fuck did you just say to me?"

Warning bells are ringing through my head, but I ignore them. "I said—if you don't want to fuck me then let me go so that I can go find someone who will," I repeat.

The words seem to have the same effect as waving a big juicy steak in front of a starving man. As hard-pressed as I am against the door, I didn't know it was possible to feel as though the scant distance between Theos and I could be closed in less than an instant. I don't see him move. I don't even hardly feel it before he's simply *there*. All over me. All around me.

His scent permeates the very air that I breathe. Theos spins away from the door, and I twist my ankles together at the small of his back, locking onto him as he strides the rest of the way across the room to the bed I'd made dozens of times before. Who knew when I first stepped into the Dark-havens' world that I would somehow end up here?

As always, the small kernel of guilt that he doesn't truly know who I am, who he is sharing his flesh and bed with, penetrates through my skull as his mouth ravages mine. And, as I always have before, I shove it down—chaining it and locking it away in the furthest part of myself, hoping that one day, I'll be able to lie with someone and not feel it ever again. For now, his kiss is enough. For now, his touch will make everything else fade away.

The sound of fabric rending startles me to a halt as fresh, cool air wafts over my newly revealed skin. Pushing my head back against the pillows, I glare up at the hulking figure above me. "Did you just rip my fucking shirt?" I snap.

Theos doesn't answer, but then, he doesn't have to. The evidence lays around me in tatters as he finishes the task of stripping it off of me. I gasp and arch as his head dips down and he licks a path across my ribs, right beneath where the strap of my chest bindings stretches.

"No corset?" he murmurs against my skin.

My hands sink into his hair as he kisses my skin again. Little pops of fire and bursts of heat creep up along my flesh with every single one. "You can't ... wear a corset under a tunic," I murmur. Not exactly true, but corsets are uncomfortable and stifling. I can't move as fast as I need or want to with them on. I can't bend properly and I certainly have no need for the use they do to a woman's figure. So binding my chest enough to keep my breasts contained is all that's needed.

Theos untucks the band of my bindings, but when he realizes I'll have to lift up for him to unwrap them, he growls out a curse and bends to his boots. I tense as he yanks out a blade from one of the two and slices right through the bindings. The glint of sharp metal so close to my skin makes my pulse race and my hands snap to his waist, half intent on flipping the script in an instant. Instinct wars against physical desire.

It isn't until he tosses the blade down onto the sheets next to my head that I relax marginally. I'm not even all that concerned with my bare breasts now in his view as he sits up and looks down at me. Black eyes no longer cloaked in gold are fixated on the reveal. Why? I couldn't say. From what I understand, Theos is quite the rogue when it comes to those he beds. Beyond a shadow of a doubt, I know that he's seen breasts before—bigger, smaller, rounder, wider, with darker areolas. It doesn't matter as they're all essentially the same.

As he continues to look, I just lay there and let him. I don't move to shield myself or hide. There's no use in pitiable modesty. In the past, I've been stripped bare of my clothes and sprayed down with water that would take your skin off if it were any more powerful. I've been tossed about, slapped around, beaten, starved. Nothing is more important to me than life, and right now, that's what I choose.

After several more beats of silence, I start to move. Reaching up between us, I cup my breasts and squirm. "Are you just going to look all night, Theos? Or are you going to touch?"

"I'm going to do more than touch." As he speaks, his voice sounds farther away despite the fact that he's hovering right above me. From the darkness in his eyes, long tracks of black veins etch out, growing deeper and longer as the black in his gaze remains. His tone has dipped into a throaty baritone.

"Then what are you waiting for?" I ask.

Against my palms, my nipples are hard. Goosebumps rise up along my biceps and down over the flat of my belly. The wetness between my legs is still there. I rub my thighs together and as if he senses what I'm trying to do—press against my clit—Theos backs up and grips my thighs, parting them to make way for his own body.

He comes back down over me, chest to chest. His skin is burning hot whereas mine feels frosted in ice. My lips part. Hunger swells within me. "You don't seem afraid." That one sentence strikes through me with all of the raging power of a tidal wave crashing against a cliffside.

"Afraid?" I repeat. "Should I be?"

Surprisingly, his lashes are dark rather than the same pale of his hair. I suspect, were they the same color, they would appear ghostly in this light and with the gold irises now swallowed by the darkness. Hands trail down over my sides and move up until Theos takes each of my wrists in his grip and raises them over my head.

My throat tightens as his fingers clamp down. While I know some feel satisfaction from being tied down during sex, I am not one of them. I've done it too often to others right before I slit their throats to feel entirely comfortable.

"Yes," Theos whispers, coming closer and closer as he pins my hands above my head and leans down into my face until his lips are grazing mine. The weighty need that's bloomed inside of me clenches against my insides. The closer he is, the more irresistible it is. "You should be utterly terrified, *Dea*." Theos presses a light kiss to my lips and when I crane my neck for more, he pulls away. "You should have run screaming the first second I put my hands on you, but you didn't. Instead, you threatened me—told me that if I wouldn't give you what you wanted, you'd find someone else. Another man to put his hands on you this way."

"Does that bother you?" I ask breathlessly. "I'm not making any promises here, Theos. This is just sex. Nothing more. I know that the moment I walk out of that door, once it's over, I'll go back to being your Terra and you'll go back to being Theos Darkhaven, a Mortal God of Divine descent."

"Will you be doing this with someone else then after all?" The question is confusing.

"I don't know," I answer honestly with a casual shrug. "Probably? Not right away, obviously. It's not like I've sought it out, but life happens and sex is a part of life, isn't it?"

His upper lip pulls back over perfect white teeth. All Gods and their offspring are so damn pretty, it would be infuriating if I didn't know it'd be hypocritical of me considering my own origins. He transfers both of my wrists into one of his hands and I know, logically, that I could fight his hold if I truly wanted to. That, though, would reveal far too much and so, I merely lay there and wait, curious as to what he's planning. It's rare for me to be so interested in someone else—much less a Mortal God like Theos Darkhaven—but it's even rarer for me to find them difficult to read.

I find Theos and his brothers as enigmatic as my own heritage. Whoever my God parent is, she certainly left little in the way of hints to find her and I fear that, even if she had, I wouldn't want to.

With his newly freed hand, Theos finds his grip around my throat. He squeezes tight, pressing against the sides with the pads of his fingers. I swallow roughly and tilt my chin up, showing him that this, too, doesn't scare me. Feigning fear is beneficial in some instances, as I've learned over the last ten years, but Theos is like a wild animal. He can smell it and it only makes him want to tear me apart that much faster.

"From tonight on, you let no other touch you," he growls. "Terra or otherwise, Kiera Nezerac, the second I fuck you, you'll be mine."

I laugh at that. I can't help it. "You couldn't stop me if you tried," I reply. I don't say it to goad him, but because even if I'm lying about who I truly am, I won't lie about this. His grasp becomes harder, growing restrictive, cutting off my airflow.

Small breaths wheeze from my lungs. Still, I keep my eyes on his. "I told you what I expect from this night," I tell him. "One night. No holds barred. No restrictions. In the morning, we go back to the way we were."

For a change, his lips quirk up. Since my first initial claim that I'd fuck someone else if he won't do it, he hasn't cracked a smile. Now that he does ... well, I find myself feeling a little apprehensive.

Theos bends over me and kisses my lips once more. I open for him, unabashed by my own need. His tongue invades, tangling with mine. He starts slow rather than fast and heavy and then alters, growing harder and deeper the longer he kisses me. Yes, he certainly has experience. By the time he releases me, I've no air left inside of me and I'm trying and failing to pant around the palm at my neck. My head feels light, dizzy.

"After tonight," he says, dropping another kiss at the corner of my mouth before moving to my chin as his grip finally eases ever so slightly. I gulp down a fresh breath of air. "You won't want to look for someone else."

So confident. "We're not engaged, Theos," I tell him. "This is just one night of pleasure."

He licks over my jawline and removes the hand at my throat completely to set his teeth in the crook, the place right between where my neck and shoulder meet. "You won't want to go back to the way we were," he warns me. "You'll want to be in my bed every night from this one forward."

I chuckle. "If we didn't already have a bet going, I'd offer another wager that you'd be wrong," I mutter. My breasts rise and fall and I grit my teeth as he bites lightly at my throat and moves down. When his teeth settle over one hardened nipple, my back arches off the bed.

Sharp, violent tendrils of pleasure shoot from the tip of my breast down into my cunt. I strain against the hand still holding me down, fighting to not do so too hard. I move against him, undulating my hips, enticing him to drag my pants down and thrust inside me.

"Theos..." His name is a plea on my lips. One he ignores

as he switches to my other breast and bites it rather viciously. A half scream echoes out of my mouth and I feel the curl of his lips around my sensitive flesh. "Bastard," I growl.

He laughs, the sound playful. Finally, he seems to decide something. He releases my hands and I lower them to his upper back as he ravishes my breasts. Kiss after kiss is pressed to my soft skin and then down between them as he peppers them over my ribs and the markings left behind from the bindings. Theos moves further still until his chin bumps against the waist of my pants.

I inhale sharply as he lifts his head and the sunset gold of his irises is back. "Last chance," he whispers.

I shake my head. "That ship has sailed," I say. "There's no stopping."

His fingers graze the ends of the ties, eyes settling on mine as he pulls until they loosen and then come free. The fabric tight to my hips slackens and finally, between the both of us, the trousers come off. "*Fuck*." Theos' low curse is ripe with pleasure and anticipation as he grips either side of my hips. "You're godsdamned beautiful."

I smirk. "You could've found that out sooner if you weren't such a fucking talker."

He glares up at me for a moment, but the heated look dissolves just as quickly as he bends and settles each of my thighs over his shoulders. *Oh yes,* I think as I recline back on the bed that is softer than any I've ever laid in. The first stroke of his tongue up my folds is soft. My eyes slide shut and I bite down on my lower lip to stifle the oncoming moans.

Theos is talented. More than that, he's a practical sex God himself. No halves at all.

Careful of my legs, but rough with his mouth and

fingers, he drives me higher and higher. Theos licks over my entrance and laps up the juices that spill from me. My own tongue touches the edge of my lips, soothing over where my teeth had bitten down a bit too hard, creating a series of divots in my soft flesh.

I reach down and smooth my hands over the head between my thighs. Theos' hair is soft, like a bird's wing. My nails scrape against his scalp soothingly as he worships at the crux of my body and I feel his responding shudder. I smile. I can't help it. I love knowing that I'm not the only one being driven insane. Sure, from the outside, it appears as though they're the ones in control, but not for long.

"Ah..." My back comes off the bed as he hits a particularly sensitive spot and just as if he'd been waiting for that reaction, Theos repeats it. A bolt of lightning travels up my spine and shoots off flames in my head. My hand goes from scraping against him to pushing.

"Enough!" I pant. Fuck, my legs are starting to tremble. The oncoming rush of an orgasm is quickly flooding my system, but I don't want it now. I want it later—with him inside of me.

Theos ignores my demand and with his amber gaze, he looks up at me from beneath his dark lashes and purposefully sucks my clit into his mouth. A scream echoes out of my throat and my head slams back into the pillow as the fires take over. Damn this man, he knows exactly what he's doing.

Halfway through my orgasm, with my mouth still gaping open, Theos drops my legs down from his shoulders and arches up over my body. Once again, Theos' hand grips my face, holding on and tightening until I can't close my lips, and then with those glittering dangerous eyes staring me right in the face, he parts his lips and lets a stream of my juices flow from his mouth into mine.

Shock. That's the first thing that hits me. Then discomfort. Then ... confused arousal. No sooner has he finished giving back what he took from me than he lowers his head and takes my mouth in a voracious kiss. Lips to lips. Teeth and tongue. It's raw and real and ... a lie. A fucking lie.

Annoyed that I've let someone take control, I rip my hands from the sheets and grip the back of his head, twisting mine as I take over the kiss. His hips are against mine, so it takes no time at all for me to wrap one leg around his side and shove. Our kiss comes to a crashing halt as I flip the two of us and his back is the one that hits the mattress as I rise over him.

My braid slaps my spine, the little flyaways sticking to my temples and neck as sweat coats my skin. I can only imagine what I must look like—panting, face flushed, hungry. Theos' lashes lower as he stares down our bodies where my pussy is hovering just over his still-clothed cock. His lips are wet and slowly—oh-so fucking slowly—he licks them.

"You taste like Divinity, *Dea*," he murmurs. "Are you really mortal?"

Panic slams into me. In one part of my mind, I recognize that he can't truly mean that. There's no way he could know what I am because if he did, I'd have been reported long ago. But the fear that's been ingrained within me for my entire life doesn't acknowledge the logic. Instead, she wants to do anything and everything to ensure our survival and that means distracting him, so distract him I do.

Reaching between us, I rip at the ties binding his cock within his trousers. Fast movements, no resistance from the man beneath me. He's not the only one who wants to forget. He's running from the loss of his friend, but I'm running from every-fucking-thing else.

His cock springs free, arching up and slapping at the underside of his abdomen, nearly touching his belly button. *Shit.* Long. Thick. He's definitely got the size down. My insides clench both in anticipation and trepidation. The ones I had sex with before were easily seduced and therefore, it came as no shock that they weren't exactly of the same endowment as Theos Darkhaven.

As if he knows the direction of my thoughts, Theos grins as he reaches down and fists his own cock, holding it up as he slides his palm down the shaft, pumping himself once, twice, three times before he speaks. "Cat got your tongue?" he asks, his voice amused.

With a scowl, I lift up one leg and move over him. "Not at all," I lie, brushing his hand out of the way as I take him into my grip. The vein in his jaw jerks against the surface of his flesh and then pulses. I breathe out as I settle the head of him against my cunt and then slowly lower myself down.

"Gods—*fuck*!" Theos' head snaps back against the pillows as I drop my weight, sinking completely over his lap and onto the hard rod that is his cock. My pussy clenches around the sudden burn. Placing both hands over the hard ridges of his abdomen, I pant through the stretch as my inner muscles contract around him. It's too much and yet, it's also just right. Perfect. He fills me so much that I swear to the Gods that I can feel him in my lower belly.

Leaning back, I lift one hand to my abdomen and whimper. If the world ended right now—a mass of raining fire and waves of the ocean over this forsaken place—I wouldn't even notice. All of what I know is right here upon the cock currently stirring up my insides. After what feels like a lifetime, the searing stretch against the thick length of him in my depths eases somewhat and I feel confident enough to lift up. Once I do, however, little pinpricks of pain and pleasure dot my flesh. With a gasp, I lower back down, taking him back to the hilt in one startlingly fast movement. That, too, fills me with new sensations.

"You're fucking tormenting me," Theos curses.

Blinking, I lift my head and finally get a look at his face. With his brow pinched tight, and his upper lip pulled back over a row of straight white teeth, he looks like he's in more pain than pleasure. Yet, at my sides, his hands contract into fists and release with repetitive movements. It's as if he wants to touch me, but fears doing so will break me.

Unable to stop myself, I reach for his hands and settle them on my hips. "Then make me stop," I tell him. "Take me, Theos Darkhaven. Forget everything and fuck all of your anger"—*and your sorrow*—"out on me. I can take it." It's probably one of the few good things being a Mortal God is good at—taking pain and pleasure that no mortal could survive.

That's all the encouragement he needs. Theos' hands latch onto my sides and the bite of his grip reaches all the way to my bones. They practically creak as he lifts me back up and slams me over his cock. Shock waves pour into my veins, ripping apart my sanity. I arch, crying out, but he doesn't stop. He continues, pounding into me over and over again until black-and-white dots speckle my vision. He fucks into me like an animal or a madman possessed. I love every bit of it. He doesn't treat me like a weak creature but takes me at my word and thrusts harder and harder. So much so that I pray he's had enough to drink to forget that this type of strength would break a true mortal.

All the while, I crane my neck and rake my nails down his chest. I ride him through the harsh thrusting and feel my clit collide with his pubic bone on each descent. A fresh scream builds within me, something I've never experienced before. It's not a carefully crafted false cry of pleasure, but one that rises within my core like a violent phoenix coming back to life after being burned to ash. The trembling from earlier invades my bones, taking over.

I hear Theos' grunts beneath me. His muscles tense under my hands. His fingers tighten on my sides. Before I realize his intention, Theos shoves his body up and over— spinning us just as I had earlier. My back hasn't hit the mattress for more than a second before he reaches down and lifts my leg over one shoulder. He pushes it down, cupping his hand under my thigh as he shoves my knee into my chest. The sudden change and tilt of his cock drives me ever higher.

I claw at the blankets around us. "Harder!" I scream. "Oh, fuck!" Thank the Gods, but he listens to me. His hips don't stop or stutter, not even when I feel his cock swell within me and a warmth floods my body. His face twists into indescribable pleasure, his lips parting as he slides into my cunt, painting my insides with his seed.

All over, I feel the tiniest bites of pain. As if all of my limbs have fallen asleep only to be woken up in the most visceral of ways. I shudder through my own orgasm, tears pricking my eyes and slipping free of the corners. With a growl, Theos slides his arm completely under the leg against his chest and shoulder and locks his hands together behind my neck. His hips never stop thrusting through my release and it goes higher and higher than I ever thought possible until the whole world explodes and all I see is white and darkness colliding into one another.

I come to an unknown amount of time later and find myself flat on my back with Theos at my side, our chests rising and falling as we try to catch our breaths. The both of us are spent. A wince comes to me as I reach down, gingerly feeling around my pussy's opening. Wetness leaks from my insides and when I lift my fingers back to my face, I find the white cloudy substance of his cum is the cause. Turning my head towards him, I try to tamp down my newfound panic. It hadn't occurred to me earlier, but...

His chuckle halts my thoughts. "Don't look at me like that, *Dea*," he murmurs. "You've wrung me dry. I couldn't try again right now even if I wanted to."

"That is *not* what I was thinking," I say.

"Then why the stare?" he asks, turning his head to meet it.

I hold my hand up dripping with his cum. "We forgot something."

He shakes his head and stretches against the mattress. "No, we didn't," he says.

I scowl. "This is serious," I snap. "I have no intention of bringing another Mortal God into this world. You and I both know that Mortal Gods don't stay with their parents." And even if that wasn't the case, I'm an assassin—and a blood servant at that. Ophelia would never allow this. It's bad enough that I don't have complete control over myself, but the idea of bringing a child into this world, forsaken and tyrannized by the Gods ... I can't bear it.

His once calm expression darkens before he shuts his eyes. "Their *mortal* parents," he corrects me. "But it doesn't matter regardless, Mortal Gods are infertile."

"Don't lie to me," I snap. "I know for a fact that there are Mortal Gods of quarter descent or less."

"There *were*," he agrees, emphasizing the past tense of his statement. "Thirty years ago, the laws of Mortal Gods changed. The Gods no longer wanted to dilute their bloodlines. All Mortal Gods in the Academy underwent infertility herb treatment. Thankfully, it doesn't affect our abilities to actually fuck and find release." He opens his eyes once more and peers at me. "We're all animals," he reminds me. "Mortals and Mortal Gods alike. Fucking is what we do. Didn't you ever find it strange that no one ever got pregnant? Even if we, as a whole, are careful, there are still accidents."

I'd never truly thought about it, but at least his explanation has given me relief. I sag back into the bed. "Thank fuck."

He chuckles at that and the worry is forgotten. I know I should get up, clean myself, and leave, but exhaustion has worn me thin. For his part, Theos doesn't demand that I leave either. I promise myself after each minute that I'll do so, but as the time stretches on, I find myself teetering on the precipice of consciousness and eventually, I lose the battle.

CHAPTER 31

KALIX

The morning sun rises early and as it does, I watch our little mortal servant dash across a courtyard, heading for the front gates. Curiouser and curiouser. Where could she be going? Turning my head, I call up one of my little familiars and send him after her. Wherever she plans on running to, I'll make sure to keep my eyes out. I find that the creature we've been keeping as our very own Terra is by far unlike the others we've had previously. Even if that makes me want to break her open to see what lies inside her bones, there's another overpowering part of me that reminds me if I kill her just to dissect her insides then she won't be bringing me any more entertainment, and I can't have that. So few things keep my attention and interest these days anyway. I'd hate to have to lose her for the momentary pleasure of seeing if there's anything physically within her that makes her so different.

Once I'm sure one of my serpents is on her path, I turn back the way I'd been walking and head towards the north tower. After several minutes, when I make it to the top and open the door to my brothers' and my chambers, I find them awake and standing across from one another in our shared rooms with scowls on their faces. Tension is thick and it merely makes me giddy at the prospect of more outbursts.

A tingle of awareness creeps along my spine as I let the door behind me swing shut. The familiar scent of sex hovers in the room. I turn my head, noting that several pieces of furniture and artwork have been completely removed. I don't have to have been here the night before to know that it's because Theos destroyed them.

"Morning, brothers," I say, announcing my presence, since neither of them has turned to greet me.

Ruen sighs and scrubs a hand down his haggard-looking face. Unlike me, he seems as if he hasn't slept in the last several hours. I do wonder where he chose to spend his night since neither of us wanted to come back here knowing what Theos would be like. If the scent on the air is anything to go by, however, it's clear Theos didn't spend it alone.

With a curse, Theos turns away from Ruen and stalks across the room to the windows. He props himself against the glass and crosses his arms over his chest. I hum in the back of my throat. "Did you not enjoy your dalliance last night?" I ask. "If you'd only asked me, I could have sent someone to distract you."

Theos slowly pivots to face me and glares. "Shut. Up."

I grin at the venom in his tone. Holding my hands up in mock surrender, I give him a pitiful look. "I don't know why you're so angry with me," I say. "I was merely trying to help."

"You're never trying to help, Kalix," Theos snaps. "So, keep your fucking trap shut and don't bother. I don't want to hear it."

So vicious. Whoever the girl was, she obviously hadn't done her job correctly if he's still this uptight. "Is this about Darius?" I inquire. "I know you cared for the man, but what's done is done now."

"Don't, Kalix." The warning comes from Ruen this time. "You antagonize him."

I do, but only because he's so easy to rile. It's not my fault he's got a short temper. I don't know why the two of them insist on caring so much for others. It always ends up this way. They all end up fighting in the ring and they either survive or they die. It's better to not care in the first place if you already know that they're likely to meet their demise at the hand of someone's power or blade.

My hands drop back to my sides. How boring. "Do either of you know where our little Terra is running off to this morning?" I ask, swapping subjects as quickly and as easily as it takes to lose interest in one thing and move on.

Theos' head jerks, but he turns away and focuses on the horizon brightening the sky outside of the arching window. Interesting response from him.

"Going?" Ruen repeats, both his tone and face darkening. *Intriguing response.* "What do you mean? Terra aren't allowed to leave the grounds without permission."

I shrug. "Well, she seems to have gained permission because I saw our little Terra leaving through the front gates on my way here."

Ruen's upper lip curls back. I do so love the way she irritates him, even if he so rarely shows it. I move away from the door and farther into the room. "You know, she's been here for quite a while now," I comment lightly. "And since the first week, we haven't done much concerning the bet— by now, I think we've lost, don't you?"

"Fuck the fucking bet," Theos barks, finally joining the

conversation as he whips his head back around. "Do you think everything is a game, Kalix?"

I blink back at him. "You enjoyed the bets," I remind him. "In fact, you were all too happy to play with her, were you not?"

Theos has pushed away from the window and stalked across the room. In a single instant, he goes from still and detached to angry and practically blowing fire into my face as he grabs me by the collar. "What have you done?" he demands.

"I've not done a damn thing," I tell him with a roll of my eyes. In fact, that's what's driving me to the brink of boredom. I've not played with her the way I want to. There's been no torture. No sex. No danger. The short battle I'd experienced the day before was certainly not enough to appease my appetite. "But if the bet is over, then that must mean I can play now, right?" I eye him, waiting for his response.

Before I can get it, though, Ruen appears over Theos' shoulder and grabs ahold of his arm. "Don't, he's just trying to goad you," he says, his sneer gone as he directs his attention to Theos.

Ugh. How utterly boring they've become.

As Theos loosens his hold on my tunic, Ruen turns to me. "You should know better, Kalix," he chastises, ever the elder brother as if he's taken it upon himself to be in charge of the two of us just because his mother happened to birth him first.

"Just because I know better doesn't mean I want to *be* better," I tell him honestly. A truer statement there never was. I'm so tired, already, of all of these rules we've been forced to follow. If only we could break free from the chains of these Academies and their expectations. I know we could, but these two don't seem to want to risk it. And thus, I'm forced to remain behind and follow in their footsteps. Because at the end of the day, everyone needs something to entertain them and my brothers are the sole beings that can provide it consistently. They never break, not truly. Not the way others do.

That fact, alone, is what makes me respect them. It's what keeps me here when I'd love nothing more than to slaughter every being that lives within these stone walls and set the chains we're bound by aflame. It's cruel of them to take away my latest fascination.

Pouting, I stare back at Ruen. "Aren't you curious?" I ask him. "If you just let me play a little, I'm sure I could find out why she's so interesting."

Ruen's frown deepens into a scowl. "Your play is nothing but torture," he replies but sounds more frustrated than angry.

"So?" What's so wrong with that? "I won't kill her if that's what you're worried about." Not at first, anyway. Something tells me, even if I tried, our little Terra could handle herself just fine. In fact, she might surprise all of us and survive me.

Ruen shakes his head. "No, don't even think it. You'll only get yourself into trouble. I'd rather keep you here on the next break than have you stationed somewhere else where I can't keep an eye on you."

The comment reminds me of my time with Talmatia. Even if I don't get into trouble, the Gods always call us for something or other. As Azai's spawn, we're subject to a lot of interest.

"She's off limits," Theos agrees.

Twisting my head to look Theos' way, I peer at him curiously. The scent of sex. The defense of the Terra. It all clicks into place and a smile spreads my lips. "Oh, you're foul, brother," I say even as I bare my teeth at him. "I didn't take you for a cheater."

"Excuse me?" Theos stiffens, but he betrays himself when his eyes cut to Ruen for a beat before returning to me.

I don't bother hiding what I know. My smile grows. "Tell me," I say. "Was she any good?"

Ruen glances between the two of us. "What the bloody Gods are you talking about?" he demands.

"Nothing," Theos claims.

"The little Terra," I say at the same time. "Oh, how ironic." I laugh. "You fucked her and yet you still want to protect her?"

Ruen curses. "No, Theos, *no*," he snaps, turning to our brother. "Tell me he's wrong."

Theos doesn't respond, but then again, he doesn't have to in order to reveal the truth. It's too late. He's been caught.

Ruen's hands clench into fists at his sides. "She's suspicious." The words practically rip free from his throat. "She can't be trusted."

"So?" I prompt, garnering his dark glare. She could be a Divine Being sent to kill us for all I care, though the likelihood of any Divine Being, Mortal God or not, relegating themselves to servitude for such a task is impossible. She's interesting and that alone is enough to make me want to keep her.

Ruen shoves a hand through the short dark strands of his hair and grabs a chunk as if he wishes to rip them out completely. I wouldn't be surprised if he did. I've rarely seen him so upset and it's amusing to watch him fight with himself. He may think no one sees it, that he's hidden it well enough. Desire, though, is my forte. Not just sexual, but the kind of desire that rests in all souls—greedy and unholy. I see such desire in him when he looks at the mortal girl, our very own mouthy little mortal Terra.

"This was a mistake," he says.

"What was?" I ask, curious.

"*Everything*," he barks out. "Letting her be a part of your ridiculous little bet. Letting her fucking stay. She needs to go."

I roll my eyes, but before I can speak, Theos jumps forward. "You were as into the bet as we were," he reminds him.

"But it did not include *fucking her*!" Ruen yells, his entire body trembling with fury.

I scratch at the underside of my jaw. "Oh, that's right," I muse aloud, thinking back. "It was just to see how long she'd last." I count back the days and weeks. "Well, if you want to honor the original bet, then that means she won regardless."

Ruen shakes his head, releasing his hair as he does so. He turns back to me. "You said she left this morning," he says.

I nod. "That I did."

"Did you—"

He doesn't need to finish his question before I have his answer. "Of course," I reply, cutting him off. "I sent one of my familiars to keep an eye on her. We'll know where she's been by the end of the day and if need be, I can always share senses with the creature."

"The bet's off," Theos says suddenly. Both Ruen and I look to him. His face is stiff and yet there are twin spots of red over his cheeks. Ruen's face is pinched tight, as if he wants to say something to that, but he stops himself.

"Are you saying that because the timeline for the original bet has passed or because you fucked her?" I inquire.

He doesn't respond.

"You ... did fuck her, didn't you?" I clarify.

Still, he doesn't say a word.

I sniff the air. "I smell sex, you have to have..."

"Gods, could you be any more fucking crude," Theos curses.

I frown. "So, you didn't fuck her then?" Excitement fills me. Perhaps the bet isn't over yet then. Perhaps there's still a chance.

"Does it matter?" Theos asks. Of course it matters. Before I can say as much, though, he flips me off and grits out his response. "But for your information, yes. I took her, or rather ... she offered herself."

More and more surprises. Tilting my head to the side, I peer at my brother with more interest. The way he avoids looking at me, the stance he takes with his arms crossed over his chest, and his jaw tight. It all speaks to something he's afraid to show and if anyone can sniff out secrets, it's me and my familiars.

As if he can sense my inner thoughts, Ruen's arm snaps out and he grabs ahold of my bicep. "Don't even think of it, Kalix." Ugh. He always says that and it always ruins my fun. "I've told you she's suspicious. We damn well don't need yet another of us falling to her fucking whims."

Theos' face pales and then tightens. His irritation and hurt is nothing in the face of my fucking boredom. Warnings. Warnings. Warnings. With a grumble, I lift my arm and shake him off. "Must you destroy every semblance of amusement?" I demand.

"She shouldn't be a source of amusement," Ruen argues. "In fact, neither of you should be looking at her like that. She's a Terra—meant for a job here and nothing more."

"You just said you found her suspicious," Theos points out.

"Yes, and as such, you both need to leave her alone," he says. "As it seems she's forgotten the bet, you two should as well. No more fraternizing with her. Satisfy yourselves elsewhere. Other Terra if you must, but not her. Leave well enough alone and for the sake of the Gods, *don't fuck her*."

I chuckle. "That's 'don't fuck her, *again*' for you, Theos."

He shoots me his middle finger.

Ruen groans, the sound rumbling in his chest. He looks far more tired than ever before.

"Why?" I demand. "You've never cared before."

"Yes, I have," he growls. "You've simply never listened."

"What if my serpent finds something today?" I ask. "What if she's a spy sent by Azai?"

The idea must have occurred to Ruen before because he doesn't seem all that surprised by my suggestion. His face hardens and his already dark eyes turn pitch black before flashing red. "If she is then we will give her nothing, do you understand?" He practically sneers. "Azai can perish in the fires of the Divine realm for all I care. If she's working for him then it's even more reason to not entertain her for a moment more." He turns to Theos. "And that includes you. Whatever happened between you two last night, you must ensure it doesn't happen again."

Theos is quiet for a moment before he responds. "If she is working for him then she already knows about certain things." Darius' death, of course, and how it affected him.

I rock back on my heels and yawn. "Darius is already dead, brother," I remind him. "It's not like Azai could take him away a second time."

Theos bares his teeth at me. "Can you keep your foul mouth shut for a singular second, Kalix?" he demands.

"What?" I lift my shoulders and let them fall back into place. "It's the truth."

In response, Ruen sighs and grabs Theos' arm, dragging him several paces away. "Ignore him," he urges. As if I haven't heard that before. Thankfully, it's the one thing Theos is never quite able to do and one of the reasons being around him is so pleasing. Ruen's tone drops, but not so low that I can't hear from where I'm standing. "Take today off and rest, the funerals for the deceased will last the rest of the week, and if the Terra truly is working for Azai, she'll be relaying your responses and attendance to him."

Theos throws off Ruen's hand and reaches up, shoving a hand through the top of his pale hair. He grabs a chunk and yanks. *Hard*. Yes, that frustration is so good. It'll make training in the coming weeks as he battles his grief and hides it away that much more enticing.

I rock back and forth on my heels and find my mind drifting as Theos and Ruen continue to talk in low tones. Curiosity gets the better of me and I reach out a mental pathway to the familiar I sent slithering after the Terra. Closing my eyes, I meld the snake's mind with my own and take in the sights it's currently seeing.

A carriage swaying back and forth, slowing to a stop. Booted footsteps hopping down. The creature waits a beat and then follows in the shadows. Every once in a while, I watch as the Terra pauses and looks back. Almost as if she can sense me and my little familiar. A shiver moves through me.

Regardless of Ruen's warning, I know that I'll not stop until I know everything about this mortal woman. Her senses are keen. Her body sensuous beneath the man-like clothes she chooses to wear. She's got the eyes of a warrior, the bosom of a sex Goddess, and the scent of something untamable. It's enough to give me a feeling similar to that of eating ambrosia.

What, oh what, could our little mortal friend truly be, I wonder. Because one thing is for certain, she's not normal. Not at all.

CHAPTER 32

KIERA

I leave the Academy at dawn, slipping through the nearly empty corridors like a shadow. The memory of last night lingers on my skin even though I'd snuck into the Darkhavens' personal bathing chamber and washed off the scent of cum and pleasure before making my escape. It was wrong of me to stay the night. The second I'd woken and realized where I still was, I'd slipped out of Theos' bed and made my exit as swiftly as physically possible.

Keeping my head low and my hood drawn up, I don't stop until I get to the front gates. I withdraw the permission I received from Hael and hand it to the guard—an older man of Mortal God descent with a streak of gray through the side of his darker hair. He reads the note and then hands it back to me before signaling for the gates to open.

I don't look back as I step through them and start walking. A strange prickling sensation moves through me as I get farther and farther from the grounds. I pause halfway down the pathway that leads to the edge of the city and look back, scanning the brush and road. There's nothing out of the ordinary, but even if my eyes don't pick up anything, my senses are screaming at me that I'm being watched.

The tips of my fingers burn with a coldness I'm not used to. Fear? I'm not entirely sure, but I do know one thing, at least. What I'd done with Theos Darkhaven last night had been a mistake. One that I won't be informing Regis about when I see him. I pray he doesn't notice the slight tilt of my stride and ask questions because if I'm honest with myself, I've never left a man's bed—even if he were still breathing when I did—with thighs this sore or a pussy this satisfied.

Turning back towards the road, I finish my descent into Riviere. It takes a good hour for me to get to the edges of the outer streets, just far enough into the residential part of the God City to catch an early morning horse-drawn carriage passing through the alleyways. The sun crests over the hillside and farther up over the spires of the Academy's roof in the distance.

Tossing the cab driver a few denza as payment, I clamber into the interior of the carriage. My upper lip pulls back instinctively as the ripe scent of male sweat permeates my nostrils and I quickly bring my cloaked sleeve up to cover my mouth and nose to muffle the smell. The only good thing about the foul odor is the fact that it means the two other individuals currently riding inside are human. Gods and Mortal Gods don't sweat the same way mortals do.

The two other riders sit opposite one another with their arms crossed and heads down as the driver clicks his tongue at the horse and sets the carriage back into motion. I'm left with little other choice but to find a spot alongside one of them.

I thrust my back against the seat as the door swings

shut behind me and turn my face into the window to watch as the world of Riviere wakes for the oncoming day. Public transport carriages aren't necessarily my favorite method of travel, but it's cheaper and it beats having to walk the entire city to get to where I'm going.

That strange feeling of being watched or followed never leaves. I peer both curiously and suspiciously at the men huddled in their seats, but neither of them speaks up, and as time drones on, they eventually disembark at their stops and others get on.

Back and forth, side to side, the carriage clatters through the streets, swaying as it stops at various intervals. The deeper we get into mortal territory, the less shiny the streets begin to look. The gold etchings on the buildings turn to silver and then plain stone. None of the travelers that board the coach are of Divine descent. Though, I suppose that makes sense. After all, no God worth their salt would be caught dead on mortal transportation unless they were hiding their identity, and in a city such as Riviere, hiding one's Divinity is reserved for only those such as me in which I am a population of one.

Another hour or so passes until we finally get close enough to my destination that I decide to disembark. My booted foot steps out onto the cobblestone road and a moment later, the door to the cab swings closed and the driver grunts as he clicks the horse back into motion. By now, the sun has risen higher into the sky, and the whole world has woken and set about their daily tasks.

Casting a quick look around, I can't shake off the strange anxiety that creeps through me. Caution had made me jump off a bit earlier than necessary, so I take a few back-alley roads and climb a few roofs, hopping from one to another before descending back to the streets just in case I truly am being followed. Finally, after what feels like forever, I spot the grime-coated door of Madam Brione's shop. I'm more shocked than anything Regis hasn't cleaned it if he's been staying in the city as he was ordered.

I twist the handle and let myself in, finding everything practically the same. The only difference to the rather unkempt interior is the fact that the stairs leading up to the individual residential rooms on the second floor are free of any dust. Regis' handiwork, no doubt. Unbuttoning my cloak, I turn and hang it onto a hook near the front door before I head up to the second floor.

Though Regis would have no way of knowing when I'd arrive, I don't doubt that he's here. I follow the well-kept, swept, dusted, and mopped staircase up to the second-floor corridor. My lips twitch the whole way. With his distaste for the unsanitary, Regis would have been a far better choice to go to the Academy than I. It's truly too bad that he wasn't the right choice of assassin.

I find the hallway upstairs just as clean as the staircase, including my own door, and out of curiosity, I pause to peek inside. Yup. He'd cleaned in there too. I shake my head. It's a wonder how he's able to fuck so much if he's such a germophobe. One might think he'd be disgusted by bodily fluids, but no. Regis is as much of a whore as a paid prostitute when it comes to sex.

Turning away from my room and letting the door swing shut, I go to the one across from me and don't bother knocking. Instead, I turn the knob and let the wood swing inward, scraping the floor and clattering against the wall it falls against. The sharp noise causes Regis to sit upright in bed as the naked body alongside him groans with irritation.

"Good morning," I say pleasantly.

Familiar blue eyes blink at me for several moments

before Regis groans and scrubs a hand down his face. "For fuck's sake," he mutters. "You couldn't have waited for a more appropriate time of day?"

I shrug, unbothered by his clearly annoyed tone. "The rest of the world is awake," I say. "I didn't exactly expect you to still be abed like a lazy good-for-nothing asshole." Lie. I had totally expected him to still be in bed. To say I'm surprised by the woman lying next to him would be yet another lie.

I prop myself against the doorframe as the woman wakes up enough to realize that they're no longer alone. A sharp scream echoes out of her throat as the pretty brunette jerks up and grabs ahold of the blankets, yanking them nearly up to her face. It takes all of my self-control not to burst out laughing as she practically rips them free of Regis' lap as well. He barely makes the move to grab a corner and keep it over his unclothed bottom half just in time.

"Fuck!" Regis curses before pointing to the door. "Out, Kiera! Give me a damned moment to get dressed at the very least."

"You're the one who sent a message and made it sound urgent," I reply, turning away as I make my way back out into the hallway. I don't close the door, but I do keep my back turned as I hear his feet hit the hardwood floor and then stomp to the doorway.

With a grin, I glance back just as he slams the door in my face. Ah, I've missed this, I think to myself. How long has it been since I've been able to actually act like myself and not force out subservient words? Too fucking long.

"I'll be downstairs in the kitchen," I call out as I head back for the stairs. "Tell your girlfriend she's welcome to join us for breakfast—or rather, I think it's almost lunchtime now."

More cursing and scrambling noises echo from beyond the door and a rather hard thump lands against the wooden frame. I'd bet my favorite pair of leather boots that he's cursing up a storm and struggling not to come out into the hallway and attack me for that comment. One night with him and most women want marriage. As much as I don't want to personally experience it myself, that must mean he's rather decent in bed. I'd sure hope so with all of the experience he's gotten. Calling his bed partner his 'girlfriend' will no doubt cause some friction, but that's what he gets for fucking around during working hours.

With the grumbling noise from behind Regis' bedroom door following me down the stairs, I head back to the first floor of Madam Brione's shop and peer into the dark interior of her main room. Everything remains the same, including the thick layer of dust that seems to permeate every surface available. Dried herbs and flowers hang from the ceiling and books are piled in a disorganized fashion on her counter as well as in stacks that litter the floor. Poor Regis. Living here must be pure torture for him. If we could switch places, I certainly would.

Making my way down the narrow back hallway that leads to a kitchen at the rear of the building, I find the place empty of all other life. Curious. I wonder if Madam Brione is even here. As I wait for Regis to make his appearance, I rifle through the pantry in search of food and find a treasure trove of herbs and ingredients. I waste no time in cracking a few eggs into a pan and lighting a fire under the wooden stove.

I'm practically ready to dish it all up by the time a hulking figure stumbles through the doorway and I hear the front door open and close. Regis glares at me as he stomps into the room and takes a seat at the rickety wooden table that's barely big enough for two people.

"You could've sent a message that you'd be coming this morning," he complains as I slap a few fried and seasoned eggs onto a metal plate and slide them his way.

I roll my eyes and dish up my own plate before leaving the stove and taking a seat across from him. Despite the food in front of him, Regis continues to peer at me with a scowl and an annoyed tilt to his brows.

"Stop being such a fucking baby," I reply as I dig into my meal. It's been a while since I've had to cook for myself and I have to say that one good thing about the Academy is that their food is always made to perfection.

Regis mutters under his breath as he eats his breakfast and for a while, the two of us eat in companionable silence that is sweetly familiar. I'd almost forgotten what it was like outside of the Academy. It's all too easy to get used to the world in there, but now, sitting across from someone of equal standing like Regis, I find that I miss the outside world.

My actions the night before come back to me with a pang in my chest. Guilt and maybe a little bit of sorrow for Theos hit me and sours my stomach. My upper lip curls back at the last egg on my plate and with a sigh, I push it away.

"You gonna finish that?" Regis asks as he finishes licking his tin fork clean.

Without a word, I push my plate towards him, and he gladly lifts the egg onto his plate and proceeds to devour it. Setting my elbow on the wooden table, I peer around the small but well-maintained kitchen. I'm not entirely sure if it's Regis' work or if Madam Brione simply treats the place where she cooks and eats her meals better than the rest of her residence.

Once Regis is done eating, however, I decide that enough time has passed and now that his bed partner has left, we're alone enough to broach the topic of today's meeting.

"So," I start. "What was so urgent that you needed an in-person meeting?"

Regis slows down and lowers his hands to the table. For a moment, his eyes are focused on the grain of the table before he lifts them to me. I stiffen at his expression a moment before he speaks.

"Carcel is coming to Riviere."

A whole host of emotions passes through me at that single statement and none of them are good. Ophelia's son is coming to Riviere, and for both Regis and I, that cannot mean anything good. For several seconds, the two of us remain silent, and finally, after I'm sure I can respond without an outburst of anger, I say, "Why?" It's the only thing I need to know. Why the fuck would Carcel show up now? Did Ophelia send him? Does she not trust that I can handle this with only Regis as backup?

Regis picks up his plate as well as mine and then takes them over to the small sink in the corner alongside the stove. He dumps the dirty dishes inside and grips the counter. With his back to me, I can't see the expression on his face, but I don't have to, to know what he's thinking. Like me, he's no fan of Carcel's.

"I don't know," he says after a moment, "but I received word of his travel a few days ago. I sent a message to Ophelia, but there's no response which can only mean one thing..." He doesn't have to finish for me to know what he's thinking.

She sent him and there will be no argument. "Damn it." The curse slips through my clenched teeth. Of all times for Ophelia's son to make an inopportune visit. Despite her lack of marriage, it's well known among the Guild that Carcel was her first choice for taking over the Underworld when it comes time for her retirement—at least, it was until Regis. The only person Carcel hates more than me is him.

"If there's no stopping his arrival, then we need to discuss what to do when he gets here," Regis says, turning to face me once more. Crossing his arms over his chest, he leans back against the counter and settles a serious look on me. "Any ideas?"

"On distracting Carcel?" I shake my head. "He's only after one thing; you and I both know that."

Regis' upper lip curls back, baring his teeth in frustration. "This job is too dangerous for him to fuck up," he snaps. "That bastard has to know that. Ophelia wouldn't have sent him if he didn't understand that much."

"Are we so sure that she sent him?" I ask. It's a pipe dream to think that Carcel is acting on his own, though.

Regis knows that as well as I do and levels me with a sympathetic look. "Carcel isn't stupid enough to interfere without her backing him."

I slap a hand on the table, rattling the whole thing on its already rickety legs. "This is the Academy we're talking about," I say. "Not some Lower God's mansion. If I'm discovered then who knows what kind of trouble we're *all* in for." No amount of torture training can prepare for the unknown. As much as I want to believe I'll never break or that I'll manage to kill myself before it's too late, just the risk of it all is too much for me to bear.

"Maybe we should quit while we're ahead," I think

aloud. "Do we even know who the target is yet or is the client still keeping that under wraps?"

Regis shakes his head, his brows lowering once more, pinching down tight and creating a V between his eyes. "It's odd," he admits. "You've settled yourself in the Academy. You've been there for weeks. We've gotten half of the payment. We should have at least gotten a hint at this point."

With one hand still on the table, I take my other and scrub it down my face. "What are they waiting for?" I wonder aloud.

Silence stretches between us for long moments, and I can practically hear Regis' thoughts turning over the same wheel as mine. "Do you think..." Regis begins, only to drift off as he lifts his head and stares across the room. His eyes are focused on the far wall, but unseeing as if he's thinking far ahead into the future instead of seeing where we're at presently.

"What?" I press him when he still hasn't finished his thought after several moments.

"Nothing," he mutters. "Never mind. It's probably not what I'm thinking." I part my lips to demand that he tell me what he's thinking, exactly, regardless of whether or not he thinks it's right. Before I can, however, he pushes away from the counter and says something else. "Carcel's arrival will likely be within the next two weeks depending on where he's coming from," he states. "Whatever his intentions are, we'll need to prepare."

I groan and sink back into my chair, tipping it onto its back legs and maintaining my balance by my knees beneath the kitchen table. "He'll want a full report like he's Ophelia or something," I guess.

Regis nods his agreement. "I can relay that."

I snort. "Do you think he'll let you or will he call me out of the Academy to give it?" I ask.

"Carcel's an ass, but he's not a complete idiot," Regis replies. "He'll know it's not easy for you to sneak out so often."

"Is that why you had me come now?" I guess with a renewed smile.

His lips twitch and one corner drifts up. That's all the answer I need. Regis is a fucking genius sometimes. Knowing that I've already had to leave the Academy for this meeting will ensure that Carcel's hands are tied and he won't be able to call for me for a while at least. I shake my head and grin his way.

"No wonder Carcel hates your guts," I say, laughing. "You've always got to back him into a corner."

"A 'thank you' will suffice, Kiera."

I roll my eyes, but when I submit my, "Thanks," I actually do mean it. Dealing with Carcel now, with everything going on inside the Academy and especially with the mistake I made last night, is something I really don't want to think about. Tipping my head back, I stare up at the ceiling as Regis sets about heading to the back door. He heads outside, propping open the door before returning with a bucket of water—likely from a shared well. Using the water and a nearby rag, Regis begins cleaning. He wipes down the table we just finished eating on and then washes the dishes.

"So," he says after several minutes of silence, "how is it going?"

"In the Academy?" As if he could be referring to anything else. I sigh. "I don't … exactly know. I'm firmly ingrained into my role and mission, but it's not like it's real yet. I have no target, and therefore, I can't do reconnaissance. The mission has stagnated. I'm growing bored."

"How are you faring with the Mortal Gods?" he asks.

My lips twist. Yesterday's memories are heavy in my mind. Not just my unintentional night with Theos, but what happened to cause that. Darius' death. The battles. There'd be no point in broaching the topic of either with Regis, and yet, I find myself wanting to. I bite down on my lower lip, nibbling as I consider my words.

"They're not easy, that's for sure," I admit. "A part of me can't stand to be around any of them. They're all so *fucking* ... pompous." The insult, spoken so many times before, doesn't hold as much weight today as it has in the past.

Regis chokes out a laugh as he finishes cleaning the counter, even the parts that I hadn't used. "Did you expect anything less from Divine Beings and their offspring?"

I shake my head. "No, not really." But just calling them pompous isn't the full truth. They may be boastful and selfish creatures, but there's a sorrow clinging to all of them. An awareness that their lives are controlled by the Divine Beings just as much as mortals' are. My chest rises and falls with a great breath.

I sense Regis' attention rather than see it as I keep my gaze trained firmly on the ceiling above me. After a while of not talking, I hear his motions get quiet and then finally his face appears over mine. "That's quite a thought-provoking expression you're wearing," he says.

My eyes cut to his. The words I want to speak linger on my tongue, right there, but I can't seem to get them out. Instead, I just sigh again and let my legs—and subsequently the chair legs—drop back down. "I'm just tired." The lie comes easily. Perhaps because it's not necessarily a full-fledged lie. The fact is, I *am* tired. Exhausted by this life of mine. What is the point of power and abilities if I can't even make my own decisions? Even the choice to come to the Academy of Riviere was only granted by another.

Regis holds up his hand, capturing my attention. "That reminds me," he says. "I almost forgot. I've got something for you."

I peer at him, curious. "Is it my birthday?" I ask. "You never give me gifts."

The dead look he gives me would be enough to send a lesser being fleeing, but not me. I merely give him a grin back as he rifles through his clothes before withdrawing a vial on a thin leather string. "We don't celebrate birthdays," he reminds me. "Don't be facetious."

I shrug, lifting both of my arms in the process. "Why not? You always are."

Regis rolls his eyes and tosses the vial and leather string my way. I catch it before it can hit the table and hold it up. Small and cylindrical, the vial is filled with a liquid so purple it's almost black. "What is it?" I ask.

"Poison," he says. "Nightshade, to be precise."

My eyes shoot to his. "I remember asking for a new poison, but I thought you'd give me something a bit lighter. Why are you giving me nightshade?" I demand, my fingers closing around the capsule and tightening.

"If you want a light poison, you could always use your spiders—their venom should be more than enough for something small," Regis replies.

"My spiders don't bite me," I remind him.

He rolls his eyes. "Then order them," he snaps and then taps his finger on the grain of the table hard enough for it to tilt slightly before settling back into place. "Nightshade is strong enough so if anything worse happens then it'll be of use to you. Just take the damn thing." He's referring to the caning I'd received and the challenge of making sure I maintained a mortal's rate of healing. I reopen my hand and stare at the sloshing liquid inside with a sigh.

"How many berries?" I ask, tilting it one way and then another. I'd been introduced to all manner of poisons during my training, and nightshade had been one of the higher concentrated ones. In mortals, it induced vomiting, delirium, hallucinations, higher heartbeat, and eventually … death.

"Ten," Regis answers. "Enough to kill an adult mortal, but for you … well, I figured you could drain half or all of it depending on your need. If the target is right, you could also slip it into their drink and then kill them when they're weakened. Even if it won't kill a God or Mortal God, it will weaken them for a time."

I consider his words. He's right, of course. I myself had tried this before and though I hadn't died, I had been weakened for several days following. "Thank you," I say, closing my fingers around the vial once more. I hold up the leather twine attached and slip the poison over my head, tucking it firmly between my breasts beneath the new tunic I'd retrieved from my room since Theos had shredded my last one.

Standing up, I push the chair I'd been sitting on back beneath the lip of the table. "I think it's best if we get our client to send the name of our target sooner rather than later," I state.

Regis eyes me, and for once, I don't want to look at him. He's known me as long as anyone and so I know how easily it would be for him to dive into my thoughts and guess what they are if I gave him the chance.

"I'll let Ophelia know," he murmurs. "I'm sure you don't

want to be around those pretentious Mortal Gods any more than necessary."

I hide the wince his words cause and merely offer a nod of agreement instead. Pretentious. Arrogant. Cruel. These are all things I expected of the children of the Gods. Since actually being around them for weeks, now, though, I'm starting to wonder if they're not more like us than I ever wanted to admit.

It's a rather cold realization and one that does not make me feel good. At the end of the day, it won't matter if they're good or bad—my target will inevitably fall and someone's blood will stain my blade by the end of this mission.

CHAPTER 33

KIERA

The first person I run into upon my return to the Mortal Gods Academy is a surprise. With soft features that are dainty in their faux fragility, Niall's ward, Maeryn, blinks back at me as I round the corner of a building and stop a few feet from where she stands. The permission I received had only been for the day, but I'd taken full advantage and now the sky is tinged with a mixture of colors announcing the arrival of night amidst its twilight hue.

"I apologize, Miss Maeryn," I say quickly, bowing slightly even as my bones practically vibrate with the need to hurry back to my room. "I didn't see you there." A mistake on my part. I should've sensed her presence before ever rounding the corner. I'd been too hurried to return to the tower, too full of thoughts of whose bed I'd slipped from earlier that morning, and what my actions last night might cause in the near future.

The flower she'd been in the process of plucking from a bush to the side of the walkway in the courtyard I now regret choosing slips from her hand and flutters to the ground. In response, Niall's ward blows out a breath. "You don't learn easily, do you?" she asks without any heat or irritation despite the words.

I lift my head, confused. "Excuse me?" As the words slip from my lips, though, I recognize this very courtyard as the same one that she'd ... well, I hesitate to say 'rescued' considering that I could have very well saved myself from Rahela's temper tantrum—but not without consequence.

Maeryn closes her eyes and shakes her head. In this low light, her skin appears darker than I know it to be. Her freckles stand out and the long ringlets of red curls that descend over her back and shoulders shift with the light breeze that flows through the buildings.

"I distinctly remember the last time you were in this courtyard, you were in a bit of trouble. Did you forget that this was a Mortal God only courtyard?"

I stare back at her and then take a quick glance around, ensuring that we're alone before I return my gaze to hers. "Does it matter if you're the only one here?"

She stiffens. I watch with interest as the hands at her sides turn to fists. "I'm not sure exactly what Niall has told you about me, but even if I'm not so inclined to have you imprisoned or punished for that blatant disrespect, you should know better."

Touchy. I suppose she doesn't like being seen as weak then. Good to know. "I meant no disrespect," I reply. "I merely meant that if you were to be kind enough to let me go, then no one else would know."

Maeryn's jade green eyes watch me with a curiosity I know I should avoid. Even if she's no more than a Second Tier Mortal God in this Academy, which is damn near close enough to Terra treatment, I like that she doesn't shy away from putting someone in their place. Even if that someone is me. A beat passes in silence and then another and another until I wonder if she'll ever respond.

After what feels like an eternity and, of course, knowing that I'm unable to leave her presence until permitted, she finally bends down to retrieve the fallen bloom. The muscles of my back tighten beneath my cloak as she rises again, takes a step towards me, and holds it out. Frowning, I look down at the strange-looking flower. It's white with red tips, but its petals are skinny and far apart, and though the filaments are the same color as its petals, they stick out farther as if screaming to be noticed.

When I still have yet to take it, Maeryn chuckles and reaches down, grabbing my hand and lifting it. She pushes the stem into my palm and forcefully closes my fingers around it. "Be careful, Kiera," she whispers. "This place is just as dangerous to Terra as it is to Mortal Gods."

A rather tumultuous emotion rumbles through me as she bows her head and slips around me. She doesn't say anything more—not that she'll keep my use of the courtyard a secret but not that she won't either. I stare down at the flower she handed me as her steps grow farther and farther away. This Academy is growing more and more peculiar by the day and I'm starting to wonder if Regis' concern isn't more warranted than my abilities presumed.

I gather myself quickly and tuck the flower into my cloak as I finish dashing across the courtyard to the other side. As I do, I lift my head, looking up to the north tower that is my destination. The arching wide window at the very top of the tower is illuminated as the sun dips beyond the horizon, bathing the sky in indigo. I'm sure the other Darkhavens have returned to their chambers after last night. The memory of Theos and I still sits heavy within my flesh.

With a shiver, I drag my cloak tighter around me and keep going. Regis managed to buy me some time when Carcel arrives, but who knows how long I can keep away from that bastard or what he'll expect from me when he comes. I've been on more than my fair share of missions with him and I do not doubt that in spite of the exacerbated danger of my current job, he'll expect more work outside of the Academy from me if it's even partially feasible. He always is one to push the limits.

Sneaking into the north tower isn't difficult. In fact, it's all too easy—whereas other Mortal God residences have guards, this one is solely for the Darkhavens and their Terra. The rest of the rooms at the bottom of the tower are used primarily for storage and emergency residences. Now that I know the truth of Mortal God fertility, too, it strikes me as almost too obvious the lower count of students than anticipated. The Gods are curbing their offspring's chance to make their own spawn. Why? What changed?

I don't get a chance to think too deeply on it as I ascend the circular staircase to the floor just beneath the top one. Unlocking the door, I slide into the cold darkness of my room and shut myself in. A dull throb has started up in the back of my head. Lack of sleep will do that to a person. It takes me three wide steps to get to the bed—or at least close enough for me to toss myself upon the creaking cot. A groan rumbles up my throat as I snatch the pathetic excuse for a pillow at the top of it, stuff my face into it, and let out a frustrated scream.

Weeks, I've been here. Weeks without a clue as to who my target is. What the hell could Ophelia be thinking? And after all of that, she still sends Carcel of all people. My throat burns through another scream before I finally roll to the side and stare up at the rafters.

How much longer will I need to live on the edge of discovery? Risking my life for that denza payout? No, it's not for the denza. It's for what that money will provide me. Freedom.

I reach back, touching the invisible mark at the nape of my neck. No one would ever be able to find it even if they stripped me down, shaved my head, and did a thorough search. The mark of a blood servant is something that travels deeper than the skin. It's inside my very bones, tethering me to Ophelia. It's why she's always felt so comfortable letting me travel on my own because ever since it was placed upon me, there was no doubt that she would be able to find me wherever I went.

I am lower than a mortal in this God's realm. I am a blood servant to her. If she commanded me to kill myself, I would struggle to resist the urge to take my own blade and slice it through my wrists and throat to bring her desire for my demise to life. I'd tried enough already. After ten years, I've learned to accept it. I've resigned myself to my fate.

But here. The Mortal Gods Academy of Riviere. I've struggled not to hope that this place would bring me to my freedom. Even if I have to put up with the Darkhavens, anything is worth the price of my independence.

I shut my eyes and in turn, shut out the image of the room around me. For several long minutes, as the temperature in the room drops in response to the temperature outside doing the same, I just lay here and float. Every once in a while there's a soft thud or thump above my head. I can just picture Ruen sitting in his chair, book in hand, rocking what should be a heavy piece of furniture up on two legs as he inadvertently swivels the wingback chair he prefers to sit in while reading and then lets it slam back down on the floor.

I've never asked him what he reads. I can always figure that out myself when I go through their rooms to clean. He seems to prefer philosophical literature and even a few romances of lore. It's such a dichotomy of his outward exterior. A warrior labeled in the scars of his youth outside, and inside the comfort of the Darkhaven chambers, a book-obsessed hermit. My lips twitch. It would be even more amusing if it weren't such a tragedy.

This whole fucking world is a godsdamned tragedy. My story. Theirs. It doesn't matter who plays the role of hero or villain in it. We're all puppets at the edges of the strings played by the Divine Beings. I just happen to be the unluckiest bitch of them all to be controlled by more than just them but by mortals themselves.

Some sword I am. All the harnessing and shaping Ophelia did and here I lie, praying to Gods that no longer listen as they sleep alongside their worshippers, that the ones I am meant to kill aren't those that rest above me.

Pathetic, this sympathy of mine.

CHAPTER 34
KIERA

I don't want to do this. *The fear and words spiral in my head, but I know better now than to voice them. My wants don't matter—not to my Master.* Despite that fact, Ophelia must be able to read the emotions on my face.

"We all do things we don't want to, Kiera." Her voice is unwavering. Hard. "This is another test on your journey. Once this is complete, you'll have that much more freedom."

Freedom. *I want it so badly—have dreamed of it. Of returning home, to the Hinterlands. Even if my dad is no longer there, it's still ripe with memories of what I crave. Peace. The absence of pain and loss and danger. For all the things the Gods have wanted and have taken from this world, my father always told me that they feared the Hinterlands. Perhaps in their gilded castles and manors, they lied to themselves and everyone else about their disinterest in a backwoods, savage land, but my dad had told me the truth. The Hinterlands were the oldest of the lands and the place that held the most secrets. They feared it, though no one could say why. That fear of theirs was going to be my salvation. My home.*

As the old memories fade from my mind, I close my eyes and try to recall the little cottage we'd lived in before those bandits had burned it to the ground. The images are foggy, old. Just a simple outline of a doorway and shadows. All around me, there are shadows. They hide my dad's face and the finer details, and trying to bat them away, even if only mentally, has them pushing back, erasing the whole image at once. I can't even remember what that small one-room building smelled like. My eyes open in panic, unseeing of what's around me. Was it always damp? Did it smell of mold and wood or herbs and rain?

Freedom is why I'm here, but I can't even recall what that feels like. What was it like to choose where I slept? Where or what I ate? My breath rushes into my chest and back out in the same instant. Even if I do this tonight, I may never see the Hinterlands again. Ice fills my veins. Tonight changes things for me. Though I hope this is my first step home, it could very well lead me farther away.

"What if I'm not ready?" I ask, speaking slowly so my words don't all rush out in one breath. Tipping my head up, I look out from beneath the hood of my cloak to the tall woman standing at my side, slightly in front of me. Her face is unflinching and if I didn't know better, I'd say she wasn't a woman at all. Not a mortal at all but a statue made of granite.

I continue to peer at the woman at my side. Ophelia and I, though we don't look alike, stand as close as two people can without actually touching. In the dim light provided by the low lanterns and the moon peeking through the clouds above, I let my gaze rove over her supple skin. It's practically a mirror image of the clouds above. Dark and smooth, clouded by nothing—not a singular blemish. If I didn't know better, I'd think she was an immortal Divine Being herself.

Since I met her, she's seemed that way. Perfect in many ways. Beautiful. Cold. Powerful. She uses her looks as a weapon and she's told me that I'll have to do the same. I know that *means that, eventually, more than just putting a blade to some-one's throat. It'll mean undressing and seducing someone. My insides roil at that thought. It's an inevitability that will come to pass if I want a future within the Underworld, and someday, beyond.*

"You're ready when I say you are," is Ophelia's only response. That's it. No comment on what I'm about to do, about the line I'm about to step over. Once crossed, I know I'll never be able to come back, and I'm struggling to see this as anything other than me making the final decision to take a life.

This isn't training. This isn't practice. This is real.

Even my dad had apologized as he had killed animals for the sake of filling our bellies. She doesn't. Ophelia apologizes for nothing. How many people has she killed, I wonder, to treat the act of taking a life with such indifference? Almost as soon as that thought crosses my mind, it flies away.

The truth is, I don't want to know how many people she's killed because, at the end of the day, the next person is all that matters. Making sure that the next person isn't me.

The back of my neck twinges. I know it's not real, the feeling of pain, but I reach back and touch the space where the brand she'd placed on me lies beneath the surface of my skin anyway. The sliver of brimstone that sits under the surface is indiscernible to the naked eye, but I'm still viscerally aware of it sitting there beneath my skin, an ever-present reminder of my ownership. It's a bad habit to keep touching it. My fingertips are cold whereas the skin above the contract mark is hot.

Remember why you're still alive, *I tell myself.* It's because of what you can do. *Only* you.

Sure, I know mortals can't kill Mortal Gods that easily, but if I've learned anything at all, it's that even if Ophelia can't physi-cally end my existence, she can do so much worse. She can make me take my own life if she so wished, and that *frightens me.*

So, here and now, I need to make a choice. It's either them ... or me.

"This is a simple job," Ophelia continues. "I chose this specifically for your first time."

I look up at her from beneath my hooded cloak. The night clouds above our heads swarm with darkness—little shadows dancing across them as they shift to cover the moon. The street lanterns are dim, flickering in low pulses as the flames inside sway to and fro.

By this time of the month, the God Lord of this territory has yet to replace the gas within them to keep them going and there are more snuffed out due to lack of fuel than there are those that remain lit. That's why she chose tonight of all nights, I'd wager. It's darker, and therefore, it will be harder for anyone to identify me if I make a mistake and am somehow caught.

She's risking a lot too, *I remind myself. Though it doesn't truly feel like she's risking anything, not from the way she acts as if nothing can touch her. Not even the Gods.*

Ophelia's head tilts slightly to the side, her chin lifting an inch as if she's listening for something. I'm left to stare up at the sharp underside of her jaw that, despite her decades of experience within the Underworld, holds not a single scar or wrinkle. Her equally black hair is braided back into twin tails down the sides of her head, disappearing into her cloak. The more I learn of the world outside of the Hinterlands, the more I realize how strange it is for a woman of such beauty to have such a position as head of an assassin Guild.

"Come." Ophelia offers her hand as she gazes across the street. Knowing I have little choice, I slip my fingers against hers—the paleness of my skin shining like the moon against the midnight sky of hers.

Unlike her face and neck, Ophelia's hands are where I see the evidence of her humanity. They are littered with tiny little scars.

Nicks and cuts. Along the inside of her right wrist, too, there sits the deepest one. Even now, when it's long since healed, the ragged line where a blade had once cut so deep as to have left a mark on her skin forevermore is a slightly lighter shade than the rest of her skin. I've often wondered who could have caused such a wound, but to ask an assassin about their battle scars is to ask them to reveal their secrets and vulnerabilities—an impossibility.

So, I tuck the curiosity away into the back of my mind and cross the road as the first droplets of the night rain begin to fall over us. The wafting aromas of cooking meat filter out of someone's chimney and my stomach rumbles with hunger. Ophelia ignores the sound and so do I. If I fail my duty tonight then I'll have more to worry about than an empty stomach.

Together, the two of us hurry down a small pathway and then around a series of small houses, lined up one by one in a row. They're peasant houses, each of them sharing a wall between them to offer the individual families some sense of privacy.

It's such a strange idea to me when once I'd only known the single-room hut deep within the Hinterlands that I shared with my dad. With each passing day, week, month, and year ... I miss it and all that it represented then and represents for me now.

Freedom.

A thing I will not have if I don't learn to take up the blade of an assassin and make this first kill.

Ophelia's footsteps slow to a stop and mine along with her. There, sitting at the top of the hill, far beyond these rows of compressed houses, is a much larger dwelling. The manor of our target. My throat works as I shoot a quick glance to her face and back again.

"The documents said it was a man, right?" I ask, proud of

the way my voice doesn't shake despite my insides doing just that.

"And a woman," Ophelia replies. "A couple. You will have to kill one and then the other, so I suggest you make your first kill as silent as possible so as not to awaken your second target. If you fail and are captured by the Gods' authorities…"

She doesn't need to finish her sentence for her words to take effect. I pull my hand from hers and cross my arms around my stomach as if I can protect it. The not-so-distant memory of brands being pressed into the sensitive flesh of my abdomen and arms and thighs and legs returns. I blink hard as I reject the tears that burn at the backs of my eyes.

A shiver overtakes me. "I won't fail."

As much as I don't want to do this … I can't afford to fail.

It's them or me, I remind myself. Them … or me.

Regis' words of warning return to me as I stare up at the double-storied dwelling atop that hill. Always choose yourself in the worst-case scenario, he told me. That's what everyone else will do too. You can't trust them. So, trust the one person you can—yourself. Be selfish.

"Are you coming with me?" I ask as I unwrap my arms from my waist and reach down to double-check that my blades are in place. My hands tremble against the handles, but it's fine. I've done this before … in theory. I've trained for this. I've fought with Regis and many others. I've been taught where each and every weak point is. Every artery and blood vessel that could be used to drain a man or woman of their blood. This is simply putting my lessons into practice. That's all this is … practice.

Inside my chest, my heart hammers away, driving strange piercing sensations through my body. Like the sharp ends of a carpenter's nails. Over and over again, it stabs into me until I swear if I reached down and felt across my rib cage that it'd be leaking blood instead of rainwater, and the remains of those nails would be protruding from my flesh, jutting out from even my clothes. Evidence of my heart's fear.

"I will wait here," Ophelia answers me. She glances down and though she doesn't spend long looking me over, I know she's seen all she needs to. Every tremble in my limbs, though I try to hide them. Every nervous tic that I haven't yet managed to find and exterminate. She sees all and if I hadn't seen her bleed myself on the rare occasions she was wounded in practice and watched with careful eyes to see just how long it took those minor cuts to heal, I might think she was more Mortal God than I am. Sometimes, it feels as if she is more than that—like some Goddess whose soul was accidentally placed in the body of a mortal and not a Divine Being.

Ophelia is never afraid. Always confident. Cruel, but not without reason. I could have been purchased by far worse mortals or ... I could have been sent to the Gods themselves. I shudder to think of that. Even if they are afforded more luxuries, being unable to walk the streets with others, breathe air in the Hinterlands, or even recall my dad's face. Those are all priceless to me and worth every bit of pain in my current life. That's why I need to make this choice. If I ever want to get the peaceful life I remember in the Hinterlands back, I need to be able to survive.

"There is a time limit to this," Ophelia continues after a brief pause as she assesses me. "You have until sunrise to complete your task. Kill the couple and come back here before the first stretches of gold have reached the sky and your training will be complete."

I pause at that. I knew this was like some final test, but I wasn't aware that this singular act would mark the end of my time as an assassin's apprentice. "Does..." I hesitate to ask it for fear that I already know the answer, but the desire to be sure swells within me, giving me no relief until I have the answer. "Does this mean I'll be free to leave the Guild?" I ask. "That if I *kill these people, I won't have to sleep in the cells anymore? That I can go out on my own?"*

Ophelia's dark gaze settles on me once more. Her full lips purse together, the edges tipping slightly down as she assesses me ... or so I assume. It's so difficult to tell with her enigmatic expressions. Unlike me, she's already mastered the act of outward apathy. It's as if nothing fazes her. No question too bold. No act too repulsive.

"You will never be free, Kiera," she says. "Not until your debt to the Underworld has been paid in full. But with this, you will have proven that you are capable of taking your place amongst the other assassins in our Guild. You will be given jobs and paid for those jobs. You've completed your instructions on what you are to do should your lineage be revealed." My body tightens all over once more at that reminder. "I'm sure I don't have to tell you again that this is a different matter. Once you've taken your first blood, your destruction along with the Underworld's will be mutually assured. You will become an assassin of the Guild and you will cease to be Kiera, the nomad. So, yes, if you are so concerned with sleeping in the cells—after this night, should you complete your mission to satisfaction, you will be permitted more liberties."

She bends slightly, arching over me as I tip my head back and stare up into her half-concealed gaze. Though I can see her eyes, pick out the individual strands of brown and red and gold within her irises, I can't see the true intentions behind her words. In fact, it feels as if she's hiding something. As if she has always been veiling whatever it is that lays dormant within her.

"Do not, however, mistake what might very well be your newfound liberties for freedom, Kiera," she warns me. "True freedom comes when you are able to make any and all choices on your own without anyone else's command or influence. Do your *duty well tonight and you will be rewarded. Fail ... and you shall understand why there are no failed assassins in existence."*

I frown. *"But I've never met a failed assassin. There aren't any at the—"* One shapely brow lifts over her eye and I stop talking. *"Oh,"* I finish lamely, realizing my oversight.

Ophelia stands back up and looks back to the manor in the near distance. "Run along now," she commands. *"I shall wait here for the news of your success."*

I swallow the lump in my throat, but it doesn't go down without a bite of pain. Instead of complaining, though, I turn towards the manor and start across the street. Almost as soon as we've separated, I look back and it's as if Ophelia manages to intertwine herself with the shadows. I no longer see her, even if I know she's there.

Keep moving. *I've long since passed the point of no return. This is no different.*

Still, despite that warning, the closer I grow to the manor the harder my heart beats against my rib cage. It's as if the crazy thing can stop the oncoming death of my target with the noise of its fear alone.

Fat chance.

My legs move swiftly, devouring the route between Ophelia and the manor. Once at the iron and stone gate that surrounds the Gods' home, I quickly scale the outside and drop down into the shadows on the other side. I mold myself to anything and everything on the landscape, becoming one with the shadows. I can feel them reaching out, touching along my skin, whispering for me to come closer. To give myself in to them completely and let them feed upon me for sustenance.

I shake off those wayward emotions and the tingling of my own power as I close the space between me and the building I'm meant to enter. It takes no work at all for me to pick the lock of a side door and slip inside. Gods, I realize, are far too confident in *themselves. There are no guards. No sentinels striding through the quiet house around me.*

I close my eyes and send out a burst of power, seeking out my little friends. Several spiders respond to my call. I meet their tiny little minds, and together, our collective consciousness combines. Behind my closed lids, I can see the outline of the home I'm standing in. Through the different hallways and rooms to the sleeping chamber of the God couple I've come for.

The spiders are anxious. They don't speak so much in human words, but I can sense the direction of their thoughts and something else has made them all too frightened. What could it be...?

The bite of fear slams into me and I stumble, nearly slipping as my back smacks a wall. The ricochet of pain seizes my spine and lungs. My breath stops in my throat and freezes as one of the spiders shrieks in my mind. Tiny, grubby little fingers smash it to bits—exterminating its life. Several other spiders, the ones around it, physically flee from whatever the source of danger is. As they do, however, they share with me the vision of that spider's murderer.

A small child with long hair donning a bloody and dirt-stained face slaps at the floor of his room. Tears cut clean tracks down their too thin cheeks. Fear. The child is just as afraid of the spiders as they are of him.

What is he? A prisoner? Why would a God keep a child so dirty within their home?

Stay on task. *Ophelia's voice appears in my mind. A reminder that anyone other than my target is to be forgotten. My insides tighten, but I wave away the image of the crying child and step through the manor. I trail the scent and feeling of Divinity until I find where it's strongest—behind a large ornate set of wooden doors.*

Silent as can be, I approach. Here is where the danger truly begins. If I'm caught, I'm dead. If I'm not, I'm that much closer to freedom. I suck in a deep breath and pause outside of the door. As I lean into the shadows, they come alive for me. Squirming and sliding down my calves and forearms as if they're living, breathing creatures. I look down at them, both confused and alarmed. They've never reacted like this in training. I didn't even know I could do this. Or ... perhaps it's not my power at all but power from the Divine Beings in the room waiting for me.

Do these little creatures answer to them? Will they reveal me? I hold my breath, but nothing happens. The shadows continue to wiggle against me like little puppies seeking affection. Oddly enough, when I reach out and pat one, my fingers move through the darkness as if it's not tangible. The misty black turns and circles my hand as if whining for more. Their excitement grows, but so too does my anxiety. I need to get this over with quickly.

I pick the lock on the Masters' room and let myself into the darkened interior. Shadows surround me, speak to me, their desires swallow me whole as they shroud my physical body. I shiver as they separate and disperse when I step closer to the bed that is set in the middle of the room.

Moonlight pours in through the window across from me, gauze curtains masking very little as it practically illuminates the path left for me to the two beings slumbering in the four-poster bed. My heart is hammering now in my chest, racing so fast, like a frightened horse, that I'm afraid the two might wake up because of it.

The very breath of silence, I slip my blades from their sheaths and hold them up. Metal glints in the moonlight. I'm so close and yet, my feet refuse to move forward another step.

You are a sword, Kiera. Once again, I hear Ophelia's voice in the back of my mind. Not mortal. Not Mortal God. A sword. Swords do not feel pain. They do not feel regret. They simply act as the weapon they were meant to be.

My insides clench and contract and release. Over and over again as beads of sweat pop up along my spine beneath my cloak and clothes. The blood contract brand on the back of my neck burns, an ever-present reminder that I don't have a choice in this. There's no point in hesitating.

One of the figures on the bed rolls to their side—the man. His face is clear even in the darkness of the room. Perfect in shape. Unblemished. Slack with sleep. I have to kill him first. Silently. Without hesitation.

I step forward. One foot and then the other until I find myself at the side of the bed. His pulse jumps beneath his throat. I go for that first, letting everything else fall away. My body moves, but I don't feel it. Instead, I let the skills that I've been trained in for the last five years take over. The sharp edge of my blade touches the God's throat and I slice through the flesh there —blood flows, down over the sheets and blankets.

Eyes shoot open and his lips part as the pain registers. It's too late, cutting his throat as well as his vocal cords ensures that he won't make a single noise, but just to be on the safe side, I quickly round the bed to the opposite God. Her face is far more dainty than the man's. Her nose is high and tiny, barely even there. Her brows are a light blonde, and across her cheeks, there are hints of sunspots. She's beautiful, I realize. She hardly looks like the kind of person who would hold human children captive and torture them. But I know from experience that looks can be deceiving. Not only am I evidence of that fact, but Ophelia had ensured that I would understand why these two were on an assassin's list.

The client that wanted them dead was a woman who'd lost her child to their tantrums and parties. Parties where they had invited young human children, only to prey upon them and turn their screams and cries into entertainment for their other Divine friends. It doesn't seem fair that this one's face is so serene, so immaculate that the only mar to her perfection is my dagger as I set it to her throat and then slit it with a much cleaner, steadier hand than I had her husband's.

The only remaining question in my mind as the red liquid pours in a stream down the side arch of her throat to soak into the bedsheets and pillows beneath her head is this: Why can I do this and no one else? Why does the Divine Blood flowing in my veins let me kill what it contains? Divine Blood against Divine Blood. It's a sick irony and an answer I don't think I'll ever find or understand.

I don't think about it for too long or too hard as my thoughts and attention drift back to the male, who remains wide-eyed, dying at a much slower pace likely due to my initial hesitation.

I watch as the man jerks back and forth on the bed that I'm sure he felt safe in when he laid down earlier this evening. His body twitches as he thrashes, gurgles cutting off any screams he might make as he chokes on the blood spurting from his neck, showering down the front of him and across the sheets. The woman, on the other hand, never wakes. Instead, the light crease of her brow as she slept and dreamed just fades away and the breaths in her chest cease completely. Twin pools of red drip down the bed and flow towards my booted feet.

It's over. My first kill and my second.

I look down at my hands, half expecting something—some form of emotion to hit me. Nothing does. There are little dots of red from the slices I made that speckle my knuckles, but I quickly rub them against my cloak, erasing the evidence.

The aftermath of death is silence, and it echoes, fills each and every room in this manor, each and every pore in my skin. I stand there as the two bodies I just turned from living beings to corpses stop twitching and begin to grow cold. I still wait for some emotion to overtake me. Guilt. Remorse. Nothing of the kind comes for me. Perhaps the Gods of those emotions have forgotten my existence.

I turn away from my targets, less quiet now as I open the door and leave the same way I'd come but not in the same form. I walk with more confidence and less fear than before down the hall. A buzzing starts up in my veins. A power I'd never known existed before now. Is this why Ophelia is the way that she is? Is this how killing makes a person?

My feet come to a slow stop as I reach the outside and I turn back with a frown, but even if I feel for the mortal child contained within the manor walls—full of fear and anger and sorrow—he is not my target. He should be none of my concern. Ophelia is waiting.

Still, I look back anyway. Wondering who he is and why he's there. I step away from the manor and rescale the wall, dashing across the streets and back into the shadows. I'll tell Ophelia about him, I decide. Even if he's none of my concern, maybe he's the reason those two were put on her list to begin with.

Maybe, in killing them, I did something good. Maybe I saved him. Or maybe that's just a hope on my part to excuse the lack of repentance I feel after killing two people. Good people are supposed to not want to hurt people, but as I stood over the Gods, sleeping in their bed, it didn't matter to me. The us versus them —the them or me I'd relied on so much before seeing them before me, under my blade. It faded away.

It didn't matter anymore who they were or what they'd done. All I knew was that I hated them, the Gods and what they represented. I killed them because I was ordered to, but I didn't cry for them because I didn't care to.

Maybe Ophelia is right, *I think to myself.* Maybe I *was* made for this.

CHAPTER 35

KIERA

"Who is he?" The sudden sound of a male voice jolts me awake. I sit up, my hand immediately beneath my pillow to grip the dagger I keep there before I realize who it is that's woken me. It's only the familiarity of the voice that stops me from whipping it out and throwing it in the following second.

Slowly, I turn my entire body towards the intruder. I don't know how, but Kalix is in my room and somehow, I never heard him enter. A quick glance at the door tells me that it's not open.

"How did you get in here?" I demand, my voice sharper than I normally would let it be. The part of me that knows it's important to keep up the pretense of subservience is warring with the part that can't possibly understand how someone managed to sneak up on me when only two people have ever been able to do so—and I suspect it's because I've known both Ophelia and Regis for long enough that somewhere, deep down in my psyche, I trust them. Even if I shouldn't trust anyone.

I do *not* trust Kalix Darkhaven. So, there should be no

excuse for how he managed to sneak into my room without waking me.

"Answer my question," Kalix responds, his tone deepening as he steps forward and out of the shadows. The moment his face is revealed by the moonlight pouring in through my window, his eyes glow an unnatural green. "Who. Is. He?"

"Who is who?" I shake my head and carefully withdraw my hand from my pillow, hoping he doesn't notice its placement.

"The man you were with," Kalix growls.

My lips part and I think back, trying to understand the meaning behind his words. I must take too long, though, because in the next second, Kalix takes two giant steps forward and slams both of his palms on my bed. The mattress squeaks in protest as he presses down, leaning over me and blocking out the moonlight. Twin pools of moss bore into me. The various shades of jade swirl and twist, entrancing me, making me feel as though I'm falling into an alga-infested ocean.

Seduction. Enchantment. Persuasion. Fuck. It only takes me a moment to realize what's happening. Kalix is trying to use Divine persuasion on me, and I'm the only one between us who knows it won't work. It's never worked on me. At least, never before now. Any time I've run into a Divine Being and felt them pushing their persuasion and will upon me, I've been able to wave it off. It never mattered if they were Lower God or Upper God or even one of the few Mortal Gods I'd come across. Now, though, I find myself struggling under the weight of his will. Why?

I don't have a chance to figure it out. Kalix lifts one hand and cups my face, tilting my head back until his eyes are all I can see. "You can tell me, little mortal," he whispers. "Who was the man you were with? Is he your lover?"

His breath brushes over my face. "I don't know who you're talking about," I say, forcing the words out.

The muscle in his jaw twitches. Irritation? Probably. I wait, curious to see his reaction. Instead of repeating the question or offering more details, Kalix changes tactics. His fingers become pliant against my face, stroking rather than holding. A shiver slithers down my spine as the spark of Divinity spreads from where he's touching me. I've never liked the way someone else's Divinity felt, but Kalix's is different. Rather than invasive, it feels like warm water washing away the dust and grime that always seems to permeate me.

I'm filthy. Dirty. The lowest of the low. Living and breathing in squalor and he's here to lift me out. How kind of him. My eyelids sink down. Curiosity and comfort swaddle me, wrapping around me and forcing me to sway towards the man above me.

"You were allowed out of the Academy grounds, were you not?" he asks.

I nod. My head feels so damn heavy. My lashes flutter. My mind battles for and against the need to give him every-thing—whatever he desires. It's as if there's a deep-rooted *need* inside of me, a *knowing* that tells me giving in to this man will bring about the most wondrous pleasure I've ever known.

Lies.

Lies.

Lies.

All I know are lies.

I shake my head, squeezing my eyes shut before I realize what I'm doing in an effort to cut off the strength of his power. My hands curl into fists where they rest on the thin mattress beneath me and a sharp sting right over the top of one of them brings me, haltingly, back to reality.

I open my eyes and look down in time to see a small black little spider scurrying over the top of my bedsheets and disappearing into the wall my bed is shoved against. The little red bump on my pale skin and the quickly fading pain of the venom that the small creature unleashed is all that remains.

Thank you ... my little friend.

"Look at me." My head swings back around and Kalix's deep green eyes are right there and angrier than ever. "Did you break my persuasion?" he demands.

I swallow before I respond. "Not on purpose." It's the truth. As much as I'd love to claim credit for thwarting him, it was one of my spiders that did it for me. I make a mental note to leave a treat out for him and his friends in the near future as a sign of my appreciation.

Kalix's lips turn down even further. His scowl doesn't detract from his beauty, though. A pity. I figure it couldn't hurt for these Darkhavens to be less attractive; it would certainly make them easier to deal with.

"You are not what you seem, are you, little mortal?" Kalix's question strikes fear deep in my heart. I don't move for several seconds, not even to respond.

Finally, after what feels like an eternity sitting there staring at him staring at me, I dip my head and jerk my chin to the side. His hand immediately falls between us, but it doesn't leave me completely. No. He wouldn't let me win just like that. Instead, his fingers weave through the thin fabric of the tunic I wear to bed. He tugs, bringing me closer.

"I don't know why you came to my room this late,

Master Kalix," I grit the words out through my teeth, anger and frustration filling each syllable. It's so damned demeaning having to prostrate myself before these vile half-blooded Gods. The irony of my own lineage makes no difference. "But you should know as well as I do that this is completely inappropriate."

A deep chuckle resonates within his chest. "Inappropriate?" Kalix's fingers tighten on the fabric over my chest and he pulls it taut. I resist, not following the movement even though I know all it does is stretch the neck opening out so that there's no doubt he can see straight down over my bare breasts underneath. "You should know as well as I do," he repeats my words in that mocking tone of his, "that *inappropriate* is what I do best. Now..." He slides forward, one leg lifting onto the mattress as he moves up and grabs ahold of my face once more. "Tell me the truth—you requested time off to travel outside of the Academy grounds to meet a man."

I gape up at him. "Did you follow me?" Was that why I'd been feeling so odd? As if there were invisible eyes on me the entire time? I knew I wasn't fucking crazy, but how had he done it? I'd never caught sight of him, or anyone else for that matter. More than that, Mortal Gods were even more restricted than Terra.

He tilts his head. "In a way," he hedges. "But I digress. You met a man in Riviere City. A mortal." His grip hardens, as if steel is pressing into the sides of my cheeks. He glowers down at me. "Who. The. Fuck. Was. He?"

Breath squeezes into my lungs. How much does he already know? What can I tell him? Will he believe a lie? Each question shoots through my mind with lightning speed. "He's no one," I try, only to have Kalix click his tongue at me and lean down into my face.

His tongue comes out, slowly, capturing the entirety of my attention as it swipes across his lower lip before disappearing back into his mouth. "Another lie like that and I'll have to punish you, my sweet Terra," he warns. "I want the truth. Who was that man?"

I know which one he's talking about. There's only one man I met in the city, only one man I suspect would earn this sort of reaction from him. I could just give over the cover story. It would play out fine if I did—after all, all paperwork and witnesses that know me in this city know only what they've been told, save for Madam Brione, and she is the one who helped to come up with my background in order to gain access to the Academy. It's on the tip of my tongue to tell him that Regis is nothing more than my brother—the only family I have left, and he's nothing that Kalix needs to concern himself over.

So, I don't know why the fuck something else comes out of my mouth.

"Why are you so curious about a mortal man, Master Kalix?"

A bolt of pleasure pierces me at the confused surprise that immediately converges on Kalix's expression the very second the question escapes my lips. His mouth opens, lips parting and closing in utter shock.

"You asked me if he was my lover," I press forward despite the danger bells ringing in my head. "Does that bother you? Do you not want him to be?"

The sound of rending fabric reaches my ears and I blink once before, together, both Kalix and my heads bend down to find that he's ripped my shirt clean down the center. He releases it immediately and drops his other hand away from my face, but the damage is done and either side of the raggedly torn pieces fall over my breasts, forming a deep v as it barely covers my nipples.

"So, he is then..." Darkness grips his expression. Anger. Irritation. Like a child who's just been told someone else was playing with their toy. "And after your night with Theos. Tsk tsk tsk."

That cannot be what this little visit is about, but it's good to know that Theos didn't keep what happened between us a secret. It makes the decision for it not to happen again that much more solid.

Kalix doesn't leave the bed, nor does he move off of me. In fact, curiously enough, he doesn't move at all. He remains right where he is, still as a statue, save for where he dropped my now ripped shirt, his eyes locked on my exposed flesh.

With a deep sigh, I shift beneath him and shake my head. "No," I answer, finally. "He's not my lover." I can't help the disgusted twist of my lips. As if I would ever be with a manwhore like Regis. The thought is grotesque. "He's my brother."

Kalix's head jerks up. "Your brother?" he repeats.

"Yes." I nod. "And while I don't know what's expected of Mortal Gods and Divine Beings, I can certainly tell you that we, mortals, do not fuck our siblings." I shift beneath him, turning my head away. "Now, I suggest that you—"

Whatever I was about to say is suddenly cut off as the shadow that is Kalix falls over me. His hands lift to my face, grabbing hold and turning it towards him. When his mouth crashes against mine, my whole body grows cold and then hot.

What. The. Fuck.

My hands land against his massive shoulders and I push. For all the good it does me, Kalix doesn't fucking move. Instead, he sinks down deeper, lowering himself over me as he pins me beneath his body. So, I do the only thing I can think of—I bite him. *Hard.*

Kalix finally drags his head back. The taste of rawness and blood lingers on my tongue. His grin is unabashed, unashamed, and certainly not angry anymore. Bewilderment continues to assault me. "You said he wasn't your lover," he reminds me.

I gape at him. Is he actually serious? "So?" I demand, pushing against him again. "That doesn't mean I want to make *you* my lover!"

"You didn't seem to mind Theos," he replies.

"You wouldn't know fuck all about me and Theos," I snap back. "But for your information, it was a one-time deal. It's never going to happen again."

He clicks his tongue at me. "Oh, sweet little mortal, never say never."

The blade beneath my pillow sits just within reach. I contemplate using it but then think better of it. No. I need to get Kalix out of my room and I need to do it the peaceful way—even if my preferred method would be to gut him and drag him out by his intestines.

"My answer is no," I seethe. "No. No. Fucking. No. Get *off* me!" I bow my body under his and all that seems to do is press the hardness of his erection against me.

"Now, now, no need to pitch a fit, little mortal." Kalix chuckles as if he's amused by my resistance. I'll be honest, I'm not using the full breadth of my strength on him and it's partially because I'm not entirely sure it would work. I've never had a God's, much less a Mortal God's, persuasion work so well on me. To say that I'm unsettled would be an understatement.

"Why did you have me followed?" I demand, biting down on my fury.

Kalix cracks his neck to the side, shadows dancing along the olive tone of his skin, revealing hollows along his throat. "Curiosity?"

His answer sounds more like a question than a certainty. I narrow my gaze on him. "I was given permission to visit my brother," I snap. "You had no right to follow me."

He laughs, the sound deep and throaty. "I have every right, Terra, darling," he replies. "You're a mortal—you don't have rights, at least not the ones you think you do. If I find your actions suspicious, then of course I'll follow you."

"You find my actions suspicious?" My heart pounds against my chest. What does he know? It can't be the truth if I'm still here, lying beneath him. Certainly, he wouldn't know. But then again, as I look up at him and the glittering hue of his moss green gaze, I have to wonder. Kalix's eyes are deeper than the average man, threaded with an empty void that lacks conscience. If it amuses him, I have no doubt he'd protect that dark barrier he keeps around him to his very last breath.

As if he senses my internal thoughts, Kalix leans down again, bringing his face back to mine. "Oh, I find you incredibly suspicious, little mortal," he murmurs. Whatever I plan to say, however, is swallowed by the sound of three hard, repetitive knocks on the door across the room. As one, our heads turn towards it. "Expecting company?" Kalix asks, lowering his voice.

I shake my head. "No."

He hums in the back of his throat and then, as if he's made some silent decision, he disappears from my body. I jolt up in bed as I look around, but he's just gone. Something wet and scaly touches the side of my leg and I practically catapult myself out of the thin cot of my bed and onto the floor. A slithery little creature slides from beneath my sheets and plops onto the floor. It pays me no mind at all as it slides around my still-booted feet—as I'd fallen asleep completely clothed from my day out in Riviere—and into the shadows.

The person on the other side of the door knocks again, this time louder and harder. "Kiera Nezerac?" The voice is low and masculine, booming with strength and command.

I hurry across the room and fling open the door, only to come face to face with a tall well-built Mortal God. He takes up practically the entire doorway, but from the slight lines around his eyes and mouth, I realize he's not a student. A guard, perhaps? Why would a guard be banging on my door?

"Yes?" A cold sweat has broken out across my shoulder blades.

His deep burgundy eyes scan me from top to bottom. "You've been called to the dean's office for reprimanding."

"Reprimanding?" I repeat as confusion clouds my mind. "I'm sorry, what's this about?"

"You've been called to the dean's office," he repeats. "You will be told the reason for your punishment within. I am to take you there now."

There is so much wrong here and no time to consider it. Reprimanding? That can't mean what I think it means, but what else would it be? "I'm not in uniform," I say lamely as I try to think of any excuse to not go or at the very least, delay it.

The man tilts his head to the side, those dead eyes of his spanning down to the torn shirt I'm still wearing. "You will be given two minutes to adjust yourself," he says. "No more."

I assume the clock starts now so I slam the door shut and practically race to rip off the torn shirt and replace it with a new one—the only other one I have. I grab my cloak and put it back on and just as the knob of my door turns, I return to it.

"You will come with me now," the man states as I swing the door wide open again and stand before him, panting and sweating from the rush. Then he turns and starts walking.

Shit. Shit. Shit.

I rack my brain for any reason to be called to the dean's office, but all I come back with is a blaring warning. This is not fucking good. I consider my options as I lean back on my heels. How fast could I take this guard out? How fast could I scale the walls of the Academy? Or go under the sewer system? Do I have a chance or do I follow him anyway?

If they've found out that I'm a Mortal God masquerading as a mortal Terra, the Gods wouldn't send a lone Mortal God guard to bring me in and I certainly doubt it'd be to the dean's office. The more I think of the reason for his being here, the more baffled I am.

"This way," the man states, turning and striding down the hall. It's clear he expects me to follow and I doubt I have any other choice if I wish to remain in the Academy.

So, with my heart in my throat, I step out of my room and trail after the guard. All the while, I can feel a now familiar pair of eyes watching me. *Kalix.* I'm sure he'll alert the other Darkhavens, but if they're even capable of doing anything ... would they?

CHAPTER 36

KIERA

Fear makes you stupid. Stupid gets you killed. It's practically the first rule I was taught in the Underworld. So, as I'm led through the maze-like corridors of the Mortal Gods Academy of Riviere, I shove that shit down. I count my steps back from the north tower and find that I'm being led towards a section of the Academy I've never been to before.

Regis' map had helped when I'd first arrived here and I'd memorized it top to bottom. Memorizing an outline on parchment, however, is vastly different from watching the darkened stone corridors turn to wide hallways with more and more ornate wall sconces lit with gas and fire to illuminate them. The stained glass windows we pass depict more and more outlandish images. Gods battling ancient monsters—some of the sea with a dozen tentacles, some of the land with great big teeth and glowing yellow eyes.

I turn my head away from them and face the Mortal God in front of me. If nothing else can alleviate my anxiety, it's the fact that he's got his back to me—clearly unaware of the danger I present. That sets me at ease. If the Gods knew my true identity then there's no way they'd send one measly Mortal God to have me brought in nor would I be unchained.

The word 'reprimand' circles my head again and again. I'm so focused on putting one foot in front of the other as well as trying to think of any reason I could be brought before the dean for reprimanding that it takes a moment for me to realize that we've stopped. I look up as the Mortal God guard in charge knocks heavily upon a thick wooden door painted in red and etched in gold. There's a plaque at the center of the door, but I don't manage to read it before the door creaks open and the Mortal God turns, shoving me through the opening.

The front of my boot catches on the lip in the doorway all too suddenly, sending me sprawling out on the floor. Even though I'd planned it to appear as mortal and clumsy as possible, when my knees crack against the hard black flooring, it fucking hurts. I stay down on the ground, though, only peering up through the threads of my hair to ascertain who's present.

Dauphine stands a few steps behind Dolos, her form bent ever so slightly to keep her head as far below his as she can while she stands. Her long uniform skirts, a charcoal gray, disappear behind the God's desk. The dark color of her clothes makes the pale dimpled hands she clasps before them appear that much paler. Her straight hair has been pulled back and is held in a low ponytail at the base of her skull. It's not her attire or stature that causes concern, though, but the deep lines on either side of her half-hidden mouth as she bows her head. It's the rapid thrum of her heart racing that I can see ticking in the vein in her throat.

She's afraid, and that cannot mean anything good.

Dolos stays sitting behind the massive desk that takes

up a solid half of the width of the room. Unlike Caedmon's office, Dolos' is pristine, wiped clean of any small trinkets or plants or books that may belie his interests. Instead, the floor is made of solid black marble, and the only thing that hangs on the walls is the tapestry behind him depicting Tryphone, the King of the Gods.

The shroud of darkness that surrounds Dolos is there, thankfully. It's probably the only reason Dauphine is able to stand so still as she, too, peers up at me from beneath her lashes. As soon as her gaze connects with mine, her eyes flare as do her nostrils. She'd seemed to be obsessive and worshipful of the Gods at orientation, amidst all of the other Terra, but right here and right now, I see nothing but a terrified human woman.

I frown slightly, but then she jerks her chin down— almost as if she's warning me to do the same. I hadn't expected that, not from her, but I follow the silent communication and I shoot my eyes back to the black marble. Sweat gathers on the back of my neck beneath the weight of my hair.

That same dense air from the battle arena washes over me in waves. Thankfully, though, it's not my first time experiencing this level of pressure. I swallow reflexively, stifling the desire to vomit. Even if he's repressing his ability, I can still sense it. It sits upon my back and shoulders like heavy weights dragging me down. I keep my lips sealed shut as I wait for the God to speak.

A moment passes and then another. Finally, in my periphery, I watch as Dolos' hand appears from the shadows, flicking towards the guard at my back. The man bows and then backs out of the room, closing the door behind him and sealing me in the room with Dolos, God of Imprisonment. I temper the rapid beat of my heart as it races in my chest, breathing slowly—in through my nose and out through my mouth.

I can't see Dolos' expression, but the sweat gathering at the top of Dauphine's forehead is enough to have me nervous. Even without being able to visually see the God in full, there's a certain amount of intimidation that comes with silence. I know it well. I've trained in it. So, I know exactly what he's trying to do. He's trying to unsettle me, and unfortunately, it's fucking working.

Breathe, I order myself. *In and out. Just breathe.*

I've killed his kind before. He has no idea the power I wield. I flex my hands into fists against the dark marble flooring at that reminder. The silence is combined with a stillness and in stillness, I find a lot of information.

The quiet of the room allows me to focus on my other senses. I want to look around, but I don't want to break the sudden spell cast over the room. There's someone else in here. Does Dolos know? He has to, and yet, he doesn't acknowledge them.

"You are Kiera Nezerac," Dolos finally speaks, his voice far less loud than it was at the arena, but no less deep. It rings with that same confidence I expect most Gods to have, especially those of the Upper God echelon.

"Y-yes, sir." It's not difficult to force a bit of a stutter into my voice. Any mortal in my position would be pissing their pants terrified right now.

"You are a new introduction to our Academy, are you not?" he demands.

I jerk my head up and down in answer. A moment later, Dauphine's high-pitched, offended tone responds. "Speak," she practically shrieks. "The God Lord, Dolos, asked you a question."

"I apologize," I say quickly. "Yes, sir. That is correct. I

am a new Terra." A bead of sweat travels down the side of my face from the hairline at the edge of my temple to my jaw. My skin itches.

"Do you know why you've been brought here?"

In a burst of amusement not befitting my current circumstances, I wonder if he knows just how like a mortal he sounds. Those words are exactly the same as those spoken to me by Ophelia—of all people—the day I'd been sold to her Guild. Slowly, I lift my head and settle my gaze on where I expect Dolos' face to be in the mass of shadow and darkness sitting in his chair, as if he's an actual person and not an outline of obscurity.

Dauphine looks at me, her already tight face growing more and more pinched as if the skin over her cheekbones is sucking into her very skeletal frame. If she were near enough to shove my head down, I have no doubt she'd try. The fear coming off of her in waves is enough for me to know just how threatened she is by the presence of Dolos.

"No, I do not, sir." This time, I keep my voice even and flat.

The wisps of shade and shadow sway as the outline of Dolos tilts his head to the left. My skin—once itchy—now feels hot. Impossibly hot. As if someone has poured boiling water down my spine and over my chest. My breaths come in shallow gasps as I fight through the pain.

"You are a brave one, Kiera Nezerac," Dolos states. "Rarely have I ever seen a mortal face me with such unflinching eyes."

Even if it's a mistake, I can't drag my gaze away now. "You did not command me not to look at you when you were talking, sir," I say.

The chuckle tinged with brass that follows my statement doesn't relieve me. In fact, it makes me feel as if the bones in my body are quaking together. What is wrong with me? The pressure he exerts without even trying is so damn powerful. Dozens of invisible boulders crash into my back and shoulders. My head throbs with agony. My mouth goes dry and still, I keep my neck high.

"You are correct," Dolos says as his amusement tapers off. He's quiet for another moment and then he turns to Dauphine. "I've changed my mind about this one," he says to her. "Prepare a cell in the dungeons. I will decide a new punishment."

Punishment? I think. *For what? What have I done to earn this sudden call from him? To earn a cell in the dungeons?*

I'm so focused on Dolos' words that I almost miss the sudden shift of the silent interloper. Whoever they are, though, it's clear they didn't expect this. What that means, however, remains a mystery to me.

Dauphine nods to Dolos, bows, and then quickly rounds his form and desk—her gaze cutting to me as she passes where I'm kneeling on her way out the door. I can feel eyes boring into my face. I don't know if it's from Dolos or the other person secreted away inside the room, though. Considering they haven't yet revealed themselves and Dolos is acting as if they don't exist, however, I maintain my composure and focus on the God.

Leaning forward, an elbow hits the edge of the desk's surface and Dolos leans his face onto his upturned palm. The shrouds that surround him act almost like a thin veil and when he touches something beyond that veil, it opens —if only slightly—and what I see beyond it is a hint into what nightmares are made of.

"We rarely allow those from the Hinterlands into our fold," he states. "Perhaps that is the reason for your fear-lessness."

"I am not fearless," I reply.

"Oh?"

I shake my head. "I don't wish to insult you by blubbering and prostrating myself before I know if that's something you'd prefer, sir."

"True—I do hate tears. They're so very annoying. I appreciate that you wait to see what your betters prefer rather than simply assuming," Dolos says.

"Then—" I don't get a chance to finish.

"Your attitude, however, makes it clear that the claims made against you have merit. Normally, any and all Terra who disregard and break the three golden rules under which they should live by here at the Academy would either be killed or banished."

"If I may, sir," I start. "What rule have I broken?" Surely, they couldn't be referring to leaving the Academy without permission. "If this is about my recent visit outside of the Academy, I assure you I did receive permission from my senior Terra."

Dolos doesn't move and I have the distinct feeling that he's observing me. Silence does wonders for people uncomfortable with it, but I've learned to sit in it. So after I've finished speaking, I wait. Seconds tick into minutes and minutes slowly lose all meaning to me at all. It isn't until I hear footsteps outside of the room that Dolos straightens in his seat and the door behind me opens.

Dauphine appears, rounding me once more as she goes to the God's side and this time kneels down with a scroll in hand, lifting it for Dolos to take. "A cell has been prepared as you ordered," she says with reverence. "Here is the decree you requested prior to the offender's arrival."

The offender's arrival—meaning me. Yet still, I have no answer. I think back to the day I arrived at the Academy.

What had the rules been? They'd been stated for us at the orientation.

Rule one, Gods and their children are the utmost authority of the world. Their word is law.

Rule two, permission is required for any leave from the Academy grounds.

Rule three, once a Terra is assigned a ward, there are no task changes allowed.

Dolos takes the scroll from Dauphine and unravels it in front of where I assume his face is. "The Terra, Kiera Nezerac, assigned to wards Theos, Kalix, and Ruen Darkhaven of the northern tower is to be reprimanded for the breaking of the most sacred law. She has exhibited a disrespectful nature unbecoming of a servant of the Gods and has participated in fornication with a ward under her servitude." Dolos lowers the scroll and peers over it at me. "Though sexual relations between servants and wards are not unexpected," he states, "as Terra are required to provide any and all services requested of them, this was noted within the complaint we received."

"I—"

"Do not speak!" Dauphine barks, lifting and pivoting her head towards me as she cuts me off.

"There was another complaint long before this one, as well," Dolos continues. "What was that about again, Dauphine?"

Dauphine returns to her prostrated position, bowing even lower than before. "Kiera Nezerac was reported to have entered a Mortal God only section of the Academy, Your Divinity," she answers.

"Ah yes, I believe Caedmon was responsible for your punishment at that time," Dolos muses. "I do suppose he can be far kinder than the average God. Kindness often leads to a poor education it seems."

"My deepest apologies, Your Divinity," Dauphine says quickly. "I shall ensure that once her punishment is seen to, I will never allow something like this to happen again."

It doesn't require a genius to know who made the first complaint—*Rahela*. I'd definitely made a bigger mistake with those actions. My rebellious nature had taken over and now regret is slapping me in the face. Not because I am truly remorseful over my actions but because of the current circumstances. An idiotic novice mistake, Ophelia would tell me. I'd gotten complacent and thought that my time with Caedmon following my near drowning had been the end of that. Apparently not.

Knots begin to form against my shoulder blades as the tension grows inside of me while I wait to find out exactly what this all means for me and what kind of punishment I will be facing. Dolos' words, though, don't tell me anything about the stranger in the room or who else could have been responsible for this latest complaint.

There are more footsteps outside of the room. My breaths come faster and faster. The door behind me opens. More Mortal Gods spill into the room, older and dressed as guards. What punishment could Dolos be thinking of? As long as it's not death, I can handle it. Pain. Torture. Banishment, even, though it'd make my mission a bit more difficult. As long as I'm alive and still breathing, there is always a way to come back.

A hard hand lands on my back, and moves to my upper arm. Without a hint of gentleness, I'm ripped up from the floor in an instant. My hands are yanked behind me and clamped together. I stretch my limbs and nearly sigh in relief when I realize that the cuffs around my wrists are pure iron rather than brimstone. Of course, why would they use something to restrain Divinity on a mere Terra?

The relief is short-lived. "For the offense of disrespecting the Gods and violating the Mortal God only sections of the Academy, you, Kiera Nezerac, are sentenced to a hundred lashes to be performed by the God, Axlan, at dawn on the third day of your ... *imprisonment*." The last part of his announcement escapes him in a gratified rush, almost a prayer upon his lips. It's light, but the weight of it seems to spread through his body. The shadows still lingering squirm and though I can't be entirely certain, I swear they feel pleasure at that singular word.

I don't need to ask why I'm being imprisoned at all. I can practically smell the waves of euphoria rolling off of Dolos in spite of the heavy pressure his presence presents. The darkness surrounding him wiggles and slides over his body and flesh like dozens of snakes made of pure night are suddenly in heat. He is the God of Imprisonment, after all. I should not be surprised that he is so joyful over his own sentence. He gains his own power in the act of imprisoning others and I'd be willing to bet that doing so to me is like sitting down with a delicious drink at the end of a long hard day for him.

The arms wrapped around me pull me back, nearly dragging me off of my feet once more in their haste. My cloak opens and down from the folds flutters a familiar red-and-white blossom. My eyes widen as the guards holding me are called to a halt. My heartbeat increases exponentially as Dolos stands up from his chair and circles the desk separating us. The closer he comes, the more laborious it is to breathe through the dense air.

Slowly, Dolos leans down and picks up the flower. Turning it side to side, I feel rather than see his smile. "It appears the first offense of intruding upon sacred Mortal God only courtyards is a regular habit, Miss Nezerac," he states, tone ripe with amusement.

I shake my head, ready to explain how I came into possession of the flower—which no doubt is a rare one only grown within that damned courtyard. He doesn't care to hear it, though. Of course, he doesn't. The shadows clinging to his form flick at those behind me.

"Take her to the dungeons," he says. "Her punishment will be performed after three days of starvation."

Three days of starvation? *Bloody fucking Gods.* My legs tangle together as I'm dragged backward out of Dolos' office and into the corridor. I'm flanked on either side as well as front and back. Another set of hands grips my right arm and now I'm being hauled forward by two massive Mortal Gods. I look up at their stoic faces. A few scars here and there, but otherwise perfection incarnate. Who they are doesn't matter, anyway, I decide. It's not like they're going to help me now.

Dolos' 'punishment' is a practical death sentence and it damn well would be ... if I weren't what I am. This is going to fucking *hurt*.

CHAPTER 37

KIERA

S tep.

    Drip.

    Step.

Drip.

Step.

Drip.

Even with my eyes closed as I lean towards the back of the cell I was unceremoniously tossed into hours ago, I hear the intruder stop in front of the bars keeping me locked up. My nose twitches at the smell. It's the same one as the invisible man in Dolos' office. Parchment. Dust. And something else. A spice I can't name.

There he is. That motherfucker.

I don't open my eyes. It's rather wet and cold down here and it fucking wreaks. The walls are made of crude cut stone, slabs of mostly even rock, save for every few feet where old scars likely made by previous prisoners attempting to claw their way out remain even now. I won't be one of them. I have no intention of losing my sanity in this dark and damp hole. I doubt even mice climb down here in this cold forgotten place. In the hours I've been here, I've wondered when the last time they actually used these dungeons was. I haven't seen any other prisoners, haven't smelled any remains of them either. Only dust, ice, and decay.

With my eyes shut against the dark and isolated image of my current predicament, I feel my upper lip curl back slightly as the scent on the other side of those bars reminds me that I'm no longer alone. Even as he's stopped in front of me, I can still hear the dripping of water or what I suspect is sewage as it leaks from the places through the cracks in the stone ceiling above.

Thankfully, I was thrown in here with the clothes still on my back and my cloak still in place after the iron cuffs had been removed. I drag my cloak closer around me to fight off the chill. If the man standing outside my cell wants me to open my eyes and acknowledge him, then he's going to have to speak first. Otherwise, I'm not fucking cracking.

I'm already angry enough as it stands. We both know—he and I—that there was no reason for my current imprisonment, but he's a smart man. He knows just how to manipulate those around him. He knew full well that Dolos' power stems from imprisonment and therefore, I have no doubt in my mind that he manipulated Dolos into throwing me in here.

It's the *why* I don't quite get.

"Are you quite finished ignoring me?" he asks, his voice deep and rather irritated.

I crack my eyes open finally and settle a bland look on him. Barely illuminated by the pale light of a fire dancing within a sconce on the wall, I pick apart his features. Twisted and half hidden in shadow, the man on the other side of the cell peers in at me. His lips are drawn down. His brows furrowed. Despite the annoyance in his tone, his expression appears for all the world as if he's feeling something I haven't yet seen on his face.

Guilt.

"I'm not ignoring you," I say. "I was simply waiting."

"For what?" he demands. So many fucking demands.

I let my head fall against the wall at my back. "For you to talk first," I say. "I'm sure there's a reason you did this."

The figure outside of my cell turns away from me. Blue eyes flash red before disappearing from my visage entirely. I let my own eyelids fall back into place. It's nice having the upper hand for a change, especially against him.

"You were supposed to be banished," he snaps.

"Oh?" I release a bemused chuckle. "Sorry to ruin your plans."

The sharp sound of fists hitting metal screeches into my ears and I open my eyes again to see him hunched over, both fists on the bars of my cell. "Does your life mean nothing to you?" he demands.

Irony, thy name is he. What a funny question coming from the person who put me in this position. "Do I need to remind you the reason I'm here in the first place?" I ask. "My life—whatever it means to me—is whatever the Gods deem it. Unimportant. Expendable."

"How did you know?" he asks this time.

I debate on telling him the truth. That it was his scent that gave him away. I hadn't really thought about it all that much during all the times I'd been near him. But it was there. Familiar. Ever present. He, himself, was practically a beacon of his own doings.

"You were in the office when Dolos sentenced me," I say.

His head lifts and this time when he looks at me, it's with a twisted expression. Confusion and something more.

Something ... I hadn't expected. Slowly, I push my hand back against the wall behind me and use that leverage to rise to my feet.

I step away from the back wall and take another and another until I'm nearly a foot from him. Close enough that I can see the puffs of white his breath makes as he breathes rather harshly. "I didn't know about the first complaint," he says as if that changes anything now.

"Rahela likely made it."

He fixes me with a stare and I don't have to be able to read his mind to know the questions swarming in his gaze. "She found me in the courtyard a few weeks ago and attempted to drown me for being there."

Twin dark brows draw together, forming a little V between them as he frowns. "You never said anything."

I shrug. "It wasn't important then."

"I made a specific request of Dolos," he says. "You were to be banished from the Academy—not ... whipped."

I lean forward until my upper chest rests against the bars that separate us. "What did you have to offer him for that request?" I ask, more curious than upset by the reveal.

He turns his head away from me and releases the bars immediately. He never struck me as a coward, but now I realize he just might be. Cruel in his inability to foresee potential cracks in his little plan. A shiver overtakes me and I close my hands around my upper arms, pulling away from the bars as well.

"If you don't want to answer that, then why did you come here?" I finally ask after several more minutes of silence. "I know it may seem as if I have all of the time in the world being locked up here for the next three days, but I should probably get my beauty sleep if I'm going to make it through starving and whipping."

He flinches but doesn't respond. I blow out a breath and turn away from him, walking back over to my place against the wall. Slipping my cloak under my ass, I drop down onto the hard ground and fold my legs together, crossing them like a child might. The movement stretches the skin of my inner thighs, but it doesn't feel bad, especially not after all of the dense weight of being in Dolos' presence.

"Ugh." I set my elbow on my knee and prop my head up on my hand. "If you're not going to say anything, then you should leave. It's cold down here and I'm sure the Gods wouldn't want you catching anything."

"You know that's not possible," he snaps back, earning a grin from me. Of course, I know that. I just wondered if he'd say anything to the comment and he did. He's unnerved. Uncomfortable. And most surprising of all, he feels fucking guilty.

Good, I think. *He fucking should be.*

I never asked to be put in his path. I never fucking asked for this damn mission to take so long. He's full of rage and remorse, but I'm full of resignation. I've always had to be. He played a game he thought he could master to try and get rid of me—a pawn, in his mind. He wanted to walk away without spilling blood, but someone like him should know by now, this whole world is nothing but blood. The blood of our fathers and mothers, the blood in our veins, and the blood that runs in the streets when those who are most powerful rule over all.

We kill to survive even if we aren't assassins. Seduce and destroy. There is no salvation for any of us.

"You're sitting in here and you still don't seem to understand, Kiera," he snaps, voice full of venom. "In three days' time, you will be walked out to the arena and the entire

Academy will watch as Axlan whips your back bloody and raw."

I put a hand to my chin and crack my neck. "I'm well aware of what awaits me. I just don't care."

"You don't care?" I've shocked him. I take pride in that.

My free hand lifts up and his eyes follow it. I flick my fingers at him. "The Gods have always played judge, jury, and executioner ever since they came to this world," I tell him. "Are you just now realizing that your actions have consequences? I would think a man of your age would have learned that by now."

"It wasn't..." He chokes out the words before stopping.

I sigh and drop my hand. "You played the game and it didn't go your way," I state. "I'm pretty strong. I don't think I'll be able to escape pain, but I think I can live through a few slaps on the back."

"They won't be so tame," he replies. "Axlan is the God of Victory. He will go as hard as he needs to in order to feel as though he's won."

"Considering one of us will be the one in chains and one of us will not be," I say. "It sounds to me like he already has and so have you. *Congratulations.*" That last word comes out with more bite and no small amount of fury.

His head lowers once more, the dark strands of his hair falling into his face and covering the scar I know to be there, dividing his brow. "For what it's worth, Kiera," he says, sounding defeated as his shoulders sag, "I am sorry."

With that, he turns and strides away. The echo of his footsteps grows distant, but it isn't until he's completely gone that I speak. "Apologies make no difference in the light of actions that can't be taken back," I murmur. "So you can take your sorry and shove it up your ass, *Ruen Darkhaven.*"

About the Author

Lucinda Dark, also known as USA Today Bestselling Author, Lucy Smoke, for her contemporary novels, has a master's degree in English and is a self-proclaimed creative chihuahua. She enjoys feeding her wanderlust, cover addiction, as well as her face. When she's not on a never-ending quest to find the perfect milkshake, she lives and works in the southern United States with her beloved fur-baby, Hiro, and her family and friends.

Want to be kept up to date? Think about joining the author's group or signing up for their newsletter below.

Facebook Group (Reader Mafia)
Newsletter (www.lucysmoke.com)

ALSO BY LUCINDA DARK

Fantasy Series:

Awakened Fates Series (completed)

Crown of Blood and Glass

Dawn of Fate and Valor

Wings of Sunfire and Darkness

Twisted Fae Series (completed)

Court of Crimson

Court of Frost

Court of Midnight

Barbie: The Vampire Hunter Series (completed)

Rest in Pieces

Dead Girl Walking

Ashes to Ashes

Sky Cities Series (Dystopian)

Heart of Tartarus

Shadow of Deception

Sword of Damage

Dogs of War (Coming Soon)

Contemporary Series:

Break Volume 2

Break Series Collection

Contemporary Standalones:

Poisoned Paradise

Expressionate

Wild Hearts

Printed in the USA
CPSIA information can be obtained
at www.ICGtesting.com
CBHW022042240224
4654CB00001B/1